BY MARY WOOD

The Breckton series

To Catch a Dream
An Unbreakable Bond
Tomorrow Brings Sorrow
Time Passes Time

The Generation War saga

All I Have to Give
In Their Mother's Footsteps

The Girls Who Went to War series

The Forgotten Daughter
The Abandoned Daughter
The Wronged Daughter

Stand-alone novels

Proud of You
Brighter Days Ahead
The Street Orphans

The Wronged Daughter

Mary Wood

PAN BOOKS

First published 2019 by Pan Books
an imprint of Pan Macmillan
The Smithson, 6 Briset Street, London EC1M 5NR
Associated companies throughout the world
www.panmacmillan.com

ISBN 978-1-5098-9258-7

1 3 5 7 9 8 6 4 2

A CIP catalogue record for this book is available from the British Library.

Typeset in ITC Galliard Std by Palimpsest Book Production Ltd, Falkirk, Stirlingshire
Printed and bound by CPI Group (UK) Ltd, Croydon, CR0 4YY

Visit **www.panmacmillan.com** to read more about all our books
and to buy them. You will also find features, author interviews and
news of any author events, and you can sign up for e-newsletters
so that you're always first to hear about our new releases.

To my hubby, Roy.
Without you I could not achieve all I do.
You are my strength.

PART ONE

Blackburn and London, 1920–21

~

Mags and Harold

Uncertainties Mar Happiness

Chapter One

Mags held on to the back of the chair and stared across at the doctor. What he was saying didn't seem possible. *Not my dear mother? No. Mother has always been strong.*

'I'm sorry, but there's only tender loving care that can be given, to ease her passing. I can arrange for a nurse to come and stay. She will administer oxygen, when needed, and the medication that I shall prescribe. But I'm afraid Belinda's weak heart is rapidly failing her.'

Weak heart? When did Mother ever have a weak heart?

As Mags watched her father shake the doctor's hand, the thought rushed through her that he had changed, too. His back was no longer ramrod-straight, and his hair, which had been greying at the temples, was now almost white. Why hadn't she ever noticed how heavily he leaned on his stick?

Suddenly the part of her world that had always felt safe was crumbling. Life here in her beloved Blackburn was lived at a slow pace, even if for the most part she was kept busy running the mill. Always she was surrounded by familiar things, and by people she'd grown up with. Now a big part of that – her family life – was being threatened.

'Margaret, the doctor is leaving. Where are your manners?'

'No, Herbert, don't admonish her. Margaret has had a shock. You should have told her about her mother's condition. I counselled both you and Belinda, many times over the years, to do so. I'm sorry, Margaret. I should have insisted that you were told and were therefore prepared for the fact that what is happening now has always been inevitable. Your mother has had a heart condition for a long time. It has been like an unexploded bomb. Anything could have triggered it to fail – and at any time. I'm sorry, truly sorry, but she only has days left to live.'

Mags shook her head. This wasn't happening. How could she have missed the signs? Yes, Mother was frequently breathless, and her skin and lips often had a blue tinge, but she had said it was an asthmatic condition and was under control.

'Sit down, Margaret. Let yourself absorb this terrible news. Are you feeling unwell yourself? You seem to have lost a lot of weight, when you could ill afford to lose any.'

Backing into the chair behind her, Mags tried to control the shaking of her limbs.

'You've never spoken of the horrors you must have witnessed in Belgium. I thought you had recovered from them, but something has knocked you back. At the winter ball, with your nice young man by your side – Harold, that's his name, isn't it?' Mags nodded. 'You seemed your old self. But since returning from your stay at his home, I have seen a change in you each time I have visited your mother.'

Something had indeed knocked Mags back. Something that gave her nightmares. Memories flooded her mind: the war, meeting and forming a strong friendship with the lovely Flora and Ella as they set out, three young girls full of

4

courage and yet needing each other's support. Then learning how Flora was rejected by her family, and Ella abandoned by hers. And seeing Flora's happiness as her brother Harold had begun to show her a little affection, and how this had led to Mags meeting Harold herself, and being swept off her feet by him. But then . . . the awful events that led to the image that haunted Mags – seeing Harold and Flora's mother sprawled on the floor, her head smashed on the fender . . .

Without her wanting it to happen, Mags's bottom lip quivered, and stinging tears begged to be released. She looked up into Dr Lange's kindly face. His words had triggered the memories, and as she let in the full horror of what had happened, other wounds opened. Images of her wartime experience flashed before her – the sweating face of the German soldier as he raped her; she could still hear his triumphant grunting, and the cheering of his fellow soldiers as they egged him on; but above their chants, the screams of Flors, dear Flors, as she fought against another of the lusting soldiers. *How can I ever recover from that? Or from the constant stream of faces of wounded and dying men, who seem to be drowning in a sea of blood?*

'Margaret? Margaret?'

Her father's desperate voice penetrated the horrific memory. She looked up at him and saw an old man. A fearful, fragile old man – both her parents had been middle-aged when she, their only child, had been born twenty-four years ago, but never before had she noticed them getting old. Yes, she'd taken more and more responsibility for running the family mill over the last few months, and had enjoyed doing so, feeling grateful that, despite their age, her parents had been forward-thinking and hadn't felt that a daughter was incapable of having a business head. But she hadn't viewed that responsibility as Father delegating because he could no longer cope. Now she did see that, and it came as a painful realization.

'Stand back, Herbert, give Margaret some air. The shock has been too much for her. Summon a maid to bring some tea. She needs a hot, sweet drink.'

Mags felt the doctor take her pulse. Her cheeks were wet, and yet she hadn't known that her tears had spilled over.

'Margaret, you need to talk to someone. I know a young woman who has taken a great interest in the trauma experienced by people returning from the war. She is trying to develop a programme that will help them cope. I'd like to refer you to her. Not only would it help you, but you could help her – guiding her as to the kind of help that is needed.'

Is that it: Am I going mad? Me? Capable Mags, am I insane? No!

'I'm all right. I'm sorry. It was just the shock. I – I never suspected . . . well, anything this serious. I can't take it in.'

When the maid entered, they fell silent. The sound of the tea being poured echoed around the room. Once the maid had bobbed a curtsy and left them, Mags watched the doctor spoon in a further two teaspoons of sugar, to add to the one that already laced her cup. A widower, the doctor always wore his wedding band, and the gold caught the light as he stirred the steaming liquid.

The ring reminded her that soon she would be married, and doubts crowded in upon Mags once more. Taking a gulp of her tea, she grimaced at the sweetness of it, but the second sip began to steady her, and she drank the rest as quickly as the scorching heat of it would permit. While drinking, she didn't have to talk. But it didn't stop her mind working. And right now it was nagging her with the truth about her fiancé, Harold – now estranged from Flora.

'Margaret, you're shaking again. Have you drunk your tea?'

'Yes, but I could do with another.'

'Ah, you're showing signs of recovery now. What do you think of my suggestion?'

'I – I don't think so. Thank you. I'm all right; it's just the stress of arranging my wedding, being away from my fiancé and taking responsibility for the mill. I will be fine.'

'Well, you do seem overloaded. And to hear such terrible news now about your mother was probably just too much for you. Let's see how you go over the next few weeks, which won't be easy ones for you. You will need to call on all the inner strength that I know you possess, in order to come to terms with your mother's condition and to help her, too. Maybe – though I hate to suggest it – you might think about postponing your wedding? I was pleased to learn that your future husband is also in the cotton trade, as it always helps if you have the same interests. He's part owner of the Roford mill, isn't he?'

'Yes. He is in partnership with his uncle. He intends to take more of an interest – as he did during the war – once he has all his affairs at home sorted out and he moves up from London to live here.'

'That will be a good solution for you, because obviously he will take over the running of your family mill, too, and then you can be the lady of this house.'

This touched a nerve with Mags. 'Dr Lange, for one thing, my mother isn't dead yet and is still the lady of this house; and for another, I will continue to run the mill once

7

I am married. I am not the kind of woman who will leave everything of a business nature to my husband.'

A cough from her father made Mags realize that she'd spoken too harshly.

'I'm sorry, I didn't mean to snap.'

'No, no. It was good to see your old spirit back in you. Ha, you've always been independent-minded. Your father tells me that you have an excellent business head on your shoulders. Let's hope your husband is just as forward-thinking as your parents are.'

Would Harold consent to her carrying on at the mill? Mags knew one of the fears she harboured was that he wouldn't; but she hadn't let that fear take root, as she felt she could manage the situation, if that was the case. She knew Harold well; and yes, she knew that part of his motive for marrying her was to get a foot on her father's mill. So why, then, was she going through with it?

Love, that's why. For some inexplicable reason – and despite all she knew about him – she loved Harold. Needed him. And wanted to be his wife.

'Well, I'll get off.' The doctor walked towards the door. 'Belinda will sleep for at least another two hours. I will have a nurse here by then. Have you a room near Belinda's that you can make available for the nurse? She will need to sleep here and be on call twenty-four hours a day.'

'We have, Doctor. But I can help. I am a competent nurse, and I want to care for my mother when I come home from the mill.'

'An excellent idea. You are a good daughter, Margaret.'

Mags felt a blush spreading over her face. The doctor always made her feel like a little girl who needed praise, but then he could also be cutting, with a remark like her needing to take on a woman's role – almost as if he hated anyone stepping away from the norm. Even when he'd spoken of the woman psychiatrist that he'd wanted to refer Mags to, he had been derogatory in saying she might need guidance in how to approach those suffering from the effects of war.

As her father closed the door on the doctor, leaving the maid to see him out, he turned to her. 'That was a big sigh, Margaret.'

'Oh, Daddy, it's just, well . . . you know. I want to be taken seriously.' She went into the embrace of his free arm.

'Well, I take you seriously. I rely on you a lot. But maybe I have been wrong to do so. Not having a son, I naturally let you take an interest in my work. Your dear mother didn't object, as she has the same nature as you – being free-spirited and not of a mind that there are different roles for men and for women. Oh, Margaret, how am I going to live without her?'

At this, Mags felt her father slump. She helped him to a chair. 'I'll be here for you, darling Daddy. We'll manage. Don't give up.'

But as she said the words, she had a sinking feeling he was doing just that.

Shutting out her own thoughts of doom and despair, she was determined to be strong. She would be the rock for her parents that they had always been for her.

And part of that role would be to curb the doubts, block out the nightmare images and try to forget the horrors of the war, and especially what had happened after it, when it was discovered that dear Flors and her adored husband, Cyrus, were half-brother and sister. That Cyrus had been fathered by Flors's and Harold's father during an affair.

But can I ever blot out the consequences of that coming to light, – the disgust and fear when I overheard Harold and his mother planning to kill Cyrus? And how am I ever going to live with the awful knowledge that, by foiling that plan, I accidentally caused the death of Harold's and Flors's mother?

Chapter Two

'My dear, I have things I – I want to s – say.'

'Mummy, please don't try to talk, it takes so much out of you.'

'Darling, I – I know I haven't long to be with you. And I want to tell you to be very careful. D – Daddy is failing, too. You will be on your own.'

'Don't, don't! Oh, Mummy, I can't bear to think of you both leaving me. But you mustn't worry, as I won't be on my own. I will have Harold.'

'Take care. Daddy is good in many ways. I – I have brought him round to thinking that he can leave the mill to you, but he – he can so easily be persuaded otherwise.'

Mags knew what her mother was trying to say. Knew that she had reservations about Harold and his motives in wanting to marry her.

'Try not to worry, Mummy. I can take care of myself. You have taught me never to accept that I am a lesser being than a man; and to stand up for my rights. Harold loves me. And I love him, Mummy – I do.'

Mags hoped this sounded convincing. Her heart was heavy

with sadness as she noted how blue her mother's lips were, and how her porcelain-like skin looked almost transparent – signs that told the end was near.

Memories of this complex woman came to her. Her energy, when Mags was just a child. How she would play all the boisterous games that a child loved to play, despite being in her forties. Her insistence that Mags should have all the privileges that a son would have – too many, if the truth be known – joining shooting parties; straddling a horse and not sitting side-saddle; being allowed to ride at a gallop, learn to jump fences and ride with the hounds. All this Mags had loved, but nothing could surmount the loneliness of her formative years.

And yet amidst it all, her mother hadn't forgotten to teach her the graces that a young lady should have, and had been careful in not letting Mags become too boyish, but had encouraged her to grow into a strong young woman who could hold her own in a crowd of men, whilst maintaining her femininity. It had been her mother who had insisted that Mags should be taught everything about the mill, and the necessary business skills, so that one day she would be able to take over the running of her father's business.

Mags had loved every minute of the learning process: helping to unpack the bales of cotton imported from America; then the cleaning and straightening, which turned the raw cotton into yarn. There were many stages to this and it was heavy work, so she had only been allowed to watch and learn. Next had been the drawing out and spinning, which turned the cotton into stronger yarn, ready for weaving. From there, she'd moved on to learn all there was to know about exporting the yarn to many countries, as 80 per cent of their produce was sold abroad. The rest went to weaving mills in Lancashire to be woven into cloth.

Their mill was the most modern, with electricity fully installed, and working conditions that complied with all the regulations. Still, Mags worried about the health of their workers, as they toiled for long hours in the humid, dust-laden conditions. She wanted the workers to have regular hearing tests, and had lobbied her father many times to provide earplugs to combat the effect of the constant loud noise.

In many ways, her life was unconventional. The girls she went to school with had gone on to finishing schools to learn how to be a lady and how to run a large mansion – managing housekeepers, hosting parties, as well as knowing the correct dress for each occasion – while she had gone into the mill, where she'd only had Betsy Bainwright for company.

Not that she minded, for she loved Betsy. They had become close from their first meeting, when Betsy had been thirteen and had begun working in the mill. Mags, the same age as Betsy, had come to the mill during her breaks from school. They had forged a relationship that had deepened to friendship, as Mags helped Betsy sweep the floor and gather the stray bits of raw cotton, which were then spun into cheaper rough-weave for selling to the factories that produced hessian for making into sacks.

Now, having mastered the workings of the mill, Betsy worked alongside Mags in the office. Her role was to train new workers as and when needed, and to supervise the younger members of the factory staff – see to their welfare and keep a record of their progress and the hours they worked. It was a role held by a man in all other mills.

The fact that Betsy was still working, despite being married

13

with three young children, was due to her husband – Bill having been injured in a mining accident in Rishton Colliery and no longer able to work.

But for all Mags's love of Betsy and the fun they had together, with Betsy's basic education, there was no stimulating girlish chatter about the injustices to women and other political topics, as there had been with her fellow companions at school. Sometimes, before the war, Mags had longed to be at finishing school. In some ways, though, she'd welcomed the war. Welcomed being able to do something, go to different places and meet new people.

'Margaret?'

'I'm still here, Mummy. You dropped off to sleep. I left you to rest.' But the sleep hadn't been restful, as her mother had plucked at the bedspread and turned her head from side to side in an agitated way. 'What's troubling you, Mummy?'

'Never let a man steal f – from you what I – I fought hard to give you, my d – darling Margaret.'

'I won't, Mummy, I promise. I love you, Mummy.'

As her mother closed her eyes, Mags knew she wouldn't open them again. She rang the bell. The nurse, a small woman with little to say, but a caring and efficient nature, came running in.

'I have to fetch my father, Nurse. Take care of my mother.'

Running across the landing to her father's room, Mags banged on his bedroom door. As if awaiting the summons, her father opened it and stood there in his dressing gown. 'I'm ready, my dear.'

'Take my arm, Daddy. We must hurry.'

Her mother seemed to have shrunk in the few minutes it had taken Mags to fetch her father.

'Belinda, my darling, Belinda.'

It was with an aching heart that Mags watched the agony of her parents' parting. Taking her mother's other hand, she tried to keep her voice steady. 'Take our love with you, Mummy darling.'

There was no deep sigh, as Mags had witnessed with many soldiers whom she'd held as they took their last breath; just a ceasing of the shallow breathing, and a mask-like appearance as the beautiful features of her mother's face became forever still.

The room took on the mantle of a silent place of despair. Then a sob broke the atmosphere and brought other sounds of the house back into focus: a door closing, footsteps hurrying and, outside, the birds chirping. These all crowded in on Mags, letting her know that the world would not stop spinning just because of her deep pain.

Looking over to her father, she saw in him the same grief she'd seen in Harold as he had knelt over his mother's still body, and she had the sense that this was her punishment – to lose her own mother. To know the pain that she herself had accidentally inflicted on Harold.

Her body crumpled and, but for the firm hold that the nurse took on her arm, she would have slumped to the floor. 'Your father needs you. Be strong for him, Margaret.'

Her father's sobs broke the silence and, looking over, she saw a broken man. She ran round the bed to be at his side. 'Daddy. I'm here for you.' Putting her arms around him, she held him. She didn't try to move him away from his beloved Belinda, but gave him the strength to stay.

Harold held Mags as they stood around the open grave a week later. His hand on her waist reassured her that he would help her. A strikingly handsome man in a rakish way, his dark hair was sleeked over to one side, and his clothes showed his good taste – smart suits always worn with a white scarf, when outside. He stood at least six feet one and gave off an air of being in charge, wherever he was.

Mags looked up at him and smiled and nodded at Harold when he mouthed the words, 'Are you all right?', although she still felt a little cross at him for arriving so late. She'd thought he wasn't going to come, as she'd had no word that he had arrived at his uncle's house. But he was stood at the church door when they arrived.

As they walked towards the church gate, Harold's words grated on her. 'We will still get married in two weeks, won't we, darling? I can't bear to live in my uncle's stuffy house for longer than that. I'd prefer to go back to the hotel in London.'

It seemed an inappropriate question when her heart was breaking, but she nodded her head.

Once seated in the back of the funeral car, Harold held her hand. 'You do mean it, don't you? Your father won't object, will he?'

'Harold, I don't know. We haven't spoken about it, but we haven't cancelled anything, either. I have given it some thought, though. If we do go ahead, we will need to scale down the wedding celebrations to just close family and friends. We can't carry on with the full-scale celebrations we had planned – it wouldn't be proper; and everyone will understand.'

'Of course, darling. Anything you wish.'

Harold spoke as if he was finalizing a business deal, not marriage to her, and this fuelled Mags's nagging doubts. Flors's voice came to her: '*Don't marry him, Mags, please don't marry my brother. He is a monster.*'

As she was used to doing, Mags analysed the reasons for

Flors saying this, rather than taking no notice of it. Harold had not been a good brother to dear Flors, but then their mother had been the instigator of that, feeding Harold tales of Flors being a wicked girl who had caused her great stress. But did this justify his behaviour towards Flors, when he was old enough to make up his own mind? *Oh, I don't know.*

Mags put her hand to her head to ease the throbbing pain there. She wished now that she'd travelled with her father, instead of electing to go back in the same car that Harold would travel in. She feared for her father. He'd been very quiet since the death of Mother, and often she caught him sitting with tears running down his face, but no sound coming from him, as if his heart was leaking.

'You look very beautiful, darling – black suits you. Your eyes look enormous. My lovely, innocent wife-to-be.' Harold's hand squeezed her thigh.

This shocked Mags: both the gesture, in the circumstances, and the word 'innocent'. *Oh God, I've never told him about the rape. Will he know? Will it matter?*

'Harold, I'm sorry, I – I . . . well, my heart is heavy with sadness. I can't – I mean . . .'

He turned away to gaze out of the car window.

'Harold, everything will be all right. It's just not the right time.'

His sigh, and the look he gave her, with one questioning eyebrow raised, told her that Harold thought any time was the right time. She lowered her head. To her, it was very unfeeling of him to expect anything of her – today of all days.

'I'll find a moment to speak to your father. I don't want to wait any longer than two weeks. If our wedding is cancelled, it will mean me having to go back down to London until the rearranged date draws nearer.' There was almost a threat in this.

'Haven't you work to do up here, Harold? I don't want to interfere, or tell tales, but word has it that your uncle isn't capable any more. Only last week it was rumoured that he had to shut down a machine, as he was running out of cotton. He'd forgotten to put in an order in time.'

'What? I didn't know that. He's a bloody old fool. Damn and blast the man!'

'Maybe more "old" than "fool". Father is always saying that it will be a good thing when you get here, as your family mill could end up closing, if it's left up to your uncle for much longer.'

'Why didn't you write to me, or send me a wire? Everything was running smoothly when I left last time.'

'I had my hands full, helping my mother through her last hours. I thought you knew the state of things, as Father said they have been bad for a while. I didn't imagine you thought the mill was running smoothly, but that perhaps you had a plan of action. Now, with you saying you will have to go back to London, I realize that maybe you don't.'

Harold shifted in the car seat beside her. 'I'll look into it all. But I can't tear myself in two. You know I have a lot to do in London, after all that happened.'

Mags didn't say anything, as she hadn't really understood why Harold needed to be in London so much, when his business and his fiancée were up here in Blackburn. Surely his solicitor could see to whatever needed seeing to, in the aftermath of the tragedy that led to his family home being burned down? Any normal person would want to be with the woman they loved in such circumstances, rather than where it all took place, wouldn't they?

This thought unsettled Mags, as she remembered that Flors had hinted more than once that there was something going on between one of her mother's maids and Harold. *Susan. Yes, that was her name. Surely not . . . No, I couldn't bear it.*

Harold cut into her thoughts. 'Can't the driver go faster than this? It's taking an age and I, for one, am ready for a stiff drink. It was freezing in that churchyard.'

There was no tenderness in Harold's words now, only irritation. This cut into Mags. 'Harold, you won't tackle Father today, will you? He's not well. He's in deep mourning.'

'Well, I was rather hoping to. Really, darling – he's a man, he understands these things. He'll expect me to be anxious. The sooner our names are joined, the better.'

'Is that all our marriage is to you: a joining of our names?'

'Don't be silly. I can only assume you are behaving as you are because you are upset. I understand that, but yes, the joining of assets is a big part of any marriage, as well as the love that two people have for one another. Both are a big consideration for me, and should be for you, too. Once we marry, I will head the largest cotton mill in the area, as your father is no longer able to run Witherbrook's mill, and it sounds as though it is time that I pensioned off my uncle from Roford mill.'

'Oh? I don't think that will be necessary. You do know that I head Witherbrook's mill, don't you?'

'Only as a convenience, surely? Once you are my wife, your father and I will take the reins jointly for a while, and then he will hand over to me. That is the natural way of things. I will head both factories. And I imagine that you will be proud of me doing so.'

'I don't want to discuss this now, Harold, please. I have a headache, and I will be expected to host the wake for my mother, when my heart is breaking at her loss. I do have more to say on the matter, but we'll talk tomorrow or the next day.'

'I'm sorry, but we must get this clear. There will be no talking about it. As my wife, you will do as I say. That is the way of things, and the way I mean to begin and to carry on. You will be at home, making sure all is running smoothly for me. I intend to host my first hunt on Boxing Day, and I will rely on you to make sure all of that is in place for me and runs well. It will be my introduction to local society.'

Mags felt too exasperated and unhappy to respond. What local society he imagined he was joining, she had no idea. The very word conjured up lords and ladies, of which there were very few in the area. Yes, there was a meet that she belonged to, but that hunt was made up of mill owners and their sons and wealthy landowners. Their gatherings took place at the White Horse Inn in Turton, about eight miles from her home – wonderful occasions, from the first sip of the warming stirrup cup to the exhilarating chase, and the gathering at one or other of the meets' houses for a hot lunch and lashings of beer or port. The only part Mags didn't like was the kill. A caring person, she never took part in this final act, but pulled away and galloped off to a place where she could wait for the rest to catch up with her. She smiled as she remembered that the first person to do so was always Jerome Cadley – her childhood sweetheart.

She'd always suspected that the lovely Jerome didn't like the kill, either, and got away from the braying hunters as soon as he knew he wouldn't lose face by doing so. But he would join in the teasing of her, which was always done by the others in a good-humoured way. *I wonder how Jerome is.* Like so many others, he'd had his life interrupted by war, but thank God had come back safely, and she'd heard he was doing his medical studies at university. She'd noticed his mother and father at the graveside, and intended to catch up with them later and find out about Jerome and send him her good wishes.

The car wheels crunched on the gravel of their drive as they turned off Feniscowles Lane. When the beautiful house came into view, Mags took in the low winter sun glistening on the frosted roof and reflecting off the many windows of her beautiful manor home. But the sight spelled loneliness when she realized that never again would her mother grace its rooms.

As Harold took her hand to help her alight, he squeezed rather more tightly than was necessary. 'I know you are under a lot of strain, darling, but please don't be difficult. I want everything settled very quickly. Surely you do, too?'

'Of course' was all she could manage, for a little of her had died on the journey – the part that held hope for her future. Hope that Harold would welcome her expertise alongside his, as they steered their mills to greater prosperity; and hope that he wouldn't quash her free spirit, but would let her grow within the marriage. A part of her wanted to call the wedding off, and yet a big part of her wanted Harold so much. Something Flors had once said to her came to her mind – that love can surmount everything. Now she wondered if it really could.

Chapter Three

'Harold, how can you be so unfeeling? Father has said that he isn't up to giving me away, just two weeks after my mother's death. Why can't you accept that? I have to; and I love you, darling, as much as you love me, and am longing to be married to you, but . . .'

Nothing Mags said made any difference. Harold's face remained set in an expression that was unmoving.

'I'm sorry, Harold, but that's how it is. We will postpone everything for six months.'

'Well, I obviously have no say in the matter. I'm your husband-to-be, and you take no notice of my wishes. When we marry, you will no longer be obligated to your father's wishes, but to mine. I hope you understand that, Mags. I won't tolerate his rule over my wife. Now I will do as I said I would and go back to my hotel in London. I am thinking of having my home rebuilt. I consulted an architect before I came up to this godforsaken place, and it is possible to reconstruct the building. It seems the fire was put out before too much structural damage was done to the outer building.'

'So you are going to leave your mill to sink under your

ailing uncle?' This wasn't what Mags wanted to say; she wanted to scream at him, and to know why Harold didn't want to spend more time with her. Her heart was breaking with the realization that he truly did think of her as an acquisition, and if he couldn't have her yet, then he would carry on without her until he could.

'I'll appoint a good manager. There must be such men. Maybe you could help with that? Yes, I could leave that to you, as you will know who is suitable.'

'And me? Have you no desire to be with me?'

'Desire is the reason I have to leave. Being around you and not being able to . . . well, I daren't even kiss you, as you awaken such feelings in me. But you won't go against your father's wishes and continue with our wedding plans, so I must distance myself from you.'

Though these words were said in a temper, Mags felt her heart lift. 'Oh, Harold, I . . . well, I feel the same.'

Harold stood. He'd been sitting cross-legged on the deep-maroon Queen Anne couch that sat in the bay window of the lovely, restful sitting room. Mags was struck by how his handsome presence graced the room. She caught her breath at the beautiful picture he presented. His tread was soft on the deep pile of the carpet as he crossed over to where she stood. His arms opened.

Mags melted into his warm, lean body. His eyes looked deep into hers. Sometimes a steely blue, they were softened now by their enlarged pupils and held a yearning that she responded to. A feeling overcame her as he lowered his head and she could feel his breath on her face.

'Oh, Mags, Mags . . .'

His lips burned her, his tongue tantalized her, his hands caressed her back and then . . . She pulled away, as much

23

from the intense sensation that his touch on her breast had aroused as from fear.

'Mags, don't. Don't resist me. If we could . . . well, be to each other – and give to each other – everything that a man and wife should, I wouldn't go away. I would stay by your side. Don't you want that?'

'I – I do, but . . .'

He pulled her into his body once more and held her tightly. She could feel his desire pressed against her. Fear vied with the thrill of it. Fear at how painful the rape had been; fear at her deceit in allowing Harold to assume her to be a virgin; and, yes, fear that she would be with child before marriage.

'My darling, I must have you – I must.' His hand stroking her hair felt such a tender, loving action. 'Don't be afraid. I will be gentle, and I will make sure you don't become pregnant until we are married.'

Every sinew of her cried out for the release that she knew she would find in his arms. When his lips found hers, she was lost. There was no resistance in her when he cupped her breast this second time. Her body quivered its need, sending the thrill of his touch zinging through her veins.

'Can we get to your bedroom without being seen, my darling?'

His gravelly voice heightened the need in her. She nodded, her throat so tight that she found speech difficult. Her only thought was to guide Harold to her room. The fear she felt added to the adrenaline pulsing through her.

Her father was taking his rest, and the only maid in attendance would be in the kitchen, giving Cook a hand. It was the housekeeper's afternoon off, and the cleaning lady had long left. No one would see them go to her suite of rooms in the east wing of the house.

When she opened the door to her sitting room, Harold made an approving sound.

'This is nice, darling. Did you choose the furnishings?'

The remark brought normality back to her, and she wished he hadn't made it, as the situation she'd put herself in became all too realistic, and a shyness that she hadn't felt before enveloped her.

'Yes. I'm very proud of how it turned out, as Mother resisted my choice. However, she loved it, once it was done.'

'I'm not surprised, it looks very . . . chic, yes, that's the word.'

The room now became Mags's focus, and all the excitement that had gripped her and made her act in such an impetuous way vanished as she gazed around her. Yes, she had chosen well, if a little unconventionally, as she loved the effect of the moss-green furniture and pink cushions standing out against the background of the soft grey carpet and curtains. The cushions had been embroidered by her own hand with moss-green leaf motifs, and the occasional furniture and her bureau were in light oak, as opposed to the mahogany of the rest of the house, and gave the right finishing touch to it all.

'Would you like to sit down and have some lemonade? I have a jug on—'

'Darling, I'm not here for lemonade.'

The tone of his voice rekindled the spark of anticipation in Mags. As she turned towards Harold, he reached out and took hold of her arm, pulling her towards him. She caught her breath as he lowered his lips to hers.

But this time his kiss wasn't gentle. His need spilled over, in a demanding, passionate probing of her mouth and a rough rubbing and squeezing of her breasts. This increased her sense of guilt at what they were proposing to do. She wanted – needed – his gentleness, not this display of animalistic fervour. Instinctively she struggled against him.

'No, Mags. I'm not going to allow you to go back on what we agreed. We are here now. You cannot withdraw from me.'

'I – I don't know. I shouldn't have brought you here. I—'

'Don't, Mags, please don't. Let's get back what we felt downstairs. Maybe I was a little too eager, but I thought . . . well, I thought we were ready. *I* am. I want you so badly, Mags.'

Guilt bored into her. She wanted to ask him to leave, but was afraid of his temper, and thought he might do that literally and she wouldn't see him for months. Something in her suspected that the affair Flors had told her of was still going on, and if she didn't give Harold what he desired, then Susan would.

'Mags?'

His plea made up her mind. She wanted Harold with all her being. 'Yes, let's start again. Gently, like you were downstairs. What you did just now frightened me.'

'Oh, Mags, I'm so sorry. I *so* want you, I got carried away. I keep forgetting this is your first time. I'll remember that now. I promise, darling. Let me kiss you. Oh, my darling, let me kiss you.'

His tone and his gentle hold on her melted Mags's resistance. Though guilt rocked her, when he said this was her first time, she couldn't spoil that illusion for him. She wasn't practised at deceit, but maybe if she cried out as if in pain, he would think that normal?

Harold dispelled any worry she might feel, as he exclaimed

at the beauty of every limb that he bared and caressed when he undressed her.

She had seen many men's naked bodies, but always racked with pain, and thin and bony after a great toll had ravaged them, but Harold was magnificent. His body was honed and contoured. And when her eyes travelled downwards, she felt an increase in the heat that crept over her. He truly was beautiful.

His loving of her was gentle and patient, until she cried out for him to come to her. When he did, her ecstasy was such that she forgot her resolve to show this was her first time, but lost herself in the extreme pleasure that shuddered through her body, taking her to a place she had never been before or thought existed. In this place she was a different being. A pliable and yet demanding woman. One who knew what her body wanted, and one who gave herself completely to loving her man. All memory and horror of her rape were gone in that moment, and her cries were ones of joy.

This stunning world of love and sexual desire seized all her senses, making her demand more – demand something she knew she could attain, something that was building inside her. Then it came, a surge of feeling so powerful it had her begging Harold to stop, as she stiffened beneath him and allowed the sensations to release an explosion inside her of wave after wave of exquisite thrill, taking her to an abandonment of everything she'd been up till this moment.

'Oh, Harold. Harold, my love. My love.' Her tears flowed as her body embraced this release.

He looked down at her. His eyes held a question – an accusation. She lowered hers, the moment spoiled as memory flooded through her, enclosing her and prodding at her guilt as his movements became like the German's had been: a deep, rough thrusting of her. This didn't cause her pain, but neither did it rekindle the feelings she'd just experienced.

Harold rolled off her as his moment came upon him. She knew this was to keep his promise not to make her pregnant. And she knew it was a moment when she should be holding him, and praising him, but she was paralysed by other feelings now.

When he calmed, he lay on his back and reached for his jacket. His silence sliced through the air. She heard him fumbling and then the strike of a match. Sulphur stung her nostrils, before the more pleasant smell of his exhaled smoke wafted over her.

'Who was it?'

The question tightened her stomach muscles.

'I know there has been somebody. Who was it?'

His tone frightened her. 'I – I was raped.'

Once again, that silence in which she could feel his anger.

'Harold, I – I didn't . . . I mean, it was terrifying, and painful and humiliating. H – he was a German soldier. He stank of sweat and beer, and cigar smoke tainted his breath. And I had the added terror of seeing one of his comrades grabbing Flors and—'

'Good God! Flora was raped, too?'

'No. Their commander came in, woken by our screams, and stopped them. There was supposed to be immunity from capture for the Red Cross workers, but the Germans didn't care about such things. They had conquered Brussels and saw the world as theirs for the taking.'

The words poured out of her, and her body shook with sobs as they did so. Harold remained like a statue beside her, his only movement the deep inhaling of his cigarette.

Mags waited.

She wanted him to take her in his arms and forgive her. But that didn't happen. He swung his legs off the bed, stubbed his cigarette in the base of a small ornament on her side table and grabbed his clothes. As he went towards her bathroom, he looked back at her, his face clouded with rage. 'You should have told me.'

The bathroom door slammed shut behind him. Mags curled up into a ball and wept.

When Harold emerged, he said two words. 'Goodbye, Mags.'

Mags stared at the closed door of her bedroom, unable to move for the weight of grief as everything assailed her: the rape, the loss of her mother, and, above all, her certainty that she had lost Harold. And after only just discovering the real him – the gentle man and the exquisite lover, qualities that far outweighed his petulance when things didn't go his way. Or putting himself, and what he wanted, above all else, a trait of which she'd seen so much.

Why had she let herself go this far? She'd known what Harold was really like. Known him to plot a murder, to get at the inheritance he thought was rightfully his. Known him to abandon his own sister, when he must have realized that his mother's hatred of Flors was irrational. And a lesser charge: she'd witnessed his lack of drive in business, preferring to hand over to a manager than see his factory through a crisis.

But what now? *Oh God, he'll go back to her – to his mistress. I'm certain of it. And I'll be left here pining for him, raging with jealousy and hate. It will destroy me.*

Uncurling her body, Mags got off the bed. Walking with determination towards the bathroom, she told herself: *No. I won't let that happen. I must be strong. I have to be, for Father, if not for myself.*

This resolve didn't sit in her for long. As she soaked in a hot bath, her whole body wept for her loss, and she knew that love can offer pain-filled agony as well as exquisite joy.

On the hall table there was a note. The sight of it stopped Mags in her tracks as she descended the stairs an hour later. What would she read in it?

Forcing herself forward, she picked it up. A waft of Harold's aftershave assailed her. The woody, provocative aroma mocked her. His hands would have had traces of it on his palms as he applied it after his bath.

Not wanting to, but unable to stop herself, she lifted the note to her nostrils and drew in a deep breath. Her eyes closed, and emotions assaulted her in a painful rush. *I love him. Oh God, I love and need him so much.*

Going through to the sitting room, she sat down where Harold had sat, hoping to feel something of him left there:

I am appalled at what happened to you, my dear Mags, but even more appalled that you kept it from me. You cheated me of being able to come to terms with it before we took the next step.

To me, this is a rotten act on your part. I am the man you love. Didn't you trust me?

Yes, I can accept that the memory was painful to you. But if you wanted to keep it to yourself, why did you not pretend? I had so much trust in you – and love for you – that I wouldn't have guessed. You needn't even have faked extreme pain, as I know many women hardly feel a thing, but are resistant to a man entering them fully at first. You could have done that – you are

not a fool. You know the way of things. You were a
nurse, for God's sake!

But you chose not to do that for me. You chose not to
keep me innocent of what had happened. You let me
find out during what should have been a wonderful
occurrence between us.

I am disgusted with you, and I do not know if I can
forgive you.

I am going back to London and will take at least
two weeks' respite from you before I make my decision.
I will write to you then, letting you know how I think
our future looks.

Whether that will be together, I do not know.
Parting will be painful, but so will marrying a liar
and a deceitful person.

H x

She had no more tears to shed. She would write to Harold
and try to explain. In the letter she would mention Susan
and give a few ultimatums of her own. Whether this would
kill their relationship or not, she did not know – if she was
wrong about him having an affair, it would; if she was right,
then it just might help him see how hypocritical he was being.

Whatever happened, something told her that she must
stand up to Harold or lose herself. She was a person in her
own right. Her darling mother had taught her that, and she
wasn't about to taint Mother's memory by not being the
woman she had been brought up to be.

Harold had that lesson to learn. And she had to know if
his love for her was strong enough to allow her to be the
person she was. If not, then painful as it would be, she would
go her own way. There had to be life after love, didn't there?

Chapter Four

The letter arrived two days after the two-week deadline Harold had set. Alongside it was one with a French stamp on it. Mags knew this would be from Flors. She wanted to open it and find out how Flors and Cyrus were faring, but she needed to know Harold's decision first.

The last two weeks had been a time during which she had found a strong resolve not to allow Harold to crush her; and to seek his assurance that, if they married, he would not behave as his own father had done and keep a mistress.

Taking the letters off the silver salver on the hall table, Mags went up to her room. It overlooked the huge, sprawling garden, with the beautiful view of the rugged, hilly terrain.

Stealing herself for whatever Harold's letter held, Mags sat down at the bureau in the corner of the room. Slicing the seal with the pearl-handled paper knife that had been a present from her mother, she felt her hands shake and a yearning for everything to turn out as she wanted it to.

My dear Mags,
I have to apologize.

Her heart leapt. Her eyes scanned the words that followed:

I behaved very badly. I should have shown more
understanding. It was a terrible thing that happened
to you, and I have spoken to someone who pointed out
that it would have been far too difficult for you to talk
about it; and that my skill in making love to you was
such that you surrendered to me without fear, and so I
should be proud of that, and should continue to help
you to forget the rape.

Mags took a deep breath. Part of her wanted to scream
at the audacity of his words, but it vied with the part of her
that was so relieved to read them, and with the sheer embarrassment of them. Who had Harold talked to? Not . . . *God,*
don't let it have been Susan! On reading the words again,
she thought they did sound like intimate words spoken
between lovers – for who else would know about Harold's
skill at lovemaking?

Your letter shocked me. It seems that I am to take on
your desire to be independent, and your outspoken and
direct approach. This will not be easy for me. I, too,
have been brought up to be independent and to have
my own way. My father trusted my decisions, from a
young age.

Trusted them, or knew it was no use arguing with you,
Harold?

I am very upset by your insinuation that I am having an affair with someone who was nothing more than a maid in my home.

When will you see the truth about Flora? What does she have to do to finally disillusion you? Do you think a mother gives up a daughter easily? Isn't it strange to you that two sons – my dear late brother Francis and I – found Mother to be a wonderful woman, who loved and cared for us? Why she couldn't do that for Flora was because Flora was destructive, wilful and, yes, even as a child, she was evil and spiteful. And despite all she has done since – finding and marrying her own half-brother, to spite our mother – you choose to believe Flora. That hurts me. It hurts not to be trusted, and it hurts to know that you too are hurting, thinking that I am being unfaithful to you, when I love you so much and you are all I need, or will ever need.

You are warm and loving and, I know now, a deeply passionate woman. My mother wasn't those things. From what I came to understand, she used the intimate side of marriage to bargain and to punish, and the result was that father sought solace elsewhere.

I am still coming to terms with how he behaved, and the devastating consequences of his actions. It isn't every day that an unknown elder brother turns up out of the blue, in an incestuous marriage with your own sister, and takes the inheritance that you thought of as yours all your life.

If I am a little rash with my decisions and actions, and seem not to settle at anything, it is because of that, coming on top of the loss of my parents and my brother

*and, not least, the family home – the only one I have
ever known.*

*Can you not open your heart to me, my darling?
Forgive me and give us a chance at happiness, without
doubting me, and without fighting me over the silly
notion you have that, even as my future treasured wife,
you want to work for a living? I cannot come to terms
with that. How will I be perceived? Do you know of
any other couple of our standing whose wife goes out to
work? It is preposterous.*

The ring of truth in his words stung. Harold was right.
She knew she was indulged – her daddy's only child, treated
like a son a lot of the time. *Oh, how folk must laugh at me
and my efforts to thrive in the business world.* This hit her as
something she had always known, but had denied. Yes, she
had gained respect for her knowledge and her flare for making
the right decisions, but she'd known the real opinions of
the men she dealt with. Maybe Harold was right. Her heart
was heavy as this realization overcame her.

*I want a loving wife, as I know you will be, who
cares for me and is there for me, making a loving and
welcoming home for me.*

*In return, I will be a diligent businessman and will
run all our business affairs. Above all, I will be a loving
husband and father to our children – I hope we have
many. I want to make those with you, my darling, and
only with you. We have both had a taste of how wonderful
our coming together will be. I am pining to repeat that.
Just writing this, I am feeling the need of you, wanting to
hold you and be one with you. Are you feeling that, too?*

Mags couldn't deny that she was. She caught her breath as, unconsciously, she stretched out her legs and tensed the muscles in her groin. A remembered thrill tightened her throat. *Yes! Yes, I am feeling it. Oh, Harold, come back to me, and be to me the husband that I want – and need.*

*Write soon, my darling; write soon with what
I want to hear, and I will be there with you like a
shot, creeping into your bed and making exquisite
love to you.*

The feelings inside Mags intensified. Her breath caught in her lungs, and her cheeks flushed. She swallowed hard as desire consumed her. *Oh, Harold, I love you. I love you.*

*I cannot promise that I can stay with you for the
whole of the time until our wedding, my darling, as
I have such a lot going on here that I need to finalize
before our marriage. I need it out of the way, so that
nothing takes me away from you afterwards. Please
let it be that I will be there.*
Your loving H x

Rising, Mags went over to the window and looked out at the garden. The weather had warmed, and there was only a trace here and there of the overnight cold – a frosted white cobweb clinging to the hedge and an icicle hanging from the wishing well, dripping droplets of water as it melted. The low winter sun shone on her, its rays amplified by the glass of the windowpanes. Soon Christmas would be upon them – a time she'd always loved, but now dreaded. It was going to be painful to get through it without her mother. But then maybe Harold would be here. Oh, she hoped so.

Reading the letter again, she knew she was at a turning point in her life, as the pull of Harold and all that he promised was too much for her to resist. Just reading his words had caused a burning passion inside her. Her body yearned for him, and her soul ached for him.

Her decision wasn't made without foreboding, for if she took the step to marry Harold, on her head be it – she had no delusions about him.

Sighing, she returned to the bureau and picked up Flors's letter. *Please let it contain good news.*

Dearest Mags,

This is the first opportunity I have had to sit down and write to you. I want you to know that Cyrus and I are very happy. It has been difficult coming to terms with the knowledge of our sibling relationship to each other, but we cannot change that and have decided to be as we were before we knew – the same deeply-in-love couple.

I am enclosing my address, and the latest one that I have for Ella; only please, whatever you do, keep mine a secret. I say this assuming that you are now married, or going to be, to my brother Harold, who I believe would still seek to harm us. I was sorry that you chose to go into a relationship with him, but as you said: love is a powerful emotion.

I hope, with all my heart, that he makes you happy. You deserve nothing less.

I have worried about you. Please don't carry any guilt about my mother's death. I don't know exactly what you meant by 'knowing hers and Harold's plan', but I can guess from their action in attacking us that they had intended extreme harm to us both, and to Cyrus in particular. I would even guess so far as them wanting him to die, so that Father's estate would revert to Harold. But if this was the case, they were foolish to think that would happen, because our son, Freddy, would have been the natural heir.

But this is about you. Mother's death was an accident – purely that. A terrible one, as it left you so broken, but one precipitated by your need to protect Cyrus and me, and I am so very grateful to you.

I know that if you are married to Harold, you won't be able to write back, but I wanted you to know that I am your friend, and I could have no better friend than you. I will be forever grateful for the way you tried to help save my little Alice. Oh, Mags, it is so painful to speak of her. But we owe you a great debt for the way you did all that you could for her. Our home is always yours, too, please remember that.

I also wanted you to know that we were delivered of our third child, a son, Randolph. He is now six weeks old and thriving, though I took a while to recover, as it was a difficult birth. I am now back on my feet and getting our new home into shape – a neglected chateau, which stands just outside the village of Laurens in Hérault in the Languedoc province. Cyrus is busy preparing his fields in readiness to plant the grapevines he has ordered, and he is loving our new life, as I am.

Take care, my dear friend. All my love, Flors x

With a sigh, Mags took two sheets of writing paper from her pad and then took the lid off the pot of ink that stood at the back of the top shelf of the bureau and dipped her pen into it. She would write to Harold:

My dearest, darling Harold,
I have been a fool. I see that now. Nothing is worth more than having you by my side. Of course I want to be your wife, and I promise I will never keep anything from you again.

Crossing herself to negate this lie, she put the pen down and found the small knob under the side of the bureau. Pressing it caused her to jump, even though she knew the secret drawer always made a loud click when it shot open. Into it she tucked Flors's letter. She would break her ties with Flors, but she wouldn't disclose to Harold where his sister was. And yes, she would keep the letter . . . just in case.

And my darling, I can, and will be, the wife you want me to be. I will leave the running of the mill to you and Daddy.
It will work, it will – I can do this. I must.
Your letter aroused feelings in me that are still reverberating around my body. My blood is pounding sensations to every part of me.
Oh, Harold, I so want – and need – you, too. Marry me and make me yours every day. Our bed will be our loving place; a place where our children are made, a place where our bond will be so deep and so binding that no one can ever divide us again, and no past can encroach upon us.

What happened in our lives previously occurred to two very different people. We are us: the 'us' that is now; the 'us' that no one can put asunder. Come back to me soon, my darling.

Your loving Mags x

A turmoil of emotions churned through her as she sat back. How was it that she'd given in so easily, after vowing to fight for her rights within the marriage? Her signature on what she'd written changed her future. Would she be able to settle down to the routine of running the household? And what of her dream of owning the mill? *That will never happen now, as Daddy will surely think it prudent to leave it to Harold, once we are married. Oh, why am I beset with doubts?*

Rising from the chair, she picked up the letter and sealed it in an envelope. Her choice was made, and now she must live by it. Walking briskly, she took the letter to the salver on the hall stand. One of the household staff would take it to the post office.

'Oh, I was coming to look for you, my dear.'

Her father's voice seemed to compound the sadness within her. Not only at having given up her dreams, but because Father no longer spoke in a commanding way that held confidence, but as if he was apologizing. He was like a lost soul, since Mother's passing.

Changing her mind about the fate of the letter, she turned towards her father. 'I was just going out, Daddy. Come with me. I have to deliver this letter to the post office, and I thought I would drive to Queen's Park and take a walk. Mummy loved that park. We will feel close to her there.'

'Yes, but she didn't like you driving. Such an unladylike thing to do.'

'That wasn't Mummy – and you know it, Daddy. That notion is yours. If Mummy could have, she'd have taken to the wheel the moment you bought the Rolls, but she knew it would put you in a tizzy.'

'Ha, I suppose you're right, my dear. I have always had more of an old-fashioned outlook. It was your mother who made it possible for you to achieve all that you've accomplished. I would have packed you off to finishing school. But I don't regret it, as you've been like a son as well as a daughter to me.'

They were walking very slowly around the perimeter of the huge lake in the beautiful park when the subject came up again. Mags had been deep in thought about how her life had panned out, but she hadn't missed the stark winter beauty around her: the slanting grassy slopes, the variety of trees and bushes and how the evergreens gave a splash of colour to the stark trees, stripped of their summer glory.

The North of England was rarely taken seriously, being looked upon as an industrial, cloth-cap-and-clogs place that was choked by the smoke belching from its factories. Very few southerners ventured up here, if they could avoid it, and yet it was a place of stunning beauty, no matter what the season. The Pennine mountains and the Bowland hills surrounded Blackburn and produced a kaleidoscope of rich greens in summer, rustic browns and flaming reds in autumn and were now clad in icy white, which after Christmas would give way to the many shades of spring, when everywhere would be bursting into bloom.

'I never wanted you to see me as a son, Daddy, but as a daughter with skills you were proud of.'

'I know, my dear. And that is what you are. I am worried

about you, though. How will you fare in a marriage to a man who doesn't agree with his wife working?'

'Oh? You know Harold's views?'

'Yes, he has tried to get me on his side.'

'Did he succeed?'

'He did. I agree with him, but I did tell him that, like me, he would benefit from seeking your advice on all business matters. I told him he could have no better person to guide him than you.'

Mags could only smile. She didn't want to disillusion her father, but she knew that wouldn't happen. Where Harold was concerned, she had to accept that it was a man's world. But could she accept that?

'But, you know, you don't have to worry. I have made sure that the mill is yours and I didn't agree to merge it with Roford mill. I—'

'Harold asked that of you?!' *How could he, and when he knows Father is at his lowest?*

'Yes, I was shocked, too. But I told him I would want to see Roford mill in profit, and with better working conditions for the weavers. As you well know, that business is in a bad way. To my mind, Harold should have stayed up here and got things sorted.'

Her father was shocked to hear how Harold had asked Mags to appoint a manager for Roford mill.

'What the blazes for? Can't he get the job done himself? Look, if he's not going to allow you to work, then I will have to take the reins. I'm sorry, but I don't see how Harold will give our works the attention that is needed – he has to prove himself first.'

This upset Mags, for she knew her father wasn't well enough to bear the stress of the business. And yet this might be the answer. 'If you could find a time when we are on our own each day, to keep me informed . . . I – I mean, Harold won't like me being involved, even as a sort of silent partner, so he mustn't know. All decisions will have to look as though they are yours, Daddy.'

His hand patted the back of hers. 'Good girl; you will fare well, if you manage Harold that way. Your mother asked me to see that you didn't "lose yourself" – as she put it. *She* didn't, you know. She managed me well; let me keep face, as the man of the house, but I knew that she held the strings that worked me. I liked it that way, and now I feel lost. Very lost.'

'Oh, Daddy, I know.'

They walked in silence for a time. It was Mags who broke it. 'Have you thought about Christmas, Daddy? I mean we don't have to do anything as we have always done it. Not this year. I'll carry out Mother's traditions of seeing that the children of the village all get a present, but we needn't get the decorations down from the attic or make a big thing of it.'

'I haven't thought about it, my dear; but yes, I would like to be quiet and not make a fuss. Is Harold coming? He left so abruptly.'

'He had urgent business, as I told you, but I have had a letter from him, and he is coming back up. Whether he will stay for Christmas, I'm not sure. He is grieving himself and may want to spend it where he can visit his parents' grave.'

'It's been a bad year all round, and you, my darling, are bearing the brunt of it from all quarters.'

They held hands, each enclosed by their own grief. But Mags couldn't dwell too long in that sad and empty part of her. She felt the burden weighing heavily on her shoulders at the thought of her father having to take a huge role in the running of the mill once more, but couldn't see another solution. *At least this way I can keep some control. But what about my promise of no more secrets? What with keeping Flors's whereabouts from Harold, and the arrangement that Daddy and I have agreed upon, I've more than broken that promise, but what choice did I have?*

Chapter Five

'Eeh, lass, I'm not looking forward to further changes. First your da gives up the helm and you take over – not that that worried me, as you're more than capable, but this man of yours hasn't proved himself at being good at running a mill, now has he?'

Betsy was always outspoken, and the fact that she could speak this way to Mags was a mark of their friendship.

Mags feared for Betsy's future. *What will Harold do about Betsy? One thing I know: he won't want to work alongside her.* No, he'd want to appoint a male clerk. His ideas were firmly set, where women were concerned; and elevating them – especially working-class women, as he would view Betsy – was not something that he agreed with.

'I knaw what you're thinking, lass: me position ain't safe. No man of Mr Roford's standing is going to take to a woman holding such high responsibility in his factory.'

'It isn't his!' But as she said these words, Mags knew she wouldn't be able to do anything about Betsy's position, other than . . . 'Betsy, I've just had an idea. How would you take to working in my house? I – I don't mean as a skivvy, but our housekeeper is retiring age now and—'

'Eeh, lass, I would be honoured. By, I can't believe as you've asked this of me. Not that I knaw how such a fine house is run, mind, but I can learn, can't I?'

Relief swept over Mags. Her worries about Betsy and her fate evaporated. 'Oh, Betsy, I'm so glad you think it a good solution.'

'Well, I knew as I'd be a problem here. And I thought as you'd find me sommat, but to honour me in this way is more than I dreamed of. Ta, lass. You're a good 'un.'

Mags laughed out loud – a reaction to how she was feeling, at the prospect of having the lovely Betsy still by her side, as much as at the way Betsy expressed herself. Though a niggling worry came over her as to how she was going to curb Betsy's natural exuberance and keep their deep friendship from being noticed by Harold. To him, servants were servants and didn't cross over to become friends – *though they could be lovers . . . Oh God, I must stop these thoughts.*

'What is it, lass? You look troubled.'

'Nothing. Sorry. I – I was just thinking how much my mother would have loved to have had you as her housekeeper, as she always laughed when I related your antics to her.'

'Aw, ta, lass. We all looked up to your ma, you knaw. She were a good 'un an' all. Look how she started the school for the young 'uns, and the Sunday school to see to their religious teachings; and every Christmas each one of them received a gift from her.'

'I know, and I want to carry on these traditions. Not that I am aware of all that she did. As you know, my life has been spent around my father and his business, but you can help me, in keeping me informed of the needs of the workforce and their families. I already have plans to expand the healthcare available to the workers, to include their families.'

'Eeh, that'd be grand, as many a bairn has died through their family not being able to afford a doctor.'

'Oh no! Oh, Betsy, I didn't realize. Why didn't they appeal to my mother? She would have helped.'

'Pride. Aye, we're a proud lot, us working-class northerners. Our menfolk are against handouts. They fight for their dues, but baulk at taking owt they perceive as charity.'

'Well, we will have to make sure that what we put in place is not looked upon in that way, but is viewed as it should be – as the right of every man to have access to medical help when he or his family need it. What's the best way for us to do that, Betsy?'

'I could say by stopping a bob from their wages each week to pay for it, but that'd cause more hardship than benefit, so write it into the conditions of their work. Make it one of their rights. That should do it. By, lass, I don't mean to talk out of turn, but perhaps you'd be best to sort it afore your man takes over, as he might not agree to it.'

This stung Mags into realizing how she was about to lose the power to make such decisions. But she also knew that what Betsy said was true. 'Well, we'd better get on with it then. I will need to draw up new "terms of working" and get them into force very quickly, as Mr Roford is due to take over soon after Christmas.'

As Betsy left the office, the sound of the machinery below as it spun the cotton amplified, making a noise not dissimilar to a train hurtling through a station and evoking in Mags a mixture of feelings.

It would be good to have Betsy's continued support and

friendship, though something told her Harold might not approve. A deep sigh released itself from within her. *Just how many concessions am I to going to have to make, to keep Harold happy?* But she brushed this thought away as it was replaced by a heat that flushed through her at the new thought that overcame her – yes, sacrifices had to be made, but how worthwhile they would be, to know the loving side of Harold on a daily basis. Mags drew in a deep breath. *Yes, if I can keep Harold happy, I will enrich our life together.*

The interview with Mrs Potts, the housekeeper, had gone well. She was more than willing to take up her planned retirement earlier than she had expected to, and welcomed the gift of her cottage free for life and the pension she would receive. 'I'll still keep me eye on things for a while for you, Miss Margaret. That Betsy Bainwright is a good 'un, but she don't know the ropes of running a place like this. If she's a willing learner, I'll come in for a few hours a week to guide her.'

'That's very generous of you, Mrs Potts, thank you. And I hope you will help me, too, in the work I intend to do in the community. I know that I need to tread delicately and not upset the egos of the menfolk. Sadly, my mother didn't have much chance to show me those skills.'

'Oh, I knaw as you'll be well received, lass. Them's very proud of your war-work and feel as though you became one of them during that time. It made it easier for the women-folk whose sons went to war, to knaw as you were out there an' all.'

Mags blushed. She hadn't the heart to dispel this miscon-ception, as there hadn't been many British in Belgium at the beginning of the war, when she had been a VAD, or

Voluntary Aid worker, there. And besides, there was so much of that time she wanted to forget that she preferred not to talk about it.

Christmas was upon them before Mags knew it. As expected, Harold didn't want to join them until January. He said he wanted to stay in the hotel, to be close to his family home for one last Christmas. Mags didn't like this, but she understood, making her mind up to hang on to the fact that her father had relented and had brought forward the day they could marry. Not that she needed his consent, but she wanted him to be able to cope with it all. And so their wedding was set for February. Mags hoped that when Harold did arrive, it would be with the news that he would stay forever, although she accepted that he might have to make short visits to London to oversee the rebuilding of his home.

'Is that everything, Betsy?'

'Aye, we have a present for all the young 'uns and a hamper for each family. You've done the community proud – they'll be queuing up to work at your mill, when word gets out about this and the improved conditions.'

'Ha, that's if we have work for them. You know yourself that the recession is beginning to bite our trade, too. But we won't think about that now. I'm eager to get the delivery done.'

A fluttering of snow met them as they went outside and got into the car. They were to follow the horse and cart to the church hall, where the goods were to be distributed.

The atmosphere when they arrived was charged with excitement. There were no men present, just mothers and children. Betsy had warned Mags that would be the case.

But no matter, for the men hadn't forbidden acceptance of the gifts, and that's all she could ask for.

By the time all was done, Mags ached from saying 'Merry Christmas' so many times and having her hand shaken, but happiness lay in her at having contributed to spreading joy amongst them. More than that, the acceptance she'd met with had made her feel like one of them, instead of a remote benefactor.

'I really enjoyed that, Betsy. I met some lovely women. And look at all the wonderful drawings the children have made, to say thank you. I will treasure them.'

'Your ma would have been proud of you – though a bit jealous an' all, I shouldn't wonder, as she was always held in such awe that no one hardly spoke, except to say ta. Eeh, lass, they were gossiping away to you as if you were born amongst them. It were good to see.'

By the time January came, Betsy was settled in her new post, and although Mags found that her father hadn't liked the change at first – complaining that Betsy did more bobbing on one knee than working, which made Mags giggle – he, too, had begun to enjoy her lively ways.

'She's done it again!'

Mags looked up from the morning paper, in which she was reading the notice of her wedding day in three weeks' time. Her heart had fluttered on seeing it in print, and this exclamation from her father seemed like a rude interruption. 'What, Daddy, and who has done it again? Sit down to breakfast and tell me all about it.'

'That Betsy! Your mother must be turning in her grave, to see her smoothly run home all topsy-turvy.'

Mags couldn't imagine what Betsy had done.

'She was polishing the banister when I came downstairs. She really must learn that her place is not *doing* the work, but *overseeing* it. And her incessant curtsying is driving me insane!' The smile on his face belied his harsh words.

'I don't think we will ever change her, so we had better get used to how she works. I haven't come across any problems, other than Mrs Potts's frustration and yours. Everything is in order. Betsy even has a special book in which she is noting everything to do with my wedding.'

'Poor Mrs Potts, it must seem that her job has been stolen from under her feet.'

'No, that's just your assumption. You don't like change. Anyway, Harold is due to arrive today. He is going to spend time in his own factory to try and sort out the problems there, but will be here for dinner tonight.'

A 'humph' was all Mags got in response to this, and it worried her. Her father didn't seem to have any liking or respect for Harold.

'And another thing: Betsy has seen to it that your morning suit has been cleaned, ready for the occasion. You are all right about me marrying Harold earlier than you wanted, aren't you, Daddy?'

'Of course, darling. I just wish he would prove to us that he intends doing a good job with both mills. It worries me how he can absent himself when all isn't well.'

When at last her father left the room, muttering something about an early night, Harold, who had arrived earlier, swept Mags into his arms. 'My darling, I have missed you so. I am sorry – truly sorry – about my behaviour. But I understand now, and we won't speak of it again.'

His kiss melted her.

'Will your father return, or can we sneak off to your room now?'

This question both perturbed and thrilled Mags at the same time. She wanted nothing more than to be one with Harold, but asking this as soon as they had time alone together made her feel that she was needed only for one thing. No conversation had taken place between them, no meaningful conversation or even finding out how she was; just this half-hearted apology, sweeping everything under the carpet, and a lust for her body. Oh, Harold had chatted over dinner, but mainly to her father about business, cutting Mags off if she tried to express her point of view. It was all worrying and frustrating. Making her mind up to accept it and to change things gradually, as she'd spoken to her father about doing, she nodded.

'Daddy will have retired now. He said his goodnights. We can safely go to my rooms. I will serve you a nightcap in my sitting room and we can chat for a while.'

'It's not chatting that I want to do.'

His half-smile, and the touch of his hand on her bottom, saw Mags forgiving him, and clenching herself to contain the feeling that was pulsing through her. She smiled back and turned towards the stairs. Betsy appeared at that moment and, for the first time, irritated Mags. Mrs Potts would never be seen at such a moment, if she could avoid it.

'I've put a nice hot cup of cocoa in your room, sir. This way.' Her bobbing up and down released any annoyance that Mags felt. She giggled and then told Betsy she didn't have to worry, as Mr Roford knew where his room was and would retire there when he was ready. 'But thank you for your concern and your thoughtfulness, Betsy. Goodnight.'

Then, to her extreme embarrassment, Harold said in a loud voice, 'Good God! Who was that?'

'Our new housekeeper.'

'What! Well, she can go – and before I move in. What were you thinking, employing such a person? How very intrusive she was. You should have hauled her over the coals, not giggled at her – you will encourage her.'

'Betsy is learning the job. She is very good in many ways. We have known each other since we were children, so she's finding it difficult to be subservient.' *Not that I want her to be, as she is my lovely friend, but I will have to teach her a few things. Oh, Betsy!*

'Well, at least she's good to look at. But make sure you get her in check, darling.'

Good to look at – not the kind of remark a soon-to-be-husband should be making! However, Mags had to admit that he was right. Betsy was a striking-looking woman, with a figure to envy, despite birthing three children. Her waist was tiny, giving prominence to both her large breasts and her rounded hips – features that were enhanced by her uniform, which was a long, plain grey frock, held in by a wide belt. Her mop cap sat prettily on her chestnut curls, taming them at the front, leaving her forehead bare and taking nothing away from her very large blue eyes and oval face. Add to this her happy disposition, and Betsy could turn any man's head.

As she thought this, Mags felt a jealous pang touch her heart when she noticed Harold giving a backward glance at the receding figure of Betsy, who was gliding towards the kitchen area.

But then Harold reaching up to take hold of her hand banished that feeling, as did him catching up with her and pressing her against the banister. 'Forget her for now. We have more urgent things to think about.' He leaned further into her and Mags could sense his need. Part of her was repulsed as a feeling of being used descended on her, but other sensations crashed in and she responded to his kiss. A door clicking shut made her jump.

Harold looked in the direction from which it had come, leaning over the banister to gaze along the hall. 'I won't be a moment, darling. I think someone deserves a lashing of my tongue.'

'No, Harold, don't! I'll sort it out, as that's the proper way to manage it.'

'Of course, darling, but see that you do.'

Mags had an uncanny sense that Harold wanted a chance to be alone with Betsy – and not just to tell her off. *Oh, why am I dogged by such uncertainty? Why do I feel so insecure?* But then she knew why: *Flors.* Flors's warning about her brother's character was playing on her mind. *I don't want it to. I don't.*

And neither did she want to take Harold to her room now. The magic had gone. 'I'm sorry, Harold darling, but I have a headache. Forgive me, but . . .'

He stared at her. His anger showed in his eyes, and a nerve twitched next to his lips. 'That was very sudden.' As he said this, he stood as if unsure what to do.

'Well, we women have our crosses to bear; it will be the onset of . . . well, you know. It is my time of the month very soon.'

This he couldn't argue with, and she was glad to see some tenderness come back into him. 'Oh, sorry, old thing. I do understand, though I'm not happy. When we are married and can openly share the same bed, we'll get round that one. Night-night.'

His peck on the cheek sickened her. *Get round it? Am I nothing but a piece of meat for his pleasure?*

Betsy donned her coat, once the household had settled down. She was glad to have heard Mags refusing to take that husband-to-be of hers to her bed. How all that had come about, she could only wonder at. Mags was a lady, and she shouldn't be used in that way. From what she'd seen, it was as if that man had a hold of some sort over her.

As she went towards the door, a bell rang. Looking up, Betsy saw that the bell came from Mr Roford's bedroom. *Eeh, what does he want? Don't let it be to bawl me out.*

As she thought this, the door to the kitchen opened and Millie, the live-in maid, came through from the hallway. 'He wants cocoa bringing to his room. And he wants it hot and served with a brandy an' all. And he says as you're to take it up.'

'But I'm just off. You do it, Millie lass, there's a good 'un.'

'I can't, lass. I only just made it up the stairs to answer his call – me back's at breaking point. I'll make cocoa, eh?'

Annoyed at this, Betsy had a less-than-kind thought. *Millie should be pensioned off; she is ancient and not up to the job. Eeh, what am I thinking?* 'Oh, all right. Eeh, my Bill will be wondering where I am, at this rate.'

As she entered the bedroom, at Mr Roford's command to do so, Betsy was full of apprehension. And this only deepened when she saw him standing just inside the door.

'Put it down over there for me.'

Almost running to the dresser he'd indicated, Betsy plonked the tray down, noticing that his bed had already been turned down for him. She almost scampered back towards the door to leave. Before she got there, Mr Roford barred her way. 'Please, sir, I have to go. I'm due home, and me husband will be waiting.'

'What I have in mind will be far more pleasant than going home to a cripple, who I'm sure cannot do you justice, pretty lady.'

Betsy swallowed hard. The remark insulted her beyond words. Mags must have told him about Bill. But despite feeling angry, her normal feisty nature deserted her. 'Please, sir, I – I'm sure as it's just the drink making you talk like that. Let me pass, and nowt will be said about this, I promise.'

His hand caught her arm in a painful grip. 'I don't think I will let you leave. And for sure you will not speak of what passes between us, otherwise you will be out on your arse without a job. That wouldn't suit, would it? No, I thought not. Well, I am adding more duties to those that you have, and I will pay you well. You're to make yourself available to me, whenever I want you to be – understand?'

Betsy could only stare at him.

'Understood or not?'

Betsy didn't know where her audacity came from, but she spat out the words. 'Naw! And that ain't how it's going to be. Touch me and I'll scream the house down, and you'll be caught red-handed and shown up for what you are – a pig!'

His free hand lashed out, but Betsy dodged it.

'How dare you! I am your master and you will do my bidding.'

'Your bidding don't include me lying with you. I'd never do that – not willingly, I wouldn't!'

'Ha! You'll just have to do it unwillingly then, won't you?'

His grip tightened and his movement – swift and vicious –

caused Betsy's body to fly across the room towards his bed. Her breath left her body as she crashed against the corner of the four-poster. In a moment he was by her side, pushing her onto the mattress. As he discarded his dressing gown, his naked body showed his intentions. Her husband Bill came to her mind. Frail Bill, who had once had a physique like this man's. Aye, and he had once taken her to places she longed to be taken again. Feelings rose in her that had her gasping against them.

'You want it, don't you? I'm right, aren't I? It's been a long time since you saw, or felt, something like this.' He held himself and made gestures towards her. Betsy could feel herself weakening. *Don't let me. Oh God, help me.*

With this thought, strength came into her and, as he drew nearer, she kicked out, landing her foot in his groin. His cries frightened her, but she could only do one thing – run for all she was worth.

She didn't stop until she was within sight of her gate. Leaning over a neighbour's fence, she gasped for breath. Tears soaked her face. They weren't all for herself, but for her dear friend. That Mags should be marrying such a man didn't bear thinking about. And what of the future? *Will I have to leave me job?*

With an extreme effort, Betsy wiped away her tears. Composing herself, she took a deep breath. She'd go and snuggle up to her Bill. *He is worth all of them as could give me more than Bill can, and I love him enough to do without that.*

Even as she thought this, she knew that denying what Mr Roford had awoken in her was going to be the hardest thing she'd ever been called upon to do.

Chapter Six

Waking after a restless sleep, Mags kicked off the covers, shivered and pulled them back over her. The window was open, and a chorus of birdsong drifted into her room. It was a sound that usually gave her a happy start to the day, but as she stretched herself, she felt anything but happy.

Harold's anger at her, and his callous remark about getting around any problems that stopped him having his way with her, had stayed with her, and she hadn't been able to get it out of her mind that she was simply a means to an end.

This was compounded at breakfast when her father told her that Harold had left early. 'He left you a note, darling. It's on the sideboard. It seems he suddenly felt he needed to go to London to finalize something to do with the house, before the wedding was upon him.'

Father's gaze held hers and Mags cringed, as it seemed to be all-knowing. Getting up, she walked over to the sideboard, her legs feeling like jelly, her heart heavy in her chest.

The note was sealed in an envelope and lay on a silver salver alongside a paper-knife. *At least Daddy hasn't read it!*

That's a relief, though his look seemed to say that he knows what is going on.

The sound of the paper-knife slitting open the envelope grated on her fraught nerves. *Am I always to be blackmailed in this way? Oh God, if only I didn't love Harold so much – and need him. Yes, that is it. I need Harold. Want his love, and his lovemaking; and, yes, his company, but without all the shackles that go with it – the doubts, the veiled threats and the feeling that I have to do his bidding at all times.*

There was no endearment to begin the note:

Something came up; sorry, had to leave early – long drive ahead of me. Be back the day before our wedding. Maybe you can do some thinking about your actions last night, before then?

I will not tolerate you treating me how my mother treated my father. That can only lead to disaster, which will be of your making.

Once we are married, you will never retire without me, unless I do not wish to come to your bed.

Mags drew in a gasp at this.

'Are you all right, darling? Is there a problem?'

'No – no, Daddy, I – I was just surprised that Harold says he has to be away until the day before our wedding. It – it's all so sudden.'

'Well, I don't blame him, myself. These last two weeks are going to be very intense, with all the arrangements that have to be concluded, and you won't have any time to give to anyone or anything, other than seeing that all the plans are in place and the dress fittings done, et cetera . . . Sensible man, I would say.'

Mags managed a little laugh, before continuing to read:

I thought we had cleared all of this up between us.
And while we are talking about my expectations of you,
I also expect your loyalty – no matter what you hear,
I want you to believe me at all times. That silly and
incompetent housekeeper of yours got some notion or
other in her head, and behaved in an inappropriate
way when she brought me up a brandy last night.
Please inform her that in future she will only ever send
a maid to my room and will not come herself. And to
that end, I want you to engage a manservant to see to
my needs.

Mags held her breath – *Betsy. Oh, Betsy, no!* In her heart, Mags instinctively knew that Harold had more than likely propositioned Betsy. If that was the case, she knew what Betsy's reaction would have been. Harold's words were simply trying to cover up his behaviour. *Harold. Oh, Harold, why? Everything isn't about your needs. Why can't you accept that you cannot always have everything your own way?*

A deep sigh escaped her. But not wishing to provoke questions from her father, she quickly covered them up. 'Oh, Daddy, I wished Harold hadn't had to leave, but I suppose you are right. I'll throw myself into getting all my plans into place, and the time will pass quickly. Will you be all right going into the mill today? Because one of us should do so, in Harold's absence. Only I would like to go and see Betsy. It's her day off, and we could make sure that her little girls' bridesmaid dresses fit properly, and shop for a frock for her.'

'Yes, I will go in. Although much as I understand Harold

wanting to escape all the marriage-preparation palaver, I do think he could have been more considerate about the arrangements we made for him to use this next week to acquaint himself with the mill.'

'Yes, that is annoying. I'm sorry, Daddy.'

'It's not your fault, darling. You have a lot on your plate. And your mother would be pleased at how you have included the servants in your plans. Betsy will make a lovely maid of honour. She's a striking young woman.'

The way this was said opened Mags's eyes to how life for Betsy must be. Young and old men alike had an eye for her, and she wasn't the type to take them up on what they might offer her.

A lovelier, more caring person than Betsy it would be hard to find. And Mags dreaded what might have happened last night . . .

Mags's knock on Betsy's cottage door was met with a flicker of the curtain. She had to knock again before Betsy appeared, and then she sidled out of the open door and closed it behind her. Her look was one that Mags had never seen before. Defiance, and a readiness to fight her corner, showed in Betsy's expression.

'I – I, I'm sorry, Betsy. I—'

'Oh, lass. You haven't come here accusing me, then?'

'No. I know something happened, but I don't know what. Will you tell me?'

'Eeh, naw, let's forget it. Mr Roford had taken a drop too much. And I shouldn't have gone to his room. Let's leave it at that, eh?'

'I need to explain why he is like he is. Can we go shopping together? We haven't had time to get your frock yet.

I've seen one. It's in the window of Madame Ruen's shop, and it has a matching hat, too.'

'Oh, me lass, I can see you're suffering, and I understand. That man of yours is going to take some handling, or let's say that if you carry on with marrying him, you are going to have to tolerate a lot as many couldn't put up with, if you're going to have any kind of happiness with him. It ain't too late, you knaw – you could still get the upper hand. You need to break the engagement and shock him that way. If you choose to give in to him, you'll be setting a rod for your own back.'

Mags knew Betsy was right. But did she have that much of a hold over Harold's heart? Would he simply accept her breaking off their relationship and not care? She couldn't bear that, she couldn't. 'But I love him, Betsy. And I think once we are married, and guilt about my situation leaves me, everything will be all right.'

'Aye, you made a bad mistake, taking him to your bed afore you're wed. You gave him the upper hand. Now I knaw the predicament you're in, as I knaw it's not easy to live without what he gives you. We're all the same, lass.'

Though she blushed, it was a relief to have Betsy to talk to. They'd always had this kind of relationship, and shared secrets, though nothing of this nature before. Mags was glad they could talk. 'I didn't have much choice. I . . . well, I know things. We can't talk here on your doorstep, but I can explain.'

'My Bill's going out in a while. He thinks he could manage a few hours' work, and Mr Hopkins at the local shop has a notice up for someone to mind the store while he does his deliveries. That Lucy, as was from the workhouse, used to do it, but she's found herself a man and is getting her freedom-papers to go and be a farmer's wife. We're all that pleased for her. Anyroad, Mr Hopkins has agreed to give Bill an interview, to see if he's up to it. He's right chuffed with the idea, is Bill. So come in and I'll just see to a few things, then we can have a chinwag over a pot of tea.'

Betsy's house was one of a row of terraced houses owned by Mags's father's mill. When the family had been put out of the mining cottage, on the termination of Bill's employment following his accident, Mags had persuaded her father that Betsy was entitled to one of their cottages as much as any male worker would be.

The front room of the house led straight off the pavement. Stepping into it gave Mags the feeling that she was in a different world – one where the aroma of freshly baked bread, warmth from the fire, and love permeated every part of the room. It was cosy and comforting.

The pretty yellow-flowered curtains hanging at the small windows didn't stop the sun's rays beaming through; instead they formed a frame that enhanced the light shining on the plain but highly polished furniture. A dresser holding china, and a table with a lace cloth draping it, flanked the two rocking chairs, one on each side of the fireplace; and through a door opposite, Mags could see a small kitchen. Bill sat in one of the chairs. He looked embarrassed as he paused in the act of pulling on his long socks. For the first time ever, Mags caught a glimpse of his gammy leg.

'Hello, Bill. Betsy has just told me your news. Can I give you a lift to the shop?'

'Ma'am.' Bill nodded his head. 'Naw, but thank you kindly. I have to show as I can get there by meself. I've been in training, so to speak, and have hobbled along there three times this week. It's painful on me gammy leg, but I need to do it, despite that.'

'I wish you all the luck in the world, Bill. But I don't think you will need it. I'm sure you'll be taken on, but just in case you're not, we could do with a further hand in the kitchen from time to time. We need someone to peel the veg and prepare it for Cook, as my husband-to-be is planning on entertaining more than we do now.'

'I can do that as well as me job at the shop, if I get it, ma'am. I can fit it around that.'

'That's settled then. Betsy will know when we need you.'

The smile Bill gave her was thanks enough. But as he stood, his wince of pain alarmed Mags and sent her reeling back to her nursing days.

'Has a doctor seen you lately, Bill?'

'Naw. There's naw spare cash for doctor's fees.'

'But surely you can still be seen by the doctor at the mine? After all, your accident happened down the pit.'

'I was signed off by him a while back, and that's when I thought to take up some work. Once they sign you off, that's it.'

The pain that he was in showed in the grimace on his face.

'Will you let me look at it? I am a nurse, remember. And what I saw just now worried me.' As Bill sat and rolled up his trouser leg, Mags was filled with sympathy for him. 'You have an ulcer, Bill. It needs cleaning out and packing with fresh lint every day until it dries and begins to heal. And it looks as though your leg was never set properly. You need to see a surgeon. I can arrange that. Once you are in our employ, you can be looked after by our medical service at the mill.'

'I heard tell as that were being closed down.'

'What?'

'Aye, I were talking to a woman who works up at Roford mill, and she were saying they had a meeting with the Mr Roford as you're about to marry. He told them they can get the idea of a welfare system out of their heads, as he won't be setting one up and will be closing the one in his other mill – which we all took as being yours and your da's mill. But happen as she heard it wrong, as you'd knaw about it, for sure.'

Fury burned through Mags, surpassing the embarrassment she felt. *How dare Harold say such a thing, without consulting me or my father? Is this how it is going to be?*

The answer, she knew, was 'yes' and a deep sadness vied with her anger. She had to accept that nothing about her beloved mill would be shared with her, and she would not be allowed to bring any influence to bear. But she did at least have her father on her side. He had promised to talk to her, and to use her decisions as if they were his own. But a sigh escaped her, as her father hadn't been fully behind her idea of providing medical care on a free basis to all their employees, let alone extending it to their families, as she had hopes of doing in the future.

Well, she would fight this every step of the way. Even tackle Harold, if she had to. 'I think, at this stage, it is probably an idea Mr Roford put forward for streamlining things at the mill, but that doesn't make it a fact. I'll look into it. Nonetheless, you will see a surgeon, I promise, Bill. But first we have to do something about that ulcer.'

'It'll have to be when I come back. I'm late, as it is.'

'Look, I know Mr Hopkins's store, so let me take you to the corner of his street. He won't see that you've had a lift there.'

65

Bill agreed to this, which put Mags's mind at rest. 'I'll wait for you there and bring you back here, and then we'll begin treatment on that ulcer. Oh, don't worry, I've cleaned out many ulcers in a much worse state than this one, and they've healed nicely, given time. Have you any lint in the house, Betsy?'

'Aye, I've a biscuit tin full of stuff for cuts and burns, and the like – have to, with my lot. This is good of you, lass. I'll come with you for the ride and keep you company while you wait for Bill.'

This pleased Mags, and she knew Betsy had come up with the idea to give them time alone. 'What about little Rosie – is she having her morning nap?'

'Naw, she's passed that stage now, she's going on four years old. She's with me ma. Ma picked her up when she took the other two along to school, to give me a chance to get a bit done around the house. Eeh, I hope as the school don't get stopped an' all, as mine would have a fair trek to the church school, if it did.'

Mags felt at a loss as to what to say about this, as her new-found status seemed to leave her powerless to do anything to stop it happening, if it was part of Harold's plan to close the school as well. She made up her mind to tackle these issues with her father, while Harold was away.

Seeing Bill hobble around the corner aroused pity in Mags for those who struggled to eke out a living, and it pained her that this was happening to Betsy and her little family. How different her own and Betsy's lives had always been, and yet something had drawn them to each other. Mags supposed it was the lack of any female company of her own age when she was at home, and she knew their friendship was unusual. Harold would frown upon it, without a doubt. But on this, she would fight her corner. She needed Betsy in her life. The thought of life without her sent a feeling of dread through her.

'Eeh, lass, you've a lot on your plate. I knaw you're going through a lot, 'cause of what happened. That man ain't right for you, and yet I knaw as you can't help how you feel about him.'

'I'm afraid for you, Betsy. I – I don't know if . . . well, if it's right to keep you on. I mean—'

'Naw, lass, don't take me job away from me. I'd never get set on anywhere else, even though I've a lot of knowledge of mill work, as lots are laying off workers, not taking them on. You knaws that. Look, I promise as I'll keep me place. I'll work at running the house and staff, and not doing the jobs meself. And I'll not be seen – only by you, when you give me my orders. Mr Roford won't have need to come to the staff quarters, the kitchen or me office, so nowt will happen again. And while I'm on, my Bill must never find out: promise me that, lass. He'd go spare and . . . well, he ain't, can't . . . well, not often; and when he does, it ain't nowt like it used to be, as he's in too much pain.' Betsy looked down at her hands and fidgeted with her skirt. 'That does sommat to a man, you knaw. Makes him feel inadequate, and jealous of others. I'd be feared he'd start thinking as I went looking for it.'

'Oh, Betsy, I'm sorry. I promise Bill will never find out. And I need to explain why I think Harold is the way he is. It is down to his mother. She . . .'

When she'd finished telling Betsy the sorry tale of Harold's upbringing, Mags felt near to tears.

'Eeh, how can a woman send her own daughter away,

67

and you say as this Flora were only a little lass at the time? Well, I reckon it were down to her ma and da that she had the misfortune to meet and marry her own half-brother. I've heard some tales, I can tell you, but what you've just told me takes the biscuit. Is that where Harold goes to stay – with his ma?'

'No. I . . . Oh, Betsy, I killed her!' The tears Mags had shed in the past over what happened were nothing to what came from her now, as she told Betsy what had occurred.

To have Betsy holding her felt good, and yet it released more of Mags's pain. It reminded her of how her own mother used to soothe her, and that she would never do so again. Awareness seeped into her that Betsy was crying, too.

'Oh Betsy, I've upset you now. I'm sorry.'

Betsy's sobs racked her body, and Mags knew that giving comfort to her had triggered Betsy's own pain.

Betsy was the first one to calm. 'By, lass, me troubles spilled from me then. I suddenly thought of what happened to Bill, and how that's made him more like a brother to me than a husband; and of me struggles to keep a roof over me family's head. But I fear that may be nowt, compared to what you might have to face in your future. But we have to be strong. Oh, aye, the men have all the rights, but it's us women who drive them. Not that they knaw about that. And that's what you've to do, if you go through with wedding yourself to Harold. Sommat I'd strongly advise you not to do. You're a beautiful woman, you've got prospects – there'd be men lining up to make you their wife, if they knew you were available. Men as would love and cherish you. I don't think as Harold is capable of doing that, or of being faithful to you. Whether that's his fault or not, it's a fact, and one I can testify to.'

With her sobs calming and some control coming back to her, Mags felt this last remark cutting through her heart. And the enormity of what must have happened between Harold and Betsy hit her. 'I'll break off with him. I will. I'll confront him with what he did to you; only you must tell me exactly what happened, so that I can hit Harold with the facts.'

'Aw, lass, you'll come to hate me, if you use me as a stick to beat Harold with. 'Cause he's not going to leave it there. He'll blacken me name until you doubt me. Naw, if you break off with him, it has to be because of sommat he has done to you. This blackmailing that he puts you through. His taking of you before you were wed, and the way he has demeaned you, in not letting you take any part in your family business. Them's to be the reasons. You've to use the letter you told me he left you. His words in that are enough to make any woman turn against him. But please don't even hint that you knaw he tried it on with me.'

Oh God, did Harold rape Betsy – or at least try to? Mags reached out and took hold of Betsy's hand.

'I'm so sorry, Betsy. So very sorry. I won't stop your employment. I need you with me, as a friend, but we will have to manage that if . . . Well, like I say, I need to think it all through. I'm not sure if my conclusion will be to stop my marriage, but if not, I will have to assert myself within that marriage. I have to be who I am. I am sacrificing too much – I'm losing myself.'

'Aye, I knaw what you mean by that. You're not the same lass as I waved off to war, in your pristine uniform and with a smile on your face, and a look that said you were going to beat the bloody Kaiser all on your own.'

They both laughed at this, and as they did so, Mags felt

something change inside her. She was ready to stand up to Harold, to confront him; and she would do so on his own ground. She'd leave for London tomorrow. Surprise him and find out if her fears were correct. She knew where to find him. He'd be in his own home, as she was sure it was habitable by now.

At this thought she felt a little trepidation, but she brushed it aside. She had to do this. She had to find the mettle she used to have. She needed to once more become the strong young woman that Betsy had reminded her of.

'Eeh, lass, you seem to have grown ten feet tall.'

Mags smiled; yes, she had sat up very straight as this conclusion occurred to her, and she knew she was ready. Ready to face all that she had to.

I can do this – I can!

Chapter Seven

The streets of London both thrilled and frightened Mags. She wondered if she would ever get used to it, for she felt as nervous now as she had on her first visit – when she was setting off to go to war. Then she had covered up by showing a confidence that she hadn't felt. She smiled as she remembered how she must have appeared to Ella and Flors, as she'd dealt with it by being over-exuberant.

On subsequent visits to Harold's home she had travelled down in Harold's car, or had been met off the train. But now finding her way was down to her, and it had all been easier than she'd thought, as there were plenty of cabs just outside the station.

The hustle and bustle of folk who all seemed to have something urgent to attend to left her feeling like a country bumpkin. And she was struck by the vast contrast between poverty and wealth as she witnessed beggars, ragged children and the glamour of the glittering shops and gleaming cars vying with horse-drawn carriages around the streets of Knightsbridge. Newsboards were full of British troops invading Dublin, something her father thought was not

71

before time, but she thought differently about it, feeling some sympathy for the Irish cause, if not for their means of dealing with their grievances.

Her mind didn't dwell on this because soon they were passing a cinema. This fascinated her, as she'd never seen one before. The billboard advertised *The Kid*, starring Charlie Chaplin. *Oh, I'd love to go one day. It must be amazing to watch real people on a screen.*

All of what she'd seen in London was forgotten as fear-filled anticipation gripped her when they neared Harold's house. This feeling was replaced by anger, as the cab drew up outside. Before her was a splendid building, far superior to the one that had burned down. Harold had lied to her. He must have had the work begin immediately, to achieve this.

The original house had been around eighty years old and built in the plain style of the era, relying on its size to give an aura of grandeur. But this new house was opulent in every way. Elaborate stone gargoyles stared out from each corner. Bay windows, with sills that had carved stone holding them up as if they were shelves, graced the facade. A porch jutted out over the steps leading to the front door and was held up by four Roman-style columns. This house was bigger than the one it had replaced. Mags counted eight windows across each of its three storeys. The bricks were of the finest London red, with the windows and doors framed in white concrete.

Mags walked up the marble steps, and her heart quickened when the sound of the bell resounded inside the house. Shivering more from fear than from the cold, she gathered her coat around her.

The door seemed to glide open. A butler greeted her.

His expression showed a brief moment of surprise. He quickly composed himself and acted as if it was commonplace for a lady to appear, unchaperoned, on the doorstep. 'Good afternoon, ma'am. Please come inside.'

Mags nodded and stepped into the magnificent hall, unable, for a moment, to take in her surroundings. Marble columns supported the ceiling, and the beautiful wide staircase, flanked by a deep-mahogany banister and carpeted in a rich ruby-red, was a sight she hadn't expected.

'May I take your name? Is Madame expecting you?'

'Madame? I'm here to see my fiancé, Mr Roford. I'm Miss Witherbrook.'

The look on the butler's face would have been comical, had the anxiety in Mags not suppressed her sense of humour.

'B – but, Mr Roford . . . I mean, I – I think you are mistaken. No . . . I'm sorry, I didn't mean . . . Please come with me.'

His recovery was admirable as he ushered her into a withdrawing room, where once more Mags found herself gaping at the sumptuous surroundings. Her feet sank into the deep-pile white carpet. Two royal-blue wing-backed, quilted armchairs and a matching chesterfield sofa surrounded the fireplace, which was a grand, carved-stone masterpiece reaching from floor to ceiling.

The whole appearance of the room was one of opulence. Although agitated about the possible meaning of the butler's confusion, Mags took in the whole of the room. Occasional furniture finished in gold leaf with marble tops stood next to the chairs, with matching Queen Anne-style cabinets, full of beautiful *objets d'art*, statues and ornaments, placed on each side of the French windows, through which she could see the drive leading up to the house. The ambience was one of wealth. She couldn't even imagine the amount of money it must have taken to build and furnish such a place.

'May I take your coat, Madame?'

Relieving herself of her very best coat, which now seemed shabby in these surroundings, Mags walked towards the chair that the butler had indicated she should sit on. But as she heard the door close behind him, she changed her mind. Feeling too restless to sit down, she walked towards the window and gazed out. From here she could feel as if she was in the former house, as the view was the same one she'd had from the dining room when she'd visited in the past.

A shudder shook her body, but she didn't give in to the memories that assailed her. She had to stay strong, to face whatever was coming her way, for it was certain Harold was leading some sort of double life. The distress the butler had shown confirmed the reasons that had driven her down to London unannounced.

The sound of the front door opening drew her attention. Seeing who was leaving, Mags drew in a deep breath. *Susan!* The maid Flors had warned her about was hurrying out of the house and down the steps, whilst pulling on a coat that was far superior to any that a maid would expect to possess.

The sight seemed to confirm all that Mags had suspected. Her body folded. Reaching out, she held on to the handle of the window and, with an extreme effort, regained control. Preferring now to sit, she crossed over to the fireplace and sat down in an armchair that accepted her as if it were an embracing pair of arms; but she didn't feel comforted, only apprehension about what was to come.

A few minutes passed before the door opened and Harold, looking cross and agitated, stood glaring at her. She refused to cringe under his gaze.

'What is the meaning of this? How dare you come down here unannounced?'

'Good afternoon, Harold. I'm sorry, but, as your fiancée, I didn't know I had to warn you of my visit.'

'Well, y – you . . . of course you should have. It is rude in the extreme to land upon me so unexpectedly, and . . . well, to spoil my surprise about the progress of the house, as you have done.'

Mags stood. 'Oh, I'm surprised all right. No need to worry on that score.'

Harold looked taken aback. He stared at her as if she was an alien being. 'What is the matter with you? You're different. You seem to be spoiling for a fight or something.'

'No, not a fight. Just seeking the truth – and I have that now. I'm leaving. And this is goodbye, Harold. Our wedding is off. Now, where is the bell hidden in this palace of a place? Or would you please summon your butler. Ha, fancy . . . you having a butler; but then your maid has been elevated to a much higher place than simply opening the door to guests, hasn't she?'

'What are you talking about? You're mad. You're having some sort of a breakdown or something. Sit down at once and tell me what this is all about.'

'You know what it is about. You do not need to be told that you are leading a double life, as you have been practising it for some time. I am here to relieve you of one of them. You can now enjoy the life you seem to prefer, without the nuisance of having to visit the one you are building in Blackburn.'

As she moved towards the door, Harold barred her way. 'Please, Mags darling, let us talk. You have the wrong idea altogether – let me explain.'

'Explain? How can you explain this sumptuous house that you told me was still being renovated from the ruins of the fire? It must have taken a fortune – all of your fortune – to build, and for what? To keep your maid in the style she's become accustomed to? I don't think such a situation can be explained to your supposed fiancée. Do you?'

'I just don't know you. What is this all about? I am not keeping Sus – I mean, any maid, or any woman – in any style whatsoever! How dare you accuse me of such a thing? You're a naive, jealous woman from the back of beyond who has no sophistication, and no inkling of how to keep a man happy. You—'

'In which case, you will be glad to see the back of me, won't you?'

'No!' Harold's stance changed, and his arms came out. 'Oh, Mags, I can't bear to lose you. I love you. I can explain. I can. Please give me a chance to. I'm sorry, I shouldn't have got angry and said those things, but turning up here unannounced and accusing me of wrongdoing . . . well, I just lost my head, that's all. Let's talk, please.'

'Talk won't do any good, unless you are prepared to admit the truth, face what you are and decide to make a new beginning. But even then, it will take me a long time to trust you and regain the willing, wholehearted love I gave you.'

Harold slumped into a chair and buried his head in his hands. Sobs racked his body, shocking Mags out of the defensive position she'd taken. She too sat down and melted into a flood of tears.

'My dreams have been shattered, along with any faith that I had in you, Harold. Can you rebuild that?'

'I – I don't know. You have made your mind up about

me. And yes, your conclusion is partly true, but not wholly. I am not as bad as you paint me. I have been through so much. I need time, but the one thing I cannot face is life without you, Mags. I – I can't.'

Through her wretchedness, doubt trickled an element of hope into Mags. *Have I got it all wrong?*

Harold straightened, perhaps sensing her uncertainty, but as he wiped his face on a huge white handkerchief that he'd taken from his jacket pocket and blew his nose loudly, he didn't look like a man who had gained a small victory, but rather like a small boy caught out in a misdemeanour. This suggested there *was* hope, for Harold's repentance was the only way they could go forward. The only way he could make the necessary changes. And she so wanted that, for she didn't want to lose him.

'I'm sorry, Mags. I just don't know what possessed me – can you forgive me? I came down to end my long-running affair with Susan. It is taking a lot for me to say this, but I can see that only the truth is going to help us. I started an affair with her about three years ago. She's married, but only for convenience – or so I thought. I – I was in love with her, but then I met you and knew what true love really was. I don't want to lose that, but I have found it hard to break away from Susan. She was prepared to leave her husband for me, and she loves me deeply. I feel such a cad. She is uneducated and is not schooled in the way of being a mistress; she wanted to be my wife, which was always impossible, even if I hadn't met you, as such a relationship could never have suited me.'

Part of Mags wanted to hit Harold. What did he think he was doing? Making everything right? But then hadn't she asked for his honesty, and hadn't she known, deep down, that Susan was an obstacle to their love? If he truly had broken off the relationship, shouldn't she be rejoicing? Why, then, was she beset by distrust?

'Did you harbour the thought that you could keep both of us? Me up in Blackburn and Susan down here, amid this . . . this opulent mansion, which you would eventually have told me you had sold?'

'I have to admit – as you have asked for complete honesty – that I did for a while. I looked on doing so as a solution, rather than as something I desired; and my visits here would have become less and less, until Susan could cope, and then I would have made the break. I wasn't ever going to move her in here. She was to remain with her husband. I – I was just going to make the break less painful for her, that's all.'

'At the expense of my pain. Don't you see, Harold, that every time you wanted to visit here, you had to conjure up an excuse? And in doing so, you tore me apart emotionally. You made me fight for every morsel of attention. If I didn't do your bidding, you used that as a reason to run down here to your precious Susan, to soothe her pain, leaving me a wreck. And you made no bones about doing so. I can't live like that, Harold.'

'I can only say that I am sorry. I've been a fool – I see that now. I've hurt you, the last person I ever wanted to hurt. Please give me a chance to make things up to you.'

Part of Mags wanted to go to him, to be held by him and reassured that all would be well in the future, but she was still unconvinced.

'For someone who wanted to give all this up, you seem to have set yourself up nicely. It appears to me you had every intention of keeping this place forever. You even have a butler who called Susan "Madame"! That's far above what

I would expect to find, in a place you were just doing up to sell.'

'We're going round and round and getting nowhere. Yes, I set this house up in a grand manner, but it was solely with the intention of selling it. I – I told you that would happen, once Susan was able to cope. Butlers always defer to anyone who seems to hold a position in the house, and London demands more than Blackburn does, by way of saleable property. Those who have money want to live in an opulent way. An establishment that is already set up is a very good prospect. Anyway, if it makes you feel any better, I *have* to sell. I've really stretched myself financially, in more ways than one.'

So now I know the real reason I am still in the picture. I am a way out for Harold. He needs me, for what I can provide. Mags would have liked it if what he was saying could be true, but she doubted that he loved her in the way he said he did.

Could she live with that? The pull of Harold was so strong that she knew she could, if he gave up Susan for good. She was about to tell him this, when a commotion in the hall got them both standing up. The door was flung open and a distraught man of similar age to her burst in, followed by the very flustered butler. 'I tried to stop him entering the house, sir, but he pushed by me.'

'I must speak with you, Roford, it iz important.'

Harold paled alarmingly. His mouth gaped open and his stance told of his fear. The man didn't move, but looked from her to Harold. Mags had the feeling that her presence had stopped him in his tracks. For a moment it was as if they were all suspended in time, and no one knew what the next move should be.

Mags couldn't take her eyes off the intruder. His accent told her that he was French. Something about him was magnetic. She found her gaze drawn to his strong physique and his coal-black eyes, framed by thick eyebrows. Her voice didn't sound like her own as she asked, 'Who are you, and how can we help you?'

His tone wasn't aggressive as he answered, 'It iz that I need to speak to Mr Roford alone, Mademoiselle. What I have to say iz somezing we men should not discuss in front of a lady.'

Enlightenment dawned on her. 'You're Susan's husband, aren't you?'

'You know about them? And yet you are the lady he iz to marry?'

This seemed to give Harold life as he shouted, 'Yes, she is, and you have no business here. Get out!'

'Monsieur, I'm not going until we have spoken. I cannot see Suzan hurt in thiz way.'

'What is it to you, Charvet? You only took refuge with her; you don't love her – never have – and she doesn't love you.'

'Monsieur, Montel Charvet is my name. And yes, our marriage iz of the convenience, but still I care deeply for Suzan and cannot tolerate your treatment of her. She loves you. You have promized her so much. And now you say you are leaving? We had agreed that we would divorce, and you are not holding your side of zee bargain.'

Mags couldn't believe what she was hearing or make any sense of it.

'Susan saw things that weren't there. This is my fiancée, and I love her and want rid of Susan for good. I have tried to let Susan down gently, but she won't have any of it. I'm sorry, deeply sorry. I should never have started the affair, but I was young and she was willing, and it just happened.'

'Az did zee baby?'

'What? What are you saying? The child isn't mine. Susan tried to blackmail me with it, but she cannot prove that I am the father.'

'We have never had relationships. You know that Suzan took me in and we married so that I could stay az a British citizen.'

'Stop! Please stop. My God, Harold, have you fathered a child with Susan?'

'No, Mags, I haven't. She does have a daughter, but she is not mine. The two of them are blackmailing me. Montel is a displaced person from the war. Susan took pity on him. But when she recovered, after being hurt in the fire that destroyed our house, she told me she had fallen in love with Montel and she ended our affair. But she came back into my life a few weeks later, telling me she was pregnant with my child. I was still in shock and trying to deal with everything. You had gone home weeks before the fire and our only contact had been by letter, and I was alone. I had lost both parents and my brother, and my rotten sister had left with my bastard half-brother. I was vulnerable. I took the easy way out and accepted the situation, and what Susan offered me, once more. But then I came back to you, and all was right again. It was then that I calculated everything and realized Susan's child cannot be mine, and I tried to end my relationship with her.'

Mags didn't know what to believe. She looked from one to the other, and saw Harold, a pitiful, begging creature, and Montel, strong, sturdy and defiant – and yes, she could see a blackmailer in him. Why was he displaced? Had he a criminal background that made him want to hide and not return home, as had been the case with others that she'd heard of who had been discovered and extradited?

Something told her that she had a chance now of regaining Harold's love and of giving him back his dignity. She would stand by him. 'I believe what my fiancé is saying, and I advise you to leave or we will call the police.'

Her words had the desired effect. Harold stood tall and once more ordered Montel to leave the house. Montel looked for all the world like a trapped animal. His eyes bored into Mags, giving her a strange feeling of being connected to him in some way, then he turned and walked out of the room.

'Oh, Mags, my darling, I love you.' Harold's arms opened to her, and Mags went into them. She needed to know if what she felt for him had died, with all the revelations of the last hour. Finding that they hadn't elated her. Snuggling into him, she felt her love for him deepen. He'd been a victim of his own foolishness, but it was over now. Now that she believed Harold, Susan and her Frenchman had no further grounds on which to blackmail him concerning the child. Nor could Susan be a pull on Harold emotionally. It was done – she was certain of that. She and Harold could put all of this behind them and go forward together.

PART TWO
Blackburn, 1921

~

Mags, Harold and Betsy

Hard-Hitting Truth

Chapter Eight

The day of the wedding – the first Saturday in February – the sun shone weakly through a haze of cloud. Its warmth wasn't enough to melt the hard frost that had bitten during the night. Mags thought everywhere looked beautiful as she gazed out of her window.

'There, lass, you look grand.'

Betsy had dressed Mags's hair. Getting ready together had added fun to the proceedings, and Mags was glad there was no atmosphere that spoke of Betsy's dissent concerning her marriage.

Betsy had accepted that Mags's love for Harold was so strong that she felt she could surmount the problems they'd had. Mags didn't know how to reconcile that with what Betsy had been through at Harold's hands, but as Betsy was coping and was happy for her, she tried not to think about what had happened and decided never to refuse Harold again. Surely then he wouldn't feel the need to stray?

Her mind recalled all that had transpired in the ten days since her visit to Harold's house. Doubts crept in now and again. To allay them, she had taken steps to secure her future.

Her mother's will had revealed a family secret. It appeared that her mother had an old friend, an Irishman, whom she'd met as a girl. They wrote often and, when he died, he left his house in Portpatrick, Scotland, to Mother. He'd left Dublin by boat because of the growing unrest there and had found sanctuary in a house from which he could still see his beloved country across the water.

When Mags tackled her father on the subject, it seemed Colm Shangly was a bone of contention between them – not for any reason other than that her father was jealous of the attention Colm had received. Now, shamefacedly, her father admitted that he had been a fool. 'My darling Belinda never expressed a wish to visit Colm, or even to visit the house left to her, but they seemed to have so much to say to each other. Reams and reams of paper came from him, and Belinda used to sit and giggle as she read through them. Always when you were out of sight, my dear. You see, they met when she was a girl and she visited Dublin city. I had this notion that they fell in love. Maybe they did. But she loved me more, I know that. I'm sorry now; really sorry for the way I was so petulant, and for not letting you know of his existence.'

Mags reassured him that none of it mattered now.

The Scottish property now belonged to Mags, as did the legacy of a substantial amount of money and her mother's jewellery. Mags had sworn her father to secrecy about it all, telling him it was to be her insurance policy, if anything happened in the future that meant she needed to take care of herself.

Her father had readily agreed, but went a step further, by adding to the amount of money and helping Mags to secure it in a bank account that needed his firm of solicitors to access it, on her signature. 'Just in case nothing of mine comes to you when I die.'

She'd not thought this unusual. Even if Father left everything he owned to her, as a married woman, all her possessions would be half-owned by her husband – those Harold knew about, that was.

Knowing that she had this fortune and property gave Mags a sense of security – although her happiness told her she would never need it, her business brain said 'just in case'. *I must instruct the solicitors to have someone check up on the house, and authorize them to carry out any repairs that are needed. Perhaps I can add to my bank balance by renting it out, or selling it?* But the latter idea felt like a betrayal of her mother, so Mags didn't think she would do that.

'You look lovely, Mags . . . Oh, I mean Miss Margaret.'

'Oh, don't stand on ceremony whilst we're alone, Betsy. We'll always be "Betsy" and "Mags" to each other.' With this, Mags accepted the hug that Betsy gave her and leaned her head into her. 'You've always been a good friend, Betsy, and always will be. It's just that, as we have already spoken of, some things will have to change, with Mr Roford being here.'

'I knaw. And I'm prepared. I'm to call you "Mrs Roford", and him "Mr Roford" or "sir". I'm to make meself scarce whenever he's around, and not do chores around the house, but assign them to others.'

Mags would have loved to make it so that Betsy could do as she wanted, but instead she could only smile.

'Don't you worry on that score, Mags – all will turn out reet. And while I'm on, you're the best friend anyone could ever have. My Bill is looking forward to seeing that surgeon you've paid for. It's given him hope for his future, as he were at rock bottom when he didn't get that job at the corner shop.'

'I know. How's the ulcer? Has the dressing I showed you how to prepare made a difference? I'm sorry I couldn't carry on with it, but my few days in London and the wedding preparations prevented me.'

'It's grand as owt, lass. Eeh, I reckon as I should have taken up nursing. It's all but healed, and I feel proud to have been able to help him.'

'That's good. Let's hope the surgeon can fix his leg, and then you'll have your hubby back.'

'That'd be a grand day – I told you, I miss it . . . him, I mean.'

They both laughed. For Mags, it wasn't without a tinge of colour flushing her cheeks. She loved having Betsy to talk to about everything, but still felt a bit shy when such things as man–woman relationships were touched upon. Though she had to admit to a tingling excitement visiting her, at the mention of it. Tonight, and every night of her life, she would be loved in that way by Harold. Yes, they had a way to go to put everything right, but her love for him would help her. She would keep him happy.

The bells ringing out from the Church of Immanuel in the village of Feniscowles set her heart beating faster. The time was upon her.

'Stay still now, so I can fix your veil, lass. Eeh, you're like a child on Christmas Eve.'

'Are you ready, Margaret? Come along, the bridesmaids should have left by now. What are you . . . ?'

Her father's voice trailed off as she appeared at the top of the stairs. Tears filled his eyes. Unbeknown to him, Mags had chosen to replicate her mother's wedding gown. Made from cream silk, the gown fitted the curves of her body, before flaring out in mermaid style – ankle-length at the front, it flowed into a trail behind her. A simple coronet of pearl daisies held her long veil in place, and around her neck she wore her mother's single-strand pearl necklace. Her bouquet had been fashioned from snowdrops and larkspurs, the exact colour of Betsy's frock, which was an empire-line style that suited her figure so well.

'Eeh, I feel like a princess,' she'd exclaimed after she'd slipped the frock on, and she looked like one, too. Her curls caught the sun beaming through the window, highlighting the redness in her chestnut hair.

Betsy's three little girls – Rosie, three; Florrie, five; and Daisy, six – were already downstairs. They were dressed in long, cream silk dresses and looked a picture. Each had their mother's hair colour and big blue eyes: they were adorable, or at least they were when they were on their best behaviour.

When they reached the bottom of the stairs, her father took Mags into his arms. His face was now wet with his tears. 'You look just like your mother, darling.'

'I wanted her to be part of today, Daddy. I didn't want to upset you.'

'You haven't. You've warmed my heart.'

'Come on, Mags . . . Oh, I mean Miss Margaret. I need a hand with me hat.'

Coming out of her father's arms, Mags laughed as she pinned Betsy's hat on, and had to admire how beautiful she looked. The hat gave Betsy sophistication, being wide-brimmed and in a curved style that took the brim lower at the side and finished with a cluster of feathers entwined with pearls where it dipped at the front. It was lovely.

'Well, well – you look very nice, Betsy.'

'Ta, Mr Witherbrook. I feel grand as owt.'

They all laughed at this.

'Well, off you go, and take your lovely little brood with you. The second carriage is for you, but you should arrive a few minutes before we do, so hurry along.'

Left alone with her father, Mags had a moment when she so longed for her mother to be by her side. But determined not to spoil the day by giving in to her grief, she gave a wide smile at her father. 'Well, this is it. The day you give me away, Daddy.'

'Yes, darling. And the day I enter into a conspiracy with you. I'll always be there for you, darling, and together we'll tame this young man you've chosen. And once we do, then I know you will have a very happy marriage. Your love for him will see to that.'

Mags couldn't say anything as she took her father's arm and walked out of the house. His words, she knew, had been said to reassure himself as much as for her. But she felt full of confidence. Everything was sorted now. Wasn't it?

After a wonderful service, they had the wedding breakfast, during which Harold made the perfect speech, remembering her mother and his parents, which brought a moment of sadness, but then lightening the proceedings with a reference to taming his wife.

'I understand that most of you belong to the meet that my new wife hunts with. Well then, as you well know, she can be a headstrong filly! I'm looking forward to reining her in and having her by my side in all I do – that is, as the loving little wife, not the businesswoman you all know her as.'

The moment's silence could have been a disaster, if Mags hadn't taken it as she did. This, she knew, was the moment to cement her husband's authority. Picking up her gloves, which she had discarded, she hit out playfully at him. 'True, darling, you are much more capable than me of running the family business, but you'd better watch out when you come home in the evening, as I will definitely hold the reins there and you will find yourself having to do as you're told.'

Harold looked annoyed, but as all her friends burst out laughing, he joined in with them. 'You can't keep a good woman down, as we all know. Well, my dear, I am looking forward to being bossed about by you, when we are behind closed doors. And to becoming part of society here in my new home town. I give you a toast to my beautiful wife – and may the best man win!'

Once more the room erupted into laughter as they all stood to toast Mags. Harold's arm came round her waist. His look was one of love, and of feeling very pleased with himself. She smiled up at him. His eyes, veiled with desire, set a tingling through her body. The moment was one she wanted to remember forever. 'My husband, I love you.'

'My beautiful wife, I love you, too. Thank you for marrying me. I am the happiest man alive.'

The cheer that went up brought the room back into focus and coloured Mags's cheeks as she realized they had all heard them. Turning, she gave a smile that reflected her happiness. Catching her father's eye, she saw a wide grin on his face – something she hadn't seen for a long time. *Everything in my world is perfect. Just perfect.*

As she lay beside Harold later that night, completely spent after his lovemaking, Mags was troubled. Flashes of an incident during the wedding reception kept revisiting her, preventing her from sleeping.

After the wedding breakfast, she and Harold had joined the staff in the small ballroom at the back of the house, where Betsy, still in her finery, was hosting a party for them, having sent the children home with her mother and Bill.

Everything was going with a swing as Cook played the piano, belting out popular songs, many from the war years, and Betsy, two of the maids and the gardener did a kind of jig. All had drunk too much and were clowning about, when Harold suddenly took hold of Betsy and danced around the floor with her.

Mags tried not to take much notice, but saw a look on Betsy's face that showed everything wasn't right. When the dance ended, Harold left the room.

Betsy announced that she had to go home to make sure her family were all settled. 'Now, mind you don't party too long. And I want this lot and the wedding-breakfast room all cleared away – and the evening buffet prepared and laid out – by the time I return.'

Alf, the gardener, expressed his disappointment. 'Aw, Betsy lass, we're meant to have a bit of slack today. It's only early afternoon yet. I thought as we'd go on till six at least.'

'You can, Alf – and all of you – but I have a family to see to.'

Harold returned at that moment and Betsy, looking embarrassed, suddenly said, 'Now afore I go, raise your glasses to our master and mistress and let's wish them a very happy life together.'

The toast lightened the moment, but Mags, who knew Betsy so well, was sure that something had been said to upset her. Going to her side, she asked, 'Are you all right, Betsy, love? This departure seems very sudden.'

Before Betsy could answer, Harold was at their side. 'Well, thank you, Betsy, for everything today. We are sorry you have to go, for my wife and I thought to spend an hour with you all. Now, everyone – thank you for your toast to my own and my beautiful wife's happiness. I have a toast of my own. A thank you to Mrs Bainwright, and to you all. You have done us proud today.'

Using Betsy's married name had sounded cold and as if Harold was putting her in her place. Mags hadn't known what to do as Betsy turned and left the moment she'd raised her glass and said thank you.

The incident had marred the day for Mags, though Harold had soon had her smiling again, once the evening party got under way. He'd been attentive and loving, the perfect husband, and that had continued when they'd reached her sitting room, where a tray was laid for them with champagne and nibbles to hand.

Mags turned over now and sighed. Her body still felt heightened, having given her so much pleasure in the arms of Harold, whose lovemaking had been exquisite, taking her to places she never dreamed possible. And then chatting, drinking champagne and doing it all over again, with an abandonment that had her crying out her joy and fulfilment.

She was being silly to think anything could mar that. Betsy was probably still cross from the incident that had happened the last time Harold was here – whatever that was. And she couldn't blame Betsy. *She must have felt awkward, too, knowing that I knew about it, and didn't want to upset me. Yes, that's all it was.* Well, Betsy and Harold had no need ever to be in each other's company again. Betsy had decided she wouldn't appear in the front of the house in future, and Harold wouldn't ever think of visiting the servants' quarters. All would work out fine.

With this, Mags felt sleep taking her and gave herself up to its peace.

Chapter Nine

Betsy sat on the wall outside her ma's house, not feeling the April downpour, such was her sense of devastation.

She'd come here to tell her ma that Bill was to have an operation to straighten his leg. The surgeon had said he would be able-bodied once more and could return to work and get his former life back. It was as Mags had said; the break had not been mended properly, and now he was to have it re-broken and set as it should be.

Not mended right? Eeh, poor Bill were left in agony for days, with just a strap keeping a splint in place. And aye, he's been in agony since an' all. But the joy of all this coming to an end for Bill couldn't lift her spirits.

'Hey, come inside, our Betsy, you're getting wet through.'

Betsy turned and looked at her sister, a bonny lass who was not yet wed, and not showing any interest in being so. She was what was termed a bookworm, and she had big ideas about being a teacher one day. *Eeh, such things don't happen to the likes of us, but I'll not spoil the lass's dreams.*

'I am wet through, our Ciss. Me tears are soaking me insides. How are we to get through this, eh?'

'Come on, lass, we will. This ain't like you. We've to be here for Ma. She can't beat this cancer that's eating away at her, but we can help her to cope and . . . well, you knaw – when the time comes, be with her, holding her hand.'

'But why? How? I hadn't an inkling.'

'I knaw. She put on a brave face over her pain and swore me to secrecy. She didn't go a minute without her make-up, to cover her gaunt features. And as for her being skin and bones, well, she's never had much fat on her, so she managed to keep from us how she was failing.'

'You should've said sommat. I could have asked Mags to help me get a doctor to see her long afore this.'

'I didn't realize. Honest, Betsy, don't blame me. I thought it would pass. Ma's allus been so tough and able to cope with owt.'

'Aye, I knaw. I didn't mean that. But what're we to do? How're we going to cope?'

'We have to. Now, as we knaw the truth, we need to be strong for her.'

Strong? How can I cope with all that I have eating away at me – Ma dying, and me Bill terrified of the op he's facing; and aye, living in fear of Harold Roford.

Betsy's mind revisited the incident that had put her in fear.

Is it really two months since the wedding? Since that pig Mags married held me too close to him and told me that his time with me will come? Betsy's mind shut out how she'd had an answering feeling in her, as Mr Roford pressed himself closer to her and she'd felt him getting hard. He'd covered it up by leaving for the bathroom straight after dancing with her.

She had to admit there was sommat about Mr Roford – he seemed to hypnotize womenfolk. Look at how Mags adored him, despite knowing that he was being unfaithful to her. *Aye, and knowing of his behaving badly with me – though I never told her all of it.*

But for Betsy the worst thing of all was having to admit to herself that, deep down, she knew she'd be hard pressed to refuse him, if he came on strong and they were alone. Even though she knew it was likely that Bill might soon be able to look after her in that way.

Eeh, dear God, don't let me. Don't let me ever give in to Mr Roford. It'd be the worst betrayal of me lovely Mags and me lovely Bill. But Harold Roford had touched something deep inside her, and it was something she didn't think she could fight. *Look at me now, thinking of him when me ma lies on her sickbed . . . Dear God!*

As soon as Betsy had asked Mags, medical help was arranged. And now Dr Lange, who was known to Betsy, as she had dealt with him through the welfare facility at Witherbrook's mill, was gathering his instruments into his case, having examined her ma.

Once downstairs, he said, 'I've given her something that will keep her asleep for a couple of hours, Betsy. Now she is going to need twenty-four-hour care – can you manage that?'

'Aye, we can, Doctor, but . . . well, for how long? I mean, I don't want to lose her – none of us do – but we don't want her to suffer like this, either.'

'I understand. To be truthful, it isn't something any doctor can predict, but I would say that Mrs Parkin has very little time left in this world. If she is a Christian and God-fearing, I would fetch a priest or vicar to her, as that often helps to settle the dying and assists them to pass in peace.'

Betsy held on to the back of a chair. Looking past the doctor, to Ciss, she could see that the truth about their ma's condition had hit her sister, as if for the first time. Finding strength that she didn't know she had, Betsy took charge. 'Aye, we'll do that, as Ma is God-fearing and says her prayers every night, even if going to church sticks in her craw, as it seems to be the domain of the rich, instead of welcoming and helping the poor. Nevertheless, I knaw as she'd like some prayers said over her. You run down to the church house, our Ciss, there's a good lass.'

Ciss didn't protest. She went to the back door as if she was in a dream and got her coat off the hook.

'Take me umbrella, lass.'

As Ciss picked up the umbrella, Betsy thought of Mags. The umbrella had been a present from her. Not many people of Betsy's standing owned an umbrella, and she was very proud of it. But it also reminded her that she would need to hurry back to her job as soon as she could, as there was a special dinner party tonight and she was to oversee everything.

'That was a big sigh. Now I know you have a big worry on your shoulders, Betsy, but I promise I will do all I can to keep your mother comfortable. And you've no need to be beholden to anyone for my services. In fact, you can do me a favour. Me and a couple of other doctors in the area are setting up a service for those who can't afford to pay. It was Dr O'Hannigan who suggested it.'

'Aye, I knaw him. He's a kindly man and has been paid in jam and the likes, by me ma and folk around here, for a good while. Only with me ma so poorly, I wanted someone with expertise – aw, I didn't mean . . .'

'I know what you meant, don't worry. Dr O'Hannigan

97

would be the first to admit that us younger doctors have an edge on up-to-date medicine, but he's an amazing doctor, for all that he is in his seventies, and a very kind man. He's made us see that we should be doing more than simply what we are paid to do. And to that end, we are going to be holding a free clinic on the last Friday of every month. Now I know that you are covered by Witherbrook's employees medical-care system, but you can spread the word to those who aren't. The clinic will be held in the church hall.'

'That's grand, Doctor, ta. It will make a difference, especially to the young 'uns and the old 'uns.'

'And not before time. I'm ashamed of what Dr O'Hannigan has been telling us he comes across. I've been shielded all my life from the lives of the poor.'

'Well, you can make up for it now, and that's good.'

'I can. Now as I say, I'll be back often. But here is my card. You can call on me if you need me at other times, or if I'm not available, I will make sure one of the others comes out to Mrs Parkin. I'll let them know the diagnosis, and they will have the right medicine with them to keep her comfortable. Good day, Betsy.'

Left alone in the house she'd been brought up in, Betsy was assailed by memories of the happy times of her childhood: of her da, a big man who was loved by everyone and was known as a gentle giant. Looking as if he should have been a labourer, he'd been a baker's assistant and was known for baking the finest bread. But the fire at the bakehouse had taken him. Betsy shuddered; she'd never let herself think about the fire for long. If she did, she had nightmares about what it must have been like to be trapped inside that searing heat. In a way, her ma had never recovered from losing her big Jack. Well, now she would be going to him, and this thought gave some comfort to Betsy.

Everything was ready for the dinner party, except that one vital member of staff was missing. 'Where has that silly lass got to? What are we going to do, Cook?'

'You'll have to wait on, Betsy. Have you ever done silver service, lass?'

'Naw. And I haven't a clue. And with all I've got going on with me ma, and with Bill going into hospital tomorrow, I can't stop shaking. I'd be chucking the food everywhere. Oh, where is she?'

'You did instruct her about tonight, didn't you? Only this ain't like Janet. If she couldn't come, it would have to be for a dire reason. And then she'd send her younger sister, who she's been instructing for a good while in the skills of serving on.'

Betsy felt sick. Had she instructed Janet about tonight? She couldn't remember. Janet went off three days ago on a break, richly deserved, and Betsy had felt confident she'd told her everything, although now she doubted herself.

'I'll have to run along there. We've over an hour before service, so I'll have time. I'll ask Mr Barnard if young Phil can answer any of the bells, but I reckon as he'll go spare. Mr Barnard don't like owt upsetting his routine.'

'Aye, things have changed around here. A butler? I never heard the like. Well, in larger establishments, yes. I once worked—'

'Eeh, Cook, I knaws, lass, and I haven't time to hear the tale again. I have to dash.'

'Why you don't send young Phil, I don't knaw. Surely that'd be best.'

'Naw. Mags – I mean, Mrs Roford – doesn't like me to be seen in the front of the house. I couldn't answer any of the bells, and Millie is busy, too, seeing to all the fires, as we daren't let the rooms get cold. Then, when the guests come down, she's all the beds to turn down, and their discarded clothes to hang up – she's enough on her plate. Besides, she ain't dressed right to attend to the guests.'

Composing herself and walking with a calmness that she didn't feel, Betsy went in search of the new butler. Her nerves jangled, as she had to be in the areas that she shouldn't be, or at least ones that were out of bounds once Mr Roford was home. Of course during the day her duties demanded that she tour the building, making sure her instructions were carried out and that all the daily helpers were doing their work.

Thankfully, everywhere was quiet. The overnight guests were in their rooms getting ready, and those who lived nearby hadn't yet started to arrive.

She found Mr Barnard in the green dining room, checking that everything was as it should be.

The room looked lovely. The long table was adorned in white linen, making a stark contrast with the centrepiece of deep-red roses, which it must have cost a fortune to obtain at this time of year. The surroundings were what Betsy thought of as 'peaceful'. The cream-coloured walls provided a restful background to the heavily patterned green and deep-red carpet, and the soft-green velvet curtains draped beautifully, providing elegance. As did the lovely carved, glass-fronted dresser, full of exquisite china, and the ornate fireplace in white marble, with its log fire blazing up the chimney.

'Mrs Bainwright? What brings you into my domain?'

'I beg your pardon, Mr Barnard, but I need to go out.' Betsy told him of her predicament and how she would need Phil to see to anything that anyone might need while she was gone. 'Janet usually does that while she is preparing to wait on, and I can't do it, and neither can you.'

A huge sigh told her of Mr Barnard's disapproval. Not of her, but of what he called a 'tinpot setup all round'.

'Didn't you take on extra staff? Surely an occasion like this warrants it?'

'There is no one. Oh, maybe Janet's sister could have been an extra pair of hands, but I . . . I, well, I've not thought on. I've a lot troubling—'

'Our own troubles are secondary to the smooth running of our household, Mrs Bainwright. Lord preserve us! Look, I know you haven't had the benefit of the training I have had, and it shows, but if I was you, I would get myself in line – and quickly – with how a household is run, as I see ambition in our master, and he is going to want his house run efficiently.'

'You are speaking of Mr Roford, I take it? Well, our master is Mr Witherbrook, and he don't entertain in this fashion very often; nor has he ever had need of a butler. And he's still alive and kicking, so you'd better run this household according to *his* needs and likes and dislikes. 'Cause if he takes a mind to kick off about it, you'll all knaw about it.'

'You can't even speak the King's English, Mrs Bainwright, so don't you dare to lecture me in the way of this, or any other, household. And the answer is "No". I am not relinquishing my one and only staff member to cover for your inadequacies. So now you can eat your words and sort that one out!'

Shaking more from fury than from all she'd had to

101

contend with today, Betsy stormed out of the room, just stopping herself from slamming the door after her. What now? Did she go after Janet and hope no one needed any attention? Or call Millie to leave her duties and get changed into uniform, and hope that she could catch up and have everything in order in time, once she could return to it?

Part of Betsy's problem was solved when she entered the kitchen once more. 'Oh, Cyril. Thank goodness! I have an urgent message I need you to deliver, lad.' The boy who helped the gardener was in the midst of taking a huge bite out of the sandwich Cook had made for him.

'He dropped in, on the off-chance. Allus has some excuse, but this time he was just hungry, poor lad. His dad's drunk again, and his ma's got nowt in.'

'Well, you can earn that sandwich and a basket of owt that Cook can put together, lad, if you run like the wind to Janet's house and come back with the answer.'

'I'll do owt for you, Mrs Bainwright.'

Betsy smiled. At fifteen, the lad was feeling his manhood coming on and she'd often caught him looking at her, his eyes fixed firmly on her breasts. She'd cuffed his ear and told him to learn respect for women, and not ogle them in such a way. But he was a nice lad really, and was always willing.

With Cyril on his way, Betsy breathed a sigh of relief, though she still had her fingers crossed that Janet and her sister would soon be on their way here. *I've been an idiot. Mr Bighead Barnard is reet, of course. I should have made sure we had extra staff. One of the dailies could have come in and done what Millie is doing, then Millie could have been on hand for the guests, and to do any other requests that came up.*

Realizing this, Betsy questioned if Mr Barnard wasn't right

in saying she wasn't up to the job. And yet she'd put her heart into seeing that tonight went well – at least she'd thought she had.

A ringing bell caught her attention. Looking up, she felt trepidation gripping her. It came from Mr Roford's rooms.

Since his marriage to Mags, Mr Roford had reorganized so much. And one of the changes was that he had wanted his own rooms. Mr Witherbrook had accommodated this by moving to the top rooms, from the suite he used to occupy with his wife. A nice arrangement for him as he had had his privacy, though Betsy doubted the wisdom of him climbing so many stairs to get to his rooms.

But to her, it was strange that man and wife didn't share the same space. Oh, it was well gossiped about that Mr Roford visited Mags most nights and often only crept back to his own rooms in the early hours, so she felt happy for Mags on that score. But other gossip worried her, as this arrangement gave Mr Roford so much freedom to come and go as he pleased; and it was said that he slipped out many a late night – no doubt to one of the gambling houses or . . . but no, surely he wouldn't have any need to go to ladies of ill repute?

Betsy had been in a quandary as to whether to mention anything to Mags about Mr Roford's supposed escapades, but had decided against it. She was sure it was just gossip, and she wouldn't risk hurting Mags on account of hearsay.

Taking a deep breath, she mounted the stairs. Her hand shook as she knocked on the door, then entered at Mr Roford's bidding.

'Ah, if it isn't Betsy. Well, well, I wondered how long it would be before you sought me out.'

'I – I ain't, sir. A member of staff hasn't turned up, and

so I've no choice but to take on the role of seeing to your own and the guests' needs.'

'Ha, you can see to mine all right. Come here.'

'Naw. I ain't doing nowt with you. I – I just want to carry out whatever you called for a maid to do, and that's all.'

'Ah, but I want more doing, now it is you who has come to me, Betsy.'

He walked towards her.

'Naw. Naw, don't touch me, please . . .'

'You're begging for it, you know as you are. I can feel it. I'm not daft. Now stop resisting and let's get on with it. I have a lot to give you, Betsy. It's you I think of, when I'm trying to satisfy that cold fish of a wife of mine. God, she's hard work – gives nothing and takes all. Now you, Betsy, I can see you're a giver. And I can see that you want to give what you have to me.'

Affronted at how he'd spoken of Mags, Betsy couldn't understand how he was still having such an effect on her. He was close to her now. She could smell him – the lovely smell of his cologne, something she'd thought strange for a man to splash on himself, but had known the allure of whenever she'd caught a whiff of it. As it hit her senses, she felt herself coming alive. Every part of her wanted this man. Wanted to know what it would be like to be kissed by him, fondled . . . entered. Oh God, she could hardly breathe.

His lips felt smooth as she met them, and yet they tingled sensations through her that she'd long forgotten could be so strong. Her arms went around him and she clung to him, not caring that he was moving them towards the bed, taking in his tongue and thrusting her own into his mouth. All thoughts of hurting Mags were forgotten as she drowned in this release of all her troubles – this exquisite wrongdoing, which was making her gasp for breath and had her longing for more.

When she took Harold into her, she cried out with ecstasy as her whole body betrayed her, and the ache within her flowed into a river of wondrous relief of all her pent-up womanhood.

Harold's cries joined hers, his hollers telling her he was climaxing, and inside her, but she didn't care: she wanted him, wanted to drink in all of him – she loved him in an animalistic way that she had no control of. And she knew in that moment that she would go to the ends of the world to couple with him as often as she could, no matter the consequences.

As he rolled off her, reality hit Betsy. *Oh God, what have I done? What have I done?*

'Come on – off the bed and pull your knickers up. I know you enjoyed it, but you're to go back to your duties now, as if nothing has happened . . . Here.'

The sound of the coins jingling as he threw them onto the bed aroused disgust in Betsy. She was the lowest of the low. How had she sunk to this? She couldn't blame Bill's inadequacy, as she knew it was possible that would soon come to an end. *I should have waited – I should! What kind of a person can I be, to use the shock of the news I had about Ma as a need for comfort? What I've done was vile . . . vile!*

'Get on your way, will you? For Christ's sake, my wife might come along to see me at any moment. You were good, but you weren't that good to think you can take up residence. Get out – and get out *now*!'

Lifting herself off the bed, Betsy felt hatred of this man grind into her. He'd taken her and changed her. He'd changed everything, and not for the better. She'd get her own back on him.

Standing, she faced him. She saw a beauty in his nakedness, but it had no effect on her as she grabbed the bodice of her dress where he'd undone the buttons and, with an almighty effort, tore it open.

'What are you doing? Stop that!'

Not heeding him, Betsy took hold of her hair and tugged it out of the clips that held it, before scraping her nails across her face and then across her breasts.

Harold looked at her in horror. He moved towards her, but she stopped him in his tracks as she attacked him, tearing his skin with her nails, kicking him and beating him with her fists. When finally he managed to push her off, she screamed with such force that her throat hurt.

As he stood and gaped at her, she ran for the door, letting her knickers fall around her ankles. Once outside the room, she hollered, 'Help me, please – someone, help me.'

Chapter Ten

Mags stood, looking out of the window of her bedroom, the room she hadn't left since her world had crashed around her three days ago. A place where her mind had been blank, unable to let everything in.

Even now her face was wet with tears, and yet she wasn't crying. Not in the way she'd sobbed when her mother died, or cried after so many events in her life. Her heart was crying. Crying for her beloved friend, Betsy. And yes, for her lost love. For Harold had to be lost to her now. There was no going back. For him to rape anyone would have resulted in this distress, but for it to have been dear Betsy. *Oh God, how am I ever to get over this utter humiliation?*

But no, *she* didn't matter. Betsy mattered. And Bill. What this had done to him, Mags could only imagine, and when he was facing his operation, too.

On top of that, Betsy's mother was failing fast. *And I can't go to Betsy – I can't. I can't face her. I feel so guilty. I knew what Harold was like. Knew that he'd tried before, with Betsy. How could I have carried on with my selfish wishes and put her in such danger?*

107

The pent-up emotion inside her felt as though it would choke her. Her body began to creep with a dirty feeling, as the rape of herself by the German soldier came into focus to mock her. The trembling of her body started up once more with these memories, and she went towards her bed and lay down. She welcomed the mist that descended over her, blocking out reality, leaving her unable to feel, unable to think.

'Mags! Mags, please open the door. It's all lies . . . lies. You have to believe me. Open this door before I have it broken down!'

Not even the sound of the door being felled got through to Mags. It was as if she had shut down. Oh, she knew what was happening, but she couldn't react to it, didn't want to. She wanted to stay cocooned in her own little world, where no one could hurt her ever again.

As she thought this, the residue of the emotional pain left her.

'For God's sake, Mags, what do you think you are doing? You haven't eaten for days, or come out of this room. Have you even washed? I've sent for a doctor. Your father has had an attack of some sort. You should go to him. You're being selfish, cooping yourself up in this room and not facing anything. You should listen to me, too. I didn't do what that slut said I did. I didn't.'

Harold sobbed as he slumped down on the side of the bed and buried his head in his hands. Wearily Mags sat up. 'Father isn't well? What's wrong with him?'

Harold looked up at her. His sobs hadn't produced any tears, and his voice held anger. 'Shock, I shouldn't wonder, at your behaviour. What kind of a woman are you? Running to your room at the first sign of a problem, instead of standing by your husband and sorting out the situation with dignity?'

'Situation? You raped my very best friend. Oh, that is more than a "situation", Harold. I want you to leave. I want a divorce. I—'

'Shut up and I will tell you what is to happen. If you don't believe me when I say that I didn't rape Betsy, that is your problem. Let me tell you this: you will not get a divorce. I am not giving up all of this. You will act with dignity. You will put out a statement that the hussy you engaged as a housekeeper has confessed to telling lies. That you understand she was after money and staged the rape – which she did. And you will say that she has now left our employment and that you are standing by your husband.'

'I will not!'

'Very well. Then I will put my second plan into action.'

Harold leaned over and pulled the bell cord. His butler appeared at the door, with a man Mags had never seen before.

'Thank you, Barnard. Please come in, Dr Jenkins.'

Mags looked at the swarthy gentleman who stepped into the room. Instantly disliking and mistrusting him, she instinctively drew herself up into a ball and clasped her knees, pulling her dressing gown around her as she did so.

'A typical behaviour of mental disorder. The patient thinks, by making herself appear small, that she can combat whatever it is she fears.'

This astonished Mags. *Mental disorder? What is this doctor talking about?*

'I have no need to examine her. She will be assigned to a psychiatrist at the asylum.'

'W – what? What are you saying? I am not mad; just very, very upset, and with good reason. My—'

'We're going to get you better, my love. You'll soon be home with me and your father, I promise.'

'No. No!' Mags's screams hurt her own ears. She couldn't believe what was happening. 'I'm not ill, I'm just distressed at my husband's vile act of disloyalty. I—'

'This is what she has been saying ever since she had a nightmare three nights ago. She woke up screaming and hitting me. Look, I still have the bruises.'

'Speak to my father, please. Please . . . he will tell you. Speak to the servants – to Betsy, and to Cook – they know.'

'Darling, my love, your daddy isn't well. Have you forgotten? He is unconscious and has been for days. He isn't expected to wake up ever again. Now that you know this, my darling, I'm so sorry. You were told and then you had that nightmare. You said everyone was leaving you.' To the doctor, Harold said, 'She lost her mother just before Christmas, poor love. Do you think it is those traumas that are causing this?'

'They could very well. But why is she fixated on you being unfaithful? That seems a strange turn for this kind of psychotic episode to take. Usually it would be that you are going to die, too.'

'Oh, that's my father's fault. He was a philanderer, and my darling wife has always held this fear that I might turn out like him. Nothing could be further from the truth. Her accusations cut me in two. I love her so much. Please – please get her better, Doctor.' This last came out on a sob.

'We will, old chap. These episodes rarely last long and, with care, hardly ever return. I have spoken to her own doctor and he said she nearly had a breakdown when her mother died, and that he thinks she is suffering from leftover trauma from her brave actions during the war. He is shocked that Mrs Roford is this ill, and to hear how ill her father is, and cannot understand why you didn't call him.'

'I didn't call him because I panicked, and then one of the guests mentioned an eminent heart specialist, who he thought would be the best person to attend Mr Witherbrook. As it happened, I knew the fellow from my university days, and so I thought that best, and then he recommended that you tend to my wife. I have been at my wits' end since, with what has been happening to my darling wife, that I haven't had time to think about calling Dr Lange to put him in the picture. And yes, Mags was so brave during the war, but what she saw and went through often visits her and sends her into a strange world, where she doesn't want to talk for days. I have tried to be understanding, but maybe I should have got help for her.'

The doctor didn't answer. Mags wanted to scream at them both again. How could they be discussing her like this, but although she knew Harold's lies were being believed, everything seemed so unreal and she felt detached from what was happening. Nothing would sink in, except that her darling father was ill and needed her. 'Please let me go to Daddy.'

'She is reverting to childlike behaviour now. It is as I said: signs of a psychotic episode due to trauma. Not a lot is known about it, but I think a spell in the institution would greatly benefit her. It will take her away from where the recent trauma has occurred – either real, as in losing her mother, or unreal, as in what she believes you have done. She needs to talk about her wartime experiences, too. If we can get her to do that, I have every hope that she will soon

111

be well. I ordered the ambulance to come here, based on what you told me on the phone had been happening. I am glad I did, as we mustn't waste a moment. They are waiting outside now.'

Realization hit Mags once more. 'No. No, please don't do this. Please. I told you, it's him. Him! *He* has done this to me. No – o – oo!'

A sharp sensation in Mags's arm stopped her screams. The room began to swim. The voices of Harold and the doctor drifted away as she felt herself floating into a long, long tunnel. A feeling of peace overcame her, and she gave herself up to the blessed relief of it.

Betsy stared at the letter from Bellinge, Solicitors. 'No. Oh dear God!'

Dear Mrs Bainwright,
We act for Mr Harold Roford of Feniscowles Manor, Feniscowles, Blackburn.
This is to notify you that our client is seeking to sue you for wrongful accusation and bringing his name into disrepute.
The consequences of your action have caused his wife to have a mental breakdown, and his father-in-law to collapse under the strain you have put the family under.
We will be asking for these circumstances to be taken into consideration, if judgement is made against you.
This case will be heard on the twenty-ninth day of April in the year 1921 in the County Court in Preston. The case will be judged by a jury, presided over by the District Judge at eleven a.m.

You are hereby summoned to attend.
Yours sincerely
For Mr Roford,
Arkwright Bellinge

Every limb shook, as Betsy backed towards a chair. *Oh, Mags, dear Mags, what have I done to you?* A holler came from her mouth. 'What have I done? Naw . . . naw!' Tears mingled with her snot as, unable to close her mouth, she gasped out the sobs that racked her body. Her mind screamed at her: *You did this, you vile creature!* And she knew the guilty truth. *Why? Why did I want him? What possessed me in those moments? I was like an animal!*

Excuses did present themselves to her: that she was in deep stress over her mother's condition, and over Bill's forthcoming operation. *Oh God, Bill!* Fear clutched her as she thought of Bill, who was at this moment going under the knife. Would he cope? He'd hardly spoken to her since he'd heard about the rape and had broken down, sobbing with anger. She'd wanted him to comfort her, but Bill hadn't been able to touch her; but then didn't men believe there was no such thing as rape? *And in my case there wasn't – oh God, relieve me of this guilt, please. Please.*

The last three days Betsy had felt sick to her stomach. She'd waited and waited for Mags to contact her, but she hadn't. Now she knew why. *Me actions broke Mags. Me lovely friend Mags is broken.*

Once more the heartbreak that she'd caused flooded through Betsy. Her body folded, and her tears dropped onto her skirt. Never had she felt such distress, and yet she couldn't get help from anyone. She could never tell the truth, not even to Ciss. There was no one who wouldn't be disgusted with her. And she couldn't blame them. Never before had she behaved in such a manner. It had been as if that Mr Roford had some kind of hold over her. *Oh, Bill, my Bill, I've betrayed you an' all.*

As she thought of hearing all the accusations in court, and of Bill hearing them, fear joined her despair. Would she lose him? Would she be able to keep up the lie under oath? As it dawned on her that the whole world would find out about her deceit, Betsy knew that whatever it took, she would have to stick to her story. Mags would get over it, and she'd kick the rotter out. That was the best thing she could do, because he was bad – evil. A destroyer of good people. Then, just maybe, everything could get back to how it used to be.

With the feeling settling in her that she had in some way helped Mags, Betsy dried her tears. She'd go to Cook and see if she would pass on a message to Mags. Together, she and Mags could sort all of this out.

When Cook opened the kitchen door, she opened her arms. 'Eeh, lass, what a terrible thing to happen. Come here, come on in. Is that Rosie as you have in the pram? By, look at her, such a little dot, and yet her coming on four years old.'

Coming out of Cook's welcome hug, Betsy manoeuvred the huge, boat-shaped wooden pram nearer to the wall for shelter. 'Aye, she's little, but strong as a horse, that one, though she runs out of steam and has to have her afternoon nap. I'll leave the pram out here; she's well wrapped up.' Applying the brake, Betsy expressed the fear she'd felt. 'I'm hoping as I weren't seen, though I came in the back way.'

'He's out, the master. Oh, Betsy lass, everything's changed.'

The warmth of the kitchen tingled Betsy's cold hands and face to life, and the familiar smell of cooking almost undid her, but hope entered her on hearing that Roford was out. 'Where's Mags . . . I mean, Mrs Roford? Can I see her? Is she in?'

'Oh naw, haven't you heard? He had her committed. Our lovely lass is in the asylum.'

'What? That bastard! Eeh, I'm sorry for me language, but he's a rotter. Why? Oh, Cook, please don't tell me Mags went mad. Naw, not that . . . naw.'

'I don't think so. She was shocked and spent three days in her room. She didn't eat and didn't want anyone to visit her, not even him. She locked her door. He broke into her room eventually, but he'd already brought a doctor over. Next thing we knew, our lovely mistress was screaming, then all went quiet and she were being carted off.'

'Eeh, naw . . . naw. I didn't mean for all of this to happen.'

'What d'you mean, lass? It weren't your fault. Though he said as it were. None of us believed him.'

'What did he say, Cook?'

'He called us all into the hall and told us that you had asked him for money. He said you'd previously asked for a large sum from his wife, as you had a notion that your husband could be cured by an operation. He said that the mistress had refused you, so you tried to get money from him. That you offered your favours for it, but he was disgusted by you. Then he said you leapt at him, taking him by surprise and ripping his dressing gown from him, leaving him naked. That you scratched and kicked him, leaving him powerless to stop you, for fear of hurting you, which he didn't want to do. He said you growled at him that either he gave you the money you wanted or you would ruin his life. When he still refused, you ripped your bodice, scratched your own face and body and pulled your hair out of its clips, before you opened the door, and then you . . . well, he said you dropped your undergarments.'

'Oh God. I have to sit down, Cook.' Pulling out one of the chairs from under the table where all the staff sat at mealtimes, Betsy lowered herself. Part of her flushed with the truth of half of Roford's story, but another part of her wondered at him making up such a lie. So that was it! Both his story and her own were half-lie, half-truth, but she knew with a sinking heart who would be believed – by them that mattered, that was.

'Look, lass, none of us believed him, nor could we under-stand why he even told us – I mean, it stinks. No one of the master's standing would normally bother about what the servants knew or thought. It's as if he's trying to make a truth out of a lie and have us back him up. Besides, you told us all that the mistress was going to pay for the surgery on Bill, a long time ago. And we all knaw you. What he says you did, you'd never do in a million years. You only answered his bell and, before we all knew it, you were screaming the place down. What's his game, eh?'

Betsy lowered her head. *Never do in a million years? But I did. I did, most of it, I did . . .*

'Oh, Cook, who's going to believe me, eh? I mean, them as can harm me. His story sounds true, and he is – like you say – a man of standing, and I'm nowt.' Taking a deep breath, Betsy decided to repeat her lie; she had to stick to it, she had to. 'I knocked on the door and he called for me to come in. He . . . he had his back to me. He was in his dressing gown. I said, "What can I do for you, sir?" Then he turned and came towards me. I – I felt scared as . . .

well, he'd tried it on me afore. Anyroad, he grabbed me and . . .'

Cook listened to her tale. Her mouth dropped open. By the end of her telling, tears were streaming down Betsy's face, and Cook was mopping her own face with her pinny.

'Eeh, lass, naw. He's a rotten sod! And you say he's suing you? What will happen if he wins?'

'I don't knaw. I don't knaw. Maybe I'll go to prison . . . Oh, Cook, I couldn't bear that, I couldn't.'

They were both quiet for a moment, before it hit Betsy afresh what had happened to Mags. 'Have you any idea where they've taken Mags – I mean, which asylum?'

'Eeh, I can never get used to you calling her by her pet name. But then you pair have been friends a long time, I knaws that. Anyroad, I've an inkling. You see, Alf were up the tree at the end of the drive – he was lopping off some of the overhanging branches – when that ambulance pulled out, and he watched it for a long time. He said it went towards Pleasington and he thought he caught a glimpse of it after that on Billinge End Road, so it's our guess it were heading for Brockhall Institution.'

'Eeh, naw . . . Naw, not there. Eeh, Cook, they say as no one ever comes back out of there. It's unbearable. And – and her dad an' all, where's he?'

'He's lain in his bed, all but gone from this world. He has a nurse caring for him. It's him as should be in hospital, but I reckon Roford don't want him to recover. I mean, think about it: with the old man dead, and his wife in a mental institute, Roford stands to gain the lot – this house and all the land that goes with it, as there's a good few tenant farmers; and that on top of the factory that he has part ownership of . . . well, he's made, as I see it.'

'The rotten swine! That's it: that were his plan all along. I knaws stuff about him, Cook. I'd like to bet it ain't long afore someone else moves in here.'

'What? Who?'

'I can't say, as I'd be breaking Mags's confidence. But one thing I do knaw. I'm going to do all I can to stop it happening.'

'What can you do, lass? Eeh, be careful.'

Betsy sat up. *I'll go to Dr Lange. But will he help? Why has he allowed this to happen?*

Before she could answer Cook, a crying from outside the door drew her attention. 'Eeh, Rosie's awake, and probably wondering where she is. Anyroad, I've to go. Me other two'll be in from school soon, an' all. Then I've to go and take me turn sitting with me ma.'

'By, lass, you've sommat on your plate. How's your ma faring?'

'I hardly dare think on it, but I'm afraid she hasn't many days left. In one way, it'd be a blessing, as she's suffering badly.'

The thought came that aye, her ma passing would be a blessing, as Betsy knew that the disgrace the court case would bring down on the family was something she never wanted her ma to witness. *Oh God, help me. Aye, I knaw as I sinned, and I'm sorry. And I knaws as I've to carry on sinning, in me lying about what happened, but I have to. I have to!*

Chapter Eleven

Mags tried to turn over, but couldn't. Something was holding her limbs so that she couldn't move. Nor could she open her eyes or cry out, as her mouth was clamped shut – by what, she did not know.

Fear encased her. She struggled, but the restrictions around her body didn't budge. Panic gripped her. She couldn't breathe.

'Calm down. If you do, we'll release you. But you can't attack us as you have been doing. If you're quiet for a while, we'll take the plaster off your eyes. Then, maybe, the one from your mouth. These were a punishment for your violence. But the straitjacket will remain on for a while. Everything depends on how you behave. It's all up to you.'

The horror of what they'd done to her seeped into Mags. She wanted to kick out at the woman who had spoken. She didn't know how long she'd been here, only that each time she'd surfaced from a drug-induced sleep, she'd fought with all her might against those trying to restrain her.

When she'd awoken the first time after arriving here, she'd found herself in a cell-like room with green-painted brick walls and a thick wooden door. The only light had come from a very high window that she couldn't reach to see out of. And apart from the wooden structure that held the mattress she lay on, there was only one other thing in the room – a bucket that stood in the corner near the door. To Mags's dismay, she realized this was for her toilet use.

The cries of the insane haunted her day and night, until at first she'd welcomed the injections, and the blessed peace they'd given her. After a while, though, her head had begun to ache, and she wanted an end to it all.

In her lucid moments she'd thought of her father, lying on his deathbed, calling for her. And all she'd wanted was to get out of here and go to him. When those attending to her refused to talk to her, she'd become angry and had lashed out at them – something she'd never done in her life. But violence seemed her only weapon, as she couldn't get through to them in any other way. When she'd fought with one man, he'd hit her. His face had come close to hers, and he'd threatened vile things that she knew she wouldn't be able to bear – one of them had been a straitjacket, and having her mouth and eyes taped. Now this had happened to her, and she was encased.

The other threat had been that he'd come in the night, when she was entrapped, and would have her – and she knew what he meant. And with him threatening this, it dawned on her what was happening to some of the other women in the cells next to hers. For their cries changed in the night, from despair to screams of 'Naw, don't – leave me alone', although some seemed to like what was happening, as cries of pleasure also echoed around her.

Barely conscious when they'd brought her in, she'd registered a long corridor with doors leading off it. Lots of doors, and from behind each one she'd heard cries, moans and weeping.

'She's waking,' she'd heard one of her stretcher-bearers say. Then they had stopped their progress and she had felt the same sharp sting of something going into her arm. The tunnel had appeared once more, and she'd sunk into it.

How long this routine had gone on for, she hadn't known. The dark was impenetrable and clawed at her.

'That's better. Reet, I'll remove your eye covers, lass. Keep still.'

Mags winced as the plaster was torn from her eyelids, stretching and pulling her lashes, till she knew most of them must have come out. Tears stung her already-sore eyes. Keeping them shut wasn't her choice, but each time she tried to open them they smarted and the light hurt.

'Now I'll be back later. And if you're still calm, I'll take the plaster off your mouth.'

Real tears joined the ones caused by the extreme pain of the plaster removal. How could this have happened? Why did Harold do this to her? He hadn't been near to visit or to check on her welfare. And what of her father? *Dear Daddy, I'm so sorry. Please don't die. Please wait for me to get out of here, as surely I must.*

Only her father and Harold would have any authority to sign her out, other than the medical staff. Harold had looked at her with glee when she'd pleaded with him. Not that he let the doctor see that.

Suddenly it began to dawn on Mags that Harold had found a way to get his hands on all that she and her father owned, without having to be bothered with her. *He's probably with his precious Susan at this very moment. Oh God, I can't bear it, I can't.*

A realization came to her that something within her had changed. Not being able to bear her predicament had nothing to do with Harold and his seedy affair. Her love for him was dead. He could go with whomever he wished to, she didn't care. But what she did care about, and couldn't bear, was not being with her father in his dying hours, and the thought of spending her life in here. *That can't happen, can it?*

But even as the thought settled in her, she knew it could. It was always being said that those brought in here never came out. *No! No, God, please – please help me.*

With her head pounding and her eyes hurting with a pain she'd never experienced before, Mags decided that she would help her own cause. She would do whatever she could to get out. If she behaved, and showed no signs of being in a poor mental state – maybe even engaged the nurses in conversation and tried to be cheerful – but how she was going to do that, she didn't know. She'd tried wailing and fighting, and protesting that she wasn't ill, and that had only worsened her situation.

As her eyes hurt less and she could look around her, she noted in more detail the small, dingy room she was in. Not that there was anything to note about it, but she counted the bricks and where the paint had dripped before it had dried; then the bars at the little window. Through this she could see that it was a lovely day. The sky was patched with blue amidst thick white, fluffy clouds. A spring day. Probably with a slight chill in the air, but a lovely day for a walk. She let her mind drift to her favourite walk around the perimeter of the woods that bordered the back edge of their beautiful garden.

Such thoughts didn't help, as her despair deepened.

Somehow she must keep herself sane. She'd ask what day it was, and by knowing this, she could keep track of time, by adding on every waking day. Then she could use this knowledge to help them see that she had her wits about her.

All of this working through a plan made her tired. Mags drifted off to sleep, praying that soon everything would be sorted out.

'Margaret, Margaret.' The voice calling her sounded soft and caring. Mags felt lulled into thinking everything had been a horrible dream. On opening her eyes, she knew it wasn't. Her temper flared, but just in time she remembered her new-found resolve. So she lay still and let the woman who'd been in earlier do whatever she had to.

A stout woman, with prominent hairs on her chin, she looked to Mags to be in her forties. Her teeth were bad and her hands grubby, but her grey uniform frock and the apron that covered it were pristinely clean and didn't have a crease in them. Mags guessed she was an orderly, as her uniform was different from that of the nurses, who wore caps on their heads, with a cloth veil hanging down to their necks.

None of the women staff had been too bad, but simply reacted to her behaviour. It was the men that Mags feared. And one in particular: a thin, weedy man, whose moustache curled into a point on each side of his mouth. His eyes were very dark and evil-looking. And although he did indeed look feeble, when he'd restrained her he'd been immensely strong. Then there were the men who were on duty at night. They were the ones who caused the most distressing noises from the adjoining cells. Mags prayed that they never visited her.

'There, that's better, lass. I'll take that plaster off your mouth, but mind: any profanities or spitting, and it'll be back in place in a shot.'

Mags braced herself, telling herself that no matter how much it hurt, she wasn't to cry out. How she managed it, she didn't know, for the stinging sensation was excruciating.

'There, all done. You've some tears to your skin, but that will soon heal.'

'Th – thank you.' With her mouth as dry as sandpaper, it was difficult to form the words. 'Can I ask what day it is and the date, please.'

'Aye, it's Saturday the sixteenth. Yesterday is being called Black Friday, as the transport and rail workers ain't coming out in support of the rest of the workers in the country. Me old man and me son are miners, and both are out on strike. They're nearly on their knees, I tell yer. And if it weren't for my wage, we'd starve. But then, happen as you'd not knaw what that feels like – you being a lass from moneyed folk.'

'I do actually. During the war I was a nurse, and I nearly starved. There was a time when I became trapped in Brussels with two fellow VADs, and we ran out of food and money.'

'Eeh, lass, you'll have to tell me more about that sometime. Well, hats off to yer. Here, let me get you a drink of water.' As she got to the door, the woman turned towards her. 'Me name's Iris. And I'm going to do what I can to get that straitjacket off yer, I promise. I'll not be a mo.'

The key turning in the lock left Mags feeling cold. The fact they thought she should be locked in had a lot to do with her own behaviour, she knew. Well, now she'd learned that far more could be achieved by being compliant. And although she realized it might take her a long time, she would prove to them all that she wasn't insane.

So I've been here six days! The incredulousness of this came as a shock. How had she lost six days of her life? Of course it had been the fault of the drugs, but they hadn't administered any of them today, so maybe things were changing for her a little. Please let them. *Please . . .*

Betsy looked across the room at Bill. His leg was in plaster and elevated on a chair. He'd hardly spoken since the ambulance had brought him home two days ago. He'd been meant to stay in hospital for ten days, but the doctor's bill had been returned unpaid, and although the surgeon had said he would wait for what was owed to him until Betsy could sort it out, he didn't think she would ever raise enough to pay for more than it was already, so he had discharged Bill early. However, he had arranged two follow-up appointments, which he said he would not invoice for. One would be to check for infection and the other to remove the cast.

'Bill, love, we have to talk sometime. I've sommat to tell you, and it ain't good.'

'Nowt you tell me can be worse than what you told me afore I went in for me operation.'

'I knaw, Bill, and I wish I could change that and have it not to have happened, but I can't. Look, there's naw way this is going to get better, so I'll have to just tell you . . .'

Bill didn't move, but just stared at Betsy. 'Court? He's taking you to court over what he did? He's not right in the head. He's evil. How can he say that about you? Mags will – oh God, she can't, for the same reason she can't keep her promise and pay for me treatment. Poor lass, poor lass.'

'It breaks me heart to think of her up there, Bill, but what can we do?'

'Nowt. Bloody nowt. And now we're landed with all of

this, as well as a debt on our hands as we'll never be able to pay. But, lass, I knaw as I didn't take it well, and that's understandable, but I've thought on it all while I lay in hospital, and I knaw as none of it's your fault. I'm sorry I took on like I did.'

'Eeh, Bill, love.'

Getting up, Betsy went to where Bill sat and sank down on the floor next to him. She leaned her head on his knee and felt some comfort from him stroking her hair.

'We'll get through this, lass, we will. When this mends,' Bill tapped his leg, 'I can look for work. Oh, I knaw as things are not good, with many a man out of work and the coal miners on strike, but I'll find sommat.'

'I knaw you will, love, and so will I. With both of us working, we'll get out of this.'

Only the spitting and crackling of the fire in the hearth disturbed their silence. Each knew their solution was no more than a pipedream, for the slump didn't look like easing, and even the mighty cotton industry was laying folk off.

'Would they let you visit Mags?'

'I doubt it, but I might try. It's not an easy place to get to, but I made a few friends among the delivery men; happen one of them would give me a lift.'

'Naw!'

This came out so sharply that Betsy read what lay behind it, and the implication hurt her. 'What's up: are you thinking I'll go with any Tom, Dick or Harry? I've never given you cause to think that of me, and now, although you say you believe me, you don't really – not in your heart, you don't, Bill.'

'Eeh, lass, I'm sorry. I don't knaw what got into me. I didn't mean owt, other than how it would look. Everything

126

you do will be watched by someone; and aye, could be used against you an' all.'

Betsy knew he was telling the truth and realized it had been his fear *for* her, not his fear *of* her, that had prompted his response. She sighed. Life was tough, but in a couple of weeks it stood to get a lot tougher.

No sooner had this thought died in her than the door was flung open. 'Eeh, our Ciss, what's to do . . . Naw. Not Ma?'

Ciss could only nod. 'She's gone, our Betsy. She's gone.'

Rising, Betsy took the sobbing Ciss into her arms. 'Eeh, naw . . . naw.' And as she said the words, she knew that nothing – no matter what it was – could hurt her more than this. Her beloved ma, gone.

'I'll come along. I'll put Rosie down with you, Bill. The young 'uns'll be in soon. There's a fresh-baked loaf; tell Daisy to cut some chunks off it and spread it with that jam as Cook gave us. That'll do for your teas. I'll be back when I can.'

In the front room of her ma's small cottage, a beam of sunlight fell across Ma's face. In that moment she looked like an angel, and peace settled in Betsy.

'Will you look at her, our Ciss? Have you ever seen owt so beautiful? Has doctor been sent for?'

'Aye. He—'

'I'm here. Now, ladies, I'm sorry for your loss, as I can see before I examine her that your ma's gone.'

Dr Lange stepped further into the room. 'Hello, Betsy. I'll see to the sad business I'm on, then I'd like a word with you, if you feel up to it.'

The doctor and Betsy stood in the small back yard. Betsy was shivering with shock, trying to pull her cardigan around her.

'Now, Betsy, I heard what happened. It was a bad business. I know you have a lot on your plate, but whatever possessed you to behave as you did?'

'So, you believe what he told you, without hearing my side then? Well, he's a liar, and rotten to the core. But I'll never convince the likes of you, will I? Aye, and it's that as makes me think as me fate is a foregone conclusion. 'Cause they'll all be of your standing as sit in judgement of me.'

'What do you mean – judgement?'

'He's suing me. That swine as you would rather believe has me up in Preston County Court on the twenty-ninth of April.'

'But that's ridiculous. What does he hope to achieve, as you can't pay any compensation?'

'Naw, but I can still be judged as having to pay it; and when I can't, I can be brought before the debtors' court and could then go to prison. And all for a pack of lies.'

'Are you saying that Roford did rape you?'

'Aye, he did. But I don't care about that any more. I care about Mags and her father. They're the ones that are important. Please help them, Doctor. He's done this on purpose. He planned from the start to get all they had. Well, as I see it, he did. I reckon as he saw the main chance fall into his lap when I answered the bell. You see, he had a go at me afore, and Mags knew of it.'

'I take it that by "Mags" you mean Margaret? Mrs Roford.'

'Aye, I'm sorry, I allus call her Mags, as me and her are good mates. Oh, I knaw as it's unlikely, but that's the way of it. Anyroad, you have to help her, Doctor. Only you can. If you can't, she'll never get out of that asylum, and her dad will die and that swine will take everything.'

'I really don't think you should be so disrespectful, Betsy.

I never heard you speak like this when I visited the mill. I know you are upset, but you have to understand that Margaret is ill. Her breakdown is real. Yes, what happened tipped her over the edge, but you have to take some responsibility for that. As I heard it, you had come on to Mr Roford before, and had been forbidden to attend him in his room. It doesn't look good that you went to him that evening.'

To her despair, Betsy realized that the doctor was like the rest of them. He wasn't about to bite the hand that fed him and take the side of one of the working class. She turned away from him and started to go inside.

'Betsy, I'm not saying that I don't believe you.'

A spark of hope warmed a small bit of the coldness inside her.

'Look, I will visit Mrs Roford. I have a right to, as her doctor, and I'll make my own mind up as to how she really is. If there is a spark of truth in what you've told me, then I will not only help her, but will help you as well. But I have to have what you say proven to me. Can you understand that?'

Oh aye, she could understand that. Weren't it the way of all men? None of them believed that a woman didn't want what a man had to offer, when he offered it.

'I'm just so relieved to hear that you're going to see Mags. Please give her my love and tell her not to give up hope. But please don't give her hope, if you haven't any to give. Oh, I knaw as, being a woman, she won't have the power she used to have, now that she's married; but she's still a person, and at this moment all she has is those of us who care about her. Trouble is, the majority of us can do nowt for her. You can, though, so please don't let her down.' Feeling she might have said too much, Betsy changed the subject. 'Now, I thank you for coming to me ma. She has a bit put by in her pot on the mantel shelf. I don't think it's much, but you're welcome to it.'

The doctor looked taken aback and Betsy knew she'd overstepped the mark, but she didn't care.

Clearing his throat, the doctor said, 'I am on your side, Betsy, and I don't need paying. I told you before about our scheme. I just happened to be the doctor on call. And I'm glad I was. You've unsettled me, and I think someone needed to, where Mrs Roford is concerned. Now don't you worry – I'll do all I can for her.'

This eased Betsy's mind, though she wondered what he could do against the might of Roford. All she could do was hope, but to her mind, Harold Roford was going to be the only winner to come out of this. Releasing a sigh of anguish rather than relief, she turned her attention to her ma. For she had the laying-out of her mother to see to. Aye, and the pain of a loss that had split her heart. Nothing could be worse than that – nothing.

Chapter Twelve

Susan stood out of sight behind the door of Mr Wither-brook's bedroom, which led to her room. Something hadn't felt right about what was going on, and she felt guilty about having been brought to this beautiful house, which belonged to Harold's wife's family. At least it had done. Harold seemed certain now that it was all his.

She hadn't wanted to come. She'd tried to stand up to him, but in the end he'd persuaded her, threatening to expose Montel if she didn't. And she hadn't wanted to leave her daughter, but Harold had promised her that when everything was finalized, and legally in his name – not just as the husband of Mags, but signed and sealed as his right of ownership, which he said could only happen after the death of Mags's father – then she could have her child with her.

She was here as the nurse in attendance. Not that she was qualified, but there wasn't much to be done for poor Mr Witherbrook, other than keep him clean and comfortable, and she could do that.

However, when the doctor was in attendance, she had

been given instructions to keep out of sight. It was all a worry to her, though she had to admit that having Harold visit her bed every night more than compensated. She loved him so much. If only his plan for them to be together didn't entail hurting Mags in this way. She liked Mags.

Harold's voice cut into her thoughts. 'Tell me, Dr Lange, how much longer can my father-in-law live like this? There is no dignity in it. He is just as if he is dead already, but his body won't stop breathing.'

'That is because he has a strong hold on this earth. I believe he is waiting to hear his daughter's voice, and to know that she is safe. He hasn't had any contact with her since . . . well, since Margaret had her breakdown. You really should have called me then. I know the family well. I might have been able to help, in particular where Margaret was concerned.'

'I have told you my reasons why I didn't, and I have apologized for not informing you sooner. But both doctors who attended Mags and her father were eminent in their field.'

'Of course. But Margaret could be cared for in her own home, and if you want to give Mr Witherbrook a peaceful ending, then I suggest that you bring his daughter to him.'

'How can I? You don't seem to realize that she isn't well enough. There have been better reports these last two days about how well her treatment is going. I have been told that even to think of interrupting it could make her take a massive step backwards. I couldn't bear that. I miss her so much. It tears me apart that I can't even visit. Until Margaret realizes the truth of what took place, and learns to understand that I am not like my father, my presence will only upset her. I could kill that Bainwright woman. This is all her fault. She's nothing but a whore, and by Friday the whole town will know that.'

'Is that when the court case is?'

'Yes. It can't come soon enough for me. I'm living in hell. Well, just look at what she has caused.'

'Quite. Now, let me examine Mr Witherbrook. By the way, I intend to visit Margaret tomorrow.'

'Oh. Will you be allowed? Surely her care is now in the hands of Dr Jenkins?'

'It is, but as her family doctor, I have the right to visit. No one has deregistered me as her practitioner.'

'Well, I will do that, if you persist in interfering. In fact I'll take Mr Witherbrook's case to another local doctor, too. One who will assist him, in his hour of need, and will not allow him to linger on and on.'

'Only Mr Witherbrook, and Margaret, can sack me as their physician, and I do not like the implications of your words, sir. Kindly retract them. You're practically saying that I should end Mr Witherbrook's life!'

'I am not. I am saying that you should do more for him than allow him to vegetate, as he is doing. And as for him or my wife sacking you, neither of them are capable of making such decisions for themselves. I have power of attorney over both of them. And so I can make this decision for them – and I am doing so. Barnard will show you out. And I will instruct Dr Jenkins that you're not to be given access to my wife, under any circumstances.'

Susan held her breath. Was there nothing Harold couldn't, or wouldn't, do?

Stepping away from the door, she went and sat on the chair by the window. The room that she was housed in held a double bed, a range of wardrobes, a sofa and a chair. She was comfortable and happy, because once more she was with her Harold. Although that happiness was marred not only by her heartache where her baby Sibbie was concerned, but by the sense of being a prisoner. She feared for Montel and what would happen to him, if Harold turned him in. She'd wished a thousand times that she hadn't told Harold Montel's story.

Montel had been judged a coward and a traitor, and had been sentenced to execution. He'd refused to lead his men into what he knew was a senseless battle and would have led to the deaths of them all. It had happened during the latter part of 1916, when many French soldiers were turning tail, and mutiny was the order of the day. Montel tried to keep his troops together but, being left with only ten men, the attack that he was meant to carry out would have been suicidal. Brought before a court martial, he was found guilty and the death sentence was passed, when really he was a hero. Thankfully, some of his men helped him to escape and, by a miracle, got him away from the coast of France in a fishing vessel. Once in England, Montel slept rough on the streets, using a crutch to disguise that he was able-bodied.

Susan had met him one evening on her way home from her job as a maid to Harold's mother. Montel had been sitting in the same doorway every evening, and she'd begun to feel sorry for him. He always spoke to her, and those early greetings led to conversations, and then to her bringing him food. As she listened to Montel's story, she felt akin to him, as she too felt a lost soul, having been brought up in an orphanage and then put into service at a young age, in a failing household where she had to work long hours. When she eventually got a job with the Rofords, she'd had to find lodgings in London – a cheap attic flat in Brixton.

It wasn't long after meeting Montel that Susan offered him shelter. He slept on her sofa and began to take care of her, as he wasn't able to get work. She couldn't say when the idea of marrying him came about, but it seemed like a good solution to his problems and it didn't matter to her. She was already deeply in love with Harold, but knew he would never marry her. Her marriage to Montel was therefore one of convenience, but over time he became the best friend she'd ever had. He knew, from the start, all about Harold. He didn't find it strange, because where he came from affairs were commonplace and he saw it as the normal way of life.

Once they were married, Montel was able to apply to become a British citizen at the end of the war. Somehow he managed to hide that he was a war criminal. Not that it was difficult, for everyone's personal records were in a mess. And he assumed that he was considered dead in his own country, as this was the fate of many deserters, because it was impossible for most of them to survive. They couldn't go home, they couldn't get work, and they were hounded by those who chose to carry on fighting to the end, and by the families of those soldiers who'd lost their lives.

All in all, it had been a good arrangement. Montel had asked nothing of Susan, and their relationship was a platonic one. How he satisfied the sexual side of himself, she didn't know and never asked. He was her friend, and that was that. When she found herself pregnant with Sibbie, Montel had assumed the role of father. Susan had been bitterly hurt by Harold's rejection when Mags had turned up, although he made her understand that was how it had to be, until he could come for her. Well, he'd done that now – but at what price?

Susan didn't altogether believe his story that he hadn't raped that young woman. She knew her Harold and loved him, despite his ways. Her heart went out to Mags, as she knew Mags also loved him, but expected too much of him. What had happened that night – well, what she could glean of it – must have hurt Mags so much. And yes, it could have caused a breakdown; but to lead to her being committed, that didn't seem right.

Montel came to Susan's mind again. And she thought of his reaction when he'd met Mags. He'd been smitten. She smiled as she remembered him coming home. She'd expected him to be angry, as he'd had no joy with Harold, but no, his head was in the clouds. '*Mon Dieu*, I have met the love of my life. The most beautiful woman in the world. Majestic, elegant and in command. *Je l'adore – je veux lui faire la mienne.*' 'In English,' Susan had demanded of him. 'Oh, Susan, I adore her – I want to make her mine.'

This memory brought a smile to her face, but her mind raced on. *What if Montel comes up and goes to visit Mags? He could say he is a cousin, and that his father married her aunt. He will be able to tell if Mags is insane or not and, knowing him – a brilliantly trained army officer, who gained the honour of being mentioned in dispatches before he was disgraced – he might find a way of helping her escape.* Susan's romantic side came to the fore then. *And what if Mags falls in love with Montel? There was definitely something between them, as he told her he had a special feeling when their eyes met, and he knew Mags felt it, too.*

Laughing to herself, Susan knew life wasn't that simple, but she wished with all her heart that Mags could get out of the asylum. *Oh, I'd feel so much better then, as nothing seems right now. Even when Harold makes love to me, I have Mags's plight on my mind.*

Getting up, Susan decided to write to Montel – right now – to see if there was anything he could do. But she was foiled in doing so, as the connecting door flew open and Harold burst in. His expression was difficult to read; it was akin to triumph, and yet she detected fear in him.

'He's gone.'

Harold was red in the face and sweaty, as if he'd been exerting himself. *No! He hasn't . . . not . . . Oh God.*

'Dead? How? I mean, what happened? How did it happen?'

'Why are you asking that? He – he just stopped breathing.'

Susan hurried past Harold. In Mr Witherbrook's bedroom her eyes took in the way the cushion on the chair looked as though it had been thrown there, whereas it was always neatly placed, and Mr Witherbrook's head was on one side. That wouldn't have happened if he'd 'just stopped breathing'. His head wouldn't have moved. Her voice failed her, as a hoarse whisper came from her. 'You killed him!'

Without registering Harold moving, she felt her body being shaken violently by him. His face was a mask of anger. His spittle sprayed her cheeks as he ground out, 'Shut up! Do you hear me? Shut your mouth. He died naturally – you witnessed his death. I wasn't even in the room. Understand?' His hand pinched her chin. His evil eyes bored into hers. 'Understand?'

She couldn't speak. Shock held her rigid. Who was this monster that she loved?

Her shock turned to disgust as Harold's expression changed. 'Susan. Oh, Susan, I've never felt so exhilarated. I'm free.' His hands groped her breasts. 'At last I'm free –

I'm the top man. No more deferring to my father, my father-in-law, my bastard rotten half-brother or my stupid wife. It's all mine – mine – and I want you. I want to celebrate by making love to you. Oh, Susan, my Susan.'

She was lost and didn't resist when he took her hand and led her back into her bedroom. There she gave in to his demands.

During his taking of her, there were moments when she thought of Harold as an animal – a passionate, complex animal, who gave her experiences that she drank in. On and on it went, giving her extreme pleasure, made even more so by having to suppress her cries when she wanted to scream her joy. When the feelings built to unbearable levels, she did holler, and her hollers were joined by Harold's, till she knew they must have been heard by all members of staff in the house. But she didn't care.

Rising as soon as they could, they adjusted their clothes. Then Harold giggled. 'Our hollers will be interpreted as grief.' With this, he put on a distraught face and ran for the door, yelling, 'Oh God, he's gone – gone!'

Susan heard him running down the stairs, even though his tread was muffled by the thick carpet. To her, the world that she'd briefly left, to wallow in sensations that had blocked everything out, became acutely alive once more.

Getting off the bed, she dressed quickly and went back into Mr Witherbrook's room. She straightened the cushion, then leaned over the body of the man, who had never woken up to speak to her since she'd been here, but whom she'd cared for tenderly. 'Forgive me.' As she said the words, she moved his head and fully closed his half-open eyes, taking two coins from the neat piles that were on his bedside table – piles that she'd never disturbed, and had liked to think of him creating neatly each evening as he retired. She placed the coins on his eyelids, before closing his mouth. It dropped open again, so she crossed the room and reached for one of his ties from his wardrobe, and tied it around his chin and above his head. These were traditions she'd learned to keep a dead person's eyes and mouth closed until rigor mortis set them like that. These simple actions gave a person dignity.

'There's no more I can do for you until the doctor has been, and then I will give you your last wash-down and see that you are dressed nicely. I know we would have got on well. I don't know why, but I have felt that the whole time I have cared for you. Rest in peace. I will make sure your daughter is freed and safe, I promise.'

The sound of voices cautioned Susan to move away from the bed. She must look like the nurse they thought her to be, and nothing else. But only Harold came into the room. His manner had changed. He had an air of authority about him that was different from the one he'd previously assumed. He truly was in command now, and all the staff knew it, she could tell. She knew Harold better than he knew himself.

The voices she'd heard had been Harold instructing his butler. She'd heard the last part of the conversation, just before he appeared. 'Oh, and Barnard, I know it's early days, but rest assured things will change around here. From now on, this will be run as a proper household should be, and I am relying on you to make those changes for me. I know it hasn't been easy for you, with all that has been going on, and with the sloppy way things were done here, but I want you to start thinking about employing a good housekeeper who knows her stuff, and whatever other staff you think we will need.'

Barnard's 'Yes, sir' told of a very happy man.

Susan sighed. Harold's tendency to think himself into a much higher position in life than he occupied was his downfall. And she wondered how long it would take for him to lose all that he'd gained by his murderous act.

Chapter Thirteen

When the cell door opened and Iris came in, Mags couldn't make out the expression on her face – the small smile that wasn't quite a smile. Hope rose in her that the straitjacket was to be removed, as Iris had promised that she would try to get permission to release her.

'I'm so sorry, lass, but I ain't come with good news.'

Mags stared at her. Since the night she had opened up to Iris about what had happened to her in Brussels, Iris had become her friend, keeping her calm and even making her smile. Giving her drinks of water and washing her, to keep her as comfortable as anyone could be in a contraption that restricted her from doing anything for herself.

But now, as Iris's expression changed, fear rose in Mags, as she realized the news Iris had for her had nothing to do with the straitjacket. 'No, it's not . . .' She could hardly ask the question, and didn't want it confirming. 'Dad . . . Daddy?'

'Aye, I'm sorry, really sorry. But, Mags, please, please hold it together, love.'

Mags gasped in a lungful of air. Her heart ached with the pain of loss and the feeling of being robbed of her father.

She wanted to scream that it was all Harold's fault – everything. But Iris was talking again, shaking her head and saying words about Betsy.

'Betsy's mother, too? Oh God, help me, help me.' *No, I mustn't let go, I mustn't. I mustn't let go.*

That the news of both demises was brought to her at the same time would be Harold's way of loading the maximum sadness on her. And yes, Mags knew that by doing so he would feel a sense of triumph over her and Betsy, and he would be hoping that she would react in such a way as to make the doctors think she had regressed.

Iris made clucking noises that spoke of her sympathy. 'Hold yourself together, Mags. I knaw as this is sommat that could break you, but don't let it. Remember how courageous you are. Do this for your father. 'Cause if you break again, you'll never get out of here.' She moved closer and Mags thought for a moment that Iris was going to hug her, but she reached behind her for the straps of the terrible strait-jacket that held her rigid. 'I've been granted permission to take this off you, as I've given good reports of your behaviour. How you react to this bad news is going to be a telling point for the doctors. Don't give them – or that husband of yours – a stick to beat you with, as he sounds a right one to me. And there's some cruel buggers running this place, who wouldn't have any sympathy with you if you broke.'

Keeping herself still and holding her emotions within her, Mags waited until the hated garment was removed. Her arms ached, and her shoulders stiffened with the restriction they'd been under.

'Now, let's rub your limbs to get your blood circulating.' The feeling of being touched by another person felt good, as the sensation gradually came back into her arms. 'Now

I'm going to make circular movements with your shoulders, lass. It may hurt at first, but as they loosen, you'll feel the benefit.'

The movement did hurt, so much so that Mags cried out more than once, but Iris carried on until at last Mags's shoulders began to move more easily and less painfully.

'Now, that's better. Eeh, you've lost weight, lass. And you look peaky. We've to build you up, and some fresh air wouldn't go amiss. What I want you to do is save your grief. Oh, I knaw you want to holler it out of you, but don't. Hold your father in the honour he deserves, with dignity. Cry, yes, but don't wail and call out. And I want you to eat. Aye, it's the last thing you feel like doing, I knaw. I remember the pain of losing my parents. But do it for yourself, and for your father. The only way out of here is to get well. Your dad would want that for you, wouldn't he? He wouldn't want to be the cause of prolonging your stay here. And while you are here, you can do nowt about owt. Out in the world, you can start to put some of the wrongs right.'

With this, Iris left her. But courage did seep into Mags. She would bear this parting from her father, until such a time as she could really vent her grief. She'd come to terms somehow with him being laid to his rest without her, but once out of here she would hold her own service for him. And what of Harold now? Hatred welled up inside her, even just thinking of him, but she would be strong. Yes, he now owned all that should be hers, but he couldn't take what he didn't know about; and he didn't know of her mother's legacy – her house in Scotland – or of the money that her mother had left her.

Suddenly her future seemed set. She would go and live in Scotland. She knew she had enough money to keep herself, but she also knew the house was quite large. She'd ask Betsy and Bill to go with her, and there'd be plenty of room for the children. They could all start their lives afresh, away from the evil that was Harold.

With these thoughts, it was as if a light had been turned on, and the darkness that had encased Mags began to lift. How this could be, when she'd just found out about her beloved daddy's death, she did not know, but maybe she was doing what Flora always did – looking for something positive in the bleakness that clothed her.

Thinking of Flora brought another idea to her. She would visit Flora in France. Yes, that would be wonderful. *Oh, Daddy, please don't worry about me – everything in my life is going to come right. Please rest easily with my beloved mummy. Nothing you did brought this on me. You never wanted me to marry Harold. And you teaching me how to run a business will stand me in good stead. I thank you for that, and for Mummy's foresight in letting me have the freedom that no other young woman of my age was ever afforded. I love you, Daddy, and I will make you proud of me yet.*

With this thought, the tears started to flow. Gentle, sad and yet healing tears, because Mags felt in charge of her emotions, of her life and of her future; and she could make a difference to the future of her dear friend Betsy, too. Make up to her for what Harold had done to her.

Something of her old self seeped into Mags. That this should happen at a time when her life was crumbling around her, she couldn't understand; she only knew that the inner strength that she used to possess was rebuilding itself and giving her all that she needed to move forward.

* * *

Betsy gave off an air of being all right, but inside she was crumbling.

She looked across at Bill, and his smile of encouragement helped her. But when she looked over at the jury, she felt her courage desert her.

There was far more going on in her life than this – her ma being laid to rest tomorrow, in a pauper's grave, for one. The notice that was served on her to quit the mill cottage they had lived in since their marriage, granted to her by Mags and her father, for another. *Oh, God, what are we to do?*

With all this weighing her down, she couldn't give any thought to all the other terrible things that had happened.

Her eyes travelled around the room, where it felt as if the very walls were condemning her. The high ceiling had a domed window in the centre of it, and through this came the pitter-patter sound of rain, as if the heavens themselves were crying for her plight. The walls were clad in oak, which shone as if polished daily. The benches and the stand for the accused, where she stood, and the one for giving testimony, as well as the judge's bench and the jury's seating, were all in matching wood. But none of it produced an air of dullness; instead, a feeling of grandeur was the overall impression.

A few folk sat in the public gallery – mostly women. Betsy wondered why they hadn't brought their knitting with them.

Mr Roford's lawyer stood, and the room came to a hush after the initial bustle of everyone seating themselves, once the judge had done so.

Dressed in a gown and wearing a short-curled wig, his voice demanded attention and stopped Betsy's mind wandering.

As he read out the charge, Betsy felt herself giving way, but knew she must not do so. Most of it was lies – wicked lies.

'We want the court to consider the destruction brought about by this woman's actions. Whilst we think it admirable that she wanted the money that she tried to extort for the purpose of freeing her husband of pain, her vile method has caused more pain than one family should have to bear. As a result of her false cry of rape, my client's wife had a nervous breakdown and is now a patient in Brockhall Institution, where the diagnosis is bleak; and the prognosis is that she may never recover. Especially as she has now been dealt a second blow, which can be considered to be caused directly by this woman's actions – the death of Mrs Roford's beloved father. The late Mr Witherbrook was an upstanding member of the Blackburn cotton industry, who collapsed immediately following the incident we are referring to and never recovered.'

There was an audible gasp that rippled around the courtroom. Betsy kept her head down.

'And so what Mrs Bainwright did on that night was not only injurious to my client's good name, but has subsequently robbed him of his new-found happiness with his young wife and has killed his father-in-law. In the light of this, my client is not only suing for defamation of his character, but for the loss of his life as he knew it. My client's claim is for restoration of his good name, and monetary compensation for lost revenue, due to his inability to work because of the huge stress placed upon him, m'lord, as well as for the mistrust of him by business associates. To my mind, what the defendant has done amounts to criminal extortion and should be referred to the Crown Prosecution for sentencing, and no less than a prison term should be served on her, given the outcome of her action.'

There was a hush as the lawyer sat down. Betsy stared in horror. *Oh God, naw . . . naw.*

After a moment the duty solicitor stood up. Assigned to her only minutes before the court sat in session, he knew nothing about Betsy, and very little about her side of the story.

Walking on wobbly legs that didn't feel as though they would hold her up, but with her head held high, Betsy reached the witness stand and took the oath. In doing so, she wondered if she could still lie. But one glance at her Bill and she knew that she must.

'Mrs Bainwright, you have heard the accusations against you. What have you to say?'

After making up her mind to speak up for herself, Betsy found that she couldn't speak, for it was as if her throat had dried and closed up. The judge leaned forward and spoke to her.

'Mrs Bainwright, these are very serious allegations: false defamation of a character, which led to the ruination of the defendant's life, and possible charges of attempted extortion. If you do not say anything in your own defence, then I will have to take your silence as an admission of guilt, and sentence you accordingly.'

'I – I didn't do it, sir.'

'"M'lord", not "sir". And if you didn't do it, you need to speak up and tell us what happened. That is what justice is all about – each party having their say, and the jury having the chance to weigh up which is the truth.' Turning to her solicitor, the judge, whom Betsy now thought of as kindly, told him, 'I would expect you to help your client out. Oh, I know there is no fat fee in this for you, and you take on this work out of the goodness of your heart, but that doesn't mean you shouldn't do it to the best of your ability. Now, without leading her, help her to voice her version of events.'

The solicitor cleared his throat. 'Mrs Bainwright, let us start at the beginning. What led you to be in Mr Roford's bedroom in the first place?'

Betsy started to tell him how she came to be there, when Roford's lawyer stood up. 'M'lord, may I just say that this wasn't the first incident my client suffered, at the hands of this woman.'

As Betsy listened to the lies Roford had conjured up about his first assault of her, her blood boiled, but a sense of hopelessness overcame her temper. Everything he said damned her.

'That occasion led to a temporary split in my client's relationship with Mrs Roford, who was at the time his fiancée. When that was resolved, Mrs Bainwright was banned from ever attending to him, if he rang his bell whilst in his bedroom. Clearly she saw a chance of breaking that rule on the evening in question.'

'It weren't like that! I didn't, I – I mean, I had to break the rule – another maid hadn't turned up and I was the only person available.'

'My client's butler was not on hand then?'

'Did I give you leave to cross-examine Mrs Bainwright, Mr Plaid-Armstrong?'

'No, m'lord. Sorry, m'lord.'

'Well then, please sit down and allow your learned friend, Mr Fitzgerald, to continue.'

Betsy wanted to shout out against the unfairness of it all.

Roford's lawyer might have sat down and shut up, but he couldn't undo what he'd just said.

'Why didn't you send for the butler, Mrs Bainwright?'

So far, all she'd said was the truth, and Betsy was so grateful to the solicitor for asking this, as she could truthfully say that she did seek out Barnard.

It was when he asked her to say, in her own words, what had happened that she faltered. She hoped those who mattered would think it was because what she had to say wasn't easy for a woman of any standing to talk about.

When she finished, there was silence once more. Then her solicitor indicated that he had nothing more to ask her, and the lawyer whom she now thought of as the Devil stood up.

'So, this is the story you have concocted. Well done. For someone of . . . well, I imagine, little education, you have done well. You have exposed what a sly nature you have, madam.'

He then almost reduced her to tears, as he tore holes in her story. 'You said that my client ripped your clothes and tore off your undergarments, leaving you exposed, and himself able to rape you. As I understand it, your undergarments were around your ankles when you stood at the door, screaming. And we can produce a witness who saw that. Indeed, in his statement, my client says that the last thing you did, after attacking him, was to pull down your undergarments.'

Betsy curled up inside, unable to answer. *Oh God, did I say as he tore me knickers off? 'Cause he didn't. I remember struggling with them and only getting them half up, before me plan came to me to cry rape, then I let them drop down as I opened the door.*

'He didn't rip them right off. He couldn't, 'cause I struggled and kicked him. He only got them to me knees afore he got on top of me.' Fear spilled over her tears.

'Mrs Bainwright, I would offer you a chance to have a break, but I think you should carry on, if you can.'

She nodded at the judge and was heartened by his look of understanding.

'You also state that Mrs Roford said she would pay for your husband's treatment, and so you had no need to extort money from Mr Roford. And yet I understand that you are in debt for his surgery. That you went ahead, even though you couldn't afford it, and that you are lying about how you were going to pay for it.'

'I'm not, sir. Mrs Roford arranged it all. You can ask the surgeon who did it. And I hadn't an inkling as all this would happen. I thought Mrs Roford would come to me after. I didn't knaw as her husband had had her committed to an asylum, so I had naw reason to cancel the operation. It were done afore I found out what had happened to Mrs Roford. And aye, what happened weren't down to me. Mags – I mean, Mrs Roford – was betrayed by her so-called loving husband!'

During this outburst the lawyer had repeatedly said her name and even appealed to the judge to stop her, but Betsy managed to get it all out.

'Mrs Bainwright, you will not make such an outburst again. However, I was interested to hear what you had to say, and I think it vital that the surgeon who carried out this operation is called as a witness. If what Mrs Bainwright says is true, then the whole motive being presented is negated.' Banging his gavel, the judge called for the session to close and for all parties to reconvene on Monday, the second of May. Before he finished he instructed both the lawyer and Betsy's solicitor to attend him in his chambers.

As he went to leave, the duty solicitor came over to Betsy. 'I believe you, Mrs Bainwright. And because I do, I'm going to do my best to defend you. Now I want you to gather some character witnesses. People of note; people who will speak for you. This latest development tells me that the judge is beginning to believe your version of events, and so we may yet win. If we do, I will counter-claim for compensation for you, because in effect your name has been slandered, too.'

'Aye, and I've suffered loss an' all. Mr Roford is me landlord and he's given me notice to quit, so I'm to be homeless. And, well, me ma died. I ain't putting that at his door, but it's breaking me heart.'

'Yes, yes, well, I'm sorry. I can do nothing about that, but about you losing your house and your livelihood, I can. So go home, get busy finding those witnesses, but leave the surgeon to me. Give my clerk his name, and the name of the hospital he works at, and then try to get a good night's sleep. Because I think your troubles may be over. Good day.'

Betsy climbed down from the witness box. *My troubles over?* Naw, they were just beginning, as she saw it, no matter the outcome.

For aren't I without me ma now, and jobless, with few prospects; and me Bill will find it hard to get work. It might be as I can keep me cottage, but there is still the rent to pay and five hungry mouths to feed. And all that on top of what is happening to Mags. Eeh, naw, me troubles won't be over — they'll just be getting bigger.

Chapter Fourteen

Moans and sobs kept Mags awake. Since being moved to the general ward, life had got worse, not better. Now she was housed in a long ward that contained rows and rows of beds, almost head-to-feet. This was meant to be a progression, but although she never thought she would, Mags longed to be back in her solitary cell.

The stench reminded her of her time in Brussels, as it assaulted her nostrils – human excrement, sweaty, dirty bodies and urine clogged the air around her. But worse than the smell was the sense of misery. The atmosphere was heavy with the emotions of these poor lost women. Somewhere inside their minds they remembered a different life, as their agonizing cries were for their babies or their mothers. Mags longed to help them, but if she tried, they became suspicious of her and lashed out.

The sound of shuffling feet alerted her. One of the women had got out of bed. She raised herself onto one elbow and looked round, peering through the dim light. The figure came towards her. Mags pulled her covers over her and fear clenched her stomach muscles.

Feeling the covers being torn from her compounded that fear. 'What – what do you want? Please go back to bed.'

'You're pretty. I like you.'

With her eyes growing more used to the dim light, Mags could see that it was the woman called Aggie and knew that she liked to fondle the other women, often causing outbreaks of violence as the women fought her off. But Aggie was strong, and her physique was more manly than feminine.

'D – don't touch me, please, Aggie.'

But Aggie wasn't listening. She sat down on the bed and leaned over Mags. Her breath stank as she panted, open-mouthed, bringing her ugly face, covered in warts and hair, closer and closer to Mags, who cringed away, pushing the woman with her hands. 'No. Please, go away.'

'Me want you. You touch Aggie and make her feel nice. Me touch you and make you feel nice.'

Screaming out for help brought none to Mags. Helpless as to what to do, and not wanting to hit out, she lay still. The wet kiss on her cheek made her want to heave. The weight of Aggie leaning across her had her gasping for air, but even worse was feeling Aggie's hand massaging her breast.

'Please don't. Go back to bed. I – I can't give you anything.'

'Yes. Touch me.'

The grip Aggie had on Mags's wrist was strong, and Mags found it impossible to stop her hand from being forced between Aggie's legs. Repulsion shuddered through her, as the effort became too much and her fingers touched Aggie's bare vagina. 'No, I don't want to, leave me alone.'

Others began to stir. Some cried out in distress. Wanting to increase this, Mags knew that only a full disruption of the ward would bring staff to assist her. 'Help me, help me!'

153

Her cry did the trick. Women began to holler in fear, some of them agonizing cries, and although Mags felt sorry to upset them all, she'd never felt so grateful in all her life to have the door open and light flood the room.

'What's going on?'

'Help me, I – I can't get her off me.'

'Aggie, you at your tricks again? Well you'll not get away with it this time – not touching the princess of the ward, you won't.'

Aggie laughed. Spittle sprayed from her mouth onto Mags's face. Still Aggie kneaded her breast, but thankfully she'd let go of Mags's hand, and Mags could now withdraw it. 'Please get her off me – please.'

'Not easy. If Aggie wants to play, she plays.'

The light went out and the door shut. Mags felt despair enter her, but then anger boiled inside her. With an almighty effort, she bent her leg under Aggie and kicked her in the stomach. Aggie let go and slipped off the bed. The sound of her gasping for breath propelled Mags into action. Jumping out of bed, she ran towards the door, only to find it locked. Banging on it didn't bring anyone to her aid.

Exhausted, she leaned on the door and looked back towards her bed. Aggie hadn't risen. Fear of a different kind dried in Mags's throat. *Oh God. Please let her be all right.*

Floorboards creaked as if they were firecrackers in the now-quiet room, as Mags crept back towards her bed. Aggie lay on her back. The sound of her breathing was that of someone asleep. Afraid to wake her, Mags fetched the blanket from Aggie's bed and covered her with it, then ran to the bathroom and washed herself till she felt herself tingle all over. Creeping back into her own bed, she daren't lie down, but decided to stay awake so that if Aggie woke, she could escape and run, before Aggie could get up.

The morning brought the sun streaming through the high windows and across Mags's bed, waking her from a sleep she didn't know she'd fallen into. Remembrance shot open her eyes. Looking down on the floor, she saw that Aggie hadn't moved. Her breathing had the pace of someone in a deep sleep.

Horror and repulsion shuddered through Mags as she thought of what had happened. Somehow she had to escape from here – she had to – but how? *Dear God, how? They can see I am sane. I have done nothing to make them think otherwise. What am I to do? How can I ever get out of here?*

Denying the tears that she knew would never stop if she let them flow, Mags got out of bed and walked towards the bathroom. Having splashed her face in cold water, she felt better able to cope. But on getting back to the misery of the ward, she wondered if she really could.

As she reached her bed, Aggie stirred. Mags held her breath. Aggie rolled over and looked up at her. Her eyes were blank. Nothing about her seemed threatening as she struggled to get up. Putting out her hand, Mags saw Aggie hesitate before taking it, and then allowed Mags to help her up. 'Go back to your own bed, Aggie.'

'Aggie wants to pee.'

'All right, go that way to the bathroom.'

Aggie stared blankly in the direction Mags had pointed her in. Taking her hand once more, Mags gently persuaded Aggie to go with her. 'There – there's the lavatory. You'll be all right now.'

Aggie smiled and then walked into the bathroom.

Mags leaned heavily on the wall. Her head pounded and her throat ached for a drink. Glancing up at the clock, she saw that it was an hour until breakfast – the first time they would get a drink – but she daren't drink the water from the tap. Many of the women did so and sickness was rife as a result. *Why can't they give us basic human care? Or even a little kindness?* This made her think of Iris, and she prayed that Iris would be on duty today. Iris was different from all the other staff and brought whatever influence she could to bear. She made this whole ordeal slightly bearable for Mags.

It was three hours later when Mags realized her wish. She was in the communal sitting room, staring out of the window, when she saw Iris cycling up the drive. Never had she been so relieved to see anyone in her life.

Within half an hour Iris was by her side. 'I hear you had trouble during the night, lass. The report doesn't look good. It says you woke the whole ward and caused a disruption. What was all that about, then? I thought we'd made progress.'

'Oh, Iris, please help me. It wasn't like that.'

Iris listened as Mags told her what had happened. 'Right, we've to sort that out. But the report is damning, and I can't do much about it. It puts you back a step or two.'

'I have no control over my own destiny, Iris. In that room there's incidents all night long. I try not to be involved, but what else can I do?'

'I knaw. But that ward is a stepping stone. I had to wrangle with a lot of the staff to get you in there. You have to bear it and do so quietly, it's the only way.'

The despair that had visited Mags settled deep in her heart.

'Look, lass, I do have sommat as will cheer you. Yesterday I gained permission to take you out in the garden for a little while each day, and that's not been stopped – not as yet, anyroad. So I'll go and get your coat and we'll go out. How does that sound, eh?'

Mags felt joy filling her and it blotted out her despair. How often she'd gazed out of the window and longed to walk in the lovely gardens, although part of her knew they were so well kept to create the impression that this was a good, peaceful haven for those who were sick in their mind, which angered her.

The breeze caught Mags's hair. She knew it must look a mess, as she hadn't been able to wash or comb it, only try to keep gathering it into a bun with the clips she had been given.

Her mind was in turmoil about how she was going to get through this ordeal, until the day came when they finally released her. Would that day ever come? Her thoughts turned to Betsy, and she wondered what other punishment Harold would have dished out. How would Betsy fare in a court of law?

Harold's cruelty knew no bounds, and Mags knew that he would delight in the little notes he wrote and had delivered to her. He knew how heart-wrenching it would be for Mags to know that he was suing Betsy, putting her through as much as he possibly could. Oh, how she hated him with a passion that she'd once loved him with.

By counting the days, Mags knew that the court case was yesterday and longed to be made aware of the outcome. No doubt, if it all went Harold's way, he would soon make sure she knew.

She closed her eyes and tried to let the sounds of the

birds chirping soothe her. And although the sun was weak, she leaned her head back, to feel whatever warmth it gave touch her face. When she opened her eyes, it was to see Iris coming across the lawn. Her heart sank, as this probably meant that she had to go back inside. For a moment she was seized with the urge to run – run for all she was worth across the vast lawn towards the gates, and then climb over and never stop running. But she stayed still.

'By, that's put some roses into your cheeks, lass. I reckon as that's done you good. Now I'm on me break, so although I said as you could only sit on the bench until I came back, as long as I'm with you, you can have a walk. So come on, let's get started.'

'Oh, Iris, thank you. I just don't know what I would do without you.'

'I do me best. But it ain't easy. If I upset too many of me colleagues, I could find meself hounded out, so I have to take it steady. But, to me, your plight is the saddest I've known. I knaw as you're not a sick woman, and I want to help you. What happened last night doesn't help, though. Oh, I knaw as it weren't your doing, but nonetheless it's now on your notes, and that bothers me.'

'Is there no way I can talk to someone and tell them what really happened? Does no one ever listen to the patients?'

'Naw. You have to realize that those in here are classed as not being sound enough in mind to be able to speak for themselves. It's wrong, I knaw, but that's the way of it.'

Frustration gripped Mags. 'Iris, if I am doing wrong by asking something of you, please forgive me, but at the moment you are the only person in the world on my side and the only person who can help me.'

Iris didn't answer. She kept her head down and her pace

steady. A little hope entered Mags. Iris had neither invited her to say how she could help, nor told her that she shouldn't ask.

'Please, Iris, if what I say upsets you in any way, just forget it and let us carry on as we are. Because without you and the little help and hope you give me, I would go under and be lost forever.'

Iris still remained silent.

'There are people who would help me. Our family doctor. He wasn't called to attend me. My husband brought in a doctor I'd never seen in my life, and who knew nothing of me. The doctor only saw the distress I was in and believed my husband's lies.' Feeling afraid at there being no reaction from Iris, Mags told her what Harold had said. 'He never mentioned what had happened to my friend Betsy. He said I was distressed after a dream that I had; that I often revisited my time during the war; and that I was irrational in believing him to be a philanderer. The doctor took my protests as symptoms of a psychotic episode. It is clear to me now that this outcome was my husband's intention.'

'Eeh, lass, but what I don't understand is why a man would go as far as having his wife sectioned?'

'Because he wants all that was mine. And now he has it. With my father dead, he has my home, the family business and the land. Everything. And I know now that is all he married me for.'

'Eeh, it sounds like sommat as should be in one of them mystery films that me hubby goes to watch. I can't be doing with them meself. I like to go and see a Charlie Chaplin, as he makes me forget everything and have a good old laugh.'

'I know, but I am telling the truth, Iris – please believe me. Would you consider going to see my doctor for me?'

'By, lass, now you're asking sommat. Look, tell me his name and I'll think about it, but can I trust him? Is he likely to shop me to me boss, because I can't lose this job. I can't.'

'No, Dr Lange would never do that. He's known me since I was a little dot, and although he did help in a small way to get me in here, it was unconsciously.' Mags told Iris then how the doctor who sectioned her had said he'd spoken to Dr Lange, and why Dr Lange would have believed Mags's breakdown to be possible. 'But if you go along to Dr Lange and tell him the truth of why I am in here, and that I am not ill in my mind, and tell him the lies Harold told, I know he will believe you and will help me.'

After a long pause Iris nodded. 'I'll do it. Aye, I may lose me job as a consequence, but I can't stand by and watch what is happening to you any longer. Oh aye, it shouldn't happen to anyone, sick or not, I knaws that. But all I can do for them as are really sick is me best to alleviate their suffering. But for you – well, I'll try to put right the wrong that has been done to you.'

'Oh, Iris, thank you.' Impetuously Mags threw her arms around Iris and kissed her cheek. 'I'll never forget what you've done for me, Iris. I'll help you all I can in return, I promise.'

'I don't want paying, lass. I've allus wanted a daughter and, if I had been lucky enough to have one, I would have liked her to be like you. And aye, if she got into trouble, I'd hope there was someone there to help her out.'

As they walked back towards the hospital building, Mags felt herself fill with hope. *Surely Dr Lange will help me. Please, please make him do so.*

Chapter Fifteen

Betsy stood with her sister, Ciss, on one side of her and Bill on the other. Bill leaned heavily on her arm, causing her shoulder to ache, but she didn't mind. She'd support him for the rest of her days if she had to.

Three weeks had passed since the court case came to an end. Dr Lange and a host of neighbours and local shop-keepers had come forward to speak about Betsy's character, although none of them were needed, once the surgeon who had operated on Bill gave his evidence. What he had to say about Mags having engaged him, and telling him that the bill was to go to her, collapsed the case against Betsy, as it destroyed the motive Roford had created for Betsy having come on to him. It wasn't altogether clear whether or not the rape had happened, leaving a shadow over Betsy. But she knew that was par for the course, as very few people believed there was such a thing as rape; most thought the woman had wanted it, then changed her mind when it was too late for the man to stop. She could live with that, as those that mattered believed her story of events, even though they weren't true.

Looking down on the mound of earth that covered her ma, Betsy let a tear spill over and run down her cheek.

'She's at rest now, love. And not in a pauper's grave, neither. With what you were able to promise from your compensation and what Ma had in her pot, we managed to get her a decent resting place, didn't we?'

'We did, Ciss.'

Stopping the funeral from going ahead when it was scheduled to had been arranged by Betsy's solicitor, after the hope that was given to her on that first day of the trial. He'd been so confident that Betsy would win, and be awarded compensation, that he'd even paid the mortuary fees. As a result, Ma was now lying in a proper grave after a lovely service had been held.

'Aye, and we can pay the surgeon with the rest. But where we're going to live is another matter, ain't it, Betsy?'

'Aye, Bill. We've to sort that problem out, and even though I've enough to pay a couple of weeks' rent, which might secure us a place, how are we going to pay after that?'

'Look, why don't you move into Ma's house with me, eh?' Ciss suggested. 'I've had a word with the landlord and he said that as long as I keep up the rent, I can have it. I were thinking of taking up Patrick Finnigan's offer of marriage as I told you of, and of us moving into it. But if I do marry him, he tells me that he can get a farm cottage, and then you can have Ma's to yourselves. But you've to sort jobs first, and I can stay and pay the rent till then.'

'Oh, our Ciss, ta, lass. Eeh, you've saved me bacon.'

'Don't cry, our Betsy lass, don't . . .'

But it was too late, for the floodgates had opened, and the sisters collapsed into each other's arms. Bill held the sobbing girls as best he could, but his own tears wet his face as he did so.

Betsy recovered first. 'Eeh, look at us. I ain't cried proper since Ma left, but I feel better for it. Come on, let's walk to the corner cafe and treat ourselves to a bun. We deserve a little bit of sommat nice out of that swine's money.'

Once seated in the cafe, Betsy followed up on what Ciss had said. 'So you've a fancy for Pat then, I take it?'

'Aye, I have, but I haven't shown him that yet. I've been biding me time. He likes the drink a bit too much for me liking, and I've given him an ultimatum: he modifies his ale-swilling or I look for someone else. So far he's conformed, but I wanted to leave it a while, to make sure he keeps to it.'

'By, you're asking a lot of him; like you say, he's partial to his ale, that one.'

'Well, if he thinks I'm worth it, he'll do it. It's up to him.'

Betsy laughed, but she thought marriage to someone who took to the drink would be fraught with problems. Aye, Pat might keep to it while he had the carrot of marrying Ciss dangling in front of him, but what about when he got that carrot for good an' all. Might he slip back into his old ways then? But she couldn't give any thought to it, for she wanted to talk about something that was very much on her mind.

'I'm worried about Mags. It's been six weeks or more now, since she were taken to that place. I've been too wrapped up in me own problems to think much on it, though it's never left me. But now, with everything seeming to be solved one way or another, I can't get Mags off me mind. I'm going to talk to Dr Lange. He told me, on the day as Ma died, that he'd try to do sommat for Mags. Surely he knaws by now how she is. I need to knaw what's happening with her.'

They both agreed. 'She's a lovely lass and she deserves

better, but if we don't help her, who will? I reckon as we owe it to her to do all we can, Betsy. I'm with you on that.'

'Ta, Bill. It helps not to have you telling me to leave well alone, as I thought you might, after what I've put you through. Well, there's naw time like the present. I'll go up to his house now and find out if he'll see me.'

'Right-o. But help me home first, as we can't leave our Rosie with Mrs Bray much longer. If we fetch her home, I'll mind her till you get back. Then I need to rest up – me leg's giving me gip the day.'

That it should do so worried Betsy. 'Thank goodness we're going to see that surgeon tomorrow. It were good of him to just accept the cost of the operation and not charge for further appointments. You knaw, there's kindness in most folk.'

'Look, you get to Dr Lange's house, as we're not far from there, our Betsy. I'll see you home, Bill.'

'Ta, Ciss, that'll be a big help. I'll let you knaw how I get on.' With this, Betsy kissed them both, then turned from them and went in the direction of Blackburn town.

Trepidation filled Betsy as her feet crunched on the gravel of the drive leading to Dr Lange's house. Those such as her didn't go calling on the likes of folk of the doctor's standing.

The housekeeper opened the door, prompting the thought Betsy had had many a time that it was a wonder the doctor had never married again, after losing his wife so young. But with this ogre in charge, no young woman would stay long enough to get to know the doctor. 'Betsy? What are you doing here?'

The question wasn't without a touch of disdain. Betsy held her head high. 'I have to see the doctor – it's urgent.'

164

'He doesn't do charity work, as well you know.'

'Well, that's strange, as I knaw different. Anyroad, it ain't charity I'm after. I just need to speak to him. Please, Phyllis, I knaw as you look out for him, and you do a good job, but I have to have a word.'

'Very well. Stay there and I'll speak to him.'

To Betsy's relief, Dr Lange came to the door. 'How can I help you, Betsy? I thought everything was settled for you. Oh, I know you have to move, but that's a small price to pay.'

'I have nowt to pay for, Doctor, and it's a pity as the likes of you can't take that in. I'm a victim. Anyhow, that's not what I came about. I want to talk to you about Mags – Mrs Roford.'

'Come in.'

He stepped back, allowing Betsy to enter the hall. A smell of polish assailed her, and she found herself in a nice-looking brown-painted hall, which was a bit dingy, but lightened by the colourful tiles on the floor.

'Go into that room there, it's a waiting room – we can talk in there.'

The same tiles covered the floor of the waiting room, but there was a lighter, more airy feel about this room, provided by the large window and the light green-painted walls. A row of chairs was placed against three of the walls, and a table stood in the corner with a neat stack of magazines on it.

'Sit down.'

Betsy took a seat near the window.

'I have thought about talking to you before on this matter, Betsy, but you had so much to contend with. Forgive my remark – I didn't mean it as it sounded. I only meant compared to what could have happened to you, guilty or not. But that's not the issue here. Mrs Roford is. I'm afraid my hands are tied. You see, Mr Roford dispensed with my services, and that is why I was able to come to the court and speak for you. Had he still been a paying customer, I might not have been able to agree to do so.'

'Does that mean as you can't help Mags?'

The doctor didn't pull Betsy up on her use of the name. 'It makes it more difficult. I did want to visit Margaret, as her doctor, and that would have been the right and accept-able thing to do. You see, I feel responsible in a way. And as I am no longer her doctor, I can tell you: Margaret had been through a lot during the war, and she'd just lost her mother, so when I was approached by a psychiatrist who had been called to see her, I affirmed that Margaret was in a low state of mind. I had no idea then that he would do anything other than treat her, and I thought it would be in her own home, as at that time I didn't know about the incident between you and Mr Roford.'

'Aye, well, you were only trying to help her. But the truth, as I see it, is that that swine Roford saw his chance to get his hands on everything, and that was the only reason for him marrying Mags. He probably thought he'd have to wait years to be the full owner of it all, but then saw his chance in the way Mags reacted to what he did to me. It all fell into his lap, so to speak, especially with poor Mr Witherbrook dying an' all.'

'Why do you say "the only reason"? I thought Roford was very much in love with her?'

'He's one as can make people think whatever he wants them to. But I knaw sommat as was confided in me by Mags. If it will help to convince you, then I knaw as she'd want me to tell you . . .'

166

The doctor listened to the story about Susan and her child, without interrupting. His expression veered between incredulousness and enlightenment.

'My God, a mistress! Even before they were married? And possibly a child? I can see it all now. The reason he dispensed with my services, too. Well—'

The doorbell clanging stopped the doctor in what he was going to say. 'Oh, dear, there's someone else needing my attention now. Can you wait a few minutes for me, Betsy? I'll be as quick as I can, only I think we need to come to some conclusion about how to proceed.'

As the door opened and Phyllis Woodrow stepped in, without being bidden to, Betsy knew the housekeeper would be thinking that she'd no need to stand on ceremony for the likes of Betsy. Her look said as much. 'Doctor, there's someone else to speak to you. She says she's from Brockhall Institution.'

'Oh? Show her into the withdrawing room. I'm sorry, Betsy, but I'd better see what this is about.'

It wasn't long before he returned, with a woman who looked to Betsy to be in her forties. She had a bonny face, despite the hairs that stuck out from her chin, which Betsy had an urge to pull out; and her smile gave an impression of kindliness, even though her teeth were in a bit of a state.

'Well, well, this lady is Mrs Iris Rudley. She is on the same mission as you are – to rescue our dear Margaret. She is an orderly nurse and takes care of Margaret.'

'Eeh, thank the Lord. Well, I'm pleased to meet you, Iris. How's Mags faring? I'm worried out of me mind for her.'

'She's a lass of great courage, that one, but I fear that if we don't get her out of there, she'll break good and proper. She's not mentally deficient and, in my opinion, hasn't suffered a mental breakdown and she shouldn't be in that institution. She sent me on this mission, but if I'm found out, I'll be for the chop – and me with two menfolk on strike and bringing nowt in.'

'I'm Betsy. I knaw as it don't seem likely, but me and Mags have been mates since we were thirteen. Mags never had anyone else; well, only horsey types, but most living a good way from her, and she only sees them now and again.'

'Aye, she's spoken about you. She told me everything, and I'm sorry for what happened to you. She's worries over how you are.'

'Tell her I'm doing all right, and that I'm doing all I can for her.'

'Well, let's hope she will soon be able to do that for herself, Betsy, though we do have a number of problems to surmount. For one, I am no longer Margaret's doctor, as I have told you. Now it may seem to you that I have influence, but when it comes to interfering in the care of another doctor's patient, then I have no power whatsoever. That is, unless I am engaged by the patient, or by the person who has power of attorney over the patient. In this case, Margaret is considered incapable of making such decisions, and her husband, who is the only one who can make them for her, has already discharged me and isn't likely to re-engage me. And I now know the reason why.'

'Eeh, Doctor, is there nowt you can do?'

'There is one thing, Betsy. Whether it will help or not, I don't know. But I will contact Dr Jenkins, the psychiatrist who sectioned Mags. I assume he is still in charge of her case, Iris?'

'Aye, his name's on her notes, but he never visits. Reports are sent to him, and they ain't allus correct. Some of them nurses up there are . . . well, I mean some can be vindictive and send in reports to suit themselves. There's one in particular – he's on nights, and he seems to have it in for Mrs Roford. Anyroad, from these reports Dr Jenkins communicates to us what treatment we should give. For Mrs Roford, it's drugs to keep her calm, but I don't allus give them to her, as they make me patients like zombies; and she don't need them. There's nowt wrong with her mind, and if that lazy Dr Jenkins came to see her— Eeh, I didn't say that, Doctor. Please, I can't lose me job. I can't.'

'Don't distress yourself, Iris. Nothing we say in here will be repeated. I have known Margaret, and been her physician, since she was a child. I . . . well, I'm very fond of her, and I'm appalled it has come to this. But as I say, my only recourse is to speak to Dr Jenkins. However, if he is not visiting and is only prescribing on the basis of reports from the staff, then I'm not sure how far I'll get.'

They were silent for a moment and Betsy imagined that, like her, the other two were pondering their own worrying thoughts.

The doctor broke the silence. 'There is another consideration. Where will Margaret go, if we do manage to get her released? She can't go back to her home. That would be disastrous, if everything we believe about that husband of hers is true.'

'She has plans, Doctor. She's assured me that, with your help, she can access the means to help herself. I don't knaw any more than that, but I questioned her on what she'd do, if I did help her to get free, and that's what Mrs Roford told me.'

'Right, first thing is for me to try and get permission to visit her. Dr Jenkins shouldn't refuse me that. But, Iris, I need to know how far you're prepared to go for her. I mean, Dr Jenkins only has those reports to go on, and if they are damning – look, I know you are worried about losing your job, but if I promise you faithfully that nothing you say will go any further, will you answer me one question?'

'Aye, I will.'

'Why are the reports so damning, if you say she is well? I mean, is it possible someone is being paid to keep Margaret's notes showing that she is still unwell in her mind?'

'Eeh, is that what you think, Doctor?'

'Yes, Iris, I think – given the conclusions we have come to – that is possible, but is it probable?'

Betsy saw Iris's face go through several expressions, until she suddenly looked as though a light had switched on. 'It is. The nurse who has it in for her – well, he ain't a proper nurse, he's an orderly – he puts everything at Mrs Roford's door: any disturbance during the night, that sort of thing. And there's been rumours flying around that he's come into some money of late, as he's splashing out on stuff that none of the rest of us can afford; he's even bought a motorbike. Good God . . . that's it! By, if I get me chance, I'll give him sommat to boast of, and it won't be nowt good, either, the rotter.'

'Well, we don't know for sure that what we are thinking is the truth. We must be very careful what we say outside this room. You must carry on as if you don't suspect anything, Iris. Leave it to me. I will come up with a way out of this. Now, ladies, I do have a pressing engagement, but rest assured we will get Margaret out of that place.'

Betsy had been listening to everything with a sinking heart, but hearing the doctor sound so positive cheered her. She trusted Dr Lange; and aye, she knew how fond he was of Mags – something she'd not approved of in the past, him being twenty years or so senior to her. But now this was something she was glad of, as she knew he would do his utmost. And that was the only hope she had for Mags at this moment in time.

As they stepped outside, Betsy offered her hand to Iris. 'Eeh, Iris, I'm so glad as Mags has a friend in you. Take me hand and take me heart – you're a friend as I'd like to have as me own an' all.'

'And me you, Betsy. I'm glad I've met you, and I'm sorry for your troubles. Mrs Roford is always saying that she should have gone to you after . . . well, you knaw. She worries what you think of her.'

'Well, tell her that don't matter none. I knaw as she believes me.' As she said this, Betsy mentally crossed herself, to negate confirming the lie that she lived daily. 'Aye and tell Mags that I'll do owt for her. She only has to send a message with you, and she can consider it done.'

'I will.'

'I have news as well, but I'll leave it up to you as to whether you tell her. She'll find out anyroad. I wanted to tell the doctor, but didn't get the chance. Cook – that's Mags's cook at her house – tells me they all think there was some funny business going on between Harold and the nurse he employed to take care of Mags's poor father. It seems that the nurse didn't leave after Mr Witherbrook died. Cook tells me they have been told she is staying on, as Mr Roford is in the throes of changing the welfare system at the mill and the nurse is overseeing those changes. Now that's not what alerted me, but her name's Susan. I can't tell you why that gives me cause for concern, but if you think Mags is well enough to fight her corner – and against sommat that once hurt her badly, where her husband is concerned – then tell her what I've said. Otherwise, don't mention it.'

'Oh, I get the implication, and she's well enough all right. She hates Mr Roford now, more than she once loved him, and would welcome owt as would give her sommat to fight him with.'

'Are you sure on that, Iris? 'Cause nowt would have made Mags not love him afore. She had it bad, really bad. Even how Mr Roford came on to me, afore they were wed, didn't put her off him. She preferred to think it was all down to sommat in his childhood, and sommat she could help him to get better from.'

'Well, those rose-tinted glasses have been well and truly knocked off her nose. I think she would be better knawing what is going on. We're taught, when training, that know-ledge is power – and it is an' all. Mrs Roford could do with some titbits that give her power, that's for sure. I'll have to bid you good day now, Betsy, but I come down to Blackburn on a Wednesday afternoon and we can meet in town, if you like.'

'Eeh, that'd be grand. I go in the tearooms for a cuppa when I'm in town – not the posh one with the net drapes, but the one on the corner of Peter Street.'

'I knaw the one. Right-o, I'll meet you there next Wednesday and we can have a chinwag and get to knaw one another.'

As Betsy said goodbye to Iris, she felt she'd made a friend. Someone who wished for something that was dear to her own heart – the welfare of Mags.

Chapter Sixteen

Mags waited and waited for the promised visit. Her heart had been lifted since Iris returned with news of the outcome of her talk to Dr Lange, and even more so by knowing that Betsy had been there. That dear Betsy hadn't given up on her was such a good thing to hear.

And so it was possible Harold was paying to have reports sent that indicated she was still mentally deranged? *My God, does his wickedness know no bounds?* But then Mags knew it didn't, as she thought of the other news. Hearing it had caused pain in her heart, not that she really cared, but rejection in favour of another woman was always going to hurt, she knew that. And she didn't doubt that the so-called 'nurse' was Susan, Harold's true love – that's if he was capable of such a thing.

Every woman – including herself and Betsy – was taken by Harold to gain something he wanted. She could understand what he wanted from her, but from Betsy? *Maybe it was just sexual gratification, but hadn't I given him that? Oh, I don't know. One minute I think I have got to the bottom of Harold's true character, and the next I know that I haven't. And that is worrying.*

As she paced the garden, Mags thought of how long she'd been here now. More than eight weeks – it didn't seem possible. She knew she'd deteriorated during that time. Her hair was lank and greasy, her eyes were like dead pools of dirty water, and the whites had yellowed from lack of sleep; and the gowns they were made to wear swamped her too-thin figure. She was still not eating well, as she found it hard to stomach some of the slop served up at mealtimes, and she had lost more than the few pounds she'd gained over the period when she was so happy to be married to Harold.

'Mrs Roford.' Iris's voice brought Mags's attention back to the present. Iris always called her that when on official business, or if afraid she might be heard, even though she called most inmates by their first names. It was a precaution she took, as she said she didn't want to appear to be getting too close to her or she might be reassigned to another case.

Walking towards Iris, Mags could feel an aura of excitement in the way Iris was almost skipping, and this jolted her hopes sky-high. 'Has he come? Dr Lange – is he here?'

'He is. Oh, Mags, he is. But keep calm, lass. I reckon as we're being watched, so don't hug me, nor owt. Slow down and we'll walk back, like a nurse and patient would.'

Once inside, Iris took Mags to a room she hadn't been in before. The sign on the door announced it as being the 'Visitors' waiting room'. She'd envied those who'd had visits from family and friends. She had longed for someone to come and see her, but it hadn't happened. Harold obviously wouldn't want to see her, but she'd hoped Betsy would find a way. She'd understood why she hadn't come, as it was a long way and the only method was by car or horse and trap, and Betsy hadn't recourse to either of these modes of transport.

The room was painted pale green and had a light and

airy feel to it. The seating was of brown leather, arranged in little groups, with a coffee table in the centre of each set of four chairs.

Seeing the doctor caused tears of relief and joy to well up in Mags's eyes. *At last, at last – a face from the life I used to have.* 'Oh, Dr Lange, I can't tell you how wonderful it is to see you.'

'Dear Margaret, how did we get to this? Dear, dear, look at you. I can hardly recognize you.'

'I know. I feel dirty and unkempt. I'm sorry.'

'Don't be. You have nothing to be sorry for. I'm the one to be sorry. I should have stood up to that husband of yours. How can you ever forgive me? I had no idea it would come to this. When asked about your mental health, I thought of what I had said to you before you married, about seeking the help of a professional. I thought Harold had come to the same conclusion and had seen that you were haunted by your experiences during the war. I assumed he was getting you help. If I'd have known what happened and his real motive, I would have been very careful about what I said.'

'I know. I have never held you to blame. But what now – can you help me?'

'Let's sit down. Iris assured me we won't be disturbed. She said she will hang around outside and make sure no one tries to listen in. I assume she has told you what we suspect?'

'Yes, and I wouldn't put it past Harold. I know a lot about him. And as I have been thinking about it and remembering, I have become appalled at going along with him. He . . . well, he's even capable of murdering someone for his own gain.'

'Dear God! And you know this for a fact, Margaret?'

'Yes, I do. I overheard Harold plotting with his mother to murder his own half-brother, only . . . Well, I foiled that and . . .'

'Margaret?'

Though it cost her emotionally, she told the doctor what had happened, and how it all ended up that she caused the death of Harold's mother.

'Well, you were very brave to intervene like that, and you weren't to know the outcome of the tussle. You must think of the positive side: you saved a life. That one life was lost was a pure accident and a misfortune, but it should not make you feel guilty.'

'I know, but these things stay with you. Anyway I need to know if you can help me. I don't think I can stand another day in here.'

'You will have to, Margaret, as I cannot work miracles. It has taken a while for me to get this far. Dr Jenkins was not in agreement with it at all. Probably afraid that I would find out he hasn't been here to see you for himself, and has used reports in order to administer a treatment plan for you.'

'Yes, I know. It's all so shocking. But he did make a visit the other day. He told me he was reviewing my case, and that he was surprised to find me so coherent. And that if I made progress and stopped having episodes of the type that is regularly reported to him, then he might look at discharging me in a few months' time. It was difficult not to scream that I didn't have *any* episodes, and that he should look at the behaviour of the institution's staff, but I kept calm and told him that I was feeling much better and thanked him. I thought if I did anything else, judging by how he reacted to everything when I first met him, he would say something like, "Typical behaviour of someone in self-denial."'

Dr Lange smiled at this. 'Haven't lost your wit and sense of humour, I see. Good. Because you are going to need both qualities. Now, Iris said I could help you form your plans for your future, should we secure your release?'

Not liking the use of 'should', Mags wanted to plead with him to make it happen, but was afraid that any outburst would be misinterpreted. Kind as Dr Lange was, he would surely be looking for evidence that she really was sane.

'I need you to go to my father's solicitors. I will give you a signed request to hand over to them – that is, if you have anything for me to write with, and on.'

'I do, as it happens. I brought a notebook in my case, for just such an event. I knew that what you would need me to do would require your written permission.' While he had been talking, the doctor had rummaged in his attaché case. 'There you are.'

'Thank you. I'll write the address on one sheet for you. Then the authority on another.'

With this done, Mags told the doctor of her plans.

'Scotland! Good gracious, that was the last thing I expected you to say. But yes, you will be safe there, and I know the area; it is very beautiful.'

'Yes, I know – but I intend to go to France first . . .' Mags told him about Flors and her relationship to Harold. 'Harold hasn't a clue where she is, and neither does he care, or know that I am aware of Flors's whereabouts.'

'My God, Margaret, it all beggars belief. But I'm glad you have a friend like that. Though I – I, well, I will miss you, Margaret, as I have done while . . . Oh, I'm being an old fool. I think it is an excellent solution for you, and I cannot tell you how glad I am that you have one – and the means to put it into action. Our only obstacle is getting you out of here.'

'Look, I want you to listen to me, and not think I truly am mentally deranged because of what I am going to say. If you cannot secure a discharge – and doing so is going to be very difficult, if Harold really is working to keep me in here – then I have to escape.'

'What! How?'

'I will need both your help and Iris's. For Iris, that could mean she loses her job, if she's found out; but if she will do it, I will pay her enough to keep her and her family for the rest of her life, so that she has no need to work. But it's the disgrace she will suffer. I'm loath to ask her to risk that for me, but I may have no other way.'

'Explain the plan to me first, and what will be my own and Iris's part . . . For goodness' sake, I can't believe I'm even saying that. But I do feel despair at the prospect of you never getting out any other way, and I cannot bear that thought. I feel so helpless. If I was still your doctor, I would be able to have some influence, but Harold has closed that loophole.'

'This is going to feel as if we are a criminal gang, but I will need you to make sure that I have a getaway car . . .' The doctor's laughter spilled over her own. 'I told you it would sound like we are gangsters, but transport is going to be vital to get me away. And you are the only person on my side who can help with that. It needn't be you and your car, but if you could hire a taxi to wait for me on a given street, at a given hour, on a given day.'

'Oh, I think I could sort that out, but I can't stand the thought of this going wrong and you getting into a worse state than you are in now.'

'I have to take that chance, Doctor.'

'David. Call me David. If I'm to be part of your gang, I think first names are called for, don't you?'

Mags giggled. 'Yes. And . . . well, if this works, I will write to you to let you know how I am doing.'

'Yes, please do. I will worry about you. Now I presume you intend to go to your bank first?'

'No, that is what the letter of authority is for. My solicitors will release funds to you, as I can't do anything without money.'

'Are you sure that enough funds will be readily available? You will need clothes and money. Look, I have a better plan.'

As she listened, Mags wanted to hug David. That he should be willing to go so far for her, as he risked so much if he was caught – he could even be struck off, which would hurt him deeply. She knew he was doing this for love. And it pained her that she could not return that love. 'Oh, David, you would do that for me? I – I'll never be able to repay you.'

It showed his character that he didn't ask anything of her, or declare the feelings that she instinctively knew he harboured.

'You don't have to. All I ask is that first you give me a chance to have you discharged in the proper manner. I will seek an appointment with Dr Jenkins and will do all I can to get him to discharge you.'

'I do agree that would be the best solution, in a perfect world, David. But in my world there is an evil force, in Harold. Surely Harold would have to be consulted, and would need to agree to having me back home? He is never going to do that. Not now. He has everything he wanted: our family home, our business, even his mistress in situ.'

'You know about that, too? I'm sorry.'

'Don't be. As Iris said to me when she told me, knowledge is power; and knowing has made me even more determined to get away and start a new life. One that Harold can't spoil.'

'Yes. That's what is needed, and I'm glad you have included Betsy in your plans, because her life will be made hell after Roford realizes that she must have helped you. I only hope she and Bill agree to go with you.'

'I think she will, as Betsy only has her sister here now, and she's of an age to get married and can care for herself. Besides, her sister will be welcome to visit whenever she likes, and I would help her to do so. I don't think Harold knows anything about Betsy's family, so she'll be safe.'

'Well, I think we gangsters had better get on with putting our plan into action then.' At the mention of gangsters, they both laughed again, and this time Mags allowed herself to let go and bend over with the joy of bubbly laughter that made her side ache.

A tap on the door brought her back up. A male orderly entered. She didn't think it was the one on nights, but fear of him still froze her. How much had he heard? And how did he get past Iris?

'Oh, I heard a noise. I thought I'd check that you were all right, Mrs Roford.'

'Yes, I'm fine, thank you.'

'Good. Nice to see you have a visitor. I'm Michael, one of the orderlies who takes care of Mrs Roford. And you are?'

'I'm a friend, Charles Boneham. Well, the father of a friend, as my daughter Shirley has been worried about Mrs Roford, so I said I would visit her. I'm sorry to see her as she is. I have managed to make her laugh by telling her about my daughter's antics, but to see her so unkempt is very sad. Don't you look after the patient's personal welfare as well their mental health?'

'I – I . . . well, it is difficult, as we have so many patients and so much to do, but I'll note that you commented on it. I'll leave you to it, but please don't tire Mrs Roford. It is then that she has her worst episodes.' Michael left the room.

'That's him! It must be, otherwise why would he say that I have episodes when I don't? And although it was genius to pretend to be Shirley Boneham's father, how will you get away with it? Don't they know I am expecting a doctor to visit me?'

'I doubt it. And no one asked me to sign in or give my name. I just said that I had Dr Jenkins's permission to visit, and that Nurse Rudley knew all about it. They called Iris, and that was that. Anyway, if he doesn't believe me, he'd have to ask Dr Jenkins, and I hardly think he will do that. That man is very unapproachable.'

'All the same, I had better go now. I'll find Iris and see why she let him in and tell her what you said. Take care, David. And thank you, from the bottom of my heart.'

'You take care, dear Margaret, and be patient. I will let you know, through Iris, when to be ready.'

Mags had an urge to go to him and kiss his cheek, but she resisted and left the room.

Iris was nowhere to be seen. Puzzled, Mags made her way along the corridor. She'd go and sit in the garden once more and hope that Iris came to her. What she would do if she didn't, Mags didn't know, but whatever happened, she must keep faith. Iris was a good person and would never do anything to cause her harm, of that Mags was sure.

Chapter Seventeen

Susan looked around the hall of Feniscowles Manor, making sure that the maid who had informed her there was a telephone call for her wasn't hanging around. All was quiet. She couldn't wait to talk to Montel. She'd given him a specific day in her letter for phoning her and had waited patiently for this day to come. Harold had an appointment and had left an hour ago, saying he would be late home; and it was Barnard's day off, and she knew this was the time of day when the staff took their breaks.

With everywhere apparently clear of listening ears, Susan picked up the receiver from where it rested on the hall table. 'Hello, this is Susan Charvet.'

'*Ma chérie*, it iz zo good to hear your voice. I am missing you zo much, and zo iz little Sibbie. When are you coming home? And what iz thiz about that beast's wife – the woman of my dreams?'

'I don't know, is the answer to the first question. My heart is breaking without my little Sybil, but I have no money to get back, or I would. But it is true: Harold has had Mags committed to a mental asylum, and I feel so sorry for her. I had an idea that you could rescue her somehow.'

'Of course I can, but not with a baby in tow. I do have money, though. Oh, *ma chérie*, I sold two of my paintings. Yez, two, and I have been asked to hold an exhibition! Think of that. It iz wonderful.'

'Oh, it is, Montel. It is the recognition you deserve.' His paintings were exquisite, and although she had sat for him on many occasions, Susan had made him promise that in the nude scenes he would only show her body and would paint on a different head. She'd been amused that the one he had completed before she left had confirmed to her how smitten he was with Mags.

'You didn't sell the one with Mags's face on, did you?'

'No, I could never part with that. And I hope one day to paint her for real – her nude body as well az her beautiful face. Have you a plan to help her get out?'

'No, I thought you would come up with that – you're the soldier, after all. Look, bring Sybil to me. Arrive on the doorstep saying you cannot take care of her any longer and that you are going away: back to France or something.'

'Iz thiz some sort of ploy to get Sibbie back with you?'

'Part of it is, as I can't bear to be apart from her any longer. But not all. I really do want you to help Mags. I feel so afraid for her. Look, she has a friend who used to work here. I'll try to find out where she lives and see if she can help. But hurry, please hurry.'

'You haven't thought to ask when my exhibition iz, but I forgive you. Mags, az you call her, iz very much more important to me. Do you think she may like me?'

'She will adore you. You said she couldn't take her eyes off you when you met her.'

'Yes, that iz true, even though she was angry. But how beautiful she was in her anger. I must also paint her with that expression.'

'Oh, Montel, you are the limit! But, seriously, please hurry. For my sake and for Mags's.'

Betsy didn't know what to make of Susan. She was a lovely-looking young woman with an almost oriental look, slim, with short dark hair and fascinating hazel eyes. Betsy wanted to hate her, but couldn't. 'By, lass, if this is some sort of trick, I'll personally blacken your eye, and I'm not one for violence. You say you want to help Mags. Why?'

'I have no other reason than guilt. Oh yes, a mistress can feel guilt. And hatred of the man who doesn't think her worthy of marrying, and yet professes his love for her. I don't want to be a mistress. I love Harold, and have done since I met him, which was long before he even knew Mags existed, but I was never good enough for him – not to marry. I was a maid, like you were. I can't explain it, but even though I knew he'd never marry me, I could never give him up, as he's in my blood.'

Betsy knew exactly what Susan meant, though she also knew there was a cure for it, as it had happened to her. All feelings that she'd had for Mr Harold Roford had been replaced by hate.

'So this man who wants to help Mags escape is your husband?'

'In name only.'

Betsy listened to the tale of Montel with her mouth open. She'd never heard the like. None of it seemed real. And yet it was that – the unlikeliness of it all – that made her believe Susan. For a moment she considered telling her that there

184

was already a plan in place, but she erred on the side of caution. 'Look, I'll think about it. I mean I don't even knaw where the hospital is, or how to get there. I've heard of Brockhall, but have never been there. I haven't been further than Blackburn town centre in me life.'

'Can you not get a message to Mags?'

'Naw, I can't – I told you. I wish I could. I wish I knew how she is, but there's nowt I can do. If owt occurs, I'll let you knaw.'

Stepping back inside her ma's house – the house she'd always think of as her ma's – Betsy went to close the door.

'Please believe me, I only want to help Mags. I do.'

'You should have thought of that when you restarted your affair with Roford, knowing that Mags was engaged to him. I'm sorry, but there's nowt I can do.'

As the door closed, Betsy was sure she heard a sob. She'd never met anyone like Susan, and there was something very likeable about her – however, even thinking this, she daren't jeopardize Mags's chances by trusting the girl.

Leaning on the door, Betsy thought about the message that the doctor had sent. *Scotland! Me and Bill and the kids. Could I do it? Uproot meself from the only life I've ever known? Bring the kids up in a foreign country?*

Feeling humiliated, Susan walked back along the street. One thing she'd learned since coming to Blackburn was that northerners stuck together. She'd tried to make friends amongst the staff, but in their canny way they'd sussed out why she was really here and barely gave her the time of day. Loneliness engulfed her. She wanted to go back to London and be near Montel, because surely he wouldn't win Mags's heart. Oh, if anyone could after what she'd been through,

Montel could, but deep down she knew that she'd played on his infatuation with Mags simply to get him up here – and mostly to get her little Sybil back.

Harold was going to be furious, but she'd made up her mind. *If only Harold would agree to go and live back in London!* He hated it up here, after all, and hated the people, calling them dumb, cloth-cap-wearing idiots.

But she knew he dared not leave. He worried that somehow Mags would get possession of everything, if he did so. How, Susan couldn't imagine because, as Harold said, everything a wife owned became the husband's on marriage. So what was he worrying about?

A plaque on the door of a house that she passed caught Susan's attention: 'Dr Lange, Physician'. Though he was no longer the family doctor, he must know how Mags was.

The door opened to her, and a woman with a look of mistrust asked how she could help Susan. 'I would like to speak with Dr Lange, please. I'm an assistant to Mr Roford. I'd be grateful if the doctor could spare me some time.'

'Come in. Take a seat in there and I'll see if the doctor can see you. He's a busy man, mind.'

As Susan entered the waiting room, she felt like running out again. What was she doing? *Christ, Harold will kill me if he finds out.* And she knew there was a good chance he would. These folk gossiped amongst themselves; someone would tell Cook, then she would find a way of telling Barnard. Susan hated the sly Barnard, and thought his disdain of her filtered through to the rest of the staff and made them dislike her, without giving her a chance. But then they all loved Mags. *They see me as the root cause of all that has happened! Well, the reason for her incarceration at least. I can't do much about that, but in helping Mags, some of the guilt I feel will hopefully leave me.*

'Mrs Charvet? How can I help you?'

'I don't know where to start, Doctor. You see, it's going to be difficult for you to believe my motive in what I have come to ask.'

'Oh? Well, we shall see. What is it you have come to ask?'

'I'm going to be honest with you. Firstly, I am Harold Roford's mistress. I'm sure the rumours are rife about me being so. Well, they are true. I have been since long before he met Mags – excuse me calling Mrs Roford that, but that is how she was introduced to me. I love Harold. I am in love with him, and he with me.'

'Yes, I have heard the rumours, but where is all of this leading to? You have no need to confirm or deny such gossip to me. I don't understand.'

'I want you to see me as an honest person, with no ulterior motive when I tell you why I am here. You see, I want to help Mags.'

'What? You've admitted to being the mistress of Margaret's husband, and that means you have already caused her misery. How can you now want to help her?'

'Guilt, plus the fact that I like, and feel sorry for, Mags. She was just a pawn in the game Harold played, to get everything she would have owned on her father's death. He didn't love her; he didn't even like her, and he talks of her as being a cold fish in bed. I shouldn't tell you all this, but that's Harold. Anyway, I'm here now about my husband. You see . . .'

The doctor didn't interrupt her as Susan told him how she came to be married to Montel, and why. She finished by telling him, 'I already loved Harold, and I couldn't have him in any other way than as his lover. Montel understood that, and only loves me as a friend. We have never consummated the marriage, or wish to.'

'Well, well, I have never heard of anything like this before. You say this is about your husband? I am mystified. Please tell me why you are here.'

After telling the doctor about Montel falling in love with Mags, and how they wanted to help her escape, the doctor was quiet for a long moment.

'This all sounds preposterous, so much so that it must be true. And I must say, you do come across as an honest young lady, even though I don't condone the way you have chosen to lead your life. You say that you think Mags was attracted to Montel? I find that bit of your story hard to believe. Mags was smitten with Harold from the first time she met him.'

'Most women are – he has a magnetism about him. And if he wants something, he uses that. I have already said why he wanted Mags.'

The doctor didn't give anything away. 'I am finding this conversation surreal. And my time is valuable. Please get to the point. I have long made up my mind as to Harold's character. Why are you here?'

'Montel wants to rescue her. To break her out of that place, which is the only way she will ever get out. Harold is determined to have Mags sectioned for life – and believe me, if he chooses to, he can. I can't bear that. I told you, I like Mags. I have seen her suffer at Harold's hands, even when she was his fiancée – and I am not talking of Mags finding out that he was setting up a life in London for himself and me, with the intention of only spending the

188

minimum of time up here that he could get away with. Other things happened, too.'

By the way that the doctor didn't press for further information, Susan suspected that he knew all about Harold's mother's death and what had led to it.

'You told me Montel is a Frenchman and an ex-soldier. Well, this is England, and we don't go around breaking people out of hospital, as you well know.'

This alarmed Susan. 'You don't trust me. And I thought you would be able to help. I thought you would want to help Mags. Please, please, I beg of you, don't tell a soul why I came to you. If Harold got to know that I was conspiring against him, he would . . . Oh my God, I told Betsy. I went to her, to see if she would help me. I've been a fool. She may tell Cook. Harold will kill me!'

'I'll talk to Betsy – don't worry. Now I am sorry, but I cannot help you with your plan. And I would strongly advise you to not carry it through. You will put yourselves in danger, and will probably ruin any chance Mags has of ever getting out of there. If you have any influence over Mr Roford at all, you would be better served trying to persuade him to change his mind about her fate. Now, please excuse me.'

As Dr Lange closed the door on Susan, his sigh was long drawn out, but didn't relieve the worry the young woman had aroused in him. And yet she had come over as genuine. Yes, he believed her. She had that simple quality about her that didn't have another side. *What you see is what you get.*

He looked at his watch. Betsy would be here any minute. She was going into town to meet Iris, and he'd asked her to call, as he might have a message for Iris to give Margaret. He did have one, but now he wasn't so sure. None of it sat well with him. He was risking so much – his whole livelihood and his vocation – but felt compelled. He couldn't just sit by and let Harold do this to Margaret. This time the doctor's sigh was full of hopelessness. Not because he thought his plan wouldn't work, but because of his real motive. He loved Margaret in a way he knew he shouldn't. *I've known her since she was a child, for goodness' sake. I'm her doctor, and twenty years older than her. It's immoral*. But knowing this didn't prevent his feelings.

Did this Montel really love her?

Despite this thought, he added to his note for Mags details of Susan's visit and her proposal. *I must let Margaret make up her own mind*. He knew that part of his motivation for even half-suggesting they let Montel help was that he would feel safer if Margaret had a man with her in France. It made him feel more confident about his plan. Montel would think like him and would take every precaution. It had to work. It *had* to.

Chapter Eighteen

Aggie was on the prowl again. Mags stiffened. *Please don't let her come to me.* Since the night when she'd kicked out at her, Aggie hadn't bothered her, but today Mags had noticed her staring at her.

Aggie's shadow fell across Mags's bed. 'Go away, Aggie. Go away or I'll kick you again.'

The bed sank with Aggie's weight as she sat down heavily. 'Aggie's lonely.'

'I know you are. We all are. I can be your friend, but I don't want, or like, you trying to touch me.'

'Aggie won't. Aggie likes you.'

'And I like you, dear. Now go back to bed and don't disturb any of the other ladies. They are all tired. Let's have a peaceful night, shall we?'

Aggie got up. 'Aggie walk with you tomorrow? Aggie come into the garden and sit on the bench with you?'

Oh God, how am I to handle this? If Aggie started to trail around with her, Mags knew that would be a disaster for David's plan. A plan that was very similar to her own, only it meant that the doctor would come himself, and not send a taxi. Iris was to help her leave the premises in a week's time. She would meet Mags in the bathroom and would change clothes with her, and then get into Mags's bed. Mags would leave the hospital wearing Iris's hat and coat over the uniform's grey dress. David would have money, tickets to France, and a case full of clothes and toiletries for her. He would have used the authority she gave him to access money through her father's solicitors, and Betsy would have shopped for everything she needed. David would drive her to Dover and book them into a hotel. There she would be able to bath, wash her hair and change into decent clothes – oh, how she longed for that moment. David would then see her onto the ferry the next day and, from Calais, Mags would catch a train – or several – to get to Flora in the South of France. Not that she had Flora's full address, that was still hidden away in her bureau, but she remembered the area and part of the name of the village. And she felt confident that, armed with this information, she would find Flora. *Freedom – oh God, I can't wait. And nothing, nothing at all, is going to stop me.*

But what of this new plan of Aggie's? What if she did befriend Mags, and Aggie tried to sit with Iris when she was pretending to be her? Iris didn't care about being found out in the morning, or the consequences of that, for she was so happy to have the chance to help Mags and to be free of this place, with enough money to keep her and her family without worrying about where the next penny was coming from. David was seeing to that part of the plan, too. Everything was set.

But if Mags did anything tonight to let Aggie down, she would most likely start a riot and that would be put at *her* door, she was sure of that. It might mean she would be sent back to the solitary secure room. *Oh God, no. I can't risk that.*

'Yes, we will walk tomorrow; and yes you can sit on the bench with me, but only if you go back to bed now and don't wake anyone else up.'

Aggie shuffled away, humming a little tune. Poor, poor Aggie, lost in a child's mind. It was pitiful to think of her as lonely. Mags's heart wanted to help her, to help them all, but she had to get out of here, she had to. She consoled herself with the thought that most of the other patients didn't know they were being treated badly. That didn't excuse it or make it right, and she prayed that one day things would change for those suffering from mental illness, and they wouldn't be treated like animals. But if someone like Iris, who worked here and cared, couldn't make a difference, what chance had she? Yes, she could bring influence to bear. If she'd known of their plight previously, when she was a respected businesswoman and member of society, she would have done; but as a fugitive – as that was what she was going to be – she had to accept that she could do nothing. The thought didn't sit easily with her as she turned over, for what she hoped would be an undisturbed sleep.

The next day Aggie seemed to have forgotten all about Mags's promise and went about her usual daily routine. This brought Mags some relief, but still she worried about the nights. It was when everyone was asleep that Aggie seemed to feel the need to be with someone and to give, and receive, her kind of love. Would she want to pick up the 'friendship' then? What if it became a regular occurrence?

This worry didn't sit long in her, when Iris came on duty and sought her out. 'I need to talk with you in the garden. Aye, I knaw as it's raining, but I have a message from the doctor.'

193

Mags's heart skipped a beat. *Surely nothing has gone wrong, has it?*

'Go on your usual walk, but hurry over to the bench under the tree, as if seeking shelter. I'll come to you, making the excuse that I'm to fetch you back inside.'

Mags shivered as she waited. Her anxiety deepened when she saw Aggie staring out at her, as she had done the day before. *Should I wave to her?* Deciding that to do so might seem like an invitation, Mags turned away and glanced at the sad-looking garden, with raindrops dripping from the trees and the flowers bending their heads under the weight of the downpour.

'Mags, come inside – come on!'

She ignored Iris's call, knowing it was just a ploy.

'Eeh, I'm out of breath, having to run over here. I've already run through the rain to get to work. But not long now, lass, afore I'll never have to do it again.'

'That depends on your message. Oh, Iris, please don't say that David – I mean, Dr Lange – has changed his mind?'

'Naw, but there has been a development. He's put it in a note, but I daren't give it to you. I feel increasingly that since the doctor visited I am being watched, so I read the note and will tell you about it, while looking as if I am trying to persuade you back in. So keep shaking your head and walking away from me while I do so.'

The first part of the message was just to tell Mags that all had gone smoothly with David's visit to her solicitors, and they would have the money she requested ready for him in a couple of days. They sent a message wishing her luck and were glad to be of help to her. She knew she could trust them.

'But sommat else happened, lass.'

Mags listened with growing incredulity to the tale of Susan, and what she'd told the doctor. Montel? Yes, she remembered him. And something lit inside her, at the thought of the Frenchman and his dark eyes, which seemed to pull her into his soul. But Montel declaring his love for her! She couldn't believe it.

'The doctor wants to know if you do have any feelings for this Montel, and if you want him involved in your rescue. For some reason that he can't explain, he trusts Susan; and if you trust this Montel, then the doctor says he would feel safer if you had him by your side when you are travelling across France. Particularly as Montel is French.'

'It's preposterous, and I cannot understand David even giving any thought to this. For goodness' sake, I only met Montel once. He's married to my husband's mistress! Yes, I did find him attractive and may have given him that impression, but you know what they say about Frenchmen: give them half a nod and they are in bed with you.'

'Do they? Eeh, I didn't knaw that. Maybe I can meet him and give him half a nod, as my old man is useless.'

Mags had to turn away, as this made her laugh out loud. 'Oh, Iris. If they see me laughing . . .'

'I knaw. Ha, I could double over. Fancy me saying owt like that, and me not having thought about sex in this good while.'

'Stop it! Oh, Iris, you are funny. But if anyone sees us!'

'Don't worry, they all knaw me. I'm allus having them laughing – though I don't talk of such things, never have done . . . It's just, well, you feel more like a friend than a patient.'

'I am, Iris. I will always remember you and I will never be able to thank you. You've made my life in here bearable. One day we will meet up again. Maybe you can come and visit me? Or I might be able to come back here. Who knows. I'm sure all that will happen to you is that you will be sacked, and you don't mind that, do you?'

'Naw, I can't wait, lass. Nowt else can happen to me. Dr Lange said it isn't a criminal offence, just a gross misdemeanour against me employers. And he said, if need be, he would testify for me that he knew you to be sane, which is going to be me motive; and he will expose that Dr Jenkins an' all. With me being free from here, I'll be able to give evidence to any tribunal about Jenkins's lack of care. You never knaw, it might even come out about Michael taking money, as there's plenty of evidence of him having more money than he can earn here.'

'I want to hug you, but know I can't.' As she looked at Iris, Mags saw love in her eyes and remembered her saying that she'd always wanted a daughter. 'You've been like a mother to me, Iris.'

Tears glistened in Iris's eyes. 'Eeh, give over, lass. Meeting you has changed me life. I can't get me head around never having to work again – well, not never, because at last I'll be able to make a good home for me menfolk; and, aye, make meself look better for them an' all, as I intend getting me teeth seen to, and me hairy chin. I've heard as it's to do with hormones or sommat. You hear a lot, when you work around doctors. I knaw as they can't do owt about that, but I'll look into other ways of ridding meself of the chin hairs. You never see a rich lady with them, and some of them must suffer with this hormone-thingy. Eeh, maybe if I looked better, me old man might get interested in me again – not that he's a pretty picture himself, but I love him.'

'I think that's an excellent idea, Iris. And you will have my address, so if ever you need anything, you only have to write. And about what you were saying before: if it does come to you having to defend yourself, then I will leave a message with Dr Lange to tell him that I will come back and be examined by the best psychiatrist in the land, to prove that you were right and I shouldn't have been here. You'll end up a hero, not a criminal, you'll see.'

'Eeh, I almost want it to happen. Now let's get back inside.'

As they walked back towards the building, Mags told of her worry over Aggie.

'Leave her to me, I'll sort Aggie. I'll befriend her, so that if she does come and find me, she's happy and doesn't make a scene. It's sad, when you think about it. The poor souls are lonely. No one really understands the torment in their minds.'

They fell silent. During this silence, Montel popped into Mags's mind. Annoyed by this, she tried to dispel the thoughts she was having, but couldn't. Her mind seemed to want to dwell on him, for some unknown reason. 'Iris, I'll think about that other matter Susan proposed. I'll let you know.'

'Right-o. I can go down to Blackburn to see the doctor. I asked Betsy to tell him that if I had an answer for him, I'd come down on Saturday evening, when my old man goes to the pub.'

Settling down to sleep that night, Mags felt exhausted. Her mind had gone round and round the subject of Susan's honesty and why she should do this, but mostly she'd pondered over Montel saying that he loved her. Was it possible? Yes, she knew it was. Hadn't Flors fallen in love with Cyrus the moment she'd set eyes on him?

Despite her doubts, her dreams were full of Montel.

Waking to the sound of a ruckus going on, Mags couldn't believe that she'd had such a good night's sleep. Looking over towards Aggie's bed, she saw that she wasn't the culprit this time, as she was still snoring away. Sometimes Aggie did sleep for hours, even during the day, and when she did, peace reigned.

There was no peace now, and Mags could see the cause was that all the other women in the ward wanted to use the lavatory at the same time. Fights and scuffles had broken out. Screams assaulted her ears.

When the door opened and the orderlies came in, Mags wanted to scream herself as they began hitting out at the poor defenceless women, but although it went against all that she was, she didn't go to the aid of any of them, but slid back under her covers and lay still and quiet.

The rough yanking of the blanket from her grasp had her gasping in horror as she looked up into the evil face of Michael. Before she could react, he pulled up her shift and exposed her naked body. His hand rose and yielded a cutting blow to her face. Cringing away from him, she tried to fight him off as he turned her over, but he was too strong for her. With one knee in the middle of her back, he rained stinging slaps onto her buttocks, which had her gasping for breath and begging him to stop.

'You caused this – you always cause these upsets. Well, this will be your last one, Lady Muck, as I am having you taken to the solitary room and will have that straitjacket put back on you.'

'No, please.' Her teeth gritted with the pain as Michael's slapping didn't cease, but through them she growled, 'I know you are being paid by my husband. I'll pay you more. I can, and I promise. Speak to Iris – she will tell you.'

The slapping stopped. Her body was jerked over to face him. 'What're you saying, bitch! I ain't in no one's pay.'

'You are, I know. And I can get evidence.' In her mind, Mags wondered if Susan knew, and if she would speak up for her, if she asked.

'What evidence?'

Around them the mayhem had calmed to a sobbing mass. Michael looked up, as if it had only just dawned on him that his fellow orderly had stopped beating the women.

'I ain't, mate – she's lying. I ain't took no money for nowt.'

Mags turned her head. She could see the other orderly, a much bigger man than Michael, coming towards her bed. His movement was slow, and his face showed anger. 'So that's how you got that motorbike and all the other stuff. And you kept it all to yourself. You never shared nowt with me, and we've been working together this good while and watching each other's backs.'

'Aye, well, I were sworn to secrecy. I – I—'

'Secrecy? So you have me down as someone who'd tell on you then. Have I told before, when I've caught you raping a couple of them? Naw, and I wouldn't, even though I thought you the lowest of the low, as I wouldn't touch the dirty toerags in that way if I were paid.'

Michael didn't speak. His look was one of fear.

'I can pay you both, if you help me. And well, too.' Mags held her breath, for she was taking a massive risk. She was giving them the knowledge that she had funds. If that got back to Harold, then she would have them no longer.

'Bring her through to our office.'

Michael pulled her roughly off the bed. Pain zinged through her, but Mags kept her dignity and held her head up high. Once in the office, she saw a clock on the wall. Eight a.m. She knew Iris would be here at nine, but would that be too late to help her?

Her eyes took in the very neat office. A desk, two chairs and three wooden filing cabinets were all it contained, besides a wood stove in one corner. A high window let in light.

'Right, Lady Muck, what's all this about your husband, then?'

Mags knew she was cornered. Whatever the outcome, she had no choice but to tell them.

'By, that's a tale and a half. Sounds like sommat out of a fiction novel. Your husband wanting you out of the way, so that he can take all you have?'

'Aye, well it's true, John. That's why he pays me to put in bad reports about her. He never wants her to leave this place.'

'And you've been doing that, even though she's given us no trouble?'

Mags felt a glimmer of hope. Maybe, just maybe, the orderly called John had a spark of goodness in him, when he considered things unfair.

'Well, you would, if you had the handouts I've been having.'

The sound of the chair scraping on the stone floor, as John rose from where he had sat, grated on Mags's fraught nerves. The situation was volatile, and she felt like a pawn in the middle of it.

'You dirty rotten tyke, you. If I'd been in on this, I'd have not agreed with it. Of all the low things you've done, this one takes the biscuit. I wondered why she was still here, when anyone can see she's as sane as the next one. That's vile – vile. How would you like to be cooped up here, eh?

With all these mental cases, dribbling and spitting and stinking to high heaven, eh? She's a lady, for Christ's sake. You're scum. Scum!'

Part of Mags wanted to smile at the hypocrisy of this, but another part of her remained afraid. Was all of this some sort of ploy? If not, why didn't Iris know about this better side of John and appeal to it? But then Iris had only recently become aware that someone might be in Harold's employ, and she had no proof. Iris probably didn't trust either of them. And how was she to know that John wasn't being paid by Harold, too?

'Oh, come off it, John – you're naw saint. You're sadistic and beat the mentals more than I do. If we're to sling mud, then I can sling me fair share.'

John sat down again. Both men were quiet for a moment, then John asked Mags, 'You say you can pay us both. How much, and what do you want of us?'

Mags realized she had to be very clever here. The sum had to be tempting, especially to Michael, who was obviously getting a good amount from Harold.

'What I really want is my husband brought to justice for what he has done, but that would implicate Michael, and I don't want that. I just want to get out of here. I want to get far away and start a new life for myself. And I can pay. It would be a one-time payment to you both. Now I know as my husband has paid you well, Michael, as I heard that you had bought a motorbike, which costs around one hundred pounds. So I would pay John more, as he has missed out. Say one hundred and fifty pounds to you, Michael, and two hundred and fifty to John.'

'Naw, I ain't having that. I've taken all the risks up to now,' Michael insisted.

'Yes, risks to keep me here. John hasn't done that, and neither has he treated me badly, as you have done.'

'I reckon as that's fair,' John said. 'And if you don't go along with it, I'll shop you anyroad, so we'll both get nowt, and this lady will go free without our help. But if we stick together, there's no one who can dispute your reports to date. We can just say that from now on she's improved and we don't think she needs sanctuary here, or any more treatment.'

'No, that will take time. I want to get out of here next Friday, the first of July.'

'You're very precise, aren't you? And how do you propose we do that?'

Mags crossed her fingers. Would the promise of the money be enough for them? John she was sure of, but not Michael, as he already had a good income and didn't want to lose it. 'With your help, I can escape. You could let me out of the gates during the night. No one would know.'

'But why Friday?'

Mags felt defeated. John was much too clever for her. 'It . . . well, it just seems a good time. I plucked it out of the air really.'

'Naw, I don't think so. Sommat's happening next Friday. I can feel it. Anyroad, naw decisions now. We have to get on – we're off duty in an hour. I'll sit on it and let you knaw. But in the meantime, Michael, you're to lay off her, all right? If you don't, you'll have me to contend with. I'm still half-thinking of shopping you, you greedy bastard. Then you, Mrs Roford, would probably go free anyroad.'

'Aye, and you'd have nowt, John. If we go along with her, we both come out all right, and with our jobs intact.'

'Like I said, I have to think on it. Go back to the ward

and dress for breakfast, Mrs Roford. I'll let you knaw tonight.'

Mags was relieved to get out of there, as she needed to pee, and they were not the kind of people she was used to dealing with. But part of her was rejoicing, because now something was truly going to happen. Whether it was her original plan, with the help of Iris and those two men, or whether it was an end to the bad reports and her eventual release, she didn't know. She hoped with all her might that it was the first, as she knew Harold; and if one loophole closed to him, he would find another. *Why didn't I listen to my instincts, and to Flors's warnings – Harold is ruthless and relentless in his pursuit of what he wants.*

As she walked around the grounds with Iris the next morning, Mags told her what had occurred. 'Can I trust them, Iris? I felt confident when I was with them, but now I don't know.'

'Eeh, lass, I'm shocked. I didn't want anyone to knaw your plans, but thinking about it, this might be the best way. I'll talk to Michael when he comes on duty tonight. Our shifts cross over, and we all have a cuppa together before I go home and they take over. But I'd say that as they haven't reported the incident you've just told me of, they intend to go through with helping you. I'll find out how they are going to set about it.'

'Iris, I want you to know that even if you're not involved in my actual escape, I will keep my promise to you. I want you to leave here. I want you to have the life you have dreamed of with your family. I couldn't have got through this without you. And I'll rest easy, knowing that you were able to give in your notice rather than be sacked.'

Iris had a tear in her eye as she thanked Mags.

Mags wanted to hold Iris to her, but knew that eyes were always watching them. 'I'll never forget you, lass.'

That night Mags was woken by Michael. He beckoned her to his office. There he told her their plan. On Friday evening she was to get ready for bed as usual. They would come for her and take her to the gate. But the timing was crucial. They would clock the night-watchman for the next two nights. A man of habit, he never digressed from the route he took around the grounds, or how often he patrolled them. They would find out the exact amount of time they had to get her to the gate.

'Everything must be as normal. The plan Iris told us about – that you were to wear her clothes – was ridiculous. If we have a visit from Matron early in the evening, she'll notice. So you prepare for bed, and go to bed in exactly the same way as allus. When we come for you, you go as you are, in your nightshift. We'll not have time to go to the cloakroom to get you a coat and, even if we did have time, we wouldn't, as it would be noted that the coat was missing. And then how do we account for you getting through locked doors, to get the coat? It must look as though you woke up, saw a chance and took it. As it is, we'll get into trouble for the ward door being unlocked, but we're going to report an incident that took our attention and say that we didn't notice you get out.'

Mags just nodded. She didn't care if she left this building stark naked, as long as she escaped. *Please God, let it happen. And please, please, let it succeed and let me get away from here.*

204

PART THREE

London, Blackburn and Portpatrick, 1921

~

Mags, Harold and Montel

Loss Suffered – Love Found

Chapter Nineteen

Mags sat in David's car as he sped away, and her body shivered with cold. The damp night air had bitten through her thin nightshift. Her slippers had soaked up water from the muddy puddles in the grass as they'd sped across to the gate, but her elation made up for all these discomforts.

David squeezed her hand. Mags smiled, keeping her eyes to the front as she dared not, and didn't want to, look back.

'I've left the coat, hat and shoes that Betsy bought for you out of the suitcase, so that you can put them on top of your nightshift. They'll warm you up, and you'll look better going into the hotel in them. I'll stop when I can, but in the meantime reach for that rug on the back seat and wrap it around you.'

Mags spoke for the first time. 'Thank you, David.' The words came out on a sob.

'There now. Let it out, if you must, but it's all over. No matter what happens, I'll never allow you to go back in there.'

Saying 'Thank you' once more was all Mags could manage. She felt fragile. The whole scheme, which had given her so much hope, had felt so fragile. She couldn't believe that she was free. *Free, free. Oh God, thank you.*

After chatting on this and that, David surprised her by mentioning Montel.

'I met that young man, Montel. He and Susan didn't get away with their ploy that I told you about, in one of my notes. Harold didn't fall for the story that Montel was bringing the baby up north because he couldn't cope, and he gave Susan an ultimatum. She gave in. Montel is taking the baby back down to London. He was in despair at having his hopes dashed, about rescuing you and riding off into the sunset with you – well, you know what Frenchmen are like, very over-dramatic. Especially as Montel is an artist. A very interesting and talented young man.'

'An artist? I didn't know that.' Montel's face popped into Mags's head and, unbidden, her heart skipped a beat. Maybe when she came back she would look him up, but for now she wasn't ready. She just wanted to get off these shores and into a hug with Flors.

But David wasn't giving up. He told her about Montel winning a commission to hold an exhibition of his art. 'He's very excited about it. It's to be next year at a small gallery in Chelsea, but he's that enthusiastic you would think he was taking over the Tate gallery. He does have a vast knowledge of the art world, though. He spotted my Henri Matisse print of *Woman with a Hat*. I bought it when I visited France just before the war. It isn't worth anything, as it isn't an original, but Montel knew it immediately and told me a lot about the artist. I really enjoyed his company and think you will like him, under different circumstances. He told me how you two met and what the atmosphere was like, but despite that, he fell for you hook, line and sinker.'

Mags let out a nervous giggle. It all seemed so surreal – herself wrapped in a blanket, speeding away in David's car and talking about a stranger having a fancy for her.

'Montel gave me his address. He said he admired you for standing up to Harold on the day you met, even though he couldn't understand you doing so.'

'I don't understand it myself now. I've been a fool, David. I've lost everything. Well, I mean I'm a long way from being destitute, but the mill that Daddy built up, our family home, a great deal of money – Harold has control of it all. However, none of that matters now. I'm free and that's all I care about, and I know that Daddy would be happy with that, too.'

They drove in silence for a while. The blanket snuggled some warmth into Mags and she could feel herself drifting off to sleep. She didn't resist, as weariness ached her whole body. She dreamed of Montel: his eyes, and how they had connected with hers. She was comfortable in the dream and, as she began to stir, she tried to direct it, wanting to find herself in Montel's arms. Stretching, she asked David what time it was and how far they had travelled.

'It's two in the morning – we've been travelling for two hours. The whole journey is going to take us around eight hours, so I booked our first stopover in Sheffield. We'll be there in ten minutes or so. We can try to get a few hours' sleep, and a good breakfast in the morning. The Old Queen's Head is a pub with a couple of letting rooms. I have stayed there before when travelling to Dover. I like that it has a large bathroom and plenty of hot water. They know we are arriving late and that one of us will need a bath before we retire, so they will stoke up the boiler. Their breakfast is a wonderful affair of bacon and eggs, fried bread and sausage, and toast with lashings of butter. My mouth is watering already.'

'Oh no, don't talk of food. I couldn't touch the soup they served for tea, and now I'm starving.'

'Well, while you bath, I'll get us a plate of sandwiches made up. I always find it difficult to sleep after I have driven a long way. A glass of ale will go down well, too. Though we do need to get some sleep, as I would like to make London tomorrow and that's around a four-hour journey.'

'Hot milk for me, please. I don't think I could take any alcohol just yet. One sip would make me drunk. And perhaps best to have it served in our own rooms, and then we won't keep each other awake.'

As Mags lay luxuriating in what had become a very rare treat – a hot bath – her mind went over and over what was happening. Was she really ready to visit Flors? And to undertake such a long journey? And what about facing the painful memories that would surely be evoked?

All the time she and Flors had spent together was tainted with pain – their time in Belgium, and the horrific rape she'd suffered. Not to mention all that they witnessed: so many young men dying, and their own near-starvation as they became trapped behind enemy lines. And then the terrifying escape to England, and Flors finding out that her lovely husband was her brother! And the death of her child, Alice, and then the death of Harold's mother . . .

A sob escaped from Mags. She tried to close her mind to the final chapter that she would have to relate to Flors, but it all filtered through her – her marriage to the evil Harold, and him having her sectioned and stealing her inheritance.

A tremble rippled through her and she knew she wasn't ready. Even listing the things that she and Flors had been through together filled her with distress. Being with Flors would turn the list into a reality again, after Mags had blocked most of it out for so long. No, she couldn't revisit it. Not in her current fragile state she couldn't. But what was the alternative? London? *Yes, I could book into a hotel – maybe stay on in the one that David has booked for us.*

Thinking this idea through, she decided to take the next couple of weeks, until she had acclimatized herself to the outside world, filling her time doing ordinary things that she enjoyed – walks, theatre visits and yes, perhaps an art gallery, and shopping; yes, she needed to shop – while she mulled over what to do next. She'd already looked through her suitcase and had found that the clothes Betsy had brought for her came from a good shop, and she liked them all. But the calf-length skirts in navy and grey, the pretty satin blouses in pink, blue and cream, and the long, hip-length jacket, also in navy, which were all similar to clothes she already owned, wouldn't be enough for her. Nor would the undergarments, for which she couldn't thank Betsy enough. She knew Betsy would have chosen these matching sets to cheer her and make her feel feminine again. In white satin, the bodices and pantaloons were edged with lace, and she couldn't wait to feel them against her skin, after wearing the rough, shapeless, itchy calico undergarments the hospital provided.

But nice as these clothes were, they were only meant to tide her over. *Yes, I would love to shop. I might even visit Harrods . . . Ooh, how wonderful. And maybe, just maybe, I will look up Montel. I could go to an art gallery with him and he could teach me about all the paintings.* Something deep inside Mags warmed at the thought of this.

With her mind made up by morning, Mags met David in the small snug where the inn served breakfast. What was put in front of her, as soon as she sat down, did indeed look delicious.

'Morning, David. I've come to a decision. I'm not going to France.'

'Oh?'

Between mouthfuls of the delicious cured bacon, Mags told an astonished but pleased David of her new plans, though she didn't mention Montel.

'That's music to my ears, my dear. As it happens, I had made up my own mind to try and persuade you to spend a couple of days or more in London with me and let me take you to a theatre or two. I'm feeling too tired for just one night's sleep when we arrive.'

'I haven't the clothes to go out in, only practical daywear, and I need to shop. So maybe dinner in the hotel, as I do have something suitable for that, and then I can shop tomorrow, and you can take me to the theatre tomorrow evening. And then I need some time on my own. I need to sort out my future. I need thinking time – well, healing time, just doing as I please.'

'Yes, I understand. And I think you are right. Let the dust settle and begin to feel more like yourself. You are already looking better. Pink suits you.'

'Thank you.' Under David's scrutiny, this was all Mags could manage. She hoped with all her heart that he wouldn't speak of his feelings for her, although so far he had seemed keener on talking about Montel's attraction to her, so maybe David was healing, too.

By the time David left London, having insisted that she keep Montel's address in her purse in case she needed someone's help while she was in the city, Mags was feeling so much more relaxed. She'd loved the *League of Notions* musical they had attended together, and particularly the beautiful and glamorous Dolly Sisters who'd starred in the show. But now it was nice to be on her own.

Checking her purse, she found that she still had five pounds left of the money David had drawn out for her. Her accommodation at the hotel was paid for, for two weeks, and David was dropping off a letter to her father's solicitors that authorized them to pay the rest of her funds into a new account, which she had opened while shopping yesterday.

All was going so well, and she was getting stronger by the day. And she knew that she would be ready to make her way to Scotland, once the two weeks were up. Once there, she would book into an inn and see how everything was with the house that she owned. It had stood empty for a while, but should have been kept in good repair, if the instructions she had given her solicitors had been followed, and so it shouldn't take long to get it ready for her to occupy. Whether Betsy and Bill would agree to come up and take care of her – Betsy to be housekeeper and Bill the gardener and handyman – she didn't know; and that she was even thinking of such a job for Bill was down to the news from David, which had been so good to hear. Bill's leg had all but mended, and there was every chance he would be able to walk normally and be free from pain.

These thoughts made her impatient to get on her way, but she had to wait until the solicitors had her funds in place for her.

The hotel stood on the edge of Hyde Park, and today Mags intended to go for a walk around the lovely park gardens. Already she was beginning to feel closed in amongst so many buildings and was missing the green and beautiful, if rugged, views from her house in Blackburn. A sigh left her as she thought this. She brushed the feeling away. There was no going back; she had to go forward.

Outside the air was warm, and the hustle and bustle of the streets excited her. Turning into the park showed her a different world; yes, there were still people, but they were ambling along or riding horses at a slow canter.

As she walked along the path, with beautifully cut grass on each side of her, Mags paused, closed her eyes and took a deep breath. When she opened them, she was startled to see Montel in front of her. Beside him was an old pram, in which sat a lovely child of around eighteen months old. With one look at the child, Mags knew she was Harold's. She felt no pain at this realization, for all feeling for Harold was gone, but she did feel disturbed by being in the presence of Montel. She didn't know if she was ready to be in his company.

If she hadn't known he was French, she would have guessed it by what he wore – an open-necked shirt with a cravat tucked into the collar, and a black flat cap at a jaunty angle on his head.

His expression was that of a naughty boy. 'Forgive me, but David Lange told me thiz iz where you were staying, and I took a chance on you coming out to walk in zee park sometime today. I intended to wait around all day, if I must. This iz Sybil, only I call her Sibbie as she is too young for such a sophisticated name. I am teaching her to appreciate the beauty around her, so today was going to be her first lesson, as I show her the wonders of thiz park, which is an excuse for me to wait and hope that you would come, but now you are here.'

Not knowing what to say, Mags smiled down at the child.

'See, Sibbie iz smiling at you. Already she appreciates the beauty that iz you.'

Mags blushed. She should tell Montel to go away, as he was being very forward, but something in her didn't want to.

'May we walk wiz you?'

'Yes, I would like that.' And she knew she would, for something about Montel excited her and had done the moment she'd first met him, but even more so now that she knew he was attracted to her. But she thought that would be an odd turn-up: herself and Montel, and Harold and Susan – it would be a wife-swap. The thought amused her and she giggled.

'You sound happy, and I'm glad. I have been, how you say, distraught? Yes, I think that iz the word. In France we would say *mon coeur était malheureux* – my heart waz unhappy – at zee plight you found yourself in. Susan, too, she waz very unhappy and asked me to help you.'

'Yes, I know, thank you. David told me. I – I needed time to think. But I'm very grateful to you and Susan. It was generous of her, in the circumstances.'

'I know it iz hard for you to believe, but Susan is a good woman. A nice woman. She iz bitten by love and cannot fight it, sadly, not even for her child.'

'That will be more the blackmailing of Harold, than Susan wanting to leave her child for Harold. He is very manipulative. It is amazing that you have agreed to care for her child.'

'I love her az if she iz my own. And I owe a great debt to Susan.'

Sibbie looked up at Montel. 'Dada.' She held a wooden toy, which she wanted Montel to take.

'No, not Dada – Montel. Oh dear, you will think Harold was telling the truth, but he iz not. Sibbie iz not my child.'

'One look at her tells me that.' Changing the subject, Mags asked about Montel's family. She was wondering why he couldn't go back to France to be with them.

'I only have a distant aunt alive – an aunt of my father's. *Ma mère et mon père* were lost to me when zee Germans ransacked our village.'

'Oh, Montel, I'm so sorry. I know what it feels like not to have any parents alive. I lost mine recently.'

They walked on in silence for a while. Nothing they could say to each other would heal the pain of loss, and each had to come to terms with having spoken of it.

Montel broke the silence. 'Look, it iz that I would like you to know about me, and why I am here in your country. Can I tell you thiz?'

'Of course.'

Mags was shocked as Montel told his story, for she'd heard of French soldiers deserting in huge numbers and thought they were reviled for it, but listening to Montel, she understood why they had done so. Montel, an officer, had taken the action to save the further needless slaughter of his men.

'I'm very sorry. War scarred us all, but it clearly took so much from you. Maybe you could find out if you have been pardoned? The war has been over for three years.'

'It iz possible. I read that many are being pardoned. And my friends promised that if ever they got ze chance, they would tell how it waz that I could not lead them into attack. They were too afraid to speak for me at the time, as they may have been looked upon as deserters themselves, and I can understand that. But let uz not talk of thiz any more. I have a burning desire to get to know all about you.'

His forwardness both embarrassed and amused Mags. And she couldn't deny the effect he was having on her. She felt like a silly teenager falling in love. *Good gracious, I'm not going to let that happen*. But as they walked and talked, she knew that she might not have any choice.

'Shall we sit on that bench, then it iz that I can get Sibbie out of her pram and let her play on the grass. She iz walking, but keeps falling on her bottom, so the impact will be less.'

Again Mags found herself giggling. 'Let me.'

Undoing the reins that kept her secure, she found Sibbie more than willing to have Mags lift her, as she stretched out her hands, smiling up at her. 'I think your lessons are paying off – she is a little charmer.'

'Yes, until she poopz her pantz, then I don't like her much at all.'

Mags found herself full of joy as laughter escaped her once more. Montel was so funny.

Holding Sibbie, she had an urge within her that wanted this child to be hers. She loved children and had dreamed of having many of them. She was surprised that so far nothing had happened, because since their marriage Harold had ceased to take precautions. Sibbie began to pull away from her, no doubt finding the prospect of being on the grass very alluring, as Mags doubted there was much for Sibbie to enjoy around the flat in Brixton, which Harold had told her Montel and Susan shared.

When she sat down next to Montel she felt acutely aware of him. His arm touched hers, and she could smell the just-washed freshness of his shirt. A shyness came over her.

Montel was quiet for a moment, but what he said next tightened the atmosphere between them. 'Did David tell you of how it iz that I feel for you?'

'Yes.' Mags's throat constricted. Her heart thumped in her chest.

'And iz it that you don't mind? I mean, iz there a chance for me?'

'I – I don't know. I've been hurt. I don't trust my feelings.'

'A "don't know" iz not a no. Yes?'

Mags found herself giggling again. 'No, it isn't a no. It is a . . . well, a maybe.'

'Ah, but you have made me zo happy.'

'I – I need time, Montel. I cannot even think of starting a relationship with anyone, not yet.'

'But I understand thiz. And I will wait, but I don't want you to go out of my life. How long will you stay in London?'

'Not long. I'm moving to Scotland.'

'Thiz I know, and it saddens me. Mags, may I hold your hand?'

How could she resist? Her head wanted to say no, but her heart ruled, and she found her hand moving towards his, almost without her bidding. His touch zinged through her. *How is this possible? Am I making another terrible mistake?* The thought made her withdraw her hand.

'Do not be afraid, Mags. It iz that when we are hurt we need a friend, and I can be that to you.'

'And you won't push me to be more – not for a while at least?'

'I promise. And you saying "not now, but maybe" will keep me longing, but careful of your feelingz. I knew my own feelingz the minute I looked into your eyes. Love can happen like this, and it did for me.'

Wanting to change the subject, Mags pointed out that Sibbie had toddled quite a way from them. She got up and went over to her. Once more Sibbie greeted her with a smile, one that showed blades of grass stuck to her mouth. 'You little scamp, have you been eating grass? Are you hungry?' Sibbie's arms came out to her. Lifting her gave Mags that maternal longing once more. Holding Sybil close comforted her. *How can Susan bear to be away from her? What is it about Harold that can tear a mother away from her child? And how can he reject his own daughter in this way?* But then Harold had been taught from a young age to discard people. His mother had done it to Flors, and so it had become the natural way of things to Harold.

There I go again, excusing him, when there is no excuse. Harold is evil. The hurt he has inflicted on me will always be with me. I am one of those he has discarded, but how many more will there be? Thinking this, Mags was glad to no longer feel the hurt. *Maybe it won't always stay with me. Make me cautious, yes, but no longer give me the physical pain it did at first.* As this hope entered her, a question came to her: *Is there happiness out there for me? Maybe a future for me with Montel?*

Something inside her wanted there to be.

Chapter Twenty

Betsy felt happiness dancing through her as she walked her two eldest to school. The air held the familiar smell of factory smoke, which belched from the huge chimneys of the many mills, and the cobbled pavement shone, as the recent shower had dampened the stones.

'Mind you don't slip, me lasses.' The girls giggled as they jumped a puddle. Daisy landed in the edge of it and sent a snake of water into the air, just missing Betsy. It came to her to scold Daisy, but she couldn't dampen the girls' joy. They'd been through a lot and today was one of the few times she'd seen them looking carefree.

Her mind brought her a memory, and pleasure warmed her body and made her catch her breath. She had her own reasons to feel lifted and carefree. *Eeh, me lovely Bill, he made me soar to a place I'd almost forgotten, with his lovemaking.* The recollection got her drawing in her breath, but as she did so, the feeling inside her changed. Letting go of Rosie's hand, she had to stop for a moment. Swallowing hard didn't help, and she only just managed to bend over the edge of the pavement before vile-tasting bile retched from her.

'Ma? Ma!'

Although her throat stung, Betsy managed to soothe Florrie, Daisy and Rosie. 'Eeh, I'm all right, me lasses, I must have eaten sommat as didn't agree with me.'

Oh God, naw. Naw. When did I have me last monthly? I've been that taken with what has been happening – the court case, the eviction, losing me ma, and Mags's plight – that I've given it naw attention. Her mind began to calculate, and her heart sank as she realized she'd last seen her bleeding before she lay with Roford. *Naw, naw – don't put this on me, don't!*

But as she cried against it, Betsy knew it was upon her, and knew too this wasn't something she could deal with. And what about Bill? He'd know. These last couple of nights were the first time in a while that he'd made love to her. The first night was a bit of a disaster, as it finished before it had hardly begun, and he was full of apologies. She'd held him and calmed him, telling him that what had happened had been lovely. But then last night Bill had been in control, and she'd felt as if she'd been transported to heaven as he took her not once, but twice. And he'd given her feelings better by far than those Roford had aroused in her.

Even the thought of that evil bastard repulsed her now. Remembering how she'd wanted Roford to touch her made a shudder of self-disgust ripple through Betsy. *I've paid, haven't I? Me one lapse, and I paid a heavy price for it. Don't make me pay again, dear God, naw!*

Tears threatened. They stung her eyes and weakened her, but somehow she had to cope. Getting to the school gates, Betsy took a deep breath as flutters began to turn her stomach once more. If she could drop the young 'uns off and get away quickly, she'd be out of sight before the sickness floated over her again. As the building came into sight, something caught her attention. Mrs Barker, the head teacher, was standing just outside. That wasn't something she did as a rule. For some reason, Betsy knew she was there to speak to her.

'Ah, Mrs Bainwright. May I have a word?'

'Aye, I've got a minute.' As she said this, Betsy willed her stomach to stop threatening to erupt again. 'Go on in, our Daisy, and take Florrie with you.'

'No. I'm sorry, but the children cannot go into school. Not today – not ever. Look, I wish it was different, but I received a notice from Mr Roford that anyone who was no longer working in any capacity for him, or for any of his mills, had to have their children removed from the school with immediate effect. He actually mentioned you and your children. I'm so sorry, Mrs Bainwright, but I know they will be accepted into the church school.'

'Eeh, but that's a long way for them to walk every day. By, he's a spiteful . . . Oh, I mean . . . well, it's of no matter. I'll be on me way. Daisy, Florrie, come along. You've the day off school, me lasses.'

Betsy couldn't stop to say her goodbyes, or the thank you she knew was due to this kindly lady. Her stomach was about to betray her, and she had to get out of sight before she was sick again.

Only just making it around the corner, she threw her heart up into the gutter once more. This time the tears flowed unheeded, as between retching she sobbed. Leaning against the wall of the corner house once the bout had passed, she felt a sense of wretchedness settle in her.

'Eeh, lass, it didn't take your Bill long, once he were mended, did it? I reckon as he's after that son he allus wanted. Come on, let's help you home.'

222

'Ta, Wendy. Did you see what happened?'

'Aye, I did. There's naw getting away with crossing them as have money and influence . . . Aw, Betsy, you don't think – I mean . . . what he did to you, he's not put your belly up, has he?'

Betsy could only sob into the hanky she'd taken from her pocket. Wendy lived in the same street as her, and Betsy had known her all her life. Wendy was known as one for a bit of gossip. They'd been to the same school as lasses, but had grown apart, as Betsy had been considered to have risen in the world, with her being a friend of Mags and working in the office of the mill instead of on the factory floor. *Ha, the old 'uns used to say as no good would come from trying to get above me station, and they were right an' all.*

'I knaw as it's asking sommat of you, Wendy, but keep this and your speculation to yourself, will you? It's going to break my Bill, and he least deserves that. Besides, what you said first time could be right, as he were at me the moment his leg were done.'

She hated talking in this way of the love that she and Bill shared, but it was what Wendy would understand. Most women took what their men did to them as a penance to be put up with. Betsy had never understood this attitude.

'Well, in that case, you could get lucky, lass. Naw, I'll not say owt. And, Betsy, it's nice to have you back in the street and one of us again.'

'I've allus been one of you. I didn't change – it was how you saw me that changed. Anyroad we're to get on home. I've me young 'uns to sort out. Happen Bill will go along to the church school and book them in for tomorrow.'

'It's grand to see him walking like a man again, lass. Your connections helped him all right, but what happened to young Miss Margaret were a crying shame. Fancy her ending up as a mental case, who'd have thought it, eh? And there's rumours an' all that he ain't going short. You knaw that young nurse—'

'Eeh, Wendy, I've to go, lass. I can't be gossiping.'

'I could tell you as we walk along; it'll make your hair curl, Betsy. But then maybe not, as you've had a taste of what he's capable of.'

Betsy wanted to scream, but part of her was grateful that the womenfolk believed her story of the rape. She doubted their menfolk did, but that didn't matter. To have the women against her would have made life even harder to bear.

Glad to reach home, she didn't dawdle at the gate. Wendy's tongue was still wagging ten to the dozen, with her much-embellished tale of the goings-on at Feniscowles Manor.

Betsy opened her gate and told Wendy, 'I'll see you around, lass. I've to get in and get to the lav.'

'All right, Betsy. Eeh, the sickness has taken you badly – could mean a boy that; when I . . .'

Betsy left Wendy mid-sentence and dashed inside. Struggling to get Rosie up the three steps to the house, she was met by Bill. His welcoming smile turned to a question as he realized she still had Florrie and Daisy with her.

'What's to do, lass?' Then his expression turned to astonishment as she pushed by him. She couldn't explain anything, as she had to reach the lav in the back yard.

Once the bout had passed, Betsy leaned against the wall. *What now? Dear God, what now?* Holding her breath until she got outside, she closed the lav door behind her.

The lav wasn't a place to linger, as the stench of it was

too strong. Shared with their neighbour, it was ready for emptying by the bog-men – as the men who came each week with a truck and emptied the lavs were known. She'd never been able to understand how Ivor from next door could take his paper and fags in there and occupy it for half an hour or so. Though she supposed it was a better alternative to his Gertrude nagging him.

Bill was angry when she went back inside. 'That rotten sod, taking it out on the young 'uns now. I tell you, Betsy, leaving here and going with Mags is looking more tempting every day.'

Betsy had never thought to hear Bill say that. He'd been against them going to Scotland. She'd thought she would have to work him round to it.

'Eeh, lass, what's to do? You look awful. I knaw as this is a setback, especially for our Daisy and Florrie, but it don't warrant getting that upset about. We'll go with Mags and make a new start, eh? Come on, let me give you a cuddle. And you dry them tears. The young 'uns need us to be strong, as they've had a lot to contend with.'

Going into his arms gave Betsy some comfort, but fear clenched her and spoilt the feeling. 'I've to talk to you, Bill, and you ain't going to like what I have to say. Daisy, get yours and Florrie's pinnies down and put them on. You can go into the yard and play; you may as well enjoy the sunshine, seeing as you're not in school. You can take Granny's old baking tins and make some mud pies, eh?'

Betsy bent down and delved into the one kitchen cupboard of her ma's that she hadn't yet cleared out. Memories of when she was a little lass came to her, and she longed for the carefree life she'd had then. *Oh, aye, we had it hard, me and our Ciss, but we were happy, and well fed, as Ma were a cook to be reckoned with.* As the tears threatened again, she brushed the memories from her.

'There you go. You can keep them with the bits and bobs you play with in the garden. You'll have hours of fun with them, and Granny'll be smiling down on you.'

Once the girls were outside and Rosie wasn't paying them any attention, Betsy sighed. Bill had a worried look on his face that she knew she would only make worse.

'What is it, lass, what's troubling you now, eh? I thought we'd got through the worst and were looking towards a brighter future, or so you convinced me.'

'There ain't naw way I can make telling any easier for you, Bill . . . I – I've got me belly up.'

'What? Eeh, lass, that's good. But . . . wait a minute . . . Oh God, it ain't mine – it's not possible . . . Naw, naw, not that; not that.' Bill backed into what used to be her ma's chair. The back kitchen was overcrowded with furniture, now they'd moved some of their bits and pieces into it. They'd thrown some of ma's furniture out, but kept her lovely dresser and the fireside chair that she'd loved.

'I can't take it, Betsy. I'll allus be reminded of what keeps me awake at nights already – the thought of him inside you. I can't take it, I can't.'

'Are you going to abandon me then, Bill, for sommat as ain't me own fault?' Guilt assailed Betsy as she said this. Her betrayal of her lovely Bill burned her heart with shame. But that was something she had to live with. 'Bill, don't reject me. You've stood by me this good while, through worse than me having a babby. No one'll knaw. That Wendy up the road caught me being sick and made her mind up as to the cause, but I told her that you'd had me the moment you'd come out of hospital, and she believed me.' *Lass hadn't*

226

the knowledge of how Bill ain't been able to take me for a long time; hindered by pain, he'd seemed to have lost the ability even to be ready to make love to me, so it's taken a while since his operation to get that back. Naw, there's naw doubt whose child this is.

'Well, that's sommat, but tongues have a way of wagging till they start speculating.'

'We'll be gone from here afore I even show. You knaw as Doctor said that Mags didn't go to France, but is staying a couple of weeks in London and then going to Scotland. He said she'd be sending for us just as soon as she sees how the land lies with her house.'

'It ain't just others knawing.' With this, Bill lowered his head into his hands.

'Bill, Bill, don't – we can get through this. We have to.'

'But how am I to take to a babby that were planted in me wife by another man, eh?'

'It ain't babby's fault. You've to remember that. Poor little mite has nowt to do with what'll pain us both for the rest of our lives.'

'Betsy, tell me. Look me in the eyes and tell me you didn't want it . . . Betsy? Betsy, lass . . .'

Betsy was out of the door and running down the path. Bill's accusing eyes haunted her. She'd known; oh aye, she'd known what had been eating away at him. It were the age-old given in all men that there was no such thing as rape. But it wasn't just that Betsy was running from. She was running from the truth. The truth that haunted her every waking hour and most of her dreams.

The brakes screeching beside her shocked her. Turning and seeing Roford getting out of his car froze Betsy to the spot. 'What's got you running, slut? Your rotten conscience,

I shouldn't wonder. Well, I need to talk to you. Get into my car, and quick.'

'Naw. I'm going nowhere with you.' Though she must look defiant, Betsy was dying inside. Why was he here . . . *Oh God! Mags! He'll think as I knaw sommat.*

'I'm not going with you, and if you touch me I'll scream the place down. There's curtains twitching already, thou knaws.'

This stopped Roford in his tracks. 'Well, we'll talk here then.'

'Keep your distance – don't come near me.'

'You're a bitch. A liar and a bitch. If I had ten minutes in a room with you, I'd make you sorry. I'd rape you all right. I'd have you begging for mercy.' For a minute his eyes clouded over, and lust shone from them. It was still there as he growled out, 'But that's not going to happen, though I know you want it to. Now tell me what you know about Mags's disappearance. I know you're involved in some way, so don't deny it.'

'Mags? Disappeared? Naw, she's in that asylum you put her in, ain't she?'

'Don't play the innocent with me. She had to have help from outside. I'm warning you: if you don't tell me, something bad will happen. Worse than I've done so far – chucking you out of your cottage and banning your brats from my school. That's nothing to what I'm planning.' It was there again – that look that told her he wanted her. But what Roford said next shocked Betsy rigid. 'How would you like your brats to go missing, eh?'

'What? You can't do that! You can't. Naw . . . naw.'

'Think about it. But while you are thinking, keep watching your back and theirs. And I'm telling you, I will find that useless wife of mine. I have my ways, so you'll lose your brats for nothing.'

With this, he turned from her and got back into his car. Betsy stared after him, before collapsing onto the wall of the house that she stood outside.

'What's to do, lass? Are you all right? That were the Roford bloke, weren't it? What does he want with you? He looked threatening. I'd go to the police, if I were you.'

'Oh, Mrs Church, he – he said he'd . . . Oh God, I've got to get home. Me family ain't safe.'

'Eeh, lass. I heard about your troubles. Your ma must be turning in her grave. A God-fearing woman she was – she'd have never known the like of what went on. But why are you scared now, lass? It's over, ain't it?'

'Naw. His poor wife. She's gone missing from that asylum he put her in, and he's blaming me. He threatened all sorts. I've to go, Mrs Church, as no one knaws more than me what an evil man he is. He's capable of doing what he says.'

'Aw, not Miss Margaret? Eeh, what befell the lass, eh? Such a lovely, kind girl and a heroine an' all. How did she come to be mixed up with the likes of him? It's no wonder that she went mad, and now she might be wandering around somewhere, lost and alone, it's a crying shame.'

Betsy went to defend Mags's sanity, but thought better of it. 'I've to go. I – I were running to the church school, to book me young 'uns in, as Roford's kicked them out of the mill's welfare school. I don't want to leave Bill with the kids too long. I'll see you later, lass.'

The woman seemed satisfied with this explanation, though it must have looked as if Roford had been chasing Betsy. More rumours would circulate – damaging rumours that might one day turn the belief they had in her into knowing nods. *Oh, Mags, please hurry and take us all out of this hell on earth. Please.*

Bill was full of remorse when she reached home. 'Eeh, lass, I'm sorry. I hadn't thought that way. It just came to me, with you saying you had a babby in you. I – I, well, I thought . . . you'd got him off you afore that happened. Now I knaw as you didn't, I'm tortured all over again.'

'Well, I hope it's by the thought of what I went through, and not the thought that I could have stopped him. You saw the bruising.'

As she said this, Betsy flushed. Aye, she'd been bruised in places where she'd thought to harm herself, but her inner thighs had not been bruised. 'Look, never mind all this now. You've to wrestle with it yourself. I can't make you believe me. But sommat else has happened, and I'm scared.'

Bill's reaction to Betsy telling him what had happened was a mixture of fear and anger. He wanted to go after Roford and warn him off, but knew he wasn't strong enough for any such confrontation. His years of being crippled with pain had taken their toll on his body. His appetite had left him, and he'd turned to skin and bones.

'We've to take care, as that man will do sommat to the young 'uns – I knaw him. And going to the police will only make Roford angrier.'

'How did it come to this? How can one man bring such devastation down on us all?'

They sat in despair. The awful realization of her having a babby by that monster paled into nothing, compared with the fear for their young 'uns. And even though she knew they were safe in the small walled and gated patch of garden behind her ma's house, Betsy went to the window to look out at them. Daisy and Florrie were playing happily, and Rosie was asleep on the sofa behind her. Betsy's heart filled with love for them. Her hand went to her belly, and aye, though she knew this little one would bring trouble to their door, she knew she loved it already.

Her body shook with repulsion at how the little mite got inside her, but her heart ached to protect her loved ones. Once more she pleaded with God to forgive her for what she'd done.

Chapter Twenty-One

Susan froze. Harold had come back to the house earlier than she expected. His face was like thunder, and his whole countenance spoke of his seething anger. When he was in this mood, no one was safe. Most likely something hadn't gone the way he'd wanted it to. And judging by the state of him, it was something big.

Staying where she was, unable to run to him as he liked her to, she waited. Harold's bark at Barnard confirmed her suspicion. Her mind raced, but nothing occurred as to why he was in this mood.

The door to the withdrawing room opened, then slammed shut behind him.

'She's gone!'

'What? Who?'

'Mags! And possibly three bloody days ago, and Matron has only just found out! She said they hadn't realized, until one of the other patients went into the office asking for her. Crying, saying that she hadn't seen Mags for days. Then when they made enquiries, they found that it could have been up to three days earlier, when Mags disappeared. One of the night staff and one of the day staff usually involved in her case had been off sick, and were saying they had a bug of some sort. The management contacted them and they confirmed that Mags was there when they were last on duty. The cleaning and catering staff said they hadn't seen her and thought it was three days since they had, but Matron told me they wouldn't think anything was amiss, as it happens all the time. They aren't informed which patients have been discharged or moved to a more secure unit. All excuses, if you ask me. An escape has never happened before, so they thought it never bloody could.'

'Probably because the patients are all mentally ill and unable to think up plans to escape. Mags isn't; she was just very distressed over what she believed you had done. She shouldn't have been put in there, Harold.'

'That's none of your business. Don't get above your station. I can soon dispose of you – send you back to that impotent Frenchman.'

'Ah, impotent, is he? Well, how come I have a daughter then who is supposed to be nothing to do with you?'

'What? Oh, shut up. Don't start to grind that old stone, it's getting on my nerves. I have more important things to think about.'

'More important? More important than your own daughter?'

'Christ, if you don't shut up, *I'll* shut you up.'

'One of these days you'll have to, as I know a lot about you, Harold.' Now that she had started, Susan couldn't stop. This wasn't about Mags any more, as Mags was free. But she wasn't. She was still shackled, and without her baby. 'And no, I won't shut up. You use emotional blackmail to keep me here. Well, I'll use real blackmail to get our daughter

233

here under your roof. I'll tell all I know, if you don't agree to let me have Sybil here. And I tell you, I know far more than you think.'

'Have you gone mad? I come home, looking to find comfort and help from you, as my bloody wife is roaming free out there – where she could do untold harm by seeking a divorce and splitting the fortune I have down the middle – and you go on about your stupid bastard daughter!'

'How dare you. How dare you! My daughter is *our* daughter. Why can't you get that into your thick skull? And if she is stupid, it's because she takes after you! YOU PIGHEADED BASTARD!'

For the first time since all of this exploded inside her, Susan felt afraid of what was happening. Harold was in front of her before she even realized he'd moved. Her head stung as he grabbed her hair, twisted it round his hand and brought her to her knees. Excruciating pain racked her head, as chunks of her hair were yanked from her skull.

Through tears that stung, Susan saw Harold's knee rise, but could do nothing to stop it smashing into her face. Her nose cracked. Dazed and sobbing, she felt the blows and kicks to her body as his spittle sprayed over her.

'I'll kill you! You slut. You've hounded me for years. You've ruined everything for me. You've been like a leech clinging to me and sucking me dry.'

'Stop, stop, please stop, Harold. I – I'm sorry. I love you. I'm sorry.'

But her words went unheeded until, like a bloodied ragdoll, she fell into blackness.

When Susan came to she was in the bath. Harold was bathing her, his sobs loud, his eyes bloodshot and his face wet with tears. 'Forgive me. My lovely Susan, forgive me. How could I do this to you? It's *her* fault – that swine of a wife of mine. She's done this. She's driven a wedge between us.'

Through lips that felt as though someone had stuck a huge wobbly jelly to them, Susan managed to utter, 'No.'

'Oh, my Susan, don't say that. Margaret is to blame. None of this would have happened if she hadn't been such a cold fish, and hadn't brought in that seductress to be our housekeeper.'

It was beyond Susan how Harold could think like this. She'd always known he was selfish and needed to be pandered to, but this was a long way past that. This was the way a madman would think. It dawned on her then that perhaps Harold *was* mad. Maybe that was what made him like he was.

'Margaret deceived me, you know. Yes, that dirty bitch had been with somebody else before me. She said he'd raped her, but I wonder about that. She's a woman who wants it. A taker. She lies there and is in ecstasy when she has a man inside her, but she gives nothing back. She just lets it happen. I think she wanted that German who was supposed to have raped her. And I thought I was getting fresh meat – a virgin. She didn't even pretend. I hate her. I hate her guts.'

Through all this Harold cried like a baby. He reminded Susan of a child who was in trouble, looking for someone to blame. She thought that if he had been standing, he would be stamping his feet.

'She has to die.'

'No, Harold, not that. I don't think she will come back here. Why should she? Her father's gone, all her money has gone, she—'

'That's it – money! I couldn't fathom how, but she must

have money that I don't know about. The bitch! That's breaking the law, as everything she has is mine. She can't have money unless I give it to her, and I did make her a generous allowance. However, I have been able to get that back from the account I set up for her.'

His tears had dried. Harold wiped his face with the flannel he'd been bathing Susan with and reached for the towel. Standing, he paced the room.

'That bitch has somehow got some money that I didn't know of. She must have. She must have paid someone to get her out of Brockhall. It's the only way. But what was that bloody orderly Michael doing? I'm paying him to make sure she is kept in there. He must have been one of the nurses off sick. Christ! He should have let me know.'

Harold was quiet for a moment. Susan began to shiver, not only as a reaction to the beating and the smarting of her wet wounds, but because the water was beginning to turn cold. She hadn't the strength to get out of the bath.

'Someone on the outside helped her – they must have done. I tackled that bloody Bainwright woman on the way here, but she acted as if she didn't even know Mags was free. If not her, then who?'

Susan's body trembled uncontrollably now. But Harold couldn't come round to thinking she might have something to do with it, could he? If he did, she'd be dead – she knew that for certain. Harold had hit her before, but never like today. Today he had crossed a boundary. Oh yes, he was sorry, but that was only until the next time, she was certain of it.

'Think, Susan. Who could have helped Mags? It had to be someone who could get money for her . . . She has wealthy friends, but how would she contact them? Wait a minute. Michael told me that she had a visitor. Now what did he say his name was?'

Harold paced up and down. Susan's body ached, and the shivering was more intense now. 'Harold, please help me out, the water's getting cold.'

He turned and looked at her as if he hadn't known she was there. He stared at her for what seemed like a long minute.

'Harold? Harold, I need to get out of this water.' His strange expression was giving her the creeps. 'HAROLD!'

He jumped. Then, as if nothing had happened, he said, 'My poor darling, you're hurt. Let me help you.' Taking her hand, he tugged at her.

'I need more help than that, Harold. You need to lift me out, as you lifted me in.'

His sleeves were still rolled up, and his shirt was soaked from washing her. Unbuttoning it, he discarded his shirt and tossed it on the floor. She looked at his firm naked chest and felt nothing. He scooped her up, taking her to the bed and laying her down, and it was then that his tears flowed once more, as he looked at her.

As she went to pull the quilt around her, he stopped her. His eyes had glazed over. She knew that look, and repulsion flooded through her. But she didn't object, as she felt too afraid to. She had long learned to be compliant to his needs.

'I want to make you better, my darling. I want to love you better. I want you to love me again.'

It was agony to take his weight, and she felt nothing when he entered her – nothing except a searing pain from the many bruises covering her, and from where her skin had split under the force of his blows. Harold was like a man possessed. On and on he pounded her, taking no heed of her cries to stop.

At last he was spent, and yet he hadn't reached his climax. He slumped off her, sobbing even more than he had before. 'Why couldn't I do it? Why couldn't I finish?' Then his voice changed and became ugly. 'It was your fault! You just lay there like *she* does. Why? Why?'

'Look at me, Harold. Really look at me. My nose feels as though it is smashed, my lips feel swollen to twice their size, and my body is bruised and broken. How can you expect me to respond to you when you have done this to me?'

'Shut up! You have to take responsibility. You goaded me. You wouldn't shut up, and I warned you. Well, I'm warning you again. SHUT UP!'

A whimper escaped her. 'Help me, Harold. Please help me. I'm cold and I cannot move.'

'I have to go out.'

With this, he folded the bed quilt over her and went into the bathroom. When he came out, Susan tried once again to reason with him, asking for a glass of water, but he ignored her and left.

After a few moments, she heard his car on the gravel. Rolling over, she managed with an extreme effort to reach the bell. A maid whose name Susan didn't know came into the room.

'I need help. Please fetch me a glass of water and bring bandages and lint.'

As the maid attended to her, she made no comment. How was it that other women and men could hear a woman being beaten and do nothing? Surely Barnard and the maids had heard what went on? One of them must have prepared the bath for her, and they must have seen her being carried up the stairs, unconscious, battered and bleeding. But then it was considered a man's right to keep his missus in check. Let alone his mistress, for whom none of them had any respect.

The pain in Susan's chest was unbearable, and breathing was becoming more difficult. She suspected that she had a broken rib and felt afraid it would pierce her lung. 'I need you to go for Dr Lange.'

'We are none of us allowed to use Dr Lange – he's not the doctor of the welfare facility no more, Miss.'

'I know, but I want him, and I will pay independently. Please have him sent for.'

It was an hour before Dr Lange arrived. When he saw the state Susan was in, he was appalled that the message had said there was no hurry.

Dismissing the maid, Susan spoke openly to the doctor. 'That's because they don't like me here – they don't care if I die. None of them came to my aid, when they must have heard how badly Harold was beating me. But no matter. I have something to tell you. Harold is out at this moment, trying to find out exactly how Mags managed to escape. He is incensed that she got away, and is looking for those who may have helped her. He has deduced that she had to have money, and to get that she needed help from someone who was rich enough to give it to her, or she has hidden funds. If she does have hidden funds, then he says she won't have them for long, as he has power of attorney over her. He knows she had a visitor at the institute, and he admitted he has a man inside the asylum that he pays. I am afraid for Mags.'

'Can you contact Montel? I will try to contact Mags, but I cannot get home for at least an hour.' The whole time they were talking, the doctor had been administering to her.

'Yes, if Montel is at home.'

'Right, tell him to warn Mags as soon as he can.'

Susan expressed her surprise at this, as Montel had told her that Mags was going to France, but she was glad when she heard of the new arrangements.

'I'm sorry, but I have to go. I must get my rounds done as quickly as possible. Now, you do have a cracked rib. I have bound you up and you must rest. Do not get out of bed for a few days, no matter what transpires. I don't think I will be able to come and see you again – not when Harold finds out that I have been here. However, I will make sure that Harold's doctor knows that you need care. Is there no one here you can trust to bring me a message, if you find out anything of importance?'

'No. No one.'

'Very well. I hope you mend quickly.'

Not a word of condemnation about Harold's actions towards her had passed the doctor's lips. It was a bitter pill to swallow that these northerners seemed to think it acceptable that Harold should treat a woman in this way. But then maybe it was just her; because of her situation, they just didn't care about her.

As Susan lay back, drowsy now from the draught of medication the doctor had given her, she felt a sudden urge to escape. And she wished with all her heart that Mags would be able to carry out any plans she had, and that Harold wouldn't be able to foil her in any way.

Chapter Twenty-Two

Mags was surprised when a bellboy knocked on her door and handed her a note. He waited while she read it. *Montel is here and wishes to see me?* How strange; he'd only left her a couple of hours ago, saying that he would see her tomorrow.

It was five days now since she'd arrived in London, and it seemed as though nothing could mar her joy. The last two days had been spent with Montel and Sibbie, and she knew she was falling in love with them both.

Montel was shown into her sitting room, and the tea she'd ordered followed soon afterwards. Once it was served, the waiter told her he would be just outside the door, should she need him. She smiled at this and knew he was discreetly chaperoning her.

As soon as they were alone, Montel told her what had happened to Susan.

'That's terrible. Poor Susan. But why is David worried about me? Harold was bound to surmise these things. Logically, they had to happen for me to escape, but he can do nothing about any of them. He doesn't know I am here;

241

he doesn't know that I have money; nor does he know who has helped me.'

They were interrupted by a telephone call coming through for Mags. 'David! Montel is here and has explained. How is Susan? And why you are so worried about me?'

Mags listened while the doctor told her that Susan would be all right; and then as he explained that the solicitors had told him it would take up to a fortnight to make the funds available to her. 'The money for the orderlies and Iris was paid without any problem, but they were small sums. To have all your funds transferred is a different matter. They told me that a lot of it was invested for you, on the instructions of your father, and that a broker is working to secure sufficient sales to get you the amount you need.'

'That all sounds fine to me. I should be all right if they can advance five pounds to me for my travel, and for a hotel when I arrive in Scotland.'

'That shouldn't be a problem and, if it is, I can do that for you on a loan basis. But what is a problem is if Harold finds out that you have assets. Susan told me that he not only has a husband's rights over your money and property, but he still has power of attorney over you. I don't think we can do anything about that, as your escape doesn't give you the same status as if you were discharged. No one has declared you sound of mind. Therefore if Harold discovers that you have money and property, he can legally take everything.'

'Oh no! I will telephone Daddy's solicitors. I know they won't divulge anything and will continue with my plan; they know that money was to safeguard me, should anything such as this happen.'

'But, my dear, the solicitor cannot work outside the law. He will be struck off. Harold would see to that.'

Mags's mind went into panic mode. All sorts of scenarios played out in her head. She was worried about Betsy's safety, as David had already told her about the threat to Betsy. And then there was the orderly, Michael. Would he tell all, under pressure from Harold? If so, would Iris be safe?

'Oh, David, I am so worried now. What can I do? Where will I live, if Harold takes my house in Portpatrick, too? And what will I live on?'

'Does Harold know who your father's solicitors were?'

'No, I don't think so. They didn't do anything at all concerning the business. There is a separate firm of solicitors for that purpose. These solicitors were kept for private family matters. But no, that's silly – Harold must know. All Daddy's papers are in the house, in his desk, and if there was a Will-reading, his solicitors would have been the ones to do that. But will they have to disclose everything? Daddy promised me that he didn't keep anything to do with my estate in the house, and neither did I; all of it was kept with the solicitors.'

'Try not to worry, Mags. I'll do all I can tomorrow. I was going to go fishing, but this clandestine work is much more exciting – if concerning. I will go to Dr Jenkins with our full story. I'll see if I can persuade him to discharge you properly, as being sound in mind. I've gained his confidence, and he is a little intimidated by me, and how I know of his lack of care of the other patients in the asylum. When he is faced with the facts – and we have witnesses now to Michael being paid to falsify your reports – we might just win the day. Keep strong. We will come through this. Or if we don't, it won't be for lack of trying.'

When they said their goodbyes, Mags did feel worried, very worried. She knew Harold's capabilities, although she had never thought he would use such violence on a woman.

It incensed her to think that nothing would be done about his attack on Susan.

She looked over to where Montel sat, with Sibbie on his knee. The child was fast asleep.

'Mags, pleaze, you must not look so worried. It iz that I only heard half of that conversation, but you will always have somewhere to live. You can move in wiz me. There iz Susan's room. I will sleep on the sofa, az I always did when Susan waz home. I haven't much, but I do earn a little from my work. I paint many portraits of zee wives, and sometimes zee girlfriends, of those who have zee money to pay. But sometimes I sell some of my own paintings. I get by. There is a community of us artists, and we help each other; if it iz that one has nothing, then zee others chip in and help.'

'Oh, Montel. I don't know what to say.' Mags's anguish weakened her legs. She sat down on the only other chair in the room.

'You don't have to say anyzing. Just know that zee offer iz there for you.'

'Thank you. It is possible that Harold could take everything, and I will need somewhere to live. But what if Susan wants to come home, after what has happened?'

'We will sort that out, if it arizez. We won't worry about it now. You see, you have nozing to worry about. I am here. Montel to the rescue.'

Mags couldn't help but laugh, even though she really was deeply concerned over all that had been revealed to her – Harold, applying for and being granted power of attorney over her! He never ceased to amaze her. She knew, when marrying him, that she was in for a tough future, but she never dreamed that within weeks it would all fall apart, and in such circumstances. And what of Betsy? *Oh, dear God, I promised to take her away from where Harold can do her harm. Now it is looking unlikely that I will be able to.*

'Mags, I need to hold you. You look so frightened and fragile. Everything iz crowding in your mind. I zink you are panicking. Please will you take zee baby and free me, so that I can help you.'

'No, Montel. I cannot let you. I have to keep to what I said – I'm not ready. I want a friend, a good reliable friend. Can you be that to me, for now? Then, if anything happens in the future, we can . . . well, we can see how it all goes.'

'I zink you are in denial. I zink it iz that you do have feelingz for me and they make you afraid. Pleaze don't be. I would never hurt you.'

Somehow Mags knew this for certain. In Montel, she had found someone who would truly love her for herself. But although she knew she had strong feelings for him, she was afraid. It had been such a short time since she was betrayed by someone she'd thought to be her true love.

'Do not add to all zee thingz you have to worry over, my Mags. I will not mention again my feelingz for you. Not until you come to me ready to accept my love and give me yourz. I just want you to know that it iz that I love you, and I will be here for you to catch you if you fall, and to rejoice with you when you are happy. Alwayz – and for everyzing – I will be by your side.'

'Oh, Montel. That is a beautiful thing to say. You are a very special person and you do have a place in my heart. But—'

'I know what thiz "but" iz. And I will respect it.'

They held each other's gaze for a long moment. Mags

felt peace enter her. No matter what happened in the future, she had one certainty: Montel would truly always be by her side, and she wanted it to be so.

When David rang her the next evening, he sounded much more hopeful. 'Dr Jenkins is considering your case. He was appalled to hear of the behaviour of his staff, and I felt guilty at only telling him now, but I have been so relieved that you were free that I let it go out of my mind, not thinking of those still confined there. However, their lot should improve now, as I threatened him with exposure to the General Medical Council. As a result, he said that he would willingly examine you again and, if he felt you are of sound mind, he will certify you as such.'

Mags felt elated, but her spirits were shot down by David's next words.

'He stipulated, though, that you must return to Brockhall. There he will examine your mental health before discharging you. It seems that in this he wants to follow the correct procedure.'

'No! David, I can't. Once in there, I will be in the clutches of Harold again and at the mercy of Michael, especially if he has since received threats from Harold.'

'I will speak with Matron. I am sure that once she knows what transpired under her very nose, she will protect you. You will only have to stay in there for a couple of days while the assessment takes place.'

'You don't know what you are asking of me, David. I am shaking at the very thought of that place. I cannot return there. Please, please find another way. Surely there will be reprisals on John and Michael – and maybe even Iris, though in the end she wasn't involved in my escape. If John and

Michael are not sacked, they will be out for revenge, as I have betrayed them.'

'There is no alternative, Margaret. Your solicitor told me he will be legally bound to disclose your assets to your husband, now that Harold has power of attorney over you; and you can only have that power removed from him, and returned to you, if you are judged to be sound of mind. Not even divorcing him would give you your rights back. Though it is a different matter if you gained those rights back and did divorce him, as then they could take up your case for a settlement. And that would be very much in your favour, as your father did provide for you and you can prove your contribution to the making of the family fortune. We spoke as friends, not with the solicitor speaking in his official capacity. I have known Derek for many years. And as far as him being your solicitor, he will act as though he knows nothing, as yet, of your power of attorney being in Harold's hands, and will continue to do whatever he can for you. And thereby lies some good news, because there are around four hundred pounds of ready cash in the solicitor's holding account in your name, and he is transferring that immediately. It will be in your account in about five days. It can't be touched by Harold while in transit, so it is safe.'

'Oh, David, that is good news. I will take my chances with that.'

'Oh, I wish you wouldn't, but I do understand. And about Iris: didn't you say she had given her notice in?'

'She was going to the moment I was free, yes.'

'Well then, I will contact her and make sure that she has. I didn't mention her and, as she didn't take part in your escape in the end, it is her word against Michael's and John's that she even knew about any plans. Not that it will matter.

No criminal offence has been committed, just an internal one; and if Iris has already left the trust's employment, then they cannot do anything to her.'

Mags stood for a long moment staring at the telephone, analysing what her options were. Four hundred pounds wasn't a lot in the world she was used to living in, but she could live well within that, and for quite some time, as her experience in Belgium had shown her. She thought for a moment about her own workers at the mill, earning an average of one hundred and fifty pounds a year – and they kept their families on that. *Well, I can do the same. And I can surely secure a position in an accounts office, with the experience that I have.*

Feeling much brighter about her future, though still unsure whether to risk going to Scotland, Mags ordered dinner, noting the cost of room service for the first time. Tomorrow, and for the few remaining days she had here, she would go out and find a cheaper place to eat. *There'll be no more Ritz for you, Mags Roford! And, thinking about it, no more Mrs Roford. Once I leave here, I will change my name.* Then she giggled at the preposterous voice inside her that said: *Maybe, one day, to Mags Charvet?*

Betsy held the letter from Mags for a long time without speaking.

'Tell me, lass, what does she say, eh?'

Bill's tone wasn't his usual gentle one. Since finding out she was expecting Roford's baby, his manner had changed. Everything had changed. Their new-found loving in bed at night had stopped, with Bill turning his back as soon as they got between the sheets. No goodnight kiss, no cuddling up to her, and at least a foot of no-man's-land between them. Betsy couldn't blame him, for it was a lot for him to live with. She couldn't even blame him for doubting her, as she deserved no less, although that hurt the most. No matter that her story wasn't true, Bill didn't know that and he should trust and believe in her.

Telling him how everything had changed deepened his mood. 'Naw. Now what? It seems Roford, the swine, holds all the cards. I feel sorry for Mags, but where does that leave us, eh?'

'Where we've allus been, only a little worse off. We have to get jobs, Bill.'

'What, you in your condition? Who's going to take on a pregnant wench, eh? Tell me that, if you can.'

This stung Betsy. She had no words.

'And I tell you this much: it's going to stick in me craw providing for Roford's bastard an' all.'

'Bill, please. No matter how this babby got inside me, it's a human being, and it'll only have us in all the world to care for it. It'll be as much part of me as our lasses are. And I, for one, will do all I can to provide for it, as I have done and will carry on doing for me little lasses.'

Bill walked out of the room. She heard the front door slam and went to the window to watch him walk down the road, as he had done each day since hearing her news. He just didn't seem to want to be near her any more.

Her thoughts turned to Mags, and how sorry Mags must feel not to be able to carry out her promise to her and Bill. *Oh, Mags, love, if only you knew. It's me who's let you down. It were my lies and deceit that resulted in you being put out of your home. Oh God, when will I ever have peace inside me again?* Sighing, she told herself, 'You're to get on with it, lass. Nowt can be undone. And hard as it is to live with, you've no choice.'

A wail from upstairs told her that Rosie was waking. She was a lazy madam, that one. She'd sleep till the cows come home, but by, did she let you knaw it when she wakened.

'Come on, me lass. Are you hungry? I've kept some porridge on the go, for when you woke. And once you've had it, we'll get you in your pushchair and go and find your da. He'll be by his ma's grave, if I knaw him. He allus goes there to talk over his troubles with her. He'll sit under that tree for hours.'

'Dada.'

'Yes, that's right – your da. Eeh, lass, you're three now and should be a right chatterbox. I don't knaw what holds you up from progressing. And you're still not that steady on your feet. You're a proper slow developer, aren't you?'

'Me slow develper.'

'Ha, that's right, or nearly. Keep this up, lass, and I'll not be able to shut you up. But by, I'd be glad not to, as you've got me more than a bit worried about you.'

'Mama wor – wor—'

'W-orr-ied.'

Rosie giggled. 'Mama not 'appy.'

'Eeh, there's more goes on in your head than we knaw. Now eat that porridge.' Something in Betsy settled, on this exchange with Rosie. As she had niggled about Rosie's lack of progress, now she wondered if it was just laziness, or the fact that everyone pandered to her, as Florrie and Daisy seemed to know what Rosie wanted, without her telling them.

But although this worry felt sorted, Betsy couldn't feel happy about everything else in her life. *It's all spoiled, and I only have meself to blame.* She'd go and find Bill and try to make up with him. But how she'd ever make everything right again, she didn't know.

Chapter Twenty-Three

As she entered the churchyard, an eerie feeling made Betsy shudder. This surprised and worried her. Usually she was relaxed amongst the graves and liked remembering the folk she'd known who'd passed on, and pondering on the lives of those who'd lived long ago. Often, as Bill did with his ma, she'd sit with her own ma, talking over her worries.

Rosie looked up at her. 'Eeh, me little lass, someone's just walked over me grave.'

'Grave.' This Rosie accompanied by pointing to the grave-stones. But Betsy didn't feel cheered, as she had done earlier, by this sudden awareness that Rosie was showing.

Everything around her was still. Not even the birds chirped. No breeze rustled the trees or the hedgerows, and Betsy couldn't enjoy what she always thought of as a place of peace. Hurrying her steps, she hoped she would find Bill around the back of the church, where his ma was buried. He hadn't known his da; some sickness had taken him when Bill was a small boy. But he'd loved his ma and felt it badly when she passed away, which had happened not long after

Bill had his accident. It was said it was the shock of seeing her Bill so badly hurt, it broke her heart.

How life had changed from that day when the mine's hooter had sounded, telling of a disaster. She'd known then that her Bill was involved, and had begged a lift to get to him. The cage he'd been ascending in had collapsed, killing four men and injuring two. There'd been a lot of inexperienced men working the mines at the time, sent there to do their war service, and one of those hadn't taken enough care to report a fault.

Bill's body wasn't the only thing injured that day, as his mind had been injured, too. He felt it badly that he couldn't work or be a proper husband to her, though others never knew, because although she had Daisy as a babby at the time, she birthed Florrie a year later and Rosie two years after that, so everything must have seemed normal to them. But everything had changed. Making babbies had been a fumbling affair, and nothing like the passionate relationship they'd known before.

Coming out of this reminiscing, Betsy rounded the corner of the church. She could see her ma-in-law's grave now, but no sign of Bill. A strange feeling came over her as she gazed at the spot, some ten yards ahead of her. Something was disturbing the branches of the overhanging tree and she could hear a soft, swishing noise. Fear held her still for a moment. Then instinct told her to leave Rosie where they stood. 'Ma has to go over to Granny's garden. Rosie watch, eh?'

'Rosie buttcup?'

'Not this time, lass. We'll pick buttercups for your granny's garden another time.'

As she walked towards the tree, her mind screamed against what had flashed into it. As she neared, the thought became a reality, and a holler came from her that burned her throat, snotted her nose and sweated tears of agony from her body. 'Naw, naw. Naw . . . naw.'

She'd seen his shoes first. Bill's shoes were on the ground, highly polished, as he liked them. They lay as if dropped from a height. Next to them were his socks, strewn as if he'd just discarded them. And then she saw his bare feet dangling.

Drawing in a deep, painful gasp, she reached up. She wanted to take his weight, but she couldn't reach him. Horror entered her as she looked into Bill's bloated face and his bulging, unseeing eyes. Quiet sobs took her now. 'Oh, Bill, me beloved Bill. What have I done? What have I done?'

A scream from Rosie got her turning. Roford had hold of the pushchair and was pulling it backwards. He was taking her child, but it didn't register. Betsy's mind wouldn't – couldn't – deal with anything other than the loss of her Bill. 'He – he's dead. Me lovely Bill's dead. Help me. *Help me* . . . Please.' Saying the words drained Betsy and she sank to her knees.

'What? What are you talking about?'

Roford was by her side now. When he looked up, he turned away quickly and vomited. When he was back in control he turned to her. 'Get up – we have to fetch help. God, why has he done this? Why? Look, come on, Betsy.' This last he said in a softer tone. 'I – I saw you come in here. I've got my car outside the gate. Come on. I – I came to talk to you. Look, I'm sorry about what I said. I was angry and worried about Mags. I wouldn't harm your children, you know that.' His hands were shaking as he helped her up.

Rosie screamed even louder as he neared the pushchair. Making an extreme effort, Betsy pulled herself together. She wiped her face with her hanky and tried to smile. 'There, there, me little darling, there's nowt to be scared of. No one's going to hurt you.'

The words felt as if they were being said by someone else, as she couldn't register that she was talking, or make any sense of what she said. Her mind was filled with Bill's face – the ugliness of it, when her Bill was so handsome. His stare haunted her. *Oh, Bill, naw, naw.*

Three days later, shivering with shock and grief, Betsy watched Bill's coffin being lowered into a pauper's grave in unconsecrated ground. No vicar was attending, as Bill was classed as having committed the ultimate, unforgivable sin in the eyes of the Church.

Betsy had wanted him buried with his ma, but the vicar wouldn't even consider it. Even so, there was no shortage of mourners – Bill was well loved. All the folk from the village were there, as were a few of his old workmates, and the colliery brass band. Now that his coffin rested on the bottom of the grave, they began to play. Their music soared into the air, and Betsy thought of her Bill soaring with it. He loved the brass band. He'd be tapping his feet . . . A picture of his bare feet swinging back and forth came to her and she cried out against it. Ciss squeezed her hand on one side, and an arm came round her from the other side. She looked up into the face of Mags.

'Oh, Mags. Mags, help me.'

Mags smiled through her tears. 'I will, my dear friend, I will.'

They stood there, the three of them holding hands,

listening to the band playing 'Amazing Grace' and seeing the sun glistening on the band's instruments, and cried together.

When the music died, Mags began to say the twenty-third Psalm. 'The Lord is my shepherd; I shall not want . . .' The band joined in very gently, playing the tune as Mags spoke the words. It was the saddest and yet the most beautiful moment to seep into Betsy. And she held strong as she listened to the comforting words.

When it was done, the congregation clapped, then someone started to say the Lord's Prayer, and everyone joined in. Whether the church prayed for her Bill or not didn't matter. His people prayed for him, and that's all she needed. Bending, she picked up a handful of earth and sprinkled it onto the coffin. 'Rest in peace, my darling Bill.'

Others followed suit, and the next ten minutes were taken up with the folk she'd grown up with filing past her Bill's coffin, all helping him on his last journey.

As the crowd thinned, she saw him. Harold Roford had dared to attend. He stood twenty yards away, his hands clasped in front of him, his expression one of regret. And yet she wondered if he was capable of feeling such an emotion. Her instinct was to run up to him and spit in his face. Ciss clasped tightly the hand she held. 'Naw, our Betsy. Today's for our Bill.'

At this, Mags looked up and in the direction of Harold. Her body straightened, and a look of defiance swept across her face as she stared at him. He dropped his head, turned and walked away.

Mags looked at Betsy and Ciss. 'Together we women can, and will, beat the Rofords of this world.' They walked away then, both of them supporting Betsy.

'How did you get here, Mags?'

'I caught the train, Ciss, but I suppose you meant how did I know? David – Dr Lange – telephoned me. I – I'm going back to Brockhall.'

'Naw, Mags, you can't. Why would you, lass?'

'I have to, Betsy. But it's only for one day. I'm sleeping at David's house, not in that horrible place. I am going to be assessed and then certified as being of sound mind. David will stay with me and protect me. But I will explain all later. Oh, there's David now.'

He stood on the edge of the crowd, but came forward as he saw Mags wave. 'Well, done, Betsy. You did Bill proud. I won't ask you how you are, as I can imagine. I have been through it and there is no pain like it, and nothing that can be said to alleviate even a small part of that pain. But it must have given you comfort to see the turnout, and to feel the love extended to Bill and you. It's a wickedness the way the Church looks on these things, as I know God will open his arms to those so troubled they could no longer stay with us.'

The doctor's words cut through Betsy's heart. Bill was troubled. So very troubled. But she mustn't go down that route, or she'd be lost. She'd remember the night he made love to her, before she realized she had her belly up. Yes, that would be her focus. How he danced in a silly fashion, showing how his leg was working so well. How he swung her round and round and they fell onto the sofa. How he kissed her and undressed her, telling her of his love for her, and expressing his thanks for the way she'd got him through everything. And how he never mentioned the rape, and she thought he'd come through the black patch that had taken him over that. Yes, she'd remember that night as the last night she'd known happiness with her Bill.

They walked towards the church gates. Roford stood on the pavement. He stepped forward. 'Mags, may I speak with you, please?'

Dr Lange spoke before Mags could. 'I don't think that would be wise, as you have caused a lot of harm, Roford. You've broken lives since you arrived amongst us, and none of us want anything more to do with you. You will be hearing from Margaret's solicitor.'

Roford's face changed. Betsy thought she'd seen evil in him before, but now he was inhabited by the Devil himself. He raised his hand and within seconds an ambulance screeched round the bend. Two men jumped out and, on Roford's instruction, grabbed Mags and dragged her towards the vehicle.

'What the hell? Roford, what do you think you are doing? Tell those men they are to release Margaret at once. She is booked to return to the hospital tomorrow. Who are these men?'

'They are orderlies. My wife is sick and needs to be in the asylum.'

Dr Lange dashed over to the men. 'Let Mrs Roford go at once, do you hear me? I am her doctor and she is in my care.'

One of the men let go of Mags and looked at Dr Lange in astonishment. Mags saw her chance and pulled away from the other one. As Betsy saw him go to grab Mags again, she shouted, 'Come on, our Ciss.' Ciss didn't need telling twice; she stood with Betsy in front of the men, and between them and Mags.

'Look, Missus, I don't knaw what's going on here. We

were called to pick up an escaped patient, that's all. This gentleman came for us and told us his wife was sectioned and had escaped, and he knew where she was. I checked and he was telling the truth, so we came here.'

'Well, you ain't having her. She's staying with Dr Lange, and that's that. It's all a lie, cooked up by him!' Betsy turned, but Roford had gone. At that moment he needed to vanish, as the whole village had now crowded round, baying for blood.

'Look, we don't want any trouble. I'm sorry, Mrs Roford, we were only doing our job.'

For the first time Betsy looked back at Mags. She was in Dr Lange's arms, her face was deathly pale and although she wasn't crying, her body was heaving in much the same way as if she was sobbing. Betsy turned back to the men. 'Just get on your way, lads. No one's blaming you. We're just protecting one of our own.'

'Ta, Missus, and I'm sorry for the upheaval we caused. We didn't knaw as there were a funeral party going on, till we pulled up. Was it someone local? Seems whoever it were, they were popular.'

'Aye, it were someone local. And he were someone much loved.'

'I can see that. Well, we'll get off.'

Dr Lange called over, 'Please report that, as arranged, Mrs Roford will attend the hospital tomorrow.'

'I will, sir, and I'm very sorry.'

Betsy took hold of Mags's other arm. 'Eeh, Mags. It's all right now, lass.'

She recovered well. 'I know. And it's all going to be fine in the future. They scared me, that's all. I'm all right now.'

Betsy wondered if Mags would ever be all right again, or

if she herself would. They'd been through a lot since Mags had taken up with Roford.

'Betsy, I've had my housekeeper prepare a meal for all of us – you and Ciss, too. Do you feel up to coming? Please don't feel obliged to.'

'I can't, Doctor, as I've to pick me young 'uns up. A neighbour took care of them for me.'

Mrs Church piped up, 'I'll get the girls, Betsy. You go along, it will do you good.'

'No, better that you bring the children with you, Betsy,' Dr Lange said. 'They should be with you now, and they must be wondering what is happening. I asked Phyllis to make something for them to eat. She has a daily helper, so she will easily manage everything.'

For a moment a picture of the dour housekeeper came into Betsy's mind and she could almost feel the displeasure this request from the doctor would have caused Phyllis. 'Ta, Doctor, I'd like to be in company. And I need to hear all your news an' all, Mags. I don't like the sound of you going back to that place.'

By the time they had eaten a delicious lamb stew with thick slices of bread, and the fluffiest potatoes Betsy had ever tasted, she understood why the doctor put up with Phyllis. And Phyllis herself showed a different side to her, as she was kindness itself to Betsy.

'Well, now. Shall we go into the withdrawing room?'

'I'll take the young 'uns home now, Betsy, and then you can talk to Mags.'

Betsy thanked Ciss and, once in the hall, the two sisters hugged one another. Betsy's dry throat cracked, but she held on to her tears. Everything felt surreal to her, as if her body was going through the motions, but she wasn't really part of it. A hand took hers, and she smiled at Mags.

'You're doing well, Betsy love. You're so brave.' With this, Mags drew her towards her, and Betsy, who was only just aware of the door closing on Ciss and her unusually quiet and pliable girls, felt a moment of deep love for Mags.

Swallowing hard, she covered her emotions by gently chastising Mags. 'You're too thin, Mags, and I noticed you didn't eat much. You need to build yourself up.'

'Well, I'm hoping that if everything turns out well, you will see to that, Betsy.'

'Me? But I thought all your plans had changed and that you were no longer going to—'

'Oh, I don't know what I'm going to be doing yet. Let's sit down, and I will tell you all about what is happening.'

Seeing Phyllis coming towards them with a tray of cool drinks showed Betsy the reason why Mags had cut her off mid-sentence. The fewer folk who knew Mags's plans, the better.

Once it was just the three of them, Mags told Betsy all that had transpired. As she came to the end of her telling, Betsy felt more worried for her than she had ever felt before. 'So Roford can take everything?'

'Yes, and that's why I had to come back. Returning to that place is terrifying me, but David managed to get the concession that although I will spend a few hours of the next two days being assessed and talking to the psychiatrist, I don't have to sleep there, and I can have David with me at all times. When David told me what had happened . . . well, I felt guilty, and knew I had to get my status as a sane person back, and hold onto what assets I have, so that we can all start that new life. I felt as if I had pulled the rug

260

from underneath you – and the hope that Bill had for a better future.'

Betsy bent her head as shame washed over her. Was she never to be free of this guilt? 'Eeh, Mags, it weren't you. Bill were disappointed, but . . . well, this ain't going to be easy to say, and I don't want it to set you back in your recovery – not that I think you went mad or owt, but I knaw as you were hurt bad by what happened.'

'What is it, Betsy? Do you want to tell me first?' Dr Lange said.

'Naw, Doctor. Mags has got to knaw. I – I'm pregnant with Roford's child.'

'No, Betsy! Oh, Betsy, Betsy.'

'I'm sorry, Mags, I – I—'

'No, don't be. It's me who should be sorry. I knew what Harold was like, though I never guessed he would bring so much down upon us all. And poor, poor Bill.'

'He'd come to terms with the rape, though he did have his doubts about me – any man would. But when we realized that I had me belly up . . .'

'Well, Betsy.' Dr Lange shook his head. 'I'm so sorry. This is terrible news. I don't know what to say, other than it isn't your fault. None of it is your fault.'

'Ta, Doctor. But I can't get it out of me head that Bill weren't sure of me. It's eating away at me.'

'Poor Bill. I can understand him. I know it's not what you ladies want to hear, but it is a fact that rape isn't widely believed. He felt the shame of it. But then with you finding you were pregnant, it must have been a blow too far.'

Betsy felt as if her heart was being sliced in two, such was the pain inside her. A tear ran unbidden down her cheek.

She thought she'd shed all the tears her body could produce, but now she wanted to scream and scream. She needed release from the shackles that held her. Would she ever get it? *Please God that I do.*

Chapter Twenty-Four

Mags stood on the pavement outside the gates of Brockhall Institution. Ripples of fear clenched her stomach. 'You won't leave me, will you, David? Not even for a second – promise me.'

'I promise. Even if you need to relieve yourself, I will come with you and stand outside the door.'

This made her smile. 'Well, not that close.' They both laughed, and Mags felt better.

Someone calling her name got Mags turning her head. 'Iris! Oh, I'm so glad to see you. Are you all right? You don't . . . Please tell me you don't still work here.'

'Naw, I've left. It's been a week now, but one of me ex-workmates who lives near to me told me that you were booked in, so I wanted to come and see you. Eeh, you don't knaw what you've done for me, Mags. I feel free.'

'Was everything all right when . . . well, you know, with my escape?'

'Yes, Michael and I went on the sick, so there was no one here who could know you were missing. John said it took three days to find out.'

'Really? And there I was, terrified someone would jump out at me.'

'Well, I'm glad as you're going to get your proper discharge, then you won't have to keep looking over your shoulder. But, lass, you don't look well.'

'I'm all right. Did you hear what happened to Betsy?'

'Naw.'

Iris was shocked, as Mags had expected.

'Eeh, poor Betsy, I'll call on her. If I'd known, I would have been there yesterday. Will you tell her that?'

'We will, but may I caution you about calling on her, Iris.'

'Oh? Why's that, Doctor?'

'Well, she's already been threatened by Roford, and he's looking for someone to blame for Mags's escape. He wants his revenge – he's that type of man.'

Mags told Iris what had happened after the funeral.

'Eeh, he wants locking up, that one. I've never known the like. And I'm wary of Michael an' all, so be careful if he tries to speak to you. He transferred to daytime duty recently, which is strange for him. John's all right. I mean, he has his ways, but what you see is what you get, with John. You knaw where you are with him.'

'Well, nothing can happen to Mags today. I'm staying with her throughout, and I'm not leaving without her.'

'I hope I see you again, lass. But by, I wish you all the luck in the world.'

'I wish I had time to take tea with you, Iris. I have so much to thank you for. But once this is done, we are taking Dr Jenkins's discharge and report straight to my solicitor, and then I am leaving for—'

'Don't tell me where, lass. If I don't knaw, I can't let it

out. But be happy, that's all I ask. And maybe one day in the future we can meet again.'

Iris left them then, and Mags had a moment of feeling so grateful to her that she wanted to run after Iris and hug her, but she had to be careful. She didn't know who might be watching.

'I fear for Iris, David. If Michael informs Harold of her part in everything. Oh, I know she didn't take part in my escape in the end, but—'

Cut off mid-sentence, Mags was silenced by the gateman opening the gate. She waited while he checked their credentials. With this over, they were free to pass through. It didn't take more than ten seconds until Mags's nerves overwhelmed her.

'Mags, please try to be strong. If you show any sign of illness, Jenkins may not discharge you, and I may not be able to save you.'

'What? Is that a possibility, David?'

'Everything is possible. Now, straighten your back and think of this as a business meeting. You must have conducted dozens of them. You did it then, and you can do it now. Don't let Harold win – he is just a business rival, and nothing more.'

Thinking of it all like that helped Mags. She did straighten her back and began to think of her forthcoming ordeal in terms of a business strategy. She would be in command. She would run this show.

Although she didn't feel quite so confident when face-to-face with Dr Jenkins, she didn't show it. She answered his questions and even asked some of him. 'I want to know why you sectioned me, Dr Jenkins?'

'My diagnosis was that you were having a mental breakdown and were delusional. I stand by that.'

265

'I was deeply distressed, that's true. But I knew what was happening, and a period of rest and maybe some medication were all I needed. You should have recognized that. But you listened to my husband and took his version, concerning how I was.'

'I am not on trial here, madam. I did what I thought was best for you.'

David coughed. Mags knew the implications, but she was so incensed with this man, who could have saved her of all she had gone through within these walls.

'Do you realize how patients are treated here, Doctor?'

'I believe, madam, that they receive the very best care we can give. The job the nurses have here is extremely difficult. They are not dealing with rational people who can be reasoned with. If you can't see that, then perhaps you are still delusional.'

This frightened Mags, and beside her David shifted in his seat. 'Mrs Roford is a born campaigner, in particular where women's issues are concerned, so you had better watch out, Jenkins – she has a nasty bark when she is roused.'

Mags took the hint. 'I'm sorry, Doctor, I know how difficult it must be. Maybe the staff can be cautioned to be a little less heavy-handed, though?'

'I will look into your allegations. Now, I think we will bring this to a close. I am satisfied that you are now recovered and of sound mind. And I discharge you as of today, with no further treatment advised.'

Mags gave a sigh of relief. Happiness flooded through her; and yes, it did contain a feeling of victory over Harold, but she felt she deserved such an emotion.

'Good. I will take my patient home with me as soon as you have the paperwork ready, Doctor.'

With this agreed, the doctor left them.

'Margaret, you were very naughty. You reminded me so much of your mother, and she would be proud of you. But we cannot change the world in one fell swoop. So please stop trying – not altogether, just in situations where it is better to keep quiet.'

Mags didn't agree with this comment, but she bit her tongue, rather than get into a debate about the issues facing women. She could never forgive David for having neither condoned nor condemned Harold's treatment of Susan. But she said nothing. For the moment she was wallowing in being truly free. She couldn't wait to get back to London and tell Montel.

At the solicitors' office she received further good news.

'We will begin to have Mr Roford's power of attorney over you rescinded immediately. Now, are you thinking of divorce, Mrs Roford? I have to caution you that it is a lengthy and costly business and may not end how you would hope, but if you are willing to go through with it, it is possible you will get half of all the marital assets. However, it is rare for that to happen. You are most likely to be given a settlement dictated by Mr Roford.'

'I would like a divorce. My marriage has been a sham and a means for my husband to steal all that my father built up.'

The solicitor looked astonished at this. 'They are very strong words, Mrs Roford, and wouldn't stand well in a divorce court. It is understood – and acceptable – that many marriages are made for gain.'

'Yes, in an open way that is discussed beforehand and agreed, as in a dowry; but my marriage wasn't conducted in this way. Mr Roford wooed me with declarations of love.

I had no reason to doubt his motives, as he had come into a substantial sum of money, but he isn't an honest man. He is a greedy man and is reckless, where money is concerned. He soon spent most of his inheritance and needed a source of income. I provided that for him, but the moment he had it, his philandering knew no bounds. His mistress lives in my house with him and he has made one of my staff pregnant.'

'Good gracious!'

'Exactly. However, no *male* court of law will see his misdemeanours as anything unusual. They will consider that I should have tolerated such a state of affairs. Even Mr Roford having me sectioned will be looked upon as my own fault. So, no, I won't file for divorce and have my wretched marriage problems made public, and then lose everything. But I want to be sure that my own personal property and legacy will now be mine alone.'

'Yes, of course. And we will see to it that they are. Your personal legacy was not part of the family estate that Mr Roford married into, so he can have no call on it. It is a pity that your dear late father didn't tie up his assets in such a way that they could not be possessed by anyone marrying his daughter. There are ways of doing that, but he was so comfortable in his own marriage, and so generous with his own wife, that he never suspected there was anyone out there who would treat his daughter differently.'

Mags didn't answer this. She had yet to deal with coming to terms with her father's passing. It was still a painful part of her that she'd locked away and dared not unlock until she was ready.

The solicitor continued, 'Well, all that is as it may be, but we have to deal with what we have. I have prepared an account of what money has been advanced so far; where further assets are invested; and what money is in transit to you, as we did have a certain amount in one of our client accounts, which your father wanted readily available to you. I think you will find it all in order.'

'Thank you. May I ask: did my father leave a Will?'

'He did . . . but I'm afraid it doesn't help you. He added to your personal assets before your marriage: those already in your name, and very generously, as you will see from the accounts. But then he left everything – the house and the business, and all other assets – to you, but with no clause that would have made it difficult for them to become the shared property of your husband. They were assets you gained after the marriage.'

'Shareable, but not owned by Mr Roford?'

'That's correct. He has the same right to them as you do, as they are marital assets, especially as Mr Roford has been running the business and the estate since your marriage. No doubt that is why he took power of attorney over you, as that meant he had full control. It is possible – though I can't find out for sure – that he transferred everything into his name whilst he had power of attorney. Your father was old-fashioned and believed the husband should have control. He spoke to me on this point, saying that your marriage was to a man of assets who owned a half-share, and soon all the shares, in a mill of his own. He was very pleased about it all and felt that you would be in good hands.'

'But Daddy found out I wasn't, so why didn't he change his Will?'

'We will never know. But take heart that you have the assets you do possess. The only way Mr Roford can commandeer those is if he finds out about them and still has power of attorney. I promise you that I will do all in my power to get that state of affairs changed very quickly.'

'Please keep me informed through Dr Lange. I am happy for him to know anything about my business.'

As they drove to David's house, the pain that had been nudging Mags erupted. *Poor Daddy. He wouldn't have meant to do wrong by me, but as I well knew, he was old-fashioned in his thinking.* At this thought the tears began to flow.

'What is it, my dear? Everything is all right now. You will be able to start your new life.'

'Will – will you take me to my father's grave, please, David. I didn't even look that way when I was in the church-yard for Bill's funeral. I – I just haven't let myself . . .'

'Oh, my poor Margaret. Of course. Would you like us to pick up Betsy to be with you?'

'No, bless her, she has enough to contend with, with her own grief. I just need to sit a while with Daddy and my mother. But don't leave me, as I am afraid to be on my own.'

The mound of earth looked bare. Not even her mother's stone was in place, as she imagined the undertaker would have arranged for it to go back to the stonemason's to have her father's details added.

'It's like a nothing-place.'

David didn't answer.

'I can't believe they are both gone. So much has happened, and in such a short time. This time last year I had them both and lived in our family home. I ran the family business and – ha! – I was even looking forward to deepening my relationship with Harold. How is it possible that so much has changed?'

'You have been through a lot, Margaret, my dear, but

everything is about to improve. You have so much to look forward to again.'

Mags's glance took in the fresh mound of earth across the cemetery in the far corner, and Betsy's plight hit her afresh: alone with three children, and with another that she hadn't asked for on the way. This thought helped her to put into perspective what she'd lost. She had always faced the fact of how elderly her parents were, and that she might lose them whilst she was still young, not that that made it any easier. But she did have a lot to look forward to. Betsy didn't.

'You're right. I must be strong. Betsy needs me. I'm worried about leaving her, as I can't stay here and she will be left at Harold's mercy. He won't give up. He knows that I must have money he doesn't know about, and it will eat away at him. He'll hound Betsy, thinking he can get it out of me by intimidating her.'

'Well, all that you plan is going to take time. Couldn't you rent somewhere for you and Betsy to stay? Somewhere Harold wouldn't think to look, or find out about?'

'Yes, that is the answer. Can we go to Betsy's now? I want to give her the news of my discharge and see how she is, and I need to know if she'll be willing to come with me.'

'That's the spirit. Keep busy, keep planning – that's what your mother and father would want of you.'

'I know. I mustn't look back and regret, or think of what might have been, but must go and build a new life and think how lucky I am to be in a position to do so.' With this, Mags said her goodbyes to her parents and walked away, leaving them to their rest.

Betsy rubbed her bruised arm as she looked out of the window of her home at the sound of a car drawing up.

Feeling dead inside, she felt no reaction on seeing Mags get out of the car. Roford had visited her home and had threatened her. *He'll never give up. He wants to know how Mags escaped and how she got the money, and he doesn't care how he finds out.* He'd twisted her arm behind her back until she'd cried out with the pain of it, but she hadn't told him anything. She had nothing to tell now. Mags was back and fighting her own corner. At least she looked happy, so everything must have gone to plan for her at the asylum.

'Betsy! Can we come in?'

Making herself sound cheerful, Betsy shouted back, 'It looks like you are in. Eeh, lass, how did it go?'

'I'm free!'

'I gathered that.'

'Betsy, come here. Let's have a hug.'

In the middle of their embrace, Betsy cracked. Sobs racked her body. Roford had hurt her badly; it wasn't just her arm that stung, but he'd dug his fist deep into her belly. She feared for her child. And she didn't know how long it would be before he tried his games on her again. It was as if he was taking his time, but would pounce when she least expected it. And she didn't know if she could fight him off.

'Sit down, love. Shall I get David to give you something to help you?'

'Naw, I can't. I've to be alert for me young 'uns.'

'Look, Betsy, I'm going to take care of you. I'm not going to make you wait until we can go to Scotland, although that won't be long now. I'm going to rent somewhere for us both and the children in London. How does that sound?'

'Eeh, London – me? Naw, lass, I'd be lost.'

'No, you won't. I'll always be with you. It's exciting,

272

Betsy. I'll take you shopping and to a show. Montel will watch the children.'

'Montel?'

'Oh, I – I . . . well, you'll have to know anyway. Montel is . . .' And Mags told Betsy all about him.

'By, lass, you didn't let the grass grow under your feet, I'll say that for you.'

'Ha! It's not like that; well, it might be. He is fond of me, and I am becoming fond of him, but at the moment he is just the kind of friend everyone needs in times of trouble. Please say you will come. I – I, well, I'm frightened for you.'

'Aye, you need to be. Roford's been at me again.' Betsy showed Mags her arm. 'He's convinced I knaw sommat. He says he has information that a woman at the hospital met up with a woman who knew you. He knaws I was involved. I kept telling him it wasn't me, but he says he'll be back – only it will be at night, and he won't stop at just giving me a beating. I told him that my sister was here at night and she'd go for the police, naw matter what. So then he said by the time he was finished with her, she wouldn't be able to leave the house. He's like a madman. It's as if he is possessed. I'm scared out of me wits.'

'He knows about Iris?'

'From what he says, he only knaws *of* her. I don't think she has been named.'

'At least that's something. Maybe that Michael has a conscience after all, as it sounds as though he has been talking. Look, Betsy, I want you to pack some cases – yours and the children's, and one for Ciss. You're not stopping here another night. You are right about Harold. He is possessed of an evil streak that I don't think he can control.

I'll be back later to collect you. I just need to make a few arrangements first.'

When Mags had gone, Betsy set about packing some of their stuff into two brown paper bags. She didn't have any cases, but Mags wouldn't know that. *Eeh, please let our Ciss agree to come with me.* But then nerves of a different kind attacked Betsy. *London? Eeh, it'll be like I'm in a foreign country.* Still, nervous as she was of the big city, it had to be better than staying here and facing the wrath of Roford.

Chapter Twenty-Five

Betsy looked across the kitchen table at her sister. They sat, one at each end, staring at each other. Betsy knew that expression on Ciss's face and had a sinking feeling that this was one argument she wasn't going to win.

'Naw, Betsy, I'm not going. I've promised meself to Patrick. He's given up the drink and he's been given a farmer's cottage. He moves out of Farmer Dilly's barn tomorrow. Look, there's sommat as I haven't told you, but Farmer Dilly's wife said that when I'm ready, I can move in with her till me and Pat marry. She wants a hand, as she's expanding the dairy and will teach me to make cheese and the like. I've done a bit of the work already and I love it. Only I didn't want to leave you on your own.'

'Eeh, lass, what about your ambitions to be a teacher? I was thinking you'd find that easier in London.'

'Naw, that ain't for the likes of us, Betsy. I knaw that now. And besides, I don't think I can live without Patrick. We thought to marry next spring, just to put some time between Ma and Bill going, as it wouldn't seem right to wed before then.'

'Aw, I'm glad for you, but afraid for thee at the same time. Roford is threatening to harm you, to get at me.'

'Just let him try. As you knaw, my Patrick's built like a giant, and he wouldn't think twice of taking his hunting rifle to the likes of Roford. Naw, lass, I'll be safe as houses, and I'm looking forward to me new life. I can hand tenancy back on this house and, if you're happy with me doing so, I can take most of the good bits to what's going to be me new home in time.'

'I'm more than happy with that, as I don't think I'll ever be back, and I can't take them with me.'

'Not ever? Oh, our Betsy, I can't bear the thought of that. You'll come to me wedding, won't you?'

'I'll try. I've to get used to the idea yet, lass. The last you told me, you still had Patrick on trial. I knew nowt of all this farming business.'

'I'm sorry, our lass, but you were in a state, and I didn't want to let you think I was leaving you an' all. I never would have, until you were all right.'

'I knaw that, Ciss. Be happy, lass, and if I don't come to your wedding it's because I'd not be safe. And while I'm on, lass, there's sommat else an' all. Sommat 'as made my Bill do what he did. I'm having Roford's babby.'

Ciss's mouth dropped open, and expressions ranging from astonishment to horror crossed her face. Finally compassion won through and, with tears glistening in her eyes, she held out her arms.

Betsy went into them gladly, and the two sisters held on to each other as if for the last time. 'We'll get through this, lass. I've got Mags, and you've got your Patrick. And though I've been less than complimentary about him when he were drinking heavy, there's not a nicer bloke when he's sober, so you work on keeping him that way. Make him happy, give him plenty of young 'uns and you'll jog along nicely together.'

'Ha! Plenty of young 'uns – I don't even knaw how you go about making them, let alone having them.'

This shocked Betsy, but then Ciss had her head in a book most of the time, and it was difficult to know what she'd grasped about what happens in the real world.

'Well, I'll make it me duty to instruct you – and right now, as I've to be ready for when Mags comes. And I've to get Rosie up out of her afternoon nap and the young 'uns from school yet. Now, our Ciss, it's like this . . .'

After her telling, Ciss's eyes were open wide and a giggle came from her that didn't hold repulsion, but expectation.

'So you're in for sommat good, our lass, as long as your Patrick knaws how to go on, and most men do.'

'Well, if he don't, we'll learn. For all his appearance, he's a gentle soul and he listens to what I have to say. I feel like I'm a treasured possession of his, and he wouldn't want to lose me for the world. That's what I use to keep him from the door of the pub.'

They hugged again, and Ciss offered to run and fetch the children while Betsy finished up and got Rosie ready. She promised she would take the bag that Betsy had got ready for her and go straight to Farmer Dilly's house and stay there from tonight, only coming back with Patrick and the cart to get what they needed. 'The rest I'll ask Farmer Dilly if we can store in one of the barns that he don't use, as you never know when one of us might need it.'

When Mags arrived, Betsy was ready. As was Ciss, because Patrick drew up at the same time as Mags. Ciss had sent the neighbour's lad with a message telling him to come urgently. He couldn't have come any quicker if he'd tried.

The sisters held on to one another as if they would never let go. When Betsy finally came out of Ciss's arms, she looked up at the huge, handsome Patrick. 'Take care of her, Pat, and look out for her. Ciss'll tell you all about it, but she ain't safe down here.'

'It is that I haven't an inkling of what you mean, or what has happened that you have to flee like this. But you be resting your heart, Betsy, 'cause I'm for loving the bones of Ciss, and no one will be at hurting her while I draw breath.'

Betsy smiled up at him, and the part of her heart that Ciss occupied did rest easy. A sigh of relief left her as she turned to get into Dr Lange's car. 'I'll write, Ciss. Just as soon as I'm settled, I'll write.'

Tears ran down Ciss's face, but Betsy saw a big, strong arm go round her and knew that while this parting was painful, it was for the best, where Ciss was concerned.

'Ma. Where we going, Ma? I want Aunty Ciss.'

'Now, Daisy lass, you being the eldest, you should be looking out for your sisters, not frightening and upsetting them.'

Daisy might be the eldest, but she was timid. Florrie was of a different mettle. 'I like it in this car, Ma. Come on, Daisy, Ma said we're going on an adventure. I've allus wanted to go on one of them. We'll see Aunty Ciss soon, won't we, Ma?'

'Aye, we will.' But as Betsy said this, she wondered if they would, and was glad when Mags got their attention.

'We are going on an adventure, children. We're going to a cottage in Turton that one of my friends owns. It's going to be lovely. Like a holiday. Then we're going to London

278

in a few days, when things are settled. Have you heard of our capital city?'

'Aye, we learned about it in school, Aunty Mags. There's palaces and a big river with a special bridge, and a clock that strikes so loud most of London can hear it, and it has a name. It's called Big Ben.'

'Aye, I remember the teacher telling us that, our Florrie, and she said the palace is where the King lives, and that the important house where the government makes all the laws is by the river an' all.'

Betsy smiled, proud of the knowledge her girls had. Mags winked at her. 'Oh, you girls know so much about it, you will have to show me and your ma around.'

The girls giggled at this, and Betsy felt her heart resting, as Patrick had bid it to. They were going to be safe. Nothing could hurt them now. Though she wondered if the pain of loss would ever go away, she knew she was ready to make a new life for herself and her young 'uns, and aye, the babby nestling in her womb, too.

London was like a hurricane, whereas Blackburn had been a mild storm. It took Betsy's breath away and she could tell that Mags wasn't at home, not really. She knew the way of things, but looked intimidated by the hustle and bustle.

The smell got to Betsy, who was used to the blustery northern winds, which sometimes carried the grime of industry in their wake. Here the air hung with smog, horse-dung and the fumes from hundreds of cars, coupled with the sweaty body smells of so many folk at close quarters – and it had her wanting to retch. But she couldn't help being caught up in the excitement of the glittering shops and the street entertainers.

279

Daisy, Florrie and Rosie loved every minute. They clapped their hands and did little jigs as they watched the musicians and jugglers. And they were enthralled to see Buckingham Palace and all the places they had learned about at school. Betsy felt a pride in her children she'd never known before. Caught up in the daily grind of getting through each day, she'd never taken much notice of what was happening with their schooling. It had been enough to get them to school.

The time at the cottage in Turton had been a time of fun for them, but for her and Mags a time of talking. Cleansing all but the very corners of her soul, where her guilt dwelt, Betsy felt better for telling Mags of her feelings; and Mags let out more and more about how her weeks in the asylum had been and, as she'd never done before, told of her time nursing in Belgium.

Betsy couldn't believe what Mags had been through, and the fear she must have felt when the borders closed and she and her friends were left behind, with no supplies and no help from any senior personnel. That her Mags – a sometimes strong, sometimes vulnerable woman – should have to go through all that she did and had done since, hurt Betsy to think about. None of it should have happened. Mags was born to the fine life, not to be used in the ways she had been.

'It seems we all have bad stuff to carry around with us,' she'd told Mags, and wished with all her heart that she could unburden herself of the worst of her own baggage, but knew that would cause further pain to Mags and maybe cut them both apart. She couldn't risk it.

Now they were staying in a small hotel in Brixton and today Susan's husband, who had somehow become such a large part of Mags's life, was coming to visit with Susan's child, and they were all going to picnic together in the park.

The name of the park had given Mags the shivers at first, as it was so like the name of the asylum. Brockwell Park was just a short walk away from the hotel and, as always, Betsy was glad to get out of the hotel, as she wasn't at home in such places. She felt she should be serving the guests, not being one of them.

When they met up with Montel, Betsy saw immediately how it was that Mags could like him so much. He obviously thought the world of Mags. 'I am pleazed to meet you, Betzy. You are very lovely, just az Mags has told me. And these are your lovely girls.'

The girls all looked up at him with cheeky smiles on their faces, and Betsy knew that Montel was the type of person that everyone took to, young and old alike.

'Pleased to meet you an' all, Montel. And I've heard a lot about you.'

Montel had looked over at Mags when Betsy said this, and Betsy saw Mags blush. To her mind, these two needed some time on their own, as she could feel a tension between them. 'Right, I'll take young 'un from you and she can stay with us, we'll sit over there by the lake. You two go for a walk, then you can give all your news to Montel, Mags.'

Mags looked pleased at this, and neither of them objected. Betsy watched them walk away, after assuring themselves she would be all right on her own, in this London that frightened her so much.

Settled on the grass and looking around her, Betsy thought the park was lovely. The grass was green, lush and velvety, and the sun dappled on the ripples the ducks made in the lake as they glided by. The thought came to her that she couldn't believe there would be such a peaceful haven in the middle of the chaos of the streets around the city. As she gave the girls some crusts so that they could feed the ducks, Betsy let her mind wander. An unknown future stretched out ahead of her. One that held loneliness for her, because although she would be with Mags, there would be no Bill, or Ma, or Ciss.

Sighing, she gave her attention to the little girl whose hand she held. 'Aye, and it's the same for you an' all. You're a lost soul, with only a stepdad to take care of you, but he looks a good 'un. And if it does work out that he takes up with Mags and comes to Scotland with us, then I'll look out for you, I promise, as I liked your ma. Despite everything, I liked her, though it beggars belief how Susan could leave you and go to that sod Roford.'

Mags found that her troubles left her as she walked with Montel. They talked about everything and nothing at first – small talk that wasn't stilted or inhibited, but which gave her time and led on to the bigger issues that she had faced and was trying to sort out.

'I hope to hear later today if the power of attorney has been lifted. If it has, then I can make plans to go to Scotland.'

'Part of me doesn't want it all to be sorted, *ma chérie*. I cannot bear to think of you all those miles from me. I have suffered while you have been in Blackburn.'

Mags felt a tingle of awareness tickle her stomach muscles. 'I – I missed you, too, Montel.'

'Iz thiz true? Iz it that you really missed me?'

Mags laughed. 'Yes, I did. I missed the cheekiness of you, showering me with compliments. You make me feel worthy again.'

'It iz that I mean every word I say to you. You are in my heart, and I want you in my armz.'

'Oh, Montel. I do have feelings for you, but it is all so soon.'

'If I take you behind that tree where no one can see us, will you let me hold you? Just as a friend who wants to soothe your hurt?'

Knowing it was a dangerous thing to do, where her emotions were concerned, didn't stop Mags nodding. Montel made a sound that told of his glee, then took her hand and ran with her into the clump of trees. Once there, he took Mags's breath away by pulling her into his body and clasping his hands round her waist. She could feel his warm breath on her cheeks, and his heart beating through his shirt. Her body moulded to his, giving her pleasure that got her drawing in the breath she'd released when he'd taken her into his arms.

'Mags. Oh, Mags, I have longed for thiz moment.'

Mags couldn't speak, as her mind was screaming, *No, this is too soon, too soon.* But her body was betraying her and had her yearning to feel the touch of his lips on hers. She didn't have to wait long. His hand cupped her chin and lifted her face. She looked into the dark, beautiful pools of Montel's eyes and was lost. When his lips rested on hers, it was as if her world was suddenly put right again; but as the kiss deepened, the world was rocked on its axle once more, as feelings she couldn't control pulsed through her body.

She didn't protest as his hand found her breast and kneaded it gently, nor resist his tongue entering her mouth, but when he went to lift her skirt, Mags pushed him away and cried out, 'No!'

Montel's gasp held surprise and then his face fell in shame. 'Forgive me. My Mags, I knew not to do zat, but it

283

iz that my heart led me. I love you, my Mags. I love you and I want to spend my life with you.'

His hand came out to her and she took it. And as she looked once more into his eyes, now full of love for her, she knew that she loved him, too. Knew that he was the other half of her. It was complicated, and yes, even a little sullied – him being married to her husband's mistress – but she couldn't help any of that. She loved Montel and wanted to spend her life with him.

There was no stopping the happy smile that played around her lips.

'Mags?'

'I accept your love, Montel, and I give you mine. But your love has to be patient. I'm not ready to give myself to you. I have to feel right. I want to – more than anything in the world I want to – but I can't, not yet.'

Montel's eyes filled with tears. Stretching out his arms, he took her back into the circle of them and leaned his head on hers. '*Ma précieuse fille*. My precious one.'

For a moment Mags stayed still, cocooned in the love that enclosed her. A love she so wanted, but was afraid of, in case it broke once she let it fully possess her. She knew she had to heal first; and then, when she was ready, embrace it with all that she was.

Back with Betsy, and in the reality of the moment, Mags felt a shyness of Montel. She'd let him in too far, and yet she yearned to go further. It was a confusion that settled in her and she didn't know how to deal with it. Betsy saved the day with her matter-of-fact way. 'Eeh, come on, you two, we're near on starving here.'

'Let's open the picnic basket then. I asked the hotel to

put up some boiled-egg sandwiches for the children, and ham salads for us. There's a cloth to spread out.' Mags got on her knees as she said this and found that dealing with the picnic took away any awkwardness. Soon they were clearing away, after laughing their way through the lunch at the antics Montel played with the children.

With the children now lying on the grass and closing their eyes, Mags broached the subject of Scotland. 'I haven't spoken in much detail about it, but I have a four-bedroomed house in Scotland, with a view over the sea. Portpatrick is a lively port, taking in fishing boats and small craft from Ireland, and at night you can see Ireland lit up. Well, I only know this from my mother's letters. I had thought to get a small cottage for you, Betsy, but now I might turn the top floor into living quarters for you. The problem is that I don't know how big the house is, or what state it's in. I did give instructions that it is to be maintained, but that could just mean that outside repairs have been undertaken. We may have a lot of work to do once we are there.'

'Thiz will mean that you will need a man around the house, and if it iz beautiful, then I can paint the scenery and you beautiful ladies, too.'

Mags didn't know what to say to this. She hadn't thought Montel would come with them, but now the idea appealed to her. 'You would give up London and the exhibition you are working towards – not to mention your artistic community – to come and live up there?'

'I would give up everything for you, Mags, but I don't see that my exhibition cannot go on. I have my paintings ready. They can be stored at the gallery, and I can come down before the opening to mount them on display. It iz a simple matter and I hope that you will be able to come down with me?'

Everything was possible, in Montel's eyes. But Mags hesitated.

'It will be perfect. I am good with everyzing. I can cook, look after children, make and mend, carry in coal for the fires and still spend time painting. Pleaze let me come with you, Mags. I cannot live without you.'

Betsy looked amused. Mags doubted she'd ever dealt with anyone like Montel before.

'I'm with him, Mags. Life will be much better with Montel in it. Eeh, he'd keep us laughing, and he'd be reet handy about the place. But what about Sibbie?'

'If Susan cannot have her, then she comes with me. I cannot leave her, though I thought that pig of a man would have given in by now, az Susan iz pining for her daughter – she rings me most days. We talk of our divorce, too. She iz wanting to be free, just in case, but she fears Harold will not divorce you, Mags.'

'No, especially if the power of attorney over me is lifted, as divorce would mean he would not have a right to everything that is judged as mine.' Mags told them the position that she and Harold were in, regarding ownership of everything.

'So while he remains married to you, he can control everyzing, and he may have transferred a lot of it into hiz name already?'

'Yes, but I don't care. I have enough for my needs. Though my solicitor does want to bring Harold to task over that. The problem is that it is a costly business to do so, and if I lose, I could be left with nothing. I would rather just walk away.'

'But then you will never be free!'

The dismay in Montel's voice both heartened and embarrassed Mags. Would she ever get used to him expressing his feelings so publicly?

'I can be as free as I want to be, Montel. We will talk about it on our own. But Sibbie is very welcome in my home, because yes, I would love you to come with us.'

Montel did a skip and a dance, in an awkward fashion, making them all laugh. Betsy winked at Mags, but for Mags the statement had seemed to release the last bit of her that was still shackled. *Yes, I can do anything I want – even live as man and wife with Montel, if I so wish. And I will, and I won't care. I will choose to be happy.*

Chapter Twenty-Six

Once the children were in bed, Mags sat with Betsy at the dinner table. This was as good a time as any to broach the subject of Montel.

'About what happened today, Betsy – you know, concerning Montel and . . . well, him coming to live with us.'

'Eeh, lass, if you want to live as husband and wife, who's to knaw, eh? We can tell the young 'uns that you wed, and leave it at that. And, Mags, if I could give you one piece of advice, it would be to do it. It's plain to see as you love one another – real love, as love should be given, not the infatuation you had for Roford. 'Cause that's all it was, you must knaw that now.'

'I do. Harold does something to women; somehow he gets us to do anything for him. Look at Susan.'

'Aye, poor lass. I wonder how she is. Though I can't come to terms with her giving her babby up. Naw woman can be right in their mind to do that. I couldn't. I'll love this one that I'm carrying, just as much as I do me girls that I had with Bill.'

'You're special, Betsy. Very special.'

'Naw, I'm just an ordinary lass. I've done bad things and good things, but by, I've paid for the bad, and still am doing.'

'What do you mean, Betsy? What are you still paying for?'

'Eeh, don't ask me, Mags. Let's change the subject, eh?'

'Betsy, I feel as though you are carrying something inside that is eating away at you. Don't let it. I am your friend, and you can share it with me. Is it something that happened that triggered Bill's action? I mean, something other than the rape and its consequences?'

'Naw, they were what triggered him, but . . . eeh, Mags, you'll hate me. I . . .'

'Oh, my dear, don't cry. Come on. I've had enough to eat and it's a warm night. Let's go and sit on the wall outside.' Once there, Mags became increasingly concerned for Betsy. Sobs racked her body. 'Betsy, please, love. Whatever it is, unburden yourself. You can never do anything to make me hate you.'

'I can, and I have. But, lass, what I've done is best left unsaid. It led to you suffering so much. And . . . and, your da . . . Oh, God, I'm sorry, so sorry.'

Mags felt alarmed now. Betsy seemed to be heading for a breakdown. Willing herself to be strong, she coaxed Betsy to tell all. 'Is it to do with the rape, Betsy? If it is, I want you to know that I can, and do, forgive you. None of that was your fault, try to—'

'It was.' A huge sob shook Betsy; spittle came from her mouth, snot ran from her nose and her body folded. 'Oh, Mags, there . . . there was no rape.'

As she said this, Betsy slipped off the wall onto the floor. A passer-by stared, then tutted and went on his way. Mags looked at the crumpled figure of the best friend she'd ever had and couldn't move. *No rape? What? No . . . no, Betsy couldn't have, could she? I can't take it, I can't.*

A figure came running over from the other side of the road. 'What iz thiz? What haz happened? Betsy, Betsy. Pleaze, you must get up.'

'Montel? What are you doing here?'

'I couldn't rest. I asked a friend to watch Sibbie. I wanted to be with you, Mags. But what iz it that has hurt Betsy like thiz? Pleaze, Mags, help me with her. Let's get her inside.'

'No, it will be too embarrassing for her.' Helping Montel to lift Betsy, they steadied her on the wall once more. 'Betsy, love. Nothing is as bad as it seems. You have to tell me now. I promise I will help you. We'll help each other. Stay with Montel while I get you a drink. I think a stiff whisky for us both is in order.'

'And I wouldn't be saying no, Mags. It iz a shock to find you both like thiz.'

Mags wanted to smile, but a painful knot had formed in her chest. *Did Betsy betray me? My best and only friend? No, please God, no.*

It took a few sips of the burning whisky to calm Betsy, and for Mags to be ready to hear whatever was coming.

'I know there's naw other way but to tell you the truth, Mags. I cannot live with this guilt any more. Even if you don't forgive me, I will knaw as I've been honest with you. I can never bring my Bill back, and I caused his death. Me lovely Bill.'

All of this was said through gulping sobs. Mags's heart felt as though it was breaking. She'd half-guessed what Betsy was going to say, and though it couldn't hurt her any more, it had done; it had caused so much pain – so much.

'Harold Roford didn't rape me . . .'

Mags listened in horror to Betsy as she sobbed out the truth. 'Oh, Mags, that moment of sinning brought so much down on everyone. I didn't think at the time it would. I just wanted to punish him, and to get you to see once and for all what a swine he was. It was when he threw the coins at me that . . . I – I, well, I snapped.'

Mags sat down on the wall. Her heart seemed ready to break in two. She'd been coping. Everything was turning out all right. She was willing to support Betsy every step of the way, believing she'd brought everything Betsy had to bear down upon her, but now she knew she hadn't. Betsy had brought it upon herself. *And on me, and Daddy, and Bill. Poor Bill.*

There was a long silence, broken only by Betsy's pitiful sobs.

'Mags, thiz iz a lot for you to take in, but you can overcome it. You need to make comparisons and to think if it iz what Betsy did that was the real cause of everything that came az a consequence. It iz the only way you can get through thiz.'

Mags hadn't a clue what Montel meant. Her mind was screaming at her. Hatred for Betsy was pounding through her veins. 'I need to be alone. I have to think. This changes everything – everything.'

'Naw, Mags, please don't let it. I'm sorry. So sorry. Please forgive me. Ple-e-e-ase.'

'Betsy, I know it iz going to be hard to do, but you need to give Mags time. Go inside and go to bed. Be with your children. Come on, it iz that I will help you. Mags, wait for me. We will go for a walk. I can help you, I know thiz.'

Mags didn't answer, but neither did she move.

* * *

When Montel came out of the hotel, Mags was still sitting on the wall outside. She allowed Montel to take her arm. Her legs felt weak, but he steadied her. 'Let uz walk.'

Leaning on him, she let him steer her towards the park. Once inside, they sat down on a bench. As it was still light, there were a few people about, taking in the balmy August evening air.

'Mags, I also am shocked at what I heard, but not surprised. You said yourself that Harold iz a magnet to women. Look how you fell for him, and how he haz Susan in his clutches. Iz it not pozzible, then, that he did the same zing to Betsy? Then, in a moment of weakness, when she didn't think she would be found out, she succumbed, just as you and Susan did. Her reaction when he called her "scum" and threw coins at her, az if she was a prostitute, waz unthinking. If she had thought other than to get her own back and disgrace Harold, she wouldn't have done it. Look how she haz suffered, for that one moment of wanting revenge. In my country we would call thiz a crime of passion.'

Mags listened, and a lot of what Montel said did get through to her. She knew Harold. Knew what he was capable of; and yes, he had made her do things she would never dream of doing. Hadn't she lain with him before they were wed? And Susan – a nice girl, an innocent, naive girl who wanted nothing other than a job as a maid in his mother's house – was seduced by Harold, only somehow she got into his blood and he could not give her up. Nor she him. *Look at how Harold beats Susan and refuses to let her have Sybil – their child – with her, and yet she is still with him.*

'But I, and so many other people, suffered so much.'

'Harold waz out to make you suffer. He would have found

a way to break you. If not that night, az you had guests, then another time. Maybe he waz even priming Betsy for the purpose; only, as she said, that night she had to do duties she didn't usually do, and so Harold unexpectedly had a chance to get what he wanted. But it wasn't the right time, so he had to get rid of her – and quick. Hiz mistake was in insulting Betsy. And so she haz become zee wicked one, zee cause of everything; and yet zee real cause iz one person, and one person only. Betsy iz just another of Harold's victims.'

Montel is right. Betsy is a victim. As I am, and Bill and my poor daddy, and Flors, and yes, Susan. We're all victims of the evil that is Harold.

'Thank you, Montel, you have made the picture clear. There are many victims of Harold's evil, and we must not let him divide us. We have to stick together. I cannot imagine life without Betsy. And you must still have Susan in your life, too, as she has meant so much to you.'

'She haz been my saviour. But I have zee good newz.'

At the end of telling her his news, that today he had confirmation that he'd gained his pardon, Mags cried out with joy. 'Oh, how? That's wonderful.'

'It iz because of Sibbie. She relies on me, and it looks pozzible that she may do so for the rest of her life. My conscience was too much for me. I thought of what would happen to her, if it iz that I am suddenly found. Better that I leave her now, and Susan iz forced to take care of her, or Sybil goes into a home for unwanted and orphaned children. And zo I went along to the French Embassy a week ago, to hand myself in. But I found that my case had been looked at again. With the war won, and further evidence taken from my fellow men, it haz been judged that, far from being executed as a traitor, I am to be honoured as a hero for saving the lives of my men. I have been awarded the highest medal for bravery, the *Légion d'honneur*. I can regain my French citizenship, if I zo wish, and can arrange to have my medal presented whenever I am ready. And all thiz iz down to Susan. She had the faith in me to save me. We have never been more than the very best of friends who share a flat. I will always be ready to help her. I love her az a dear friend.'

'Oh, Montel, I'm so pleased. I know how terrible it is to be a fugitive. And I know what it is to have such a friend as Susan. I have that in Betsy, but now I have let her down. I have walked away when she needed me most. How can I ever make that right?'

'But of course you can. Your reaction is natural, and is what Betsy knew would happen. She iz probably thinking of leaving tomorrow. You must go back to her and give her your understanding – not forgiveness; don't make her feel that she needs that, az she will try all her life to be sure she haz that. But tell Betsy there iz nothing to forgive. That you realize that now. Tell her how she iz a victim az much as you are, and that you will help each other.'

'Oh, Montel, you are so wise. So wonderful. I love you.'

'My Mags, my beautiful Mags.'

His kiss was gentle. 'Thiz izn't the time for our passion. There iz hurt to heal. That iz what we have to concentrate on. But, Mags, did you hear any news? Iz it that you are free, and that man haz no further hold on you?'

'Yes, yes, I am. I was about to tell Betsy, when all this blew up. I had a call from David. Harold no longer has power of attorney over me. But he did put all the money we had into an account in his name only. He could do nothing about the house and the business – well, he has the lion's share of that, as he is the managing director. But none of that matters. I so want to leave for Scotland. And I want to do so as soon as we can. Have you spoken to Susan?'

'I have. She iz still suffering from the beating, but she says Harold cannot do enough for her and iz mortified that he lost control. She believes him when he says that he will never do it again. I was cross with her. I tried again to persuade her to make it so that Sibbie can be with her, but although she cried, Susan said she couldn't do anything, and would I take Sibbie to Scotland with me? I lost my temper and asked how she could choose her own happiness over that of her daughter. She told me: "No, Montel, I am choosing Sibbie's happiness over mine. With you and Mags and Betsy, Sibbie will be happy. Harold will never let me go, and he won't have Sibbie here or recognize her. My heart bleeds to be with my daughter, but I have no choice other than to let her go."'

'Poor Susan. In a way we are in the same position, as Harold will never let me go, either. If you and I are to be together, it will never be as man and wife. Not while I have even a small claim over what Harold wants as his own.'

'Will you be happy that way?'

'I will. Very happy.'

'Well then, we will have our own ceremony. Here and now. Margaret Roford, I take you as my wedded lover, from thiz day forward. I will love and cherish you. All that I have iz yours.'

'Oh, Montel. I take you as my wedded lover, to love, cherish and care for, in sickness and in health, for the rest of our lives. All that I have is yours.'

His kiss this time held love, and a promise of all they would become to each other in the future. His passion deepened with the kiss and found an answering passion in her. Taking her hand, he led her into the wooded area. There she became his, swirling in a love she'd never known before. He was hers. Her forever love.

Chapter Twenty-Seven

By the time they travelled to Scotland, Betsy and Mags's friendship was more tightly sealed than ever. As they sat on the train on their journey, Betsy's hand rested in Mags's.

'You shuddered again. Dear Betsy, don't. Don't punish yourself night and day.'

'Eeh, lass, you knaw me so well. I'm lucky to have you.'

'Blame everything on Harold, like I told you. He is the evil force who brought down on everyone everything that happened.'

'Aye, I knaw. But it's a bit frightening to knaw what someone like that can bring out in us. I never thought in a million years that I would end up betraying you.'

'And I never thought in a million years that I would happily deny Harold's daughter, and the mother who was in dire straits, with no job and no prospects. But I did. I believed Harold when he said Sibbie wasn't his. But I have a chance to make up for that now. We'll give Sibbie a happy life, for her and for Susan.'

'Poor lass.'

The countryside sped by and darkness fell. It seemed strange to go to bed on a train, but it was an adventure, too. The next morning brought lovely sunshine and a delicious breakfast of bacon and eggs on toast. Soon they were pulling into Glasgow station. The route was planned this way to give Mags a chance to buy a car. She and Montel were to share the four hours or so of driving to Portpatrick, with Betsy and the children sitting in the back. They had a small amount of luggage to take with them, enough to tide them over, and that would fit in the boot, and Mags arranged for the rest of their luggage to be taken into storage and delivered in a few days' time.

Finally they were on the road leading to the sea. Although they were tired and very hungry, their spirits lifted to see the glistening water and the many boats bobbing up and down in the port. Everywhere was a hive of activity, as some men unloaded fishing boats and others mended nets.

'It's lovely.'

'Oh, *mon Dieu* – an artist's dream.'

'Eeh, it's grand.'

The road ended in a T-junction, with the sea straight ahead. To the left and the right there was a high cliff, giving the port the appearance of being in a valley. Little cottages lined the quayside and an inn snuggled between them.

Looking in the direction where she knew her house stood, Mags gasped, 'Oh, look, I think that's it. The two-storey white building.'

The house, though not terribly grand, had a charm that made Mags fall instantly in love with it. Its tired exterior didn't detract from how inviting it looked, and the view was unbelievable. She wanted to go straight to it and check it over, but the children were fractious and needed attention and it wouldn't be practical to do so.

Turning away, they made for the inn.

Six weeks later, as the nights began to draw in, they were all settled. The house had turned out to be much bigger than its front implied, as the building went quite a way back on the left side, leaving a sheltered garden on the right. This annexe was being turned into a home for Betsy and her girls, while the main body of the house would be for Mags, Montel and little Sibbie.

All were rather fed up with the building work, but they spent happy days walking and exploring, though for Montel it was painting and more painting.

Mags had her own room, promising Montel that their lives together would start once they were living separately from Betsy and her family, although there were opportunities for them to be alone, as Betsy had taken to going out for a walk with the children every afternoon. Always they came back full of excitement at something newly discovered: seals playing in the sea, a rickety bridge over a ravine that led to a field of cows, and a magical castle, as they called the ruins of Dunskey Castle, sitting on the cliff to the south of the house.

But for all the happiness she'd found, Mags was beset by worry. Everything was costing a lot more than she had imagined, and she had visions of her legacy running out within two years.

Winter was upon them before the house was truly ready, giving them all their own living areas. By that time an idea had occurred to Mags. They had noticed that many tourists

299

came from England and the Scottish cities to the village, by train via Stranraer, and by boat from Ireland. The three hotels and the inn always did a roaring trade.

Looking over at Montel as he lay asleep, with the low winter sun streaming through the window and lighting up his naked body, Mags felt her happiness to be complete, but also knew that now was the time to plan to supplement their income the following summer. Betsy was soon to have her baby, but once she had recovered and could take responsibility for running the home, Mags would be free to put her ideas into action.

Montel stirred. 'What iz it you are thinking about, my darling? I can almost hear your brain ticking.'

'Ha, yes, I am scheming. But we ought to get up – it is light and so it must be almost ten.'

Montel rolled over onto his front and cupped his head in his hands. 'It is too cold. I'll light the fire in a moment. Then I'll come back to bed and make love to you while the room warms up.'

Mags smiled at him. 'Well, sometime today I need to discuss some plans that I have to bring us in an income.'

Montel moaned. 'So it iz that my lovemaking has to wait, eh?'

'No, we can do that first – as you say, once you have lit the fire. Because now that you have mentioned it, I am aching for you.'

'I think that you are a naughty girl, Mags.' With this, Montel jumped out of bed and rekindled the embers in the bedroom fireplace, soon having the dry sticks crackling away and placing coals on them. Then he laughed at what the cold had done to his ardour. 'Come here, it iz that you have to warm me up again.'

Mags giggled, and her happiness brimmed over as she went into his arms.

With the fire crackling up the chimney, they sat up against the pillows, both of them hot and filled with joy. Montel lit one of his small cigars, and Mags breathed in the aroma she'd come to love.

'Now I am ready to listen.'

'Well, we haven't long, as Betsy will be calling out that breakfast is ready.'

'Oh, of course it iz Sunday, and she hazn't to take the children to school.'

'No, but she likes her routine, even if it does start later on Sundays. Now, what do you think of a craft shop, where we can sell everything that is made locally? And, of course, your paintings of the local area. You have so many now, and not all of them are for your exhibition.'

'Hmm, I'm liking the idea. I can also offer a portrait-painting service for those who are here for a few days, with the backdrop of any scene they like in Portpatrick.'

'That would be wonderful.'

'I have all but one of my paintings ready to take to London. My *pièce de résistance* is yet to be painted.'

'Oh? And what is that – have you something planned?'

'I have. It is you, my darling. You in all your nude glory.'

'What? No, that won't happen.'

'But it must. I have to. It is my dream.'

Mags didn't know what to think. She knew he had painted Susan in the nude many times, but herself? This she wasn't sure of. 'Will my hair cover my face?'

'No, of course not. The study iz of complete and utter

wonderful womanhood. Nothing about a stunning woman in all her glory offends the art world.'

'I will let you do it, but I have to approve of it before I agree to you showing it. It may be something that we keep between us, never to be seen by anyone but us.'

'My love for every part of you will shine through. I will call it *A Man's Perfect Lover.*'

Mags burst out laughing.

'And zo what else do you plan we sell?'

'Home-knitted garments. I have seen many a woman sitting on her step in the summer with her needles clicking away. I plan to find a local outlet selling wool from the highland sheep and pay these women to knit for me. And pottery, too. I was a very good potter in my youth; it was one of the crafts we did in my school. I am going to buy all the tools I need and try to use the clay produced locally. I know Lanarkshire is renowned for its clay production, but if I can find somewhere nearer, that would be more in keeping. I would want my vases to have scenes of this lovely village, so I will need some painting instructions from you. And maybe I'll even stock a few tartan items – scarves, et cetera. Oh, and berets. Betsy is a handy seamstress. I will get her a treadle sewing machine. I need all of this done during the winter months, so that we have stock to open with, and it can be ongoing from there. I am thinking of finding out who owns that old boathouse on the edge of the village – the one that is almost falling down. I think it is an ideal setting and can be renovated to become our shop, and the back part can be our workshop.'

'I am – how you say? – astonished! It iz all planned, and all sounds wonderful. I am excited to see my paintings on sale again.'

'No, it isn't planned, it is only an idea. But oh, I'm so happy you think it a good one. I will begin the planning and research stage now, and the financial side, too. It has to be viable, and we have to see that we can make a profit.'

'*Vous êtes une merveille.*'

'Oh, I hope that isn't something rude. I do understand that you said "You are a" but after that . . . ?'

'How you say? "Marvellous", but shorter.'

'Marvel? Well, I'll only be that if it works, but I'm going to give it my all.'

'Then it will certainly work; it haz to, *ma fille habile* – my clever one.'

'I'll talk over every step that I take. I hope to start soon after Christmas, once Betsy has had her baby and is up and about.'

On cue, Betsy entered the conversation by yelling up that breakfast would be ready in five minutes. This had them both scrambling out of bed. They jollied each other for a turn at splashing themselves with water from the bowl on the dresser and then donned dressing gowns. Opening the door to their bedroom released the delicious smell of frying bacon drifting up to them. Holding hands, they descended the wide staircase together and were soon amid the hubbub of noisy children and general family life.

They had purposely chosen the biggest room to be their kitchen, so that they could fit a huge table into it. The floors were a shiny dark stone, and the walls a rough texture in cream, with many hooks drilled into them, holding strings of onions, brightly polished copper pans and bunches of herbs of all kinds. The range took up at least six feet of one wall and had a proving oven, a warming oven and a baking oven, as well as a hot plate on one side and an open fire on the other. Next to this was a dresser on one side, which displayed their best china and contained their everyday dishes in its cupboard, and a pantry on the other, with a cold slab for butter, lard and milk, as well as a cold store for meats. The table was scrubbed wood and each of the ten chairs had a cushion in blue gingham, which matched the tablecloth they put on for mealtimes, plus the curtains as well as the small curtain around the deep pot-sink. Next to the sink, which was placed under the window and between the doors, was a gas stove for when it was too hot to light the range. All in all, it was a family room, where they all congregated during the day.

Mags loved it. Memories of being an only child often assailed her, and when she compared it to this, she knew she had missed out.

'Mama!'

Sibbie had taken to calling Mags that, though she gave her no encouragement and tried to make her say 'Mags'. Montel often showed Sibbie a portrait of Susan – one of the few fully clothed portraits he had – and told her over and over again that this was her mama.

Mags looked into Sibbie's chubby face and had the urge to pick her up and hold her to her. As she went to do so, a cry from Betsy stopped her. 'Eeh, Mags, the babby's coming.'

Mags cried out with joy. So elated did she feel that she clasped the hands of Daisy and Florrie and had them skipping around: 'The baby's coming, the baby's coming.'

'Mags, you daft ha'p'orth, stop your antics and help me. I don't reckon as it's going to be long.'

At this, Mags went into nurse mode. 'I'll help you, Betsy. Let's get you to your bedroom. Montel will take over here.'

As they went through the room allocated as Betsy's living room, Mags tried to soothe any worries Betsy might have. 'Don't worry about the baby being a few weeks early, Betsy, everything will be fine.'

'I knaw. I'll just be glad to get it over with, lass.'

Hours later, Mags didn't feel quite so confident as she mopped Betsy's brow. Betsy's energy had all but drained from her. 'We'll have to send for the doctor, Betsy. I thought the baby was coming, but you don't seem able to get it any further.'

'Help me, Mags. Don't let me babby die.'

Mags knew the doctor would take an hour to get to them, as there wasn't one in the village, and even if Montel went by car to Stranraer to fetch him, that wasn't to say that he could come at once. She had no choice – she had to help Betsy herself. 'I'll get my hands around the head, Betsy, and you push. I think the child is lying face-down. If my efforts don't work, then I'm sorry, my dear friend, but I'm going to have to cut you.'

'Do what you have to, Mags, but help me . . . Help me!'

Betsy's desperation provided the extra impetus the baby needed – one push and Mags could take its head in her hands and twist gently, and this had the baby slithering out. 'Oh, Betsy, it's here, and it's a boy!' A piercing wail drowned them both out for a moment. 'Oh, and with a strong pair of lungs.' *Though more a wail of 'See to my needs', I would say, just like his father.*

Brushing this thought away, Mags shook herself mentally. She didn't want to think of the child in that way. She looked at Betsy. Though she was red and sweaty, with her hair matted to her head, Betsy's smile told of extreme joy. 'Billy – I have to call him Billy after my Bill. Eeh, Mags, a boy. Let me see.'

The tiny form, covered in blood, wriggled in Mags's arms as she cut the cord. 'Almost done, just making him a neat belly-button.'

A weak giggle came from Betsy.

As Mags wiped the baby's face, she had the feeling again of 'like father, like son', as the baby's expression showed his likeness to his father. His brow was furrowed, and his mouth was open, as if in protest that this entry into the world wasn't going his way. But the likeness didn't end there, as he had his father's features and his black hair and eyes.

Mags could feel a repulsion growing inside her, but she didn't want to feel that; she wanted to feel love for this precious new life. Wrapping the still-yelling Billy in a warm blanket, she handed him to Betsy. The baby immediately settled and snuggled into his mother. At this, a feeling of warmth did enter Mags, although it was tempered by the thought that now that he had what he wanted, Billy – like his father – had changed into a little charmer.

I must stop thinking like this. It's unfair of me to compare this baby, only minutes into life, with his monster of a father.

Seeing the lovely picture of mother and son helped her. Everything would turn out well, of this Mags felt sure. Billy would have the influence of Betsy, herself and, above all, Montel, to shape him. Thinking like this gave Mags a yearning she had felt for months now – to find herself pregnant with Montel's child. Montel was a born father. He'd become just that to Daisy, Florrie, Rosie and Sibbie, and now she knew he would take on Billy, too.

Oh, my darling Montel, the day I met you was the day I began to live – really live – and now I want to make you a father for real. But can I? Her mind reminded her how nothing had happened when Harold stopped taking care not

306

to make her pregnant, and yet he had proven he could father children. *Please God, don't let it be that I am barren.*

But no, she wouldn't think like that. She would throw herself into making a magical Christmas for her lovely family, as that's what they were: Betsy and her four, Sibbie, and the wonderful Montel and herself – family. Afterwards, she would devote all she could to building a family business and supporting Montel in the art world. Whatever the outcome for herself – her own children or not – she would be fulfilled.

PART FOUR
Portpatrick and Blackburn, 1924–25

~

Mags and Montel

A Broken Heart – A Glimmer of Hope

Chapter Twenty-Eight

Since opening Charvet's Art and Craft Products two years earlier – the name was chosen to honour Montel and to emphasize the huge part that his work played – the business had gone from strength to strength. The summer season takings were enough to show a profit on the year and that was boosted by trade coming to them from those taking a winter break, especially the rich among the Irish people who sailed across in their yachts whenever the weather permitted. His portraits were proving so popular that those booking them sometimes had to return on a second visit to be able to fit in an appointment. Mags was so proud of him and rejoiced in the self-worth it had given Montel as the main breadwinner of his family.

His exhibition had gone down really well, although for her own portrait Mags had insisted on buying lengths of lace and wrapping herself in it. In the end the effect was tantalizing, as the contours of her body were visible as if seen through a mist. The painting was beautiful and had been bought by a wealthy Londoner, who wanted to know who the model was. Montel had told him it was his wife, to which the man expressed extreme regret, but joked, 'If I was an Arabian, I would offer you all the camels in Arabia for her.' This had made Montel laugh out loud when he had related the story to Mags.

Betsy had become more involved in the business than Mags had originally envisaged, because besides making a Scottish tammie hat each day, she helped with the pottery-making and had proved to be very talented at it, as well as artistic. Her paintings on the pieces of pottery were a realistic depiction of scenes around them. Montel had complimented her and given her tips. Now Betsy's pieces were sought-after. She preferred this to working with the tartan cloth, which she found too thick for her sewing machine, and had to stitch the hats by hand, often doing it in the evening, with her girls making the pompoms for the top of the hats.

They engaged daily helpers to clean the house, cook for them and look after the children, and that and the employment of many knitters and seamstresses skilled at working with tartan meant they were all loved and accepted by the villagers, who saw them as furthering the prosperity of their neighbourhood.

But, joy of joys, Mags was certain that at last she was pregnant. She'd now missed two of her periods and was feeling very queasy in the mornings.

Opening her bedroom curtains let in the sunlight. Its warmth held the promise of a lovely late-May day. All the family were out, except for four-and-a-half-year-old Sibbie and two-and-a-half-year-old Billy. How different these half-siblings were proving to be, with Billy living up to her first assessment of him as demanding and determined to have what he wanted, and Sibbie being much more like her father's lovely sister, Flora: gentle, kind and always giving in to Billy. Mags loved them both dearly, but felt guilt inside her concerning them. She had never been able to write to Flors to tell her and Cyrus that they had a niece and nephew. If only she had remembered Flora's letter, with her address on it, when she had finally escaped and left Feniscowles. Susan could have got it for her. But since then Mags had become wary of entrusting Susan with something so important. She'd even cautioned Montel not to tell Susan exactly where they were, when he contacted her. If Susan knew, she might be forced to disclose it, under the threat of a heavy beating from Harold.

Putting her hand on her stomach, Mags prayed her little one was truly nestled there, and that all would be well. Maybe now, with so much time having passed and no trouble coming their way from Harold, it was possible to trust Susan with getting Flors's address for her. There had been no news of any further beatings, and Montel had said that although Susan ached for Sibbie, she was otherwise very happy. *Can I risk Harold finding out where Flors is?* For sure, he would still harbour feelings of bitter revenge against Flors and Cyrus, and could bring terrible consequences down upon them for their continued incestuous relationship.

Mags had tried writing to Ella at the address Flors had given her, as this she had been able to record in her address book without any problems. The book had been lying openly on her bureau, and not long after they had settled in Scotland, Susan had given the book to David to send on to her, along with some of her other personal possessions. At the time, although it was lovely to have her mother's jewellery and her father's watch and cufflinks, it had felt as though Harold had instructed Susan to clear Mags and her parents out of

313

the house. Bitterness settled in Mags for a time afterwards, but she'd come to terms with it, with the help of Montel.

Sadly, the letter she had sent to Ella had been returned with 'Addressee not known at this address', and so unless she could get hold of Flora's address, she would never again have contact with either of them. All she could remember was that Flora was living in the Languedoc area, in a village called Laurens something-or-other, and it was there that she had planned on going when she first escaped from the asylum. But as for sending post to such a vague address, she just wasn't sure.

Going through to the small room that she used as her office, Mags set about tackling the mound of paperwork that had piled up. Invoices needed paying, receipts booking in and correspondence replying to. All was to do with the business and it now formed a major part of her own contribution. She'd have loved an office in the boathouse, where their shop was, but all available room was taken up with the pottery and the stockroom, as well as the shop itself and a studio for Montel.

After making separate piles of urgent and non-urgent post, Mags sat back. She felt restless. Her mind wasn't on paperwork today; it was as if she had a premonition of something bad going to happen. Rising, she decided that she would go for a walk. Maybe the two little ones could go with her, if they weren't resting.

She found Cook and the children's minder in the kitchen, having a cup of tea. 'We were about to shout up to see if you wanted a wee drop of tea, hen. There's plenty and it's only just brewed.'

'Thank you, Helen, but no. I thought I would get some air; it's stifling up in that office. Where are the children?'

'Och, they're playing in the garden . . . well, squabbling that is. But, as usual, yon Sibbie has given in.'

Mags looked out of the window. 'They look happy enough now, so I won't disturb them. Have you the sandwiches done for Betsy and Montel? I'll drop them off, if you have.'

'Aye, that'd be canny of ye. Save me walking that way. Me legs are screeching at me the day.'

'Oh? I'm sorry. Well, get off when you like, Cook. I can see to dinner tonight.'

'It's all ready for ye, all but the cooking of it.'

When Mags took the basket containing the sandwiches and lemonade, she thought as usual that there was far too much for Betsy and Montel, but was glad, as she could sit outside on the wall with them and share their lunch.

She walked down the slope, passing the time of day with her neighbours as she went. It was as she reached the bottom and was about to turn left, to take her to the boathouse, that she spotted a car parked a little way along the seafront. There was something familiar about the figure at the steering wheel, facing towards her. Mags's heart dropped into her stomach as if it were a concrete brick. *It can't be! Why, after all this time?*

Harold got out of the car and walked towards her. 'So, my little wifey, I've found you.'

Mags looked around her. Apart from strangers milling around, there was no one she knew who she could ask to run and fetch Montel.

'Why have you come, Harold? Couldn't you just leave things as they are? You have what you wanted – and I have a happy life. Or is it that at last you want to do the right thing by Susan and divorce me and marry her?'

'What? Me marry someone as low-birth as Susan? No.

I'm ridding myself of her. I have met someone. Someone of my own standing.'

'Harold, you are the meanest man I've ever come across. I doubt you will give Susan up, but someone has something you want, and you're willing to hurt poor Susan once again until you get it. Well, I hope this time she sees sense and finds someone who will love and cherish her, and your child.'

'I haven't got a child.'

Mags wanted to tell him that he had two, but it wasn't her place, as Betsy had never said that she wanted Harold to know about Billy. 'Well, you can divorce me whenever you want to. But remember that I am entitled to my share in the divorce settlement, and I will fight for it.'

His smile showed how sure he was of himself. 'That's what I wanted to talk to you about. There is very little left to share, of what there was. The mill is failing rapidly and is likely to go into liquidation or bankruptcy. There are hardly any assets, and I'm overdrawn at the bank to my limit. However, I have made enquiries, and you have plenty of assets – and therefore the same goes for me, as I am entitled to half of what you have.'

Mags wanted to laugh out loud, as for once she had the upper hand over Harold. 'If you are referring to the business we run here, then I only actually own a one-third share. And I know that you cannot touch my house, or any personal money that I have, as they are assets that I had before our marriage.'

Harold's face changed from one of victory to the ugly mask of hatred.

Mags seized the moment to taunt him further. 'Daddy told you that I had a good business head, but you wouldn't believe it. Well, I think my astuteness in this matter proves it. I always suspected something like this might happen, and I made sure that I was ready for it. Have you any contingency plans, Harold?'

'You bitch!'

'Yes, a very happy and comfortably-off bitch, thank you very much.'

'You won't be.'

Mags shuddered as Harold turned on his heel and stormed over to his car. But she didn't want to leave it there. 'By the way, how did you find me?'

Harold was in his car. He set off at a roaring pace, heading straight for her. Mags jumped back. His brakes squealed as he pulled up inches from her. 'I happen to go to London a lot and I was asked to dinner at a friend's house. What should be on the wall but a disgusting painting of you. It was only a matter of complimenting the artist and pretending that I didn't know him, but would like to commission a painting, and *voilà*, as he would say.' Harold revved the car. 'So now I know where you are, and there will be no hiding from me. You will be begging me to take your money, before I am finished.'

Pebbles shot in the air as he sped off. Mags stood for a moment, fear pumping around her veins. Harold was capable of anything. Anything!

'Ah, but iz it that the paperwork is already done? I thought it would keep you buzy all day . . . *Mon amour*, what iz it? You don't look well. Come and sit next to me.'

Sitting on the wall next to where Montel had his easel and paints, Mags couldn't stop her limbs from trembling.

'Tell me, *mon amour*. You look as though you have had a fright.'

317

'I have, Montel. Oh, I have, and of the worst kind.'

After Mags explained what had happened, Montel went quiet before muttering, 'I should have thought – it iz that I exposed you to being found.'

'No. How could you ever dream that the buyer of the painting would be connected to Harold in any way? But what are we to do? His threats were very real. He has been thwarted in what he wants – and by me – and he won't be able to stand that. He will want his revenge.'

'If it iz that I live to be a hundred, I don't think I will meet another man az wicked az he iz. Hiz threat of revenge iz very real. I think he will want to destroy what you have: all of thiz, and maybe your home, too. We cannot sleep until we know zee threat iz passed. I will stay over here at the boathouse each night. And we will employ somebody to guard the house. Big Rory iz zee man I am thinking of. He haz a dog, and iz always about at night with hiz gun. He goes poaching, but that doesn't make him the money we will pay him.'

Mags knew Rory very well and hadn't been above buying grouse and rabbits from him, though she had left the conclusion of such deals to Cook. She knew this to be a good solution, but was anxious about the disruption to their family life. 'But for how long? How can we know when the threat has passed?'

'You say that Harold iz running out of money, which means he haz to act fast. He haz been foiled from getting it from you, zo he will have to go to London to raise it. Susan haz told me that he still haz hiz house there. He could charge it to zee bank or sell it.'

'Wouldn't he have done that already – taken a bank loan on it, I mean?'

'Possibly, but we have to hope that he hazn't acted in character for once, and still has that asset to call on. If zo, he will only be able to spare a couple of dayz here. I will contact Susan. We know that he izn't there, zo it will be safe to ring her any time. She may hear from Harold. She haz our number for an emergency, zo she can keep uz informed if he calls her, or if she hears of hiz plans. I need to tell her that she iz welcome to come here, Mags, because now I no longer have my flat, she will have nowhere to go. Are you happy with that?'

'Of course – we have always included her. I thought of that myself and nearly blurted out to Harold that would happen, when he kicked Susan out.'

'Thank you, my darling. It iz that I will always take care of Susan.'

'And I would expect no less of you.'

Montel had taken her hand and now squeezed it gently. 'I love you. *Je t'adore*.'

'Oh, Montel, I adore you, too.' She wanted so much to tell him of the possibility that they were to have a child, but now wasn't the moment. She wouldn't want her telling to be overshadowed by Harold's threats to them, or to give Montel something else to worry about. And she would rather be certain, so as not to disappoint him if it turned out she wasn't pregnant.

'I will go to zee house and telephone Susan. You go and see Betsy, and warn her about there being danger to uz all.'

Neither Mags nor Betsy felt like eating their sandwiches, but they picked at them as they sat in the sunshine.

'Eeh, lass, I'd lulled meself into thinking that nowt could touch us now. But they say a bad penny allus turns up.'

319

'I feel so helpless. What can I do to stop Harold? I don't know what he plans, or if his threats were real – no, that's not true, I know they are, but who would believe us?'

'I knaw. Well, all we can do is be careful, for a couple of days. Montel's right. Harold can't stick around up here much longer than that. And then Susan will . . . Oh, here's Montel now.'

When Montel reached them, he sat on the wall between them. 'It iz that Susan iz distraught. She says Harold haz told her to leave before he gets back. It seems he has taken up with the daughter of the same man who bought the picture, only he haz bragged that he owns two mills and a large house in Blackburn and one in London. His own mill has gone, and hiz uncle iz dead. There iz nothing left of that legacy. He haz taken to gambling and loses heavily, whilst hiz aim iz to win big. Susan said your family mill iz running into the ground, with huge debts.'

'Why didn't she tell you any of this before?'

'Mainly because Harold waz always there when I telephoned, and he haz been stopping Susan from using the telephone and monitors the bill, zo that she can't get away with it. She said she tried to get to Dr Lange to give him a message, but he wasn't in. He is away on a long holiday.'

'Yes, I know. David's last letter said he was going to travel wherever the whim took him, and that his first port of call was Africa. He was leaving on a ship from Southampton.'

'Susan iz afraid. She knows Harold will kick her out, but doesn't know when. She iz staying until she haz to go. I tried to persuade her to come here, but she dare not. She said if she did and Harold found out, then she waz afraid for her life.'

'Oh, dear God! Look, Montel, we have to protect Susan. Has she a bank account of her own?'

'No, dear Mags, she iz not of that status.'

'Well, we must get money to her somehow. I will look into telegraphing some to a post office for her. Then she can find some accommodation until it is safe to come up here.'

'Thank you, Mags. Thiz will put my mind at rest. Now I must search out Rory. He iz usually about, from around this time.'

'Can he not look after both the boathouse and our house? He can see each from the other. And he can patrol them both.'

'It iz too much responsibility for him. He can see, yes, but he cannot be in two places at one time.'

'I just hate you being down here on your own.'

'I am zee soldier! I have zee highest honour for fighting the Germans, zo I can fight off zee Harolds of thiz world with no problem. I will be ready, and if he comes, then I will surprise him. He will run off, I am sure. Especially az I will shout for Rory, who I will instruct to fire hiz gun in the air if I call out to him. It will be very funny to see Harold running. And I don't think he will come back.'

When darkness fell and Montel was ready to leave the house, Mags's heart felt heavy. She clung to him. 'Be safe, my darling. Be safe.'

His eyes held hers for a long moment. Something in her wanted to capture his look forever. It held love, trust and, yes, desire. He pulled her close. 'I will imagine all night that I am in our bed with you. Imagine me there, too.'

'I won't be able to sleep. I might sit in my office all night,

321

watching the boathouse, as that is the only window I can see it from.'

'No, you mustn't. Please promise that you will go to bed. Even if you don't sleep, it iz for zee best.'

When he kissed her, the kiss lasted for a long, long moment. To Mags, it felt as though Montel was saying goodbye.

As he turned from her and went out of the door, she wanted to beg him to come back. But she knew it would be no use. Sinking onto a chair, she put her head onto the kitchen table and sobbed her heart out.

Chapter Twenty-Nine

A flickering light woke Mags from her sleep. Two days had passed since her encounter with Harold and ever since she hadn't been able to sleep, until tonight. Earlier she'd lain on the bed, fully clothed in readiness to get up every few moments and sit by the window in the office, but after spending most of the previous night there, she was exhausted and must have drifted off. Looking at the clock on her bedside table, she saw that it was two o'clock.

The light was unusual, as it danced on her walls. Catapulted to a sitting position, Mags swung her legs off the bed and slipped her feet into her shoes. As if her life depended on it, she ran to her office. What she saw started a scream from deep within her. The boathouse was on fire!

Hollering so loud that her throat hurt, she was outside before she'd registered that she'd come down the stairs. Something tripped her up. As she fell heavily, her breath left her body for a moment. When she recovered, she felt something under her. A dog! Rory's? The animal didn't protest at her falling over it or move a limb, making Mags realize that is was dead. But where was Rory? *Oh God, where is everybody?*

Mags didn't feel the grazes and bruising she'd suffered from the fall and looked frantically around her. Betsy came through the door, a shawl wrapped round her shoulders and covering her nightshift. 'Mags, eeh, lass, what's to do? Oh God, the boathouse!'

'Rory's dog's dead . . . and . . . Oh, Betsy, we have to get down there. Where's Rory, and Montel? *Montel!*' Screaming his name, Mags ran down the slope. Betsy caught up with her and took her hand.

When they rounded the corner, Mags felt her heart sink. The flames looked as though they were licking the sky. Suddenly she realized that others were out of their houses and were trying to douse the fire.

'Montel! MONTEL!'

A hand caught her arm. 'Lassie, you cannot go in there.' Angus, a local, called out to Betsy, 'Hold yon lassie back, hen.'

'Mags, Mags – eeh, me lass, don't; please don't go near it. Stay with me, as Angus says.'

'No. No-oooo!' Mags sank to the floor as the awful truth hit her. Montel was still in the boathouse, and probably Rory, too. *Please God, no.*

She could stretch her mouth no wider, nor sob any deeper, as her body gave way to the terrible fear that was tearing her limb from limb.

Betsy knelt beside her. Through her own sobs, she tried to give Mags hope, but Mags knew there was none to be had. Her precious Montel . . .

'He's gone. Oh, Betsy, he's gone.' With this, a mist came over Mags and took her into blackness.

* * *

When Mags opened her eyes, Betsy was by her side. 'Eeh, me lass, me poor lass. Shock took you into a deep faint. Some of the men carried you back here. Try to drink this water, Mags.'

'Is – is it true? Has . . . my Montel, has he gone?'

'Oh, Mags, me lovely friend. I – I . . . well, I'm sorry, lass. Sorry to the heart of me, but—'

'No! Oh God, don't say it. Don't!' But then Mags realized she had to know the truth, had to hear it spoken. 'Oh, Betsy, has he . . . ?'

'Yes, lass. Eeh, I'm sorry. Me heart is breaking for you, but – well, they found three bodies.'

'Three?' Mags sat up. 'Who . . . ?'

'Well, Rory can't be found; and his dog, as you knaw, was lain outside, probably clubbed with sommat heavy. The third body ain't certain, but I reckon we can have a good idea; well, I hope so anyroad.'

'Harold?'

'Aye. Angus has just been and told me the news. They all knew there was a problem, and that Rory was helping by guarding us. But I told him about Harold, and what we feared. He said there's a strange car parked at the bottom of the slope, but there's a few around, as there allus is, so they want to knaw if we knaw the make of Harold's car. In the meantime the hoteliers and innkeepers are checking that all their guests are safe, and the villagers are checking all the locals.'

'I only know his car is a green one. I'm not sure about different makes. But it has to be Harold. Please God that it is. I would never wish this fate on anyone, but I would on him. And if it is, I hope he continues to burn in hell for eternity.' A huge gasp seized Mags as she finished saying this. 'Help me. Oh, my Betsy, help me.'

'I'll hold you, me lass. I'll do all I can for thee.'

Mags felt her emotions shutting down, as Betsy held her close. It was as if a shield had been put up between her and the horror of what she faced: a long, bleak future without her Montel. This shield allowed her to ask questions. 'Did Angus say what caused the fire?'

'Naw. I asked, but he said as we would probably never knaw. But, lass, you're to be strong. If this breaks you, then Harold will have won. We knaw this is his doing – it has to be.'

'Yes. The pity is that he couldn't help himself. Oh, I'm not excusing him, but his whole family, except Flors, self-destructed. His brother died by a fire set by his own hand. His mother destroyed Harold's father, and then he in turn destroyed her . . . It just goes on and on.'

'Aye, I remember you told me of them. Well, now it seems Harold has destroyed himself, and murdered others. But what of Flors? Is she like them?'

'No. If Flors only knew it, she was lucky to be the forgotten daughter, rejected by them all. Lucky to have been brought up by her nanny, and not to have been influenced by the evil that affected the rest of the Rofords. But she was scarred by them, and her ultimate happiness was marred by the actions of her father keeping the secret of his child born out of wedlock.'

'Aye, it's a million-to-one chance that Flors should fall in love with her long-lost brother. Eeh, the tangles that evil weaves. Well, please God, we're rid of Harold now.'

'Yes, please God. But . . . Oh, Betsy, how am I to live without my Montel?'

'Don't! Don't go down that road. Take it step by step. And I'll walk beside you. You will get through it, lass, you will. I knaw this as a fact.'

Mags clung on to Betsy's hand. They'd come through a lot together. Whether she could come through this, she didn't know, but she would hold Betsy's hand whenever she needed to and would try to gain strength from her. And yes, she had her baby.

'Betsy, I think I'm with child.'

'Eeh, lass . . . lass. I'm pleased for thee. Hang on to that. Hang on to knawing as you have a part of Montel allus with you.'

They went into a cuddle, and Mags felt she never wanted to come out of it, as in Betsy's arms there was safety and the strength to stop her falling into the deep, dark pit that had opened up inside her.

The rain soaked them as Mags stood, with Betsy by her side, at the open grave containing Montel's coffin. It had been a week since that horrendous night. Susan stood on her other side. A shadow of the girl she had been, she had arrived the day before.

When Susan saw Sibbie, her arms went out to her, and Mags willed the little girl to go to her, but Sibbie didn't; she turned and ran towards Mags instead, her arms begging Mags to lift her up. 'You're a big girl now, Sibbie, I can't lift you, darling.' At this, Sibbie had hidden in her skirt. Taking her hand, Mags steered her towards the portrait of Susan and told Sibbie, 'Look, that's your mama.' Then she turned the little girl towards Susan and said, 'Your mama.' Sibbie reacted by pulling her skirt around herself once more to hide her face. 'It's just shyness, Susan, give her time.'

Later in the afternoon Sibbie had taken a string of wooden beads to Susan. 'Look. Montel made these for me, so that I can count them. Do you like them, Mama?'

Susan gathered her up to sit on her knee and Sibbie hadn't left her side since, wanting Susan to bath her and put her to bed and proudly announcing to the other children, 'I have a mama, too.'

This had helped Susan, and Sibbie. Even though Sibbie didn't understand where Montel had gone, she revelled in having what the others had: a mama. Finally Susan was where she should have been all along – with her daughter.

Susan's grief for Harold was not as evident as her grief for Montel and her sadness for Mags. She only mentioned Harold once, saying that she was glad his body was identifiable as she would have wondered forever; and that the arrangements had been made for his remains to be collected by the family undertaker, who would take them and lay them to rest in the Roford crypt in London. 'I won't be attending. He was ready to cast me out again, knowing that I had nowhere to go. Well, I knew I was coming up here, but I didn't tell him that. The love I had for Harold all but died. I can't come to terms with never seeing him again, but worse than that, he has taken away from me my best friend in all the world.'

'We're here for you, Susan.'

'How can you say that, after all I have done to you, Mags? You should hate me.'

'It wasn't you – it was Harold. He sought you out. He lied to you, and to me, until he was wed to me. But let's not go over it all, as it is too painful. I just want you and me to be friends. You were Montel's greatest friend and, as such, are mine.'

Susan cried then. Some of her ramblings, as Mags held her, had been about being sorry; others had been about how stupid she had been; but most had been about the loss of her dear Montel. At this point, Mags's own tears had joined Susan's and, in this, they had cemented their friendship.

A cold hand came into Mags's hand. She gripped Susan's hand just as hard as she was already holding Betsy's, as they watched the local vicar sprinkle holy water on Montel's coffin as it lay in the gaping open grave.

A picture came to Mags of Montel sitting on the quayside, painting. So alive, so beautiful.

Tears streamed down her face. She wanted him back. She didn't want him gone. She wanted the dream of them marrying to come true. But then their hearts were married, as were their souls, and although his soul was soaring high, she knew he would never truly leave her. He couldn't. Their hearts were entwined forever. *You will live on in your child, Montel.*

This thought prompted more tears. A river flowed from her eyes, her heart and her whole body. Her very soul was bleeding tears. Montel's voice came to her. '*It iz that you must carry on, mon amour. Carry on for our child, and for Betsy, and for Susan, and for the children; they will need you. I will be with you – with you always.*'

Why Montel would speak to her of their unborn child, she didn't know. Maybe it was her own voice, bidding him to say that. But no, the voice was definitely Montel's. She was sure of that and rejoiced that, in death, he did know of his child. And she would do all she could to carry through what he bid her to.

Lifting her eyes to the sky, Mags didn't care about the rain beating on her face. Montel had taught her to let herself feel everything around her – even the rain – and to welcome it as a thing of beauty. 'Everyzing has a beauty to it, including the rain. Welcome it and embrace it.'

Betsy let go of her hand and took it with her other hand. With her free arm she held Mags to her. Susan did the same. They cocooned her in their love and steered her towards where the vicar stood, holding a handful of earth. Taking it, Mags sprinkled it on the coffin. As she did so, the urge came to her to throw herself on top of the coffin and be buried with Montel. The thud of the wet earth brought her to her senses. 'Goodbye, my darling. Take my love with you.'

She watched as Betsy threw the handful of earth she had picked up, and then Susan did the same. Her sobs were tearing through Mags. Stepping forward, she took Susan's arm and helped her to step away from the grave.

The three women in Montel's life – his dear friend, his new friend and the love of his life – formed a circle of support for each other as they hugged one another. Their hearts were broken, but Mags knew that their spirit wasn't. She knew because her own spirit was strong. And as always, when others needed her, she found deep inside herself the urge to help them. 'Come on, my dear friends, let's go and collect the children and see that all these lovely folk, who have accepted us into their community, have helped us when we needed their help and have stood with us today, are welcomed into the warm and dry to share some refreshment with us.'

'Aye. That'll be our first step to our healing.'

'It will be. We have many steps to take, but together we'll get there. Come on, Susan – no more tears till we are on our own. We have our duty to do by these lovely people.'

Together they walked towards the cemetery gates and the

carriage that would take them down the hill to the quayside inn where there were refreshments laid on, and lashings of good Scotch whisky to warm everyone through.

When they reached the quayside, Mags looked over to where the burnt-out shell of the boathouse stood, a black silhouette against the sky. By some miracle, the store at the back had hardly been damaged, and in it thirty or more of Montel's paintings had survived, as had Betsy's kiln and pottery wheel and a good stock of her vases and plates.

'We'll build it up again, Betsy. And we'll have a special room that will exhibit Montel's paintings. We will keep and preserve them, and will never sell any of them. They will be for us and everyone else to enjoy, and a memorial to Montel. And, Susan – as Montel's legal widow – you will inherit his share and be part of the business, too.'

'No! I don't deserve that, and you know I wasn't his proper wife.'

'I know you were the saving of him, and that's what matters. He told me that, but for you, he would have died in the gutter. And he loved you dearly; and, if not biologically, he was a father to your daughter. So accept it, with my love. Together we can come through this.'

'Aye, it's our only way, Susan. And you've nowt else, lass. Mags is offering you her hand and her heart, and so am I.'

Susan smiled and nodded. Her red-raw eyes didn't reflect her smile, and Mags knew it would take a while for all of them to smile again from the heart. She wondered if she herself ever would again. But she knew she would come through. She'd throw herself into sorting everything out first and would then rebuild her life, although she had doubts that it would be here, amongst the folk she'd come to love.

At that moment she heard joyful shouts of 'Ma, Ma!' And fainter ones of 'Mama, Mama . . .'

She looked a little to the left and saw Betsy's girls running down the hill, calling to their mother; and Sibbie and Billy running for all their might behind them, calling out 'Mama'. Billy had been taught this term of address by Montel.

The children's cries were a mixture of joy and relief. Mags knew all that had happened hadn't passed them by. They lacked an understanding of it, but felt the sadness of missing Montel and knew he was never coming back to them.

Her heart went out to them, and they gave her another reason to carry on. *I'm to secure their future, too. And that of my unborn child.* And she knew that her future path was set. It wasn't the one she'd thought to tread – at least, not without her beloved Montel by her side – but it was one she would take with courage, and with Montel's spirit inside her.

Chapter Thirty

Mags walked round the rooms of what was once her happy family home in Feniscowles, but now felt more like the lair of the Devil that had betrayed her. Most of her mother's and father's furniture was in store, put there by Harold and replaced with pretentious pieces that were meant to speak of grandeur. Her anger was such that she wanted to physically throw it all outside and make a bonfire of it, but she'd schooled herself to be sensible over the disposal of everything.

A year had passed, and in that time the house had been looked after by the staff, so it wasn't musty. It was found that, of her father's fortune, only debt remained. All had been gambled or squandered by Harold.

The bank was ready to take possession of the mill, such as it was. Only a few of the workers remained. But Mags hoped to pay off the estate debt with the sale of the house. Money was still coming in from the tenanted farmers, but that would cease, as all the land would be sold with the house – land that was her most valuable asset. Harold hadn't changed or interfered with the running of that part of the estate, but had simply taken the rents and squandered the money.

As Mags continued her evaluation of the place, she could feel there were still traces of the love she'd experienced with her mother and father: it was in the walls that had enclosed them, and in the floors they had trod; in the fireplaces they had sat round, and in their spirits – although she knew they must be restless, she could still feel them in each room.

She had chosen to leave her five-month-old daughter Elizabeth Flora Ella, known as Beth, in Scotland with Betsy and Susan, but was regretting that now as she felt as if part of herself was missing. Beth was named Elizabeth after Betsy, who had been christened by that name, and Flora and Ella to complete the honouring of Mags's most precious friendships.

Thinking of Flors and Ella made Mags determined to go into the rooms she'd avoided until now – those that had formed her own suite. But as she climbed the stairs she thought herself silly to imagine that her bureau would still be in its place. When she saw that it was, and that her little sitting room was untouched, she wanted to give in to the tears that tightened her throat.

Memories assailed her. *How did it all go so wrong? But then I brought evil here. I mistook charm and skill for reality. I was a fool. I should have listened to Flors.*

Going to the bureau, she found the button to the secret drawer. Its click seemed louder in the empty building as the drawer shot open. And there it was: Flora's precious letter with her address. Mags didn't waste a moment, but sat and wrote to Flors there and then, deciding to give her solicitor's address because then, no matter what her future decisions, as she had many ideas about how she was to go forward, she knew she would receive a reply.

Her heart poured onto the pages. There was so much to tell, and somehow she felt cleansed when it was all out of her. And the feeling gave her a longing to be with Flors, to be held by her and soothed by her wise words and helped to cope, as Flors always had helped; and to take pictures with her of Flors's nephew, Billy, and her niece, Sibbie, so beautifully painted by Montel. But most of all she wanted to take Beth to meet Flors. She wanted Beth to grow up knowing both Flors and Ella.

In the letter she asked if Flors knew where Ella was.

Sighing, Mags wondered if she would ever see the day when all three were reunited, but she knew that whatever happened, she would visit Ella too, once she knew Ella's whereabouts.

Sealing the envelope, she felt she could now deal with everything. She would put the house up for sale as it was, apart from the furniture in this suite – her much-loved pieces. These she would put into storage with her parents' things until such time as she had her own home, which she would ask her solicitors to find for her and Beth, as she no longer wanted to stay in Scotland. She hadn't been happy there since the fire, as Portpatrick held so many memories. And even though the boathouse was rebuilt, its ghostly past haunted her. No, she wanted above all things to restore the mill to its former glory.

With everything decided here, Mags set out to go to her solicitors to instruct them on the sale. While there, she would also instruct that Harold's house in London be sold and she would pass the proceeds of that sale, together with the small amount of money in Harold's own personal account, over to his children, Sibbie and Billy. It would go into a trust for them, where it would mature over the years to a nice fortune for them to share when Sibbie reached the age of twenty-two and Billy twenty-one.

She would match the sum raised at the time of the sale and put that into trust for Daisy, Florrie and Rosie. They would have a little less, there being three of them, but being girls, hopefully they wouldn't need as much, just enough to give them some independence. For her own daughter, Beth, Mags had already set up a generous trust fund.

By the time Mags arrived back in Scotland there was already news of a buyer in the pipeline for her parents' house and land. She was thrilled.

In answer to her solicitor's letter telling her this, she again reiterated the minimum she would accept. She knew what she would need, in order to appease the bank and invest in the mill, as well as buy herself another house in the Blackburn area. Now, she just had to tell Betsy and Susan of her decisions, but that was a small hurdle. There was so much for her to get down to, once she had the capital.

'Eeh, lass, you have been busy. But I don't like that you're going back. How am I to manage without you? Aw, I don't mean financially or physically, but as a friend, whose allus been by me side?'

'We will only be a phone call away, love. And I will visit often. Or, if you want, you can come and live back down there with me.'

'Naw. Well, I've made me life here now, and I thought you had an' all.'

'I have – did – but all that has gone for me. You and Susan are doing very nicely with the business.' She couldn't

336

bring herself to call it by its new name, Montel's Arts and Crafts, given to it by Susan and Betsy to honour Montel. Although she had agreed, it was painful for her to think of it as that, with Montel not being there.

'I need something to keep me occupied – I mean *really* occupied. Just helping you out and doing the books doesn't do that. I promise that we will see a lot of each other and be in contact all the time.'

'Aye, we will, that's for sure. I'm sad – I can't pretend I'm not – but I feel it is the reet thing for you, lass. I don't think you'll ever rest until you restore your father's pride in Blackburn. And what you've done for me lasses and for Billy, well, I can never thank you enough. Here, give me a hug.'

'And I've to thank you as well, Mags, for giving Sibbie her rightful inheritance, with her half-brother. There was no way they could ever benefit without you from anything their father owned, as Harold never recognized Sibbie and didn't know about Billy.'

'Come here, we'll have a group hug,' Mags suggested, 'as it seems our immediate futures are settled. How mine will pan out, I don't know. I only know that I must try. But before I begin that task, and while everything is going through, and it can take a while, first I am going to France. I'm going to see Flors.'

'Eeh, at last. Aw, I'm pleased for you.' They had come out of the hug, and Betsy had busied herself putting the kettle on. 'By, lass, you've wanted to do that this good while. Well, you go, lass, and enjoy every minute. Everything can be put on hold for you for a time.'

'Well, not too long. I do have to move quickly on the mill, before it goes under, but I was able to persuade the bank not to pull the rug from under it. And I have asked my solicitors to negotiate with the creditors to accept half-payments until my estate is all sorted out. If they do that, everything can be left to tick over as it is, until I am back from France. I really need a break.'

Beth stirred gently in her pram and let out a wail, as if on cue.

'Eeh, that one lets you know what she wants – she takes after you, Mags: determined, and strong-willed, yet with a loving streak that melts your heart.'

'Ha, that's what I am like, is it? Well, both my determination and my strength have regularly let me down. I hope they never let my Beth down, too. Not that they will, if I can help it. I am going to give Beth what my mother gave me, but allow her to make her own choices, not follow the way my father steered me into his business as if I was a son. That scared away all the likely suitors I might have had.'

'Eeh, it's water under the bridge now, all of it. You have your good memories, as we all do. Look at us? Three widows, but we have a thriving business, a family to be proud of and future prospects to look forward to. Not bad in this day and age, I'd say.'

Mags's laugh wasn't as enthusiastic as that of the other two. Yes, she was a widow, but of the wrong man. But she joined in the banter about who was the bossiest, and whose children were the cleverest and the best behaved. Billy lost the last one, as he was always a tartar, but a lovable one, and between them they were steering him in the right direction. However, Mags had to admit to being worried about how he would turn out, and how his half-sister, the gentle-natured Sibbie, would cope with him as time went on.

Once they'd drunk their tea, Betsy took her cardigan off the hook on the back door. 'Well, me lasses, I've to fetch the young 'uns from school. It's my turn. I'll call by the docks to see if I can buy us some nice fish for tea. Cook's going to try to make chips. I cut all the spuds up for her, and we filled the large pan with lard, so we're in for a treat t'night.'

Mags and Susan looked at each other. They both knew that the trip to the docks was more Betsy hoping to catch Angus, to have a chat once his boat came in. When she'd gone out of the door, they both giggled. 'Fish, ha, if I never see another one, I'll be happy. We've had it every night while you were away, Mags: fish and mash, fish pie, fish stew, fish and beans. I tell you, if fish is good for the eyesight, I'll never go blind.'

Mags joined in Susan's laughter. 'Oh dear. The way to a man's heart is through his stomach, but Betsy seems to think it's by buying his fish!'

'Bless her. I hope that works out for her, 'cause, even though there is the three of us, you can still feel lonely.'

'Oh, Susan, don't. My loneliness eats away at me. It drives me to search for something to fulfil me. I know getting the mill up and running will do that, but as that's a while away, I'm pinning my hopes on my trip to France and making all the arrangements for me and Beth to travel. What about you: how do you combat loneliness?'

'Well, I was leading to that, because I too have a liking for a local man.'

'Oh? Well, that's good news. Does he like you, and who is it?'

'It's Rory's son, also called Rory. He . . . well, he knows our story, Mags. I'm sorry, but you see I bumped into him up at the churchyard and we got talking. It became a regular arrangement to walk up there together.'

'Oh?' For a moment Mags felt a pang of fear that the villagers would hear, and what would they make of it all? To those living in a village and leading an ordinary life, without such drama, the whole thing would sound very sordid.

'Don't worry, Mags. Rory won't say anything to anyone – he promised me, and I believe him. Only I wanted to be honest with him when he asked about my connection to Montel and what my name was. He thinks it's all a very sad tale, and he admires you. He doesn't know how you surmounted it all to take care of me, but he says he's glad you did.'

'This sounds serious – not Rory knowing about us, but him being glad you are here.'

'I think it is, Mags. Well, I hope it is. I – I think a lot of him. He looks on me as a victim of Harold, and said, as you did, that we were all victims of that evil man. And Rory counted himself in that, too, as he can't get over losing his father.'

Mags smiled at Susan. 'They were Montel's words that I was repeating. But at least good is coming from it all. You have Sibbie and you've met Rory, whom you never would have met, but for what Harold did. And Betsy looks as though she is healed from her Bill's passing, and Billy is an addition to our little family, too. Not only has all that good come from all the bad that happened, but I have this little darling as well – and a chance to rebuild my father's dream, and to see my friends again. None of it can make up for what we've lost, but it is all a victory over the evil that was Harold.'

They carried on chatting, speculating as to whether Angus would be willing to take on a brood of four children and hoping that he would. And Mags thought, *Yes, good has come from all that Harold tried to sully, and I hope with all my heart that it works out for Betsy and Susan. And that my plans work out, too. They must, as I'm throwing everything I have at this and looking on it as being my saviour.*

Chapter Thirty-One

A few days later Betsy walked down the slope. The fishing boats were coming in, but she had been banned from buying any more fish for at least a week, so she had no excuse to meet the boats. A few women were gathered on the quayside, but she would have to leave them to it. She turned in the direction of the school. Today marked its breaking up for the summer holiday, 31st July – how had they got more than halfway through 1925 already? And how was it that her Billy would be starting school when the new term began? Sibbie couldn't wait, bless her; she loved her half-brother so much – with all she had to put up with from Billy, Betsy thought she'd be glad to get away from him for a few hours, but she hated it every morning when she had to leave to go to school without him.

Eeh, they think the world of each other, and I'm that glad. Sibbie will be a steadying influence on Billy as they get older, I'm sure of it. But even as she thought this, Betsy hoped she was right. She looked down at Billy, feeling the tug of his hand. He wanted to get to the school to be with Sibbie, and she wasn't walking fast enough for him. 'Mama, hurry – you walk too slow!'

Betsy had never been comfortable with the way Billy copied Sibbie and used the term 'Mama'. She was his ma; 'Mama' was not for the likes of them. But correcting him only brought on the sulks. Every trait he had showed how he liked to have his own way, and in this she feared many a time that history might repeat itself.

The children were full of joy once they were let out of the confines of the school gates, as they had six whole weeks in front of them before returning. Their antics got Betsy laughing, as they chased one another down to the quayside. Then the younger ones engaged in play-fighting with the cloth bags they all took their books in. Daisy had let Billy have hers, as she and Florrie felt themselves far too grown-up, for Daisy was now ten and Florrie was nine.

'Eeh, stop that, you young 'uns, or you'll end up hurting each other and then falling out.' All of them stopped except Billy. He landed Sibbie a real whack across her legs. She went down.

'Eeh, Billy lad, now you apologize.'

'No. I was only playing.'

'But, lad, I told you all to stop. Rosie and Sibbie did, and so Sibbie wasn't ready – you caught her a blow she couldn't get away from.'

'Sibbie's too slow. And she's always getting me into trouble.'

'Naw, lad, you must take the responsibility. You should have stopped when I told Sibbie.'

Billy stamped his feet. 'I didn't want to stop!'

'Now then, what's all this, eh? Are ye having trouble with your brood, hen?'

343

Billy immediately cowered into Betsy's flowing skirt.

'I ken there's a mutiny. Now we can't be having that in Portpatrick. We're all seafaring and fair seamen. What is it that ails ye, lad?'

To Betsy's surprise, Billy stepped forward. 'I didn't want to stop play-fighting, and I hit Sibbie when she wasn't ready.'

'Well, thee's an honest lad, and that makes for a good seafaring lad. Now, help Sibbie up and shake her by the hand. Och, it's a wee gesture, but it shows the man you are.'

Betsy couldn't believe how Billy did Angus's bidding, but the reason for it soon became apparent. Billy wanted what Angus could give him.

'Please can we go on your boat one day, Angus?'

Aw, why does I think like this – Billy's just a little child. It's natural he'd want to do sommat as lads enjoy, like going for a ride in a fishing boat.

'Aye, ye can. But I need to know as ye've behaved yourselves for at least a week. When your ma reports that to me, then I'll tek ye out to sea.'

Billy jumped for joy.

'By, you have a way with children, Angus.'

'Aye, ken as I do. But I have the practice of me sister's wee brood – she's nine of them.'

'Eeh, and I thought I had me hands full with four.'

'Och, them's fine wee bairns; you've done a good job, Betsy. D'yer get to go out in the evenings any time, hen? I was thinking of asking you to walk with me.'

Betsy couldn't believe what she was hearing. She looked up into Angus's rugged, handsome face, framed with his curly hair and beard, both just a little more ginger than her own colouring, and smiled. 'Aye, I can. And I'd like that.'

His smile brought a twinkle to his hazel eyes. 'Then would the neet suit ye?'

'Aye.'

'Well, I'll meet ye here, me bonnie lassie, in two hours. I've to wash the stink of the fish off me and have me tea.'

'Naw, you don't stink. I like the smell of fish.'

His eyes twinkled even more as he said, 'Och, I know you do, hen. Don't you come down to the dockside enough, or is there another attraction?'

'Go away with you – there's nowt down there for me but the purchasing of fish.'

'Ha! Well, we will see.'

With this, Angus turned and went in the direction of his ma's cottage, and Betsy was left feeling as giggly as if she were a young girl again.

'Ma, if you walk out with Angus, does that mean you'll marry him?'

'Eeh, Daisy, shush. Naw, he's just a nice person, and I like his company.'

'Well, Roddie at school said he wants me to walk out with him, and he said that his sister walked out with her boyfriend and now they are getting wed. He said he wants us to wed one of these days when we've grown. He's canny, is Roddie.'

This made Betsy chuckle even more. All the children had picked up the Scottish way of expressing themselves, but to think of her Daisy having a romance really tickled her.

'Eeh, lass, you've time enough to think of walking out with lads. Though I agree, Roddie is a nice lad. And talking of that, I'm to have a few words with you. And Florrie. There's sommat as I have to prepare you for.'

'Aw, Ma, what? You sound as though this "sommat" is a big thing.'

'It is, lass. We'll have a talk when we get home, eh?'

Betsy thought back to her own time of becoming a woman. She'd been eleven, but their Ciss had only been ten, so Daisy could be starting her monthlies any time.

With Ciss brought to mind, Betsy thought of how it did her heart good to hear from her sister, and she loved the letters they wrote to each other. Ciss was so happy with her Patrick. Pat had kept off the booze, and Ciss was to have her second child. *By, our Ciss with two young 'uns – I can't believe it.*

A longing went up in her to see Ciss, and her thoughts went to Mags going back down to Blackburn in the near future. *Eeh, I'll visit then. I'll stay with Mags and see our Ciss. That'll be grand.*

After being teased mercilessly by Mags and Susan, Betsy set out to meet Angus. The lovely evening meant she could wear a light frock, and she'd borrowed one of Mags's dresses – yellow, with little rosebuds dotted all over it. It flowed to her calf and had a cut-out square neckline that showed a very small glimpse of her cleavage, which was the only place the frock was a little tight. Her lovely curly hair flowed to her shoulders, with the side lengths plaited and pinned under a bow on top of her head. It was her shoes that the others laughed at most. Wedged cream sandals, they were hardly walking shoes, but Betsy was going for pretty, not practical, so she ignored them telling her to put on a pair of flat sandals.

She could see Angus's appreciation the moment they met. His long whistle made her giggle.

'Will I do?'

'Aye, hen, ye'll more than do. I ken ye're a sight to wonder at.'

'Eeh, ta, Angus. I wasn't sure.'

In his eyes she read his admiration, but Betsy wanted more than that. She'd fallen for Angus. At first it was just an attraction, for he was handsome in a different way from those who usually attracted her – the dark, handsome type. But although he was a big, muscly man, Angus was gentle, and she loved the way he'd handled Billy, and it had warmed her heart that he was used to having a lot of young 'uns around him, too.

They chatted as they walked, about this and that. Angus told her of growing up in Portpatrick, and of the sea being his life. Of how he was part of a group of like-minded men who formed the offshore rescue service.

Betsy kept her tale to just her and her Bill, feeling her guilt and the ache she'd long buried rise up once more. In her telling, she hadn't accounted for Billy's age.

'So, ye were pregnant with Billy when yer man died – that's awful sad, Betsy. Like poor Mags. The village sent its heart out to ye all, the day of the fire.'

Something in Betsy wanted to be truthful with Angus. She knew she risked him not wanting to know her after he heard the truth, but she had to take that chance. She wanted him to feel as she felt for him, and that could only be built on truth. The lies she'd told had destroyed so many people's lives: her beloved Bill's and Mags's in particular.

'Eeh, it's warm, can we sit on the grass a while?' They'd climbed the slope leading to the rickety bridge that took them to the ruins of Dunskey Castle, and to their left was a grassy area.

'Aye, and I know ye feet must be killing ye, hen.'

'They are. Eeh, I was a daft ha'p'orth to think of wearing them, but I wanted to look nice for you.'

Once they were seated, with the sound of the sea far below them lapping gently on the rocks, Angus took her hand. A feeling zinged through Betsy that made her gasp a breath deep into her lungs.

'Ye allus look beautiful, me lassie.'

Betsy couldn't speak. She looked into his eyes, saw there the same feelings she was experiencing, realized his face was coming closer to hers and longed for the moment of contact. When it happened, she melted into his strong body and accepted his kiss. A light touching of their lips soon deepened into a passionate kiss, which set Betsy yearning to be taken by this man. Feelings she had suppressed flared up inside her, engulfing her and not allowing her to think straight. Only appeasing the powerful ache inside her would make her world right.

She didn't object when Angus's hand found her breast and his thumb rubbed her nipple, but arched towards him in a gesture that gave him her permission to go further. He didn't. Releasing her, he apologized. Turning his body, he sat up and stared out to sea. His breath laboured, and his face, though naturally ruddy, had a glow, as beads of sweat stood out and glistened in the late-evening sun.

'Naw, don't apologize. I – I were to blame. I have a powerful feeling for you, Angus.'

He turned and looked at her. She could see the hunger in his eyes, but could feel his determination not to take her. 'I think a canny lot of ye, Betsy. But it ain't reet to take advantage of ye. I feel ye's a lonely lass. I want more than just to be a balm to that loneliness.'

Betsy was quiet, for she knew the time had come to be truthful with him, but it wasn't easy. She drew a deep breath. 'Ta, Angus. I . . . well, afore we go further, you need to knaw sommat about me. I told a lie once, and it caused a lot of heartache to them as I love most. Naw, not just heartache, but it took two lives an' all.'

Angus's look changed to one of doubt. *Please God, let him not reject me.*

After her telling, his hand wiped the tears from her cheeks. 'Och, me wee lassie, that's a terrible thing for thee to deal with. But Mags is reet. That Harold was to blame. And I'm reet glad we didn't save him that neet. Though heartsore as the lovely Montel perished; and, aye, Rory. Rory was a character. A strong man, who had some ways he followed that weren't within the law, but he kept us villagers in meat, when it was hard for some to afford it. A good man at heart. And a sad loss.'

'Are you saying as you don't condemn me?'

'Aye, and I think thee should forget it and forgive yourself, hen. Ye were tempted and gave in, but ye're a passionate woman; and with a man like that Harold sounds, taking advantage of ye, it would take a saint not to do what ye did. And, lassie, yer revenge were brilliant, even if it did have a knock-on effect. Ye couldn't have known that, and if ye had even suspected, ye wouldn't have done it.'

'So you still want to . . . well, you knaw . . . be me friend?'

'Betsy, lassie, I want to be more than ye friend.' His voice had deepened and his eyes misted over.

Her body swayed towards him. His arms accepted her, and gently laid her down. His kiss this time wasn't hesitant, but deep. Her mind went briefly to the last time she'd felt like this, with Bill, and it felt as if he was saying it was all right to fall in love again.

With the sun going down over the outline of Ireland on

the horizon, their love became one – binding, real and cemented, with a passionate giving to each other. When it was over, Betsy felt a peace sweep her clean of all the hurt and humiliation she had suffered. Her pain left the innermost corners of her heart and was replaced with joy. 'I love you, Angus McFlorren, I love you.'

'Betsy, me Betsy. I love ye, me lassie.'

When they walked back down to Portpatrick, they held hands. To Betsy, it felt as if she'd known Angus all her life.

'Och, me wee lassie, I'm not wanting to leave ye. Betsy, will ye do me the honour of becoming me wife? Aye, I know it is soon, but we're not youngsters, and I've waited long enough for the reet one to come to tek me heart, and ye did the moment I set eyes on ye, four years back. But I knew the time wasn't reet. You having a babby inside thee, and being a stranger here. Well, I've bided me time, but of late I saw ye were attracted to me, and now I don't want to wait a moment longer.'

'Eeh, me Angus, I will. I will. I was coping with a lot when we came here, and then got caught up in building the business, but on the night of the fire – that terrible destructive and heartbreaking fire – a fire of a different kind lit inside me, and I've been trying to convey that to you ever since. Eeh, the lassies are sick of fish!'

Angus laughed out loud. It was a beautiful sound that filled her with joy. 'Me lassie. Me own lassie. Let's wed soon. I can put the banns up tomorrow, if that's canny with thee.'

'It is, but we have a lot to talk over – where we'll live, though I knaw as Mags will be happy if you move in. She is moving on soon.' She told Angus of Mags's plans.

'That's one canny woman. We all admire her. Well, that seems a good arrangement, but what about other lassie?'

'Susan? We won't be a bother to her. She's lovely, and easy to live with, and besides, we only have to share the kitchen. I'll ask Mags if we can have her sitting room as ours; there's another one we all use and that can be Susan's, so that we all have our own place to go to. And, Angus, I have a double bed!'

Angus slapped her bottom in a way that said, 'You're my woman now.' His smile held desire. 'Well, ye tek yeself to that bed now, bonny lassie, or I'll want me wicked way with thee again.'

When he held her and kissed her, Betsy knew the desire he felt for her. She had an answering feeling in her own groin, but there was nowhere for them to go and she'd been out long enough. Mags and Susan would have had to put all her brood to bed, as well as their own young 'uns. 'Good night, me love.'

''Neet, bonny lassie. I'll call tomorrow to tek you over the hill agin.'

Betsy giggled. The gate squeaked as she opened it, and she saw the twitch of the curtain being put back into place. *Eeh, they've been spying on me. Well, me plans'll come as naw surprise, then.*

Chapter Thirty-Two

Everything had been a whirlwind since Betsy's announcement four weeks ago. And now, as if that was only yesterday, here they were on this late August day in the little Scottish Free Church.

Mags couldn't believe this day had come. She stood behind Betsy and Angus, side-by-side with Susan and Ciss, who were dressed in identical lilac, long satin frocks to the one she wore. In front of them stood Daisy, Florrie and Rosie, dressed in the same colour but different designs, and, sat in her pram, little Beth, who hadn't been left out, was clothed in a baby version of the same frock that the girls wore. Susan had made them all. She was a wonderful seamstress.

Betsy looked lovely in her long cream-lace gown and a huge hat of lilac – the hat was one of Mags's that had started life as a plain straw summer bonnet, but was now swathed in the same lilac satin that the frocks were made of.

Angus stood proudly by Betsy's side, dressed in a kilt of his family's tartan, and had treated them to a little jig while they had waited outside the church for Betsy to arrive. Happiness and joy shone from him.

Mags sighed, as memories tried to assail her, and regrets of the wedding she never had to Montel, but she placed them in a compartment inside her heart for now. This was Betsy's day – one she so deserved.

Susan, too, was planning a similar day in the future. Rory, on hearing of Angus proposing, had promptly gone down on one knee and proposed to her! So it was wedding bells all round. They weren't having their day until Mags returned from France, but all four would be making the changes to the house that would suit them.

Mags thought of her own home: a five-bedroomed house standing in its own grounds on the Darwen road out of Blackburn, which her solicitor had found for her and was so convenient for the mill in Darwen. The house was in need of renovation, but there were some rooms that she and Beth could move into. At the moment these were being given a fresh coat of paint, and some of the furniture would be moved into them in readiness for her move.

Everything was now sorted, regarding the sale of her family home, and on her last visit to Blackburn, Mags had had productive meetings with her bank, and with the manager of the mill. The latter she'd found to be a very capable man, one she felt confident to leave in charge while she took her long-awaited trip to France – something that Betsy's plans had delayed. Mags knew, though, that on her return she had a long, hard road to travel to get the mill solvent again, and she had been cautioned that the cotton industry was experiencing a slide, which she was already aware of, but her answer had been, 'Those who survive will be all the stronger, and I intend to survive!' But the best part of that trip had been making sure that Ciss knew of Betsy's wedding plans, as Betsy had been anxious that a letter might not reach her in time.

Mags looked over at a smiling Ciss. Her face showed her well-being. The long journey hadn't fazed or tired her, and she looked lovely, with her little stomach mound protruding.

As the service got to the part of making the vows, there was a hush, interspersed with little happy-sobs from herself, Ciss and Susan. Mags wanted to remember for the rest of her life the picture that Betsy made as she said 'I do' to her Angus. It was a beautiful image of a beautiful woman, looking up to her man with pride and love. A lump in her throat threatened, which wasn't provoked by feeling happy and moved by the proceedings, as Mags felt a sharp awareness of her own loneliness. But she kept herself in check and smiled heavenwards, as inside her heart she made her wedding vows to Montel.

'Eeh, Mags, you all look so lovely. I'm the proudest bride there ever was.'

'And the most beautiful.'

'Ta, Mags. I wish—'

'No "I wish" today. You have everything you've dreamed of. Be happy, my dear friend. That will make up for all that you wish for me that cannot happen.'

'Oh, Mags.' They were in each other's arms, their tears wetting each other's bare shoulders, but it didn't last long.

'Eeh, no crying on your wedding day. It's unlucky, our Betsy!'

'Ciss. Oh, Ciss, I'm so happy that you came, lass. And look at you. I tried to imagine what you looked like when you were carrying a babby last time, but I couldn't. But you look a picture of health and happiness.'

'Aye, I am happy, our Betsy. Happier than I've ever been. Patrick is a wonderful husband and daddy to our little Jobe, who's a fine lad, an' all. Well, I knaw he ain't a fully grown one yet, but he's . . . well, just a lovely bundle of fun. Mrs Dilly is looking after him while I'm away, as it would have been too much for me to cart him here. I'm missing him, though, and I'll be glad to get on that train tomorrow to take me back to me menfolk.'

'That makes me so happy. All I ever wanted for you was that you'd be happy, lass. And I'll come down to see you soon, I promise.'

Mags crossed the room and left the two girls talking. They were in the back room of the local inn for the wedding breakfast, but most people had gone out to sit on the lawn. Mags looked for Susan and found her with her Rory.

'Mags, come on over. There's some cool lemonade on a table over here.'

'Oh, that would be very welcome. Hello, Rory. Soon be your big day.'

'Och, I cannae wait.' With this he slipped his arm round Susan, and Mags's loneliness deepened.

'Susan, I'm going to pop home for a while. I'm so hot, I thought to freshen up. I won't be long, but if I'm missed, you can cover for me.'

'Oh, Mags . . . I—'

'I'll not be long. See you in a mo.' With this, Mags escaped through the gate without looking back. She couldn't stay. Her pain had cracked and left her exposed. Tears flowed down her cheeks. Picking up the hem of her skirt, she ran towards the churchyard. Once there, she made her way to Montel's grave and sank down onto her knees. 'Oh, Montel, my darling, I tried. I tried to get through today without breaking. But I miss you so much. Come back to me – come back to me.'

'Can I be of assistance, Mags?'

'Jerome! What on earth?' Dabbing her eyes with her handkerchief, Mags looked up in astonishment at Jerome. A member of the same hunt meet that she had belonged to, they had been friends for years, but she hadn't given him a thought for . . . well, she didn't know for how long. How could he be standing here! Was she dreaming?

'Sorry to startle you, old thing.'

'But how?'

'Let's sit down on that bench over there. Oh, Mags, I can't say how good it is to have found you.'

'You've been looking?'

'Yes. Well, since I've been back home, that is. I graduated from medical school and am now a doctor. I wanted to write while I was away, but . . . well, I heard you were married. Anyway, why the tears? Is that someone you loved? It broke my heart to see you like that.'

Mags told him all that had happened.

'My God, Mags! I – I just don't know what to say. And all of this happened to you because you made friends with another nurse in Belgium? Well, I mean, it led to this – of course it wasn't the cause.'

'Yes, it was a fateful day, the day my friend Flora brought her brother to our house. But I'm still mystified about how you came to be here. Look, I've been missing too long from Betsy's wedding. I made the excuse that I wanted to freshen up, but I think they would have guessed the real reason.'

'Loneliness is a terrible thing. Montel sounds like he was an amazing person. I'm sorry for your loss.'

'Thank you. Shall we walk to my house, where I can change? I've soiled my dress, lying on the grass like that. It's only over the road. And yes, loneliness does eat away at you.'

When they were walking along the road, Jerome explained how he came to be here. 'I saw your family home for sale, and . . . well, I bought it.'

'What?'

'Yes, I always loved it. And recently I lost my grandparents – well, as you know, they were as rich as stink, lovely grandparents that they were. And they only left it all to me. I have their house and grounds, a manor house in Berkshire, and pots of money: lucky me. Though I will miss them, as they were adorable.'

'Oh, I remember them; they were free spirits, always going off to exotic continents and being very flamboyant and bohemian. I'm sorry to hear of their passing.'

'Yes. Anyway, when I signed the papers for your place, there it was: your address. I had a compelling urge to come and look you up, Mags. I heard that your husband had been killed, but I didn't know that you had another.'

'No. I was living in sin, and that isn't something you write home to the neighbours about.'

'No, I suppose not. But the main thing is that you found happiness with Montel – not what convention dictates.'

Mags smiled up at Jerome. He was always a little like his grandparents. He hadn't wanted to follow a conventional route, either, but he'd given in and done so to please his parents.

'What happened to your music, Jerome?'

'Oh, I still play. I've brought my violin with me, as it happens. I had visions of wooing you on top of one of these cliffs, by playing my violin and seeing you come from wherever you were and running up the hill into my arms.'

Mags blushed. She'd avoided the 'why' he was here, and had only asked the 'how'. Jerome had always been sweet on her, from when they had been twelve years old and had kissed in the bushes of his garden during one of the many parties his mother used to throw.

They had reached her gate when she asked, 'Where is your car?'

'It's parked along the quayside. I've booked into the hotel up on the cliff there.'

'Oh, the Portpatrick Hotel – it's lovely. Well, while I freshen up, why don't you fetch your violin? There's a wedding reception that would greatly benefit from your playing and, in particular, your lively folk music.'

'I would love that. I'll meet you back here.'

Mags watched Jerome go towards his car – a Rolls-Royce. *Well, well. Jerome Cadley! I never expected that, in a million years.* But somehow his appearance had pleased Mags and had edged the loneliness away. *Ha! Hark at me. I'm being a daft ha'p'orth, as Betsy would say.*

Betsy's expression turned from concern to amazement when Mags walked back into the reception with the handsome Jerome. Tall, with fair hair, he had a sportsman's physique. His grey eyes twinkled, as if he was always amused, and the indentations on each side of his mouth gave this impression, too.

'This is Jerome, Betsy. He is an old childhood friend who just happened to be holidaying here, and I bumped into him. I hope you don't mind me bringing him. He can play for his supper, as he is a violinist.'

'Eeh, pleased to meet you, Jerome. Of course you're welcome, lad, and especially if you play for us.'

'Hello, Betsy, nice to meet you. I guess you're from my area, Blackburn? And is this your new husband?'

'Aye, I am; and this is Angus.'

'Well, you two, as this is a romantic day, I will come clean and tell you that I actually came searching for the love of my life, Mags.'

'Jerome!'

'Eeh, Mags, that is romantic.'

'Don't you start, Betsy. Oh, Jerome, we'll have to talk, but first play for the guests and get the party going.'

Jerome did more than play. He belted out a few Scottish Highland reels that went down so well the place was in uproar, with all the wonderful dancing men in their kilts. Mags felt her spirits soaring from the black pit they had been in for so long. She clapped her hands and jigged with Beth on her hip, and drank the whisky offered.

When the proceedings came to an end, she agreed to go for a walk with Jerome, so that they could talk some more. Dusk had fallen and across the water the magic of Ireland lit up, throwing reflections across the shadowy sea.

'Mags, you know how I feel about you – always have. Is there a little spark in you for me? Maybe I shouldn't ask, but I have waited and hoped for so long.'

They were so near to the boathouse that it felt like a betrayal even to listen to Jerome, but then Mags wondered if that was just her, because Montel wouldn't look on this as a betrayal. *What am I thinking? I can't possibly fall for someone else so soon!*

'I know you are going to need time, Mags. But I have that. I'm not setting up in a practice. I'm going to be a landlord farmer. I never really liked medicine. Dr Lange influenced my parents into steering me that way because he thought I had the right nature, but really I would have preferred to be a vet. I love animals and the land, especially

359

horses. Do you remember Romany, my piebald? Such a gypsy horse—'

'Stop. Jerome, you're rambling. Not giving me time to think.'

'I know, but it is because I am afraid of your answer. Sorry.'

'I haven't one. I'm confused. This is all so sudden. I'm afraid that my loneliness will make me say the wrong thing. I always was very fond of you, Jerome – you were my first boyfriend, my first kiss. I feel our friendship is so easy between us, and yes, I do find you attractive.'

Jerome gave a low whistle. He was funny, in an expressive way. 'Does that mean I have a chance, honey?'

Mags laughed out loud at his fake American accent.

'I had a university chum from New York. And that's how he spoke, honest.'

'Oh, Jerome, it's so good to see you.' With this, Mags leaned forward and kissed his cheek. 'You're a tonic.'

As she went to draw back, he caught her arm. 'Mags, my darling Mags. I – I've dreamed of this moment.'

She didn't resist.

'I've loved you forever, Mags. It broke my heart when I heard of your marriage. I know that I never made a move, but I was just a student with an allowance, and you had moved into the men's world of business. We seemed worlds apart, so I tried to forget you, but it didn't work.'

His face came close to hers. His lips brushed hers. She pulled away.

'I'm sorry. So sorry. I – I . . .' Jerome said.

'Don't be. I wanted you to kiss me. Oh, Jerome, this is all so sudden. Look, I am going away, for about a month.'

'When? Where?'

'To France, to stay with Flors, the friend I told you about. I start my journey on Monday. Let me think this through while I am away, and clear my head. I need that time, Jerome, and so do you. You knew nothing of how I have been living, or of me having a child. We have to let these things lie within us for a while and see if we can surmount any problems they may impose on us. And that men's world you remember me being in – well, I want to return to it. I need to save my father's pride and joy.'

'The mill?'

'Yes, the mill. I've bought a house on Darwen road. I'm moving back. We will be near to each other and can take things one step at a time.'

'But that's wonderful news. And I will help you in your quest to rebuild the mill to its former glory. Not that I know anything about cotton mills, even though I have grown up breathing in their smoke. But I can learn, and maybe that smoke has filtered into me a love of them. Who knows?'

'Oh, Jerome, you're so funny.'

'I'll drive you.'

'What?'

'I'll drive you to France. I won't bother you, once you are there. I'll go off and travel. I want to see Spain, and I may go over to Africa, as my granny and granddad did. Yes, it all sounds so wonderful. Please say yes, Mags.'

She went into a fit of giggles. Jerome was like a breath of fresh air. He saw no obstacles to him just upping sticks and going. 'What about your farmers, and your new house?' Mags asked.

'Oh, they don't need me – well, not yet. Though I am going to set up a union for them; and farmers' meetings where they can discuss things that are worrying them; and form a co-op for buying their supplies. But all of that can wait. Besides, the house needs work. The furniture is awful. Whatever possessed you to buy such stuff?'

All of this sounded so caring of the farm tenants that it made Mags feel guilty that she and her family had never given them a thought. Not really. There had been the Harvest Festival barn dance funded by her father, a real hoedown of an evening when the beer and cider flowed, but other than that, they'd paid more attention to the mill workers and their welfare.

'I know what you mean. But that wasn't me. I'm furnishing my house with all the lovely pieces my parents had. At least Harold had the good manners to put it all in store for me, when he stole the house.'

'Well, have we got ourselves an adventure?'

The idea did appeal. A whole journey of chatting and really getting to know one another again. 'Yes. Yes, we have.'

'Hooray!' With this, Jerome did a little jig.

'Oh, Jerome, stop it.'

'I hope never to stop making you laugh, Mags. You're very beautiful all the time, but when you laugh, you light up the world.'

He took her hand and steered her towards her home. At the gate he pulled her close and kissed her hand. 'I'll see you in the morning and we can make the final arrangements. Goodnight, darling Mags.'

Mags watched him walk down the slope. When he'd gone a few yards, Jerome jumped in the air and kicked his feet together. She went into the garden in a fit of laughter. Suddenly her world had changed. She felt eager to get on with the next chapter, instead of trying to make meaningful plans just to give herself something to think about, other than her heartache.

Does my heart ache now? Somehow, Mags wasn't sure that it did. *Oh, Montel, I will always love you, but I feel you letting me free.* Something settled on her arm. In the gas lighting she saw that it was a white feather: the symbol of those who have passed, trying to tell you something. A peace came over her. She clutched the feather – oh, she knew it had fallen from the geese setting off in their droves for warmer climes and carried on the wind, but to her, landing on her at that moment, it seemed as if Montel was saying, '*Be happy, my Mags.* Mon amour.'

She wouldn't put it past him to have made tonight happen – even to seeing that Susan and Betsy were happy first. With this thought, Mags looked up into the stars and blew a kiss to the brightest of them all.

Chapter Thirty-Three

The journey to Blackburn with Jerome was filled with chatter. Mags and Jerome shared old memories of when they were children, which had them giggling at their antics and that of their peers, until their reminiscing reached the war years. So many of their friends had never returned.

'I heard that you were in officer training, then I didn't hear any more for a long time, Jerome, but I was so happy when I learned you had returned.'

'The memories haunt me to this day, as I'm sure they do you, Mags. So many wasted lives. I was with Henry Moulds when he died.'

'Poor Henry, always the prankster. Such a waste of millions of lives, and so many families broken. For me, it was mostly French and Belgian soldiers that I helped, and held the hand of when they were dying, though there were some German ones, too.'

'I heard a little about what happened to you. Do you feel like talking about it, Mags?'

Surprisingly, she did. Everything poured out of her: things she hadn't spoken of, details she'd spared those she'd told and, without realizing it was happening, tears rolled down her face, but she couldn't stop talking. Never before had she released it all in this way.

She felt, rather than knew, that the car was stopping.

'Mags, may I hold you? I – I mean as an old friend?'

She slid across the bench seat and went willingly into his arms, touched to see that Jerome too had tears trickling from his eyes. She didn't register his closeness, as this wasn't a romantic awareness of each other, just two people who had grown up together and had faced their own hell in wartime.

After a moment Jerome told her the details of how Henry had died. 'His death affected me so much, and yet death surrounded us every minute of every day. What I can't come to terms with is the bodies we had to leave where they fell. Thousands of them.'

'Maybe one day someone will gather their remains and bury them properly. But here we are, seven years later, and there is still so much to rebuild.'

'Yes. One of the things I learned in medical school was a little-known technique that can match people to family members. It was discovered by a Swiss chap, Johann Friedrich Miescher. I have often thought how wonderful it would be for families to find the body of their sons and be able to lay them to rest. Most just know they are missing, presumed killed in action, which leaves them in limbo somehow.'

Listening to Jerome, Mags thought once more what a caring person he was. 'Jerome, David – Dr Lange – was right to direct you into medicine. You are the right person, with all the right qualities. Far from giving up being a doctor, you should use the skills you have to treat those who cannot afford medical help.'

'Yes. You're right – of course I should, and I will. But come on, old thing, we have a holiday to sort out first.'

With this, he pecked her on the cheek. Something in Mags wanted more than that, but she denied it, helped to do so by Beth stirring and letting out a yell.

'It's all right, darling, I'm here.' However, Beth wasn't going to be soothed. 'Oh dear, madam has woken up all grumpy. Are you hungry, darling?'

Beth's arms were out, her face wet with tears.

'I'll get her into the front to sit with you. We should reach the cafe I know of soon – it's just inside Carlisle. We can get her some hot milk there,' Jerome suggested.

'Thank you. I have some rusk, so I'll soften that in the milk for her.'

Everything about Jerome warmed her heart. Not many young men would dream of having anything to do with the care of a child, even if it was one of their own – all that was women's work, to them.

'Come on, little one.' Beth shied away from him. 'Oh, I can see a rabbit in the field, come and look.'

Beth stopped crying and looked interested.

'Yes, a grey one with floppy ears.' Jerome wiggled his fingers near his ears.

Beth giggled and went eagerly into Jerome's arms and he took her to the gate of the field. Forgetting that he was a stranger to her, Beth held on to Jerome's neck. Mags wound the window down and could hear her giggling as he told a tale about the rabbit being at work, finding food for his young – acting out the part as the story unfolded. 'And when he has something, he will do a hop, skip and a jump.' With this, Jerome turned and said, 'Shall we do a hop, skip and a jump back into the car?'

Beth giggled out loud as Jerome did just that, shaking her as he did so.

'Oh, dear Jerome, you had better pray that a car doesn't come along. They will think you an idiot, hopping around.' But although she said this, Mags got out of the car and did the same. All three then had a fit of the giggles.

'Oh dear.' Jerome held Beth away from him. 'I think we made her laugh too much.' Drops of liquid leaked from the leg of Beth's nappy.

'I'm sorry, Jerome, I – I—'

'Don't be silly. It's quiet normal, and when I did my stint on the children's ward, I had far more than that on me, I can tell you. Pass me her blanket and a dry nappy.'

Mags placed the blanket down and went to take Beth, but Jerome didn't pass her over. Instead he'd already removed the soggy nappy and laid Beth down, to pin another one expertly in place.

Mags watched in amazement, because Jerome was one of the only men she knew who would do this, although Montel would have, and she'd seen him do so for Sibbie and Billy many a time . . . She paused her thoughts there. *I can't believe how naturally I referred to Montel in my mind! And without feeling any pain.* A little guilt entered her at this, but as Jerome was calling to her to take Beth from him, Mags didn't pay it much attention.

'I need to go myself now – all this hop, skipping and jumping!'

It all seemed so natural, as if they were a family. *Yes, that's it. I feel so at home with Jerome. It does feel as if he has completed our family.* Warmth flooded through her.

'Hey, that's a beautiful smile. What have I done to deserve that?' Jerome was getting back into the car.

'Oh, just being you.'

He held her gaze. 'Please may I kiss you, Mags?'

She leaned over Beth and offered him her lips. 'Yes. You deserve one.'

It was no more than a friendly kiss, and yet Mags knew it impacted upon Jerome as it did on her. As their lips parted, they looked deep into each other's eyes.

'Oh, look, I think Beth wants a kiss, too.'

Beth surprised Mags then, by kissing Jerome and putting her arms around his neck. In the last few minutes it had been as if Jerome was her father.

Mags felt the warmth that had entered her earlier deepen to love for Jerome. Reluctantly she lifted Beth off him and sat her down between them once more. 'Come on, darling, there'll be plenty of time for cuddles in the future. Now we'd better get on our way, or it'll take us days to get to our new home at this rate.'

Jerome winked and started the car. Beth put her hand into Mags's and snuggled into her.

By the time they reached Blackburn, Beth had been asleep for a couple of hours, and both Mags and Jerome were exhausted. Mags had taken the wheel for a while, when Jerome had said that his eyes were feeling strained; and this had further pleased her as he showed no qualms about women driving. He truly was made from a different mould to most of the men she knew, and was so like Montel in his thinking and actions.

'How about you come home with me, Mags? Mother would love to see you, and there will be a meal ready, as she is expecting me. I telephoned her and gave her all the news, on having found you, and about you having a child. I told her I was bringing you back to Blackburn. And she said then that you were welcome, if you needed a bed for the night.'

'That sounds wonderful, Jerome. Thank you. I don't know how my house has progressed, and I would have to go to a restaurant to eat and then start to find bedding and make up beds. It is all so daunting that I was thinking of booking into a hotel.'

Dinner was lovely. Beth was fed and bathed as soon as they arrived at Jerome's parents' house, and was snuggled into a cot that had been brought down from the attic and put beside the bed that Mags was to sleep in.

Mags was feeling refreshed after a bath and having changed into a light evening dress, a simple straight satin frock that hung from her shoulders. The pale blue complemented her ivory skin. She'd brushed her hair and allowed it to fall in its own natural waves onto her shoulders. Pleased with the way it shone, and how the hints of chestnut amongst the darkness caught the light, she had the strange feeling of getting ready for a date, as she finished her outfit with a long string of pearls. She'd checked her appearance many times in the long mirror in the guest room that she occupied, and now felt happy with how she looked.

Mrs Cadley was a lovely person, and to Mags it was as if the years hadn't happened and she was a little girl visiting with her parents. Nothing about the house had changed. Nor about Mr Cadley, though she was sure he'd mellowed a little, as she remembered him being an abrupt man. She wasn't in his parents' company for long before she could see that Jerome had inherited his mother's gentle nature.

He had been waiting for her as she'd descended the beautiful wide, curved staircase. He'd stood in the hall, looking so handsome in his dinner jacket that she caught her breath.

To Mags, as he'd taken her hand, the feeling inside her was of coming home. Only this home was even grander than her parents' house had been – if a little old-fashioned, with ruby-red carpets of an Indian pattern, and heavy, carved furniture in dark oak.

Taking her arm, Jerome commented on how beautiful she looked, and it occurred to Mags that she could say the same about him, but she checked herself. Everything seemed to be moving along at a much faster pace than she had wanted.

As they stood out on the porch after dinner, the night was balmy in a heavy, thundery way. The smell of honeysuckle hung on the night air, and but for the gas light in the garden, they would have been in darkness, as clouds gathered in the sky.

Jerome stood very close to her, and Mags felt acutely aware of him: of how he smelt of a popular woody aftershave, of the feel of his tailored jacket and of whiffs of his small cigar.

'Remember that bush?'

The one they had kissed behind. 'Yes' was all she could manage.

'Can we repeat history?'

No words were needed as he threw down his cigar and trampled on it, then took her hand. Once behind the bush, he held her gently. 'Mags, my darling Mags, at last.'

His lips came onto hers and she was lost. Lost in a sea of feelings she never thought to experience again. There was no resistance in her, and she didn't want there to be. This felt so right, so wonderful – she was alive again. Every part of her was awakened and ready to give of her love once more.

When he came out of the kiss, Jerome murmured, 'I love you, Mags. I love you with all that is me, and always have done.'

'I love you, Jerome. I'm ready to give you the same deep love I gave to Montel.'

'Oh, Mags, that is the greatest compliment you could give me.' Pulling her to him, he said, 'I wish I could hold you every hour of every day and every night.'

Mags could only snuggle into him and drink in the feeling of being loved and cherished again. The thought came to her that if only the war hadn't happened, in the normal run of things she and Jerome would have come together. Then all the suffering wouldn't have occurred. But then she would never have known Montel, or had the gift of her beautiful little Beth. *In the end, all I suffered has been worth it.*

EPILOGUE
France, 1926

~

Mags, Flora and Ella

A Reunion

Chapter Thirty-Four

Ten months had passed by the time Mags, Jerome and Beth finally set out to France – a trip that was to be the couple's honeymoon.

The storm on the night Mags and Jerome had sealed their love prevented them from keeping to their plans. Both of their houses sustained damage, as did the mill, with a huge chimney collapsing.

It was this damage that caused the most worry, as six workers doing the nightshift were hurt. Mags was mortified and made sure they and their families were cared for. But from a business angle, it had been a disaster, as Mags had found that due to lack of maintenance, the insurers wouldn't pay out. Her decision was to stay and to be at the helm until the mill was up and running once more.

Jerome had taken the opportunity to ask Mags to marry him.

On her wedding day seven months previously, 5th December 1925, it had seemed to Mags that the last year had been all about weddings and frocks and all the palaver that went with the occasion, as she had kept her promise and had been up to Scotland to be with Susan on her wedding day to Rory in November. Once more she had been maid of honour, this time in primrose; and once more she had gone to be with Montel for a while. On her visit to the graveyard she'd sat and talked through all her plans and knew, when she left, that she had Montel's blessing.

And so she had approached her own wedding with happiness, and it had been a wonderful affair with all of the families from her old circle attending. So many of them had refused the invitation when she was marrying Harold, as most had come across him in their business activities with his uncle's mill and hadn't liked him, and so the excuses had piled up.

She had worn a beautiful cream silk suit with a draping jacket and a long pleated skirt. And her bridesmaids and maids of honour had all been in cream, too – simple silk frocks, but, like her, they all had a fur wrap to keep them warm. A flurry of snow had greeted them as they'd come out of the church in Feniscowles, and each of them had taken their flowers to the graves of their loved ones. Betsy had stood by Bill's grave and introduced him to Angus, and had then done the same to her ma. Mags had spent a little while with her mother and father before being led away by Jerome.

Some sadness had entered Mags, but she hadn't let it spoil her day. She'd wrapped one flower from her huge bouquet and had asked Susan to put it on Montel's grave for her, and that had given her peace.

It had been lovely to see them all, and Iris and her husband, attending. And for little Beth to be reunited with what Mags thought of as her family.

The one picture Mags would keep in her mind was of

all the children playing a game where they clasped hands and skipped around Beth, who sat in her pushchair clapping her hands and then laughing out loud when the chain of hands collapsed and they all fell on the ground. It was a lovely moment.

Betsy was blooming and was now about to give birth to her fifth child. Mags would have loved to have gone up to Scotland to be with her, but couldn't put off the trip to France any longer. It had been music to her ears to hear Betsy telling her about her life and singing the virtues of Angus. 'Eeh, lass, if you're half as happy with your Jerome as I am with me Angus, then you're in for a good life.'

'I will be,' Mags told her. 'Jerome is wonderful, Betsy. He is like Montel in a lot of ways, and yet different. Uniquely himself.'

And now they were standing on the steps of the magnificent *Assemblée Nationale* in Paris, looking up at the columns standing like guards over the entrance. For Mags and Beth, a momentous occasion was upon them, as Beth was to receive her father's medal, the *Légion d'honneur*. Mags had arranged it all through the French Embassy in London.

Beth looked lovely in her double-breasted light-grey coat with matching beret. Her legs were clad in white leggings and she wore shiny black shoes. Mags and Jerome stood on each side of her, and as Jerome was fluent in French, he was to translate. Mags could hardly believe that Beth was just eighteen months old, as she walked with pride and seemed to fully understand the significance of the day.

As the presentation was of a military medal, the French army was in attendance and stood to attention at the bottom of the steps. When the doors opened and Aristide Briand, the French prime minister, walked through, there was the sound of a hundred men standing to attention, with a background of squawking birds taking to the skies.

Mags's nerves clenched as they climbed the steps. Monsieur Briand greeted them in English and then, taking the medal from a cushion held by an attendant, proclaimed in French why it was being presented. A lump came to Mags's throat as Jerome whispered to her how he was praising Montel's bravery and that of his child, who was standing here about to collect her late father's medal. *Oh, Montel, I hope you can see this. Look at our little girl standing to attention. She is doing you proud.*

When Monsieur Briand bent forward and spoke to Beth, she looked up at Jerome.

'He says you must feel very proud today. Say "yes", darling.'

'Yes.' As she said this, Beth nodded her head vigorously, no doubt remembering how Mags had told her over and over again what a special occasion this was.

Monsieur Briand smiled. Then he wiped a tear from his eye and, bending down, pinned the medal to Beth's coat and kissed her on each cheek. Beth grinned up at him. 'Mush-tash tickles Beth.'

Mags was mortified. But the prime minister coughed and took out a large handkerchief and pretended to blow his nose, with his eyes twinkling as he looked at her.

After that, he shook hands with Mags and Jerome and whispered something. And later, after the band had played and the prime minister had gone back inside, Jerome told her that he'd said what a charming child they had, and he had no doubt she would go on to do great things.

'Well, that's nice – as long as it is nice things, and not

anything that requires her to be brave. Thinking of which, I can't wait to see my very brave friends.'

As they walked down the steps, Beth looked up at Jerome. 'Dada.' Her hands stretched up to him indicating that she wanted him to lift her up and carry her.

It was Jerome's turn to have tears in his eyes as he bent down to pick her up.

'You have two dadas, little Beth. One is looking down on you from heaven, and I will care for you and cherish you always.'

As Beth looked heavenwards, following Jerome's pointed finger, Mags did, too. Her eyes stung with unshed tears. *Oh, Montel . . . Montel. I know you will approve, but I miss you.*

A hand came into hers. She looked into Jerome's beloved face. 'Take comfort, darling Mags, Montel is always with us.'

The 'us' meant so much to her. 'Thank you, darling Jerome. Thank you for understanding.'

As they neared the village of Laurens in Hérault, Mags pondered on all she'd learned from Flors in her letters, and couldn't believe that she was to meet up with Ella, too. And that Ella was married – well, for the third time.

To think that Ella had gone through the death of her first husband, Paulo, a French soldier just like Montel, and had then been forced to marry Shamus, a gangster and murderer who had been hanged for his crimes just a couple of years ago. The whole story was so moving and showed Ella's courage.

The journey's end was along a dirt track of a road, with the most beautiful chateau appearing on the skyline as they rounded a bend.

In no time, Mags was in the arms of both Flors and Ella. All three were crying. All three had suffered greatly during their time in Brussels, and since they had escaped and come home back in 1915, as fresh-faced young women with an experience behind them that had scarred their generation. But all three had found happiness. Lasting, loving happiness. And at last they were reunited.

Around them children danced. Mags was introduced to them – Flora's Freddy, Randolph, Marjella and Monty, and Ella's son, Paulo – before being swept into the arms of Cyrus, Flors's husband, and then introduced to Ella's husband, Arnie.

So many memories assailed Mags, but she reflected that yes, a terrible war had been fought during 1914–18 and at an appalling cost to life, but it had brought her and Flors and Ella together. And it had meant that for their little ones, and for Betsy's soon-to-be five children and Susan's one child, there was a lifetime of peace ahead of them.

A shudder seized her as this last thought came to her, and concern for Mags caused a bustle of activity as she and Jerome and little Beth were ushered to the shade, where there was a huge wooden table surrounded by dozens of chairs. On the table were bottles of wine and fruit juice.

'Welcome to our world. Everyone who enters has to sample our wine.'

Mags smiled up at Cyrus and caught the likeness in his looks to his half-brother, Harold, but brushed it away with a smile, as Flors put her arm round her waist. 'We are going to toast you with a bottle from our very first batch of wine, darling Mags. Oh, it's so good to see you.'

'And you, Flors. I've thought of you both so often.'

'I brought hell down on you, when I introduced you to

Harold. Poor Mags. Your letters broke my heart. But it is all behind us now – everything that the three of us have been through. It is all in the past. The future can only be bright for us, so let's drink to that.'

As their glasses clinked together, Mags felt at peace. Yes, they had been through a lot, but everything had come out right.

She looked over to where Jerome was laughing out loud at something Arnie had said, and a warmth entered her. Nothing was ever going to spoil this wonderful peace they had all found – nothing . . .

Letter to Readers

Dear Reader,

Thank you for taking this journey with me; I hope very much that you enjoyed Mags's story – the third in The Girls Who Went to War series.

There was no in-depth research for this novel as much of what I had discovered for the first two books in the series stood me in good stead for this one, and we have now moved on from the war. I did have the pleasurable task of driving around the lovely northern city of Blackburn and its surrounding villages to find the right places, churches, parks and villages in which to set the scenes played out in the area. I hope my descriptions do them justice. This is the kind of research that I like doing – it beats all the searching on the internet and reading books, as interesting as that is.

The first book in the series, *The Forgotten Daughter*, tells the story of Flora, Ella and Mags: how they met and formed a deep friendship; their extreme bravery when trapped in Brussels behind enemy lines; how they coped with running a hospital that had been abandoned; and how they made their daring escape when all the patients had been despatched. It then goes on to tell Flora's story as Ella goes to France to continue nursing and Mags, the most damaged of the three girls, goes home to her family. Flora's story is a love story with a difference as she is banished from her home and her fortunes wane, leaving her to face betrayal, incest and the deaths of some of those she loves most.

The second book in the series, *The Abandoned Daughter*, is Ella's story. All Ella knows about her past is that she was born in Poland. Living in London with her nanny, she has desperately wanted to know who she is, but questions were always batted away. When her nanny dies, Ella is left with a diary that reveals most of the secrets of her family and she vows to visit Poland one day. In the latter part of the war she falls deeply in love with Paulo, a French soldier who suffers from the effects of inhaling gas during an attack by the Germans. Battling to save his life, Ella is left destitute and her life takes many twists and turns as she fights to save her family. Ensnared into a destructive relationship and facing once more the rejection of those who should help her, Ella is forced to make a devastating decision. If you missed either of these books, don't worry as they all stand alone. They can be purchased at any good bookshop or online.

The fourth book in the series, *The Courageous Daughters*, will explore the time of the sons and daughters of Flora, Mags and Ella, in a war that will pit sibling against sibling and break hearts and lives as Flora's and Ella's children, brought up in what is to become Vichy – the so-called free France – take different sides. Though Mags's girls are too young in the beginning, she is distraught when Betsy and Susan's children go to war, as she looks on them as her own. It is a story of the Resistance, the Special Operation

Executives, and how love can conquer. This is set to be published in Spring 2020.

I love to interact with my readers and to receive your feedback on my books. They say that to leave an author a review is like hugging her and I so love to receive reviews, too.

I can be contacted through my web page: www.author marywood.com.

And/or, join me on Facebook. My page www.facebook.com/HistoricalNovels is a lively interaction with my readers, with laughter and love in abundance, as well as all the latest book news, competitions and guest authors. I would love to see you there.

You can also find me on Twitter: @Authormary.

I look forward to hearing from you.

Acknowledgements

An author is nothing without her editors and I am blessed to have the wonderful Wayne Brookes and his team, and Alex Saunders and his team, at Pan Macmillan publishers taking care of me and my work. I want to give special thanks to Samantha Fletcher, Mandy Greenfield and freelance editor Victoria Hughes-Williams for all the care they take with my work. Between you, you take my creation and make it sing off the page. Thank you.

And, besides editors, others within the Pan Macmillan team work very hard on my behalf – including Ellis Keene, my publicist, and the sales team, who work so hard to get my books shelf-space. Thank you to each of you.

And thank you to my son, James Wood, who reads my work before I release it to anyone, making suggestions as he picks up on areas that may be a little flat or need to have more dramatic impact. Thank you. After your advice I feel confident to send my work on its journey to the publishers.

And thank you, too, to my agent Judith Murdoch, who is always there for me and always encouraging, as her signature words 'Onwards and Upwards' testify. Judith, you are simply The Best.

Thank you, too, to my lovely great-niece Rosie Hall, who gave her valuable time to help me with some aspects of the book.

To my darling husband, Roy, for his love and support. And our children, Christine Martin, Julie Bowling, Rachel Gradwell and James Wood, their partners and the beautiful grandchildren, great-grandchildren and added family they have given me. And to my Olley and Wood families. All of you give me support, encouragement and above all, love. You all enrich my life. Thank you.

And of course, no acknowledgement is ever complete without giving my thanks to my very special readers, especially to those who follow me on Facebook and my web page. Each and every one of you brings so much to me. Your eagerness for every book is such an encouragement, seeing me through many hours of writing. Your help with promoting me and my books is invaluable, too. I wish I could name you all. Without each and every one of you, there would be no 'Author Mary Wood'. You help me to achieve my dream. Thank you.

My love to you all x

If you enjoyed

The Wronged Daughter

then you'll love

The Forgotten Daughter

by Mary Wood

Book one in
The Girls Who Went to War series

From a tender age, Flora felt unloved and unwanted by her parents, but she finds safety in the arms of caring Nanny Pru. But when Pru is cast out of the family home, under a shadow of secrets and with a baby boy of her own on the way, it shatters little Flora.

Over the years, however, Flora and Pru meet in secret – unbeknown to Flora's parents. Pru becomes the mother she never had, and Flora grows into a fine young woman. When she signs up as a volunteer with St John Ambulance, she begins to shape her life. But the drum of war beats loudly and her world is turned upside down when she receives a letter asking her to join the Red Cross in Belgium.

With the fate of the country in the balance, it is a time for bravery. Flora's determined to be the strong woman she was destined to be. But with horror, loss and heartache on her horizon, there's a lot for young Flora to learn . . .

Available now

The Abandoned Daughter

By Mary Wood

Book two in
The Girls Who Went to War series

Voluntary nurse Ella is haunted by the soldiers' cries she hears on the battlefields of Dieppe. But that's not the only thing that haunts her. When her dear friend Jim breaks her trust, Ella is left bruised and heartbroken. Over the years, her friendships have been pulled apart at the seams by the effects of war. Now, more than ever, she feels so alone.

At a military hospital in Belgium, Ella befriends Connie and Paddy. Slowly she begins to heal, and finds comfort in the arms of a French officer called Paulo – could he be her salvation?

With the end of the war on the horizon, surely things have to get better? Ella grew up not knowing her real family but a clue leads her in their direction. What did happen to Ella's parents, and why is she so desperate to find out?

Available now

The Street Orphans

by Mary Wood

Outcast and alone –
can they ever reunite their family?

Born with a club foot in a remote village in the Pennines, Ruth is feared and ridiculed by the superstitious neighbours who see her affliction as a sign of witchcraft. When her father is killed in an accident and her family evicted from their cottage, she hopes to leave her old life behind, to start afresh in the Blackburn cotton mills. But tragedy strikes once again, setting in motion a chain of events that will unravel her family's lives.

Their fate is in the hands of the Earl of Harrogate, and his betrothed, Lady Katrina. But more sinister is the scheming Marcia, Lady Katrina's jealous sister. Impossible dreams beset Ruth from the moment she meets the Earl. Dreams that lead her to hope that he will save her from the terrible fate that awaits those accused of witchcraft. Dreams that one day her destiny and the Earl's will be entwined . . .

'Wood is a born storyteller'
Lancashire Evening Post

Available now

Brighter Days Ahead

by Mary Wood

War pulled them apart, but can it bring them back together?

Molly lives with her repugnant father, who has betrayed her many times. From a young age, living on the streets of London's East End, she has seen the harsh realities of life. When she's kidnapped by a gang and forced into their underworld, her future seems bleak.

Flo spent her early years in an orphanage and is about to turn her hand to teacher training. When a kindly teacher at her school approaches her about a job at Bletchley Park, it could turn out to be everything she never realized she wanted.

Will the girls' friendship be enough to weather the hard times ahead?

Available now

Tomorrow Brings Sorrow

by Mary Wood

You can't choose your family

Megan and her husband Jack have finally found stability in their lives. But the threat of Megan's troubled son Billy is never far from their minds. Billy's release from the local asylum is imminent and it should be a time for celebration. Sadly, Megan and Jack know all too well what Billy is capable of . . .

Can you choose who you love?

Sarah and Billy were inseparable as children, before Billy committed a devastating crime. While Billy has been shut away from the world, he has fixated on one thing: Sarah. Sarah knows there's only one way she can keep her family safe and it means forsaking true love.

Sometimes love is dangerous

Twins Theresa and Terence Crompton are used to getting their own way. But with the threat of war looming, the tides of fortune are turning. Forces are at work to unearth a secret that will shake the very roots of the tight-knit community . . .

Available now

All I Have to Give

by Mary Wood

When all is lost, can she find the strength to start again?

It is 1916 and Edith Mellor is one of the few female surgeons in Britain. Compelled to use her skills for the war effort, she travels to the Somme, where she is confronted with the horrors at the Front. Yet amongst the bloodshed on the battlefield, there is a ray of light in the form of the working-class Albert, a corporal from the East End of London. Despite being worlds apart, Edith and Albert can't deny their attraction to each other. But as the brutality of war reveals itself to Albert, he makes a drastic decision that will change both Edith and Albert's lives forever.

In the north of England, strong-minded Ada is left heartbroken when her only remaining son Jimmy heads off to fight in the war. Desperate to rebuild her shattered life, Ada takes up a position in the munition factory. But life deals her a further blow when she discovers that her mentally unstable sister Beryl is pregnant with her husband Paddy's child. Soon, even the love of the gentle Joe, a supervisor at the factory, can't erase Ada's pain. An encounter with Edith's cousin, Lady Eloise, brings Edith into her life. Together, they realize, they may be able to turn their lives around . . .

Available now

Proud of You

by Mary Wood

A heartfelt historical saga with a compelling mystery at its heart.

Alice, an upper-class Londoner, is recruited into the Special Operations Executive and sent to Paris where she meets Gertrude, an ex-prostitute working for the Resistance Movement. Together they discover that they have a connection to the same man, Ralph D'Olivier, and vow to unravel the mystery of his death.

After narrowly escaping capture by the Germans, Alice is lifted out of France and taken to a hospital for wounded officers where she meets Lil, a working-class northern girl employed as a nurse. Though worlds apart, Alice and Lil form a friendship, and Alice discovers Lil is also linked to Ralph D'Olivier.

Soon, the war irrevocably changes each of these women and they are thrust into a world of heartache and strife beyond anything they have had to endure before. Can they clear Ralph's name and find lasting love and happiness for themselves?

Available now